# HERO'S STRENGTH

*Song of Prophecy Series Book 10*

## P.E. PADILLA

OLIVERHEBERBOOKS

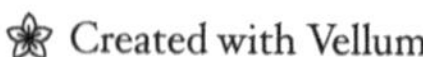 Created with Vellum

## The Great Prophet predicted you would want to read his story

Tsosin Ruus, the most renowned mage during the Age of Magic, wrote the Song of Prophecy to aid the world of Dizhelim as it would exist thousands of years after his life ended. But who was the Great Prophet, and how did he come to be the most important person in history...up until the present time?

And what of Erent Caahs, the most famous of contemporary heroes?

Get these two full-length companion novels to the Song of Prophecy and Hero Academy series for free and find out the fascinating stories that transformed ordinary boys into figures idolized by millions.

To get your free books and find out about upcoming books, please visit my website at https://pepadilla.com (top right hand corner of the page). Thank you!

# PARTIAL MAP OF DIZHELIM

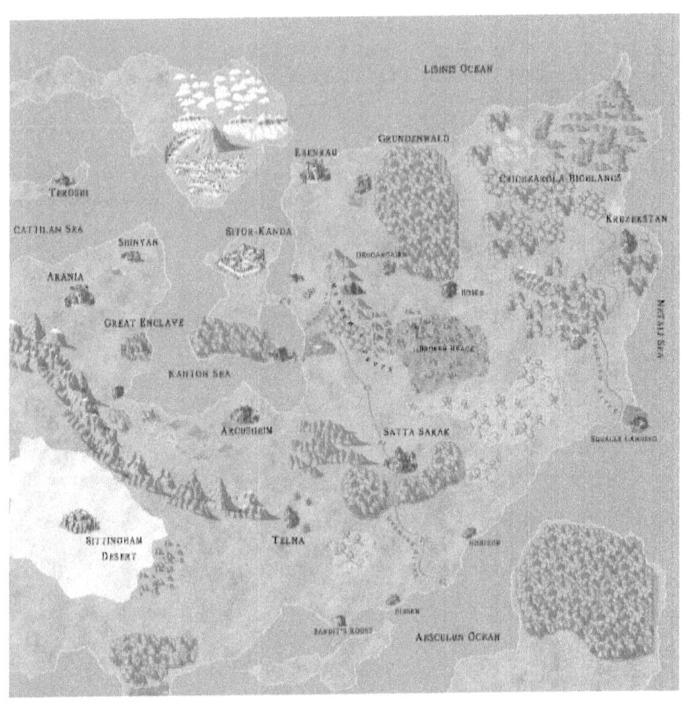

*If there is one thing I have learned in all my years of strife and hardship, it is that the nations of the world rarely understand true strength. Often it is not how much power one can bring to bear, but the resolve to do what is necessary despite all obstacles, that leads to victory."*

Thomasinus, Son of Daven (who later adopted the surname Davenson), first king of the Great Enclave, on the War of Magic.

J oceus Davenson, King of the Great Enclave, sighed into his mirror.

"Another meeting, Rumbler," he said to the image of the dog in the corner of his looking glass. "Another meeting."

The king straightened to his six-foot-two-inch height and adjusted the crown on his head, slightly shifting the brown hair that could use a trim. He stared for a moment into the face of the man in front of him, brown eyes meeting brown. At forty-eight years, he wasn't old—not quite yet—though days like this one did make him feel so.

He sighed again and turned to the one who, at times, seemed his only real friend in the world.

Rumbler lifted his shaggy head, ears hanging limply in the way that made the old dog look sad. His tail, brown with splotches of black—like the rest of his body—swung back and forth as the king met the canine's droopy, rheumy eyes.

"What do you think, old boy? You have the right of things. Sleeping next to the fire, eating scraps the children of the castle sneak to you, not worrying about anything except to hunt for scratches on the ear." Joceus squatted and gave the dog the scratches behind his ear he loved so much, and the tail became a blur.

It brought a fleeting smile to the king's face, but it dissolved into a neutral expression. At least it wasn't a frown. He stood and straightened his robes, glancing one more time in the mirror to make sure he looked suitably regal.

"I don't know why I bother. It's only a meeting of the King's Council. Not like I'll be addressing the entire court. It has been strained lately, though. I'd rather take you for a walk in the gardens, believe me. Bother. I should go. Enjoy your fire, old friend. I'll see you when my task is done."

The king took a long drink of the wine sitting on a side table, wiped his mouth, and left his chambers.

Joceus arrived precisely on time at the Council Meeting Room. It was a chamber specifically set aside for the King's Council and he'd been spending much too much time in it lately. The world was going mad, and the kingdom of the Great Enclave felt it. Ruling a kingdom had never been easy, but in a time of monsters, wild ancient magic, wars, and complete unrest, performing his duties was like carrying a large chest full of gold up a steep hill. In the rain. Barefoot. With a rope tied to a ship's anchor wrapped around him.

"Good morning, Your Majesty," Sudin Torfan said as Joceus entered the room. The portly man brought a smile to the king's face. He'd been Joceus's closest non-canine friend for close to forty years, despite the decade difference in their age. Sudin had always been like an older brother.

"Good morning, Sudin." He nodded to the others in turn. "Altor, Elnaril, Shalana, Katar."

The others bowed their heads and greeted him with a *Your Majesty* or a *Your Highness*.

A brief dizziness splashed over the king, like when he rose

too fast after lying down for a time. He blinked it away and sat.

"Let's start with any further information on the dark monsters some of the eastern nations are reporting. Have we news?"

Five sets of eyes swiveled to Altor Vondus. The man wasn't tall to begin with, but with his stick-like form and a hunch that Joceus was confident came from the man's obsession with books, he looked downright diminutive slouching in the chair at the meeting table.

Altor swung his hazel eyes around the room, noting that he had been singled out. He hopped, very like a fisher bird that had been pecked by another fowl as it focused on catching prey.

"I...uh, have received a few reports on the subject. The word is that Kruzekstan and possibly Artuyeska have been conquered by the monsters. Of course, with the time it takes for such reports to travel here, the news is already old."

Elnaril Leovaris sneered at the report. His sharp, thin face and pointed chin were made for such expressions. "Are you saying, then, that the tales of monsters suddenly appearing in Dizhelim are true? That indeed some magic has brought hundreds of them into the middle of the eastern kingdoms?"

Altor blinked at his fellow Council member. "I believe we have established the veracity of the reports of the monsters previously. Are we to rehash all we have discussed before?"

"No," Shalana Vabiros said. The only woman on the Council was a little taller than the scholarly Altor, though she wasn't a big woman. Nearly the same age as Joceus himself, she had a presence that her height and age couldn't account for. Being the only female, one with sand-colored hair and blue eyes amid the primarily dark hair in the kingdom, somehow seemed to work in her favor in relations with others. The woman could calm a pouncing ridge cat. "There's no need, Altor. It's just Elnaril wanting to start an argument again."

"I see," Altor said, relaxing fractionally. "There is also a report of some problems in Shinyan. It's unclear, but it appears that they were poised to go to war with Teroshi, and then they were not. The emperor's son, it seems, dueled with and killed his father and became emperor himself. He then opened relations with Teroshi, called the war off, and has announced an alliance with Sitor-Kanda, of all things."

"Quite a lot of activity in that one report, eh Altor?" Katar Trisric said. The large man's brown eyes twinkled and his face—set in a mischievous smile, as typical—crinkled jovially. "What, exactly, did they ally with the Hero Academy *for?*" He raised a hand, then continued. "Wait. What I mean is against whom are the two allying? I don't want Elnaril to misconstrue my question."

Altor seemed at a loss. "Why, to fight against the monsters, of course. The Academy claims these are the monsters of prophecy and that the very world depends upon alliances."

"Pure and utter nonsense," Elnaril said. "They must be angling for something else. Some power or riches or the like."

Katar's smile lessened. "I heard the Church of Vanda has begun calling their soldiers and gathering them together as well. Is this related? Thousands of Vandal soldiers just across our border is frankly more concerning than alleged monsters on the other side of the world."

Joceus silently listened to his councilors, as was his custom. It usually worked better to let the arguments and discussions fly and then formulate his own opinion and state it at the end of the meeting. He found it difficult to focus on the topics today, though, especially with the rapid-fire comments and the changes in subject. His head was a bit muzzy and his thoughts slow.

"The question," Elnaril said, "is what *we* will do about all this. I couldn't give a cup of goat's milk about what these other nations, or even the church, are doing. What will it mean for the Great Enclave?"

"Obviously, we will need to make a decision." Sudin eyed Joceus expectantly. "Will we form agreements with Arania and the church, do so with the Hero Academy, or keep to ourselves and watch to see what unfolds?"

"Sitor-Kanda's very existence is based on the Prophecy," Shalana said. "If they say the dark times have come and the monsters of legend are here, we would do well to heed their words."

"Ally with those book-hoarding hucksters?" Elnaril replied. "Where is the reward in that? We give of our resources and our military might and we gain what for our troubles? Nothing. At least the church can give us some benefit, even if it's ensuring peace along our borders."

"Peace?" Katar asked. "Can one have peace with an organization that bases everything it does on the premise that everyone who is not a Vandal deserves to die? Mark me, an agreement with them will include a requirement that everyone convert to becoming followers of Vanda."

"So what?" Elnaril spat. "Good people are already followers of the only true god."

Altor raised his hand meekly, stopping anyone else from speaking. "Pardon, but I've also received reports that priests and priestesses of the old gods are appearing, and their worship is having a resurgence. The Church of Vanda is not happy about this, of course. I thought I should mention it."

Elnaril sneered at the bookish man. "We cannot alienate the church."

Sudin put both hands up to forestall the argument. "Perhaps we should hear what his majesty has to say on the matter."

All eyes turned to Joceus, but it hardly registered. His vision had gone blurry and his stomach roiled like something was inside him trying to claw its way out. He tried to pull together the tattered string of thoughts into one that was coherent. He opened his mouth to speak and a recognizable feeling came over him. He turned his head just in time to point it away from the table.

Vomit spewed from him, more than should have been possible. He found himself falling toward the floor, but never quite made it. Arms held him up, positioning him back in his chair.

"Send for Verona," a voice said. "Quickly."

The King of the Great Enclave felt himself being lifted by many hands and laid on the council table. Images flickered in and out until his vision failed completely and he lost his fight for consciousness.

I

"Why aren't we going back the way we came?" Lily Fisher asked. "Faitar's Route was nice and wide, not to mention level most of the time." The tall, red-headed archer frowned at the road, not much more than a dirt path through scrubland. "I miss seeing the trees, too. And enjoying their shade."

Aila Ven smirked, looking away from Lily riding next to her. She'd let Tere deal with the questions.

In response, the older archer—the only male in their trio —sighed. Aila snuck a look at him as he slowed down to talk to Lily face-to-face.

"We didn't do it to irritate you, if that's what you're thinking, though if we did, I'd say we were successful." His white eyes were still difficult for Aila to look into, especially when the bright sunlight reflected off them like it was at the moment. "The simple explanation is that the distance is shorter going southeast from Vandomus to Metrovial instead of traveling more south on the Faitar's Route. Travel is faster on the highway, yes, but we'll make better time this way, overall."

"Besides," Aila added, "things seem pretty crazy in Arania right now, so we'll meet fewer troubles going this way. We'll go through less of Arania."

"Yeah, yeah," Lily said. "So you've said before. What I want to know, though, is what is the real reason? Since when did we go the difficult way to save what amounts to a few hours, maybe a day, and when did we get so sensitive to problems on the road? Traveling is full of problems. We all know that."

"Lily, dear," Tere Chizzit said, "there's really no reason to argue about it. We're already on the way. Turning back and going the other way is out of the question at this point. Let me ask you something. Why are *you* so married to the idea of going back the same way we came into Arania?"

The statuesque archer shook out her long, red hair and took a sharp breath in through her nose. Aila glanced at Tere and found the precursor to a smile on the old archer's face.

"I wanted to stop at the weapon shop in Metis again. I was thinking I'd get another knife or two."

Tere snorted and Lily's face reddened. "I thought so. You whined that you should have bought those knives during our entire visit to Arania. Aila and I both asked you if you wanted to go back and get them. You told us no."

Lily crossed her arms under her breasts, still holding her reins loosely. She was a good enough rider to control her horse with her knees. What she was not, however, was good enough to keep her lower lip from pouting.

"You did tell us no," Aila confirmed. "We would have been more than happy to go that way."

"Lily," Tere said. "We'll look for some new knives for you in the Great Enclave. I'm sure there are fine weapon smiths in Metrovial. It's one of the great cities of the world. Why are you so out of sorts? I've never seen you cause any trouble before."

She shrugged her toned shoulders while her arms were still crossed. Aila chuckled at the image of the former Falxen assassin sulking.

"It's almost time to find a campsite for the night," Tere said. "I'll cook dinner, since Aila can hardly make anything edible. I'll even rub your feet if it'll make you feel better."

Lily shifted in her saddle. "It's not my feet that's sore."

The wicked grin on Tere's face made Aila burst out laughing.

"My calves and my lower back are aching a little bit," Lily said, her face going red enough to match her hair. "Get your mind out of the privy, Aila."

The shorter woman couldn't speak because she was laughing so hard.

"I'll massage your calves and your lower back," Tere said, "after I make you dinner. Will that do?"

The redhead threw one more glare at Aila and nodded to Tere. "That will do nicely. Thank you."

Tere hissed something under his breath that sounded an awful lot like "women," but Aila couldn't be sure.

One of the nice things about traveling through the more desolate area of Arania was that they could literally camp anywhere. They didn't have to search for a clearing because almost any place would do. The wind rarely blew hard in this part of the nation, so pulling up to a small bunch of trees and setting up camp right there was no problem. There was even a stream nearby, though Aila wondered why there weren't more large trees with the ready water source.

They hadn't passed a lot of surface water since they'd been traveling the lesser populated area of Arania, but there had been enough that they hadn't had to ration their drinking water. Yet. Aila had never been through the terrain they would cross, but Tere said he had. He was arguably the world's best tracker, even discounting his magical sight, and she trusted him with her life. They'd be fine and they would get to Metrovial, the capital city of the Great Enclave, faster than if they'd taken another route.

After an uneventful night, Aila woke in the morning to the smell of food cooking.

"I told you she'd wake up if she smelled food," Tere told Lily. "It's about time. The morning is almost gone already."

"We're not in a big hurry anyway," Aila said. "All the excitement tired me out." She flashed all her teeth at the old archer. "Thanks for making breakfast—or lunch?—though."

Tere shook his head. One second he was standing over a camp pan, searing some of their already cooked venison from a kill the day before, and then he was teetering dangerously.

He swayed, putting his empty hand to his head and closing his eyes.

"Tere?" Lily dashed over and held his shoulders to keep him from falling into the fire.

"It's fine, girl. I can stand. If you want to hug me, then just do it. No need to make an excuse for it."

Lily slapped his arm. "No need for you to teeter like you're drunk so I'll rush to hold you in my arms."

"Tere," Aila said. "Are you okay?"

"I'm fine, like I said. My vision went a little crazy for a second. The magical matrix jumped around like it was standing on a hot coal bed."

"Really? How'd that happen?"

He swung his white eyes to her. "If I had to guess, I'd say it was either another one of those random magical shift things we've been having, or someone has released more magic into the world. I'm guessing it's the second one. Why don't you fetch the message tablet from my pack and ask the others if they felt it."

"Oooh, good idea." Aila pulled out the little tablet and took the stylus from its holding place on the side. "Sometimes it's hard to keep up with these things. So much is happening lately. I'll just..." She stopped as she noticed there were several messages already on the tablet.

After reading them, she looked at her two companions. "There's something in here about Fahtin having a vision. She sounds frantic, like maybe something happened with Raki. There's no response from Jia's group. I'm going to jump into the conversation."

HEY EVERYONE, IT'S ME, AILA. WE JUST FELT ANOTHER ONE OF THOSE CRAZY MAGIC SHIFTS. WHAT DID YOU DO NOW? AND WHAT IS ALL THIS ABOUT A VISION AND RAKI?

SHE EYED THE TABLET FOR A FEW MINUTES, BUT NO response came, so she set it down and helped Tere by retrieving dishes from her saddlebags and the forks from Lily's. By the time breakfast was ready, answers started appearing on the face of the tablet.

I'M HERE AT THE ACADEMY. AEDEN, FAHTIN, AND EVON ARE ALL HERE, TOO. ALMOST EVERYONE FELT THAT SHIFT, IF THE PEOPLE AROUND ME ARE AN INDICATION. IT WASN'T ANYTHING WE DID HERE, SO WHETHER IT WAS A RANDOM SHIFT OR ANOTHER WELL, IT DIDN'T ORIGINATE WITH US. JIA? IS IT YOUR GROUP?

AILA, FAHTIN'S VISION INDICATED THAT RAKI WAS HURT OR SOMETHING. SHE'S VAGUE ON EXACTLY WHAT IT WAS.

-- MARLA

NO OTHER ANSWERS APPEARED.

"I don't know what to think," Aila said. "If they released another well, that would be a good thing and they should be safe now, but not answering could be bad. What do you think happened?"

"We could conjecture all day long and it wouldn't help," Tere answered. "All we can do is wait. It's one of the hardest parts when friends are doing dangerous things."

"But all Jia and the others were doing was searching for a missing Academy operative," Lily said. It sounded to Aila like she was trying hard to make a point, possibly to ease her own concerns.

Tere clicked his tongue. "A missing person could mean danger. A trained operative didn't simply wander off or forget to send a message to the Academy." He took a bite of sausage. "I'm sure they're fine, though. Be patient. We'll find out eventually."

Tere was right, like most times. Blasted man. Later that day, as evening approached and they'd been riding for several hours, another message finally arrived.

FAHTIN, WE'RE ALL FINE. THERE WERE SOME PROBLEMS AND WE GOT SEPARATED FROM OUR MESSAGE TABLET. SORRY TO WORRY YOU. WE FOUND ANOTHER WELL. THIS ONE HAD DARK MAGIC IN IT. WE ALSO FOUND EMILIYA STERRIS, THE ACADEMY OPERATIVE WHO DISAPPEARED. SHE HAD BEEN CAUGHT UP IN A DARK BUBBLE. WE'LL EXPLAIN WHEN WE GET BACK TO THE ACADEMY.

MARLA, WE HAVE ANOTHER COGISCRO STONE FOR YOU TO INTERPRET. WE'RE LOOKING FORWARD TO SEEING YOU ALL. BE SAFE.

--JIA

.   .   .

"Great!" Aila said, considering throwing the tablet from her. "Everyone is having adventures and finding sources of magic and all we get to do is go and do stupid political stuff."

"Weren't you only doing 'stupid political stuff' in Shinyan, too? Then you ended up going back to the founding of the nation, finding another Well of Power, *and* deposing the old emperor to install a new one."

"Yeah, whatever. That was different. All we're doing is going to the Great Enclave to talk to the king. He's not trying to start a war, and he won't be trying to throw us in the dungeon."

"How do you know what he'll do?" Tere asked.

"Because...because it wouldn't make sense. He's not our enemy. The point is that we don't get to have fun like the others."

"Fun?" the aging archer said. "We've all been to at least one of the wells. Getting to them is definitely *not* fun."

"It is compared to diplomatic duty. Ugh."

Another message appeared on the tablet and Aila was thankful she hadn't thrown it as far as she could from her. She stopped her horse to read it.


Great job you two. We can't wait to hear about it. Aila? How are things going with your mission?


"Mission!" she spat, rethinking again whether she should toss the magical device. "Punishment, more like." She continued to grumble as she took the stylus out and responded.

. . .

Yes, good job Raki and Jia. Oh, and Urun. As for our mission, we took a detour to see what was going on in Arania, specifically Vandomus. We'll give a report when we get a chance. We're on the way to Metrovial to speak with the king. We'll send a message when we get there.

Aila read off Marla's message and the one she sent, then got Muscade moving again. They had two or three days before they'd be at the Clavian capital city, so she stowed the message tablet away but kept her ears open for its buzz.

The next day's travel was more of the same until the afternoon when they neared what she thought was the border between Arania and the Great Enclave. As they circled around a copse of trees, an obstruction ahead caught Aila's attention.

"Is that a bunch of tents?" she said, squinting her eyes to focus better on them.

"Looks like it," Lily answered. The archer checked her bow, which she'd been keeping strung in case she needed to use it quickly. "Tents, a few wagons, and a bunch of horses. Some kind of camp?"

"Can you see how they're dressed?" Tere asked. "Do those uniforms remind you of anything?"

The small figures in the distance were indeed dressed alike. They were garbed in white garments with shiny, silver-colored breastplates, topped with silver-trimmed white cloaks.

"Oh," Aila said, trying to keep the disappointment from her tone. "It's the Army of the Vandan church. I wonder what they're doing."

She scanned the area. It was well-suited to a small force that wanted all traffic to be channeled through them. With some rocky hills to the right of the road and thick trees to the left, anyone using the thoroughfare would have to go directly through the block of soldiers.

"Hold," one of the soldiers said as they approached. He wore a sword but didn't have one of the halberds the other guards standing by on duty carried. The insignia on his uniform showed his rank as lieutenant. "Where are you going and what is your purpose?"

Aila was going to answer—it was always best to be respectful and polite to the forces of the church—but Tere beat her to it.

"Our business is our own. What are you doing, camped here to harass travelers?"

The officer's mouth thinned to a straight line. "We are here doing Vanda's work, ensuring that undesirables do not infiltrate Arania."

"That must be special for you," Tere said. "In case you haven't noticed, we're *leaving* Arania, going to the Great Enclave. There's no reason for you to slow us down. Even if we were *undesirables*—especially so, in fact—I would think you'd be happy we're leaving."

The man sputtered and Aila's face grew warm. Why was Tere being so rude?

The officer called over a trio of guards, hand on his sword. "Dismount for questioning."

"No," Tere said.

"You refuse?"

"That's what 'no' means. Do Vanda's teachings not tell you what 'no' means? From what I understand, much of the religion revolves around the word."

Tere's body shifted visibly. He didn't *move* so much as everything in his body went loose and supple. Aila had seen it before. Hells, she had *felt* it before. It was the precursor to a violent altercation. The soldiers seemed to realize it as well, because the ones with polearms gripped the shafts more tightly and widened their stance. The officer stepped his right foot out to the side like he was going to draw and slash with his sword.

"Please," Aila said. "I'm a devout follower of Vanda's Church. We mean no disrespect and don't want to cause trouble. We actually come from Vandomus, where I wanted to visit to behold the sacred city. We're going back to the Great Enclave. Will you let us pass?"

For apparently the first time, the officer shifted his focus away from Tere. His eyes took in Aila and Lily. A slow, wicked smile crossed his face.

"One of Vanda's own. It's good to see there are those who follow the teachings among the heretics of the world. I would like to...talk with you. Get to know you better. I'm sure we can work something out that will not involve all three of you being taken into custody as members of a rebellious faction."

"Oh, good. We can talk right here."

"No. I mean that we should talk privately. You and your red-haired friend can join me in my tent. I'm sure we can resolve the issue of the rudeness of your father."

"Father? Me and her? What do you...?" Aila trailed off as it finally sunk in what the man was saying. She normally didn't have trouble catching such references, but it was the last thing she expected from an officer in service to the church. "How dare you!"

"Come join me and you'll see what I dare. What will it be? A little private time, or shall we tear you from your saddles and thoroughly beat you before taking you into custody? It'll end the same for you two, only with more bruises." He watched Tere from the side of his eye as he stepped up and put a hand on Aila's leg.

Aila glanced at Tere, who was fuming, and Lily, who had her teeth gritted and her hand gripped so tightly on her bow, the muscles in her forearm were etched like steel cables. Both of them nodded to her simultaneously.

Aila sighed, looked into the officer's beady eyes, and kicked him in the jaw. She had no sooner put her foot back in the stirrup than she dug her heels into Muscade's flanks and shot ahead, aiming for the few soldiers scattered across the road.

The three nearest guards swung their halberds toward Aila, but arrows suddenly appeared in the arms of two of them and the third yelped in surprise as another arrow clanged against the blade of his polearm. Aila looked back and both Tere and Lily had another arrow each already nocked in their bows, ready to loose.

It wasn't much of a chase. Aila flew through the edge of camp, the hard-packed dirt of the road making for a fast gallop. Tere and Lily raced behind her, letting a few more arrows fly when individual soldiers tried to grab at them or Aila as they zipped past.

Only three soldiers mounted to chase them, but after arrows sprouted from the shoulders or arms of all three of them, they even gave that up.

After several minutes of the hard pace, the three slowed their horses down to a canter, then a trot.

"Nice folks, your church has," Tere told her.

"Oh, shut up," Aila answered.

"Is that enough *fun* for you for now?" Lily said.

"You shut up, too. Leave me alone."

Aila was fairly sure they had crossed the border into the Great Enclave. Even so, having ruffian soldiers of the church that close to Clavian land wasn't good. She made a mental note to add a statement about it to what they'd say when they were in front of the king. The world was plain going crazy if she couldn't even trust the church anymore.

❧ 2 ☙

The trio finally started seeing villages and towns as they got closer to the bowl set within the mountains that gave the Great Enclave its name. Aila breathed a sigh of relief at the buildings—so different than those in Arania—they passed by. The Aranir had a liking for grand designs, sweeping curves, and beautiful facades that didn't seem to serve any purpose other than to increase the area that needed to be cleaned.

Clavian structures were more utilitarian. They did the job of providing shelter from the elements, but they also exuded strength. Any one of the simple buildings, whether a home or business, could protect its residents from attacks. They had a solidity that comforted Aila, as if by being among them she was impervious to situations such as they had faced with the church soldiers.

That had affected her more than she let on with her friends. She'd hardly thought of anything else since their escape from the roadblock. How could Vanda's church tolerate such actions and attitudes in its officers?

The night before they were to arrive in Metrovial, they

stopped at an inn within the small town of Pontilus. They'd passed through the other communities without pausing for more than the time it took to ask a passerby the name of the town or village. Even then, Aila had noted something a bit off.

"Have you picked up on a general disheartenment in the places we've passed through?" she asked her friends as they sat in the common room of the inn where they'd booked rooms for the night.

"Disheartenment?" Lily repeated.

"Yeah. People have seemed lethargic, brooding, with their heads down like they're in mourning or something. At the first town, I thought maybe they'd had a funeral or some catastrophe, but every other place we've been, it was the same thing."

"Like they're defeated," Tere said.

"Yes. Exactly."

"I can even see some shadings of it within the magical matrix. Flashes of dark colors that indicate moods or thoughts. They're unhappy about something."

"That's what bothers me," Aila said. "My father used to tell me if everyone in a town was unhappy, there was something seriously wrong and it was the responsibility of the one who governed them to fix it. In fact, he said that it was probably the fault of the leader to begin with."

"Your father said that?" Lily asked.

"Yeah. You know, before...before my parents died."

"Sounds like something a wise father would say," Tere said, taking a drink of his ale. "Or the leader of a rebellion would say."

"He was no rebel," she said, a bit too quickly and too loudly, leaning forward in her seat. She glanced around, cleared her throat, and sat back. "Sorry. He was no rebel, though."

"Okay, okay. I was just joking. Mostly." The old archer showed his teeth to her.

She suppressed a shudder at seeing his cheesy grin with his white eyes hovering above it.

As they ate dinner, Aila spoke little and focused on the sounds around her, listening for anything she could pick up from the other patrons. The room wasn't full by any means, but there were a good fifteen or twenty people scattered around.

"...and they raised taxes again," one middle-aged woman said. "How does the king expect I can make a living when I'm paying almost as much in taxes as I make? I'm going to have to close my shop down at this rate."

"It won't help you," said her companion, a man with dark hair without a spot of grey. "The newest round of taxes is independent of what you make. If you have no money coming in, you'll still be on the hook to pay them."

"It's ridiculous," another man said through a bite of his dinner. "Supposedly, it's for the army, to provide for our protection. They always protected us just fine before they started taking all our money."

"Don't forget the curfews and the limit on the number of people that can gather at one time," an older woman from another table added. "It's like they think *we're* the danger or something. I don't like it, not at all. Smells like four-day-old fish."

The first woman, the shop owner, shook her head. "Then there's the decree that we support the church, not only by attendance at the sermons, but financially as well. I'm thinking it would be better to move to Sutania. My family has lived in the Enclave since its founding, but it's almost like they're trying to force us to leave. It's a sad time, I tell you."

Aila couldn't believe what she was hearing. Clavian people had always taken pride in their nation. How could things have fallen so far that there was talk of leaving their ancestral homes?

Lily and Tere chatted, but Aila was too busy thinking. Dwelling on what she'd heard. It bothered her more than she would ever admit. Aila added asking about the discontent she'd heard to the list for when she spoke with the king. She had thought Arania was a mess with the church soldiers everywhere and harassing citizens, but this sounded worse.

"I'm going to bed," she told her friends as soon as she had finished eating. "I'm tired and just want to go to sleep."

"We'll turn in soon, too," Tere said. "After we finish our drinks. We'll get to Metrovial tomorrow. Are you excited?"

Aila swallowed, darting looks between the two of them. "Uh, sure. Excited. Yeah. We'll finally get to finish our mission. We'll probably be on the way home in a day or two. That'll be good, huh?"

Tere stared at her and Lily narrowed her eyes as if she was trying to figure out something. Aila didn't wait for them to ask.

"Well, goodnight." She darted to the stairs and went up to her room.

As planned, they ate breakfast and rode through the opening to the bowl formed by a series of mountain peaks until, just before noon, they reached the capital city. It had been a while since Aila had seen it. Her heart fluttered at the stone walls shining in the midday sun, obscured in places by trees that had grown as high as the walls. The backdrop of the high, snow-capped mountains in a massive ring around the entire area was enough to leave her breathless.

A cleared space—a killing field for times of war, as if enemies would ever be able to breach the mountains to reach the city wall—surrounded the city. From certain vantage points along the road down toward the gate, they could see the city and its walls separated from everything around it, but at other angles, the thick forest seemed to engulf the entire thing.

The road wended through the trees, walls of brown and green surging up on each side. The smell of pine, of moist soil, and of decaying leaves and forest detritus wafted around them and Aila took a deep breath, enjoying the scent and the relative calm of it all. The way the path twisted hid other travelers on the road, making it feel like they were the only ones there.

"The road was designed not to be straight," Tere said. "There are two reasons, really. One is that the builders wanted to preserve some of the massive trees that had been there for centuries. They curved the road around them so they didn't have to cut the mammoths down." He pointed to a gigantic oak the road curved left to avoid. "The other is that there are hidden grottos and archer stations at some of the turns to whittle down enemy forces advancing on the city. It's difficult to keep track of what all parts of an army is doing if it's in segments."

"Thank you for that history lesson," Aila said, softening it with a crooked smile.

"You're welcome. You know, I only came back here twice since my visit as a boy. Both times I just passed through, on the way to doing something else. It's been a very long time since I walked around the streets of Metrovial."

"You came to Metrovial as a boy?" Aila asked.

"He did," Lily answered. "Right after he left Arcusheim searching for his family's killer, he came through the Great Enclave looking for him. From here, he went into Arania to perform one of his earliest heroic acts when he captured the bandit and slaver Ossar Sattis, the Blue-Cloaked Bastard."

Tere's mouth dropped open and he stared openly at Lily. "How? What? Why do you know that?"

The beautiful redhead winked at him. "Do you think I

was exaggerating when I told you I know more about you than anyone else? I can't say I know everything about you, but it's damn close."

Aila burst into laughter. "You are amazing, Lily. Do you know what he had for breakfast when he was here or where he stayed?"

"No, don't be ridiculous." She kept a straight face for a moment, but then a smile broke through. "Not from lack of trying, though. Turns out, no one around him cared enough to note all those important facts."

"Scary," Tere said. "You're scary."

"I am and you love it."

He laughed, shaking his head as they reached the gate of the city. Aila was glad for the distraction because even as they approached the guards lining the gate, her heart was thumping so hard in her chest, she thought for sure the soldiers would hear it and arrest her for being suspicious. She pulled her hood down to shade her face and followed Tere and Lily through the open space and into the city proper.

Aila had thought—more than once in the last several days —that she should take her two friends aside and tell them what to expect when they got to the castle, but she always found a reason not to. They had almost reached the end of their journey. She, Tere, and Lily could very well be in the king's palace in as few as a couple of hours. Still, she didn't talk to them. It would go worse for her for not speaking to them before they got there, but all she wanted until then was to enjoy her friends' reactions to the city. She slowed her horse so she stayed a pace or two behind them and watched their interactions, basking in the simple pleasure of it.

❧ 3 ❧

"There's the library," Tere said fifteen minutes later, pointing out a large building where thousands of books resided.

"There's *a* library," Aila corrected, "though it *is* the main library for the city."

Tere twisted in his saddle to look at her. "To me, it's *the* library. It was the most magnificent thing I'd ever seen when I was a young boy in this city for the first time. I couldn't believe there were so many books in all the world, let alone in one place."

"That must have made you feel really small," Lily said.

"It did. I remember it like it was yesterday. The woman—she was a girl, really, but to me at that age she was a mysterious older woman—told me I could look around and read whatever I wanted. For free. I could hardly believe it."

"What did you read?"

"Nothing. I was on the hunt for my family's killer, so I walked around for a few minutes and then left. I apologized to the woman and the man who were at the desk, telling them I'd come back if I could. They must have had a laugh about that: a boy from the country in the big city, though I was actually from Arcusheim. I had always thought I lived in a *big city* until I came here."

"Do you want to go in?" Aila asked.

"No. We have a mission to accomplish. Maybe afterward we can stop by. Just for the sake of nostalgia."

As they traveled down one of the wide streets of the city, they watched the others around them. To Aila, it all seemed surreal. Many had the hoods of their cloaks down as she did, though air wasn't particularly cool. People looked around or behind them frequently, like they were afraid they were being followed or were dodging trouble.

The trio passed a large building with a sign hanging out front that read *Senod Protection Services*. As they drew even with the door, it swung open and a grey-haired man walked out. He looked fit and the clothes he wore—tailored tunic and pants—were of good quality. They weren't silk, but a rougher fabric that demonstrated he wasn't some lord who was born into money but was someone who worked for his place in society.

Tere noticed the man, too, and stopped his horse to look at him.

"Senod?" the archer asked.

The man tilted his head up to look at Tere. "That is my name. Do you wish to contract my company for protection? We are one of the top employers of skilled guards in the city."

Tere smiled widely at Senod, though Aila couldn't figure out why. "No, nothing like that. I haven't seen you in a very long time. I'm glad to see that you made something of yourself."

Senod narrowed his eyes at Tere. "I'm sorry, but I don't think I recognize you. Please forgive me."

"It's understandable. I don't look anything like I did when we met last. Tell me, Senod, have you come upon your good fortune honestly? Tell me the truth. I can tell if you're lying."

The man's face underwent a startling transformation. First, his brows drew down and he almost looked like he would take offense. Then they shot up his forehead and he leaned forward to stare at Tere.

"No. It couldn't be."

"It is. I'm so glad I didn't break your arm or turn you over to the guards. I'm proud of what you've done. You are to be commended."

"But, but...you're dead."

"Not yet," Tere said. "Though the day's not done..."

The man grabbed Tere's hand. "It's true. You are him, aren't you?"

"No, my friend. I'm not that man anymore. Just remember me as the boy I was when we met."

"You must come to dinner, meet my wife, my family. Please. We can talk more. I am wanted at an appointment right now, but tell me you will. I will not take no for an answer."

"Peace, Senod. I have business at the castle. I'll visit you here at your office when I am able. I'm not sure how long I will be occupied."

"Yes, yes. I am here most of the time. I look forward to speaking with you. Gods, it's amazing. You're still alive! Thank you. For what you did for me and for agreeing to speak with me. For all that you've done for the world as well. I look forward to it."

Tere said his goodbyes and waved the man away, then turned and walked his horse forward again, whistling to himself.

"You're not even going to tell us what that was about?" Lily asked.

"You're the scholar on all things regarding me. You tell me."

Lily growled in her throat. "You know I don't know what that was. That's why I'm asking."

"It's nothing, really. Just someone I met once."

"Someone you met once? That man looks like he'd give his life for you. That doesn't happen when you meet someone just once."

"It does to me," Tere said. "You'd be surprised. I made a few friends over the years."

Aila laughed at Lily's scowl. "Come on, Tere, you know you want to tell us. Quit teasing Lily and explain. How do you know the founder of one of the top guard companies in the capital city?"

Tere gave Lily the side eye and chuckled. "I like to remind her occasionally that she doesn't know every damn thing about me...or about the man I used to be."

"I never said I knew everything," the red-haired archer spat. Tere ignored her.

"That first time I was in Metrovial, I was walking around gawking at everything. It really was magnificent to me, bigger and grander than anything I'd ever seen. As I wandered, trying to find a guard station to ask about the man I was after, I felt someone try to steal one of my knives.

"I snatched the hand of the person doing it and found myself facing a skinny boy in ragged clothes. I asked his name and he lied to me. It was the first time I'd used my magical sight to read someone's aura in the magical matrix and figure out they were lying. I asked again and he told me a different lie. I gave him one more chance, telling him that he better not lie to me or I'd break his arm, cut his hand off, turn him into the guard for hanging, or all three.

"He told me his real name. Senod. I warned him to change

his ways and I let him go. I sometimes would wonder whatever happened to him. It looks like he turned out okay in the end."

"Senod was a street thief and a pickpocket?" Aila asked. The man was very well-known in Metrovial. He had a reputation of being honest and honorable, as well as for training and maintaining the best mercenary guards and soldiers available.

"He was," Tere said. "I'm going to enjoy speaking with him once we're able to go to dinner at his house."

"Senod knows who you are?" Lily asked. "He knows that the one who caught him stealing was Erent Caahs?"

"Apparently so. I told him my name, though I didn't think he'd remember it. Of course, right after I met him I captured Ossar Sattis, and then I trained with Arto Deniselo. Just before I met him, I helped out that caravan of encalo north of Arcusheim and escorted them to the Great Enclave. People talk. I think I started to become a little famous during that time."

"A little famous. Pssht."

Tere shrugged. "We can ask him about it when we go to his house for dinner. You two will come with me, won't you?"

"We'll go with you," Aila said. "It's a good thing for Senod that you hadn't learned yet how to be strong before you met him. Things would have gone a lot differently."

"What does that mean?" Tere asked.

"Well, once you learned to be stronger, you wouldn't have given him such a break. Or, actually, you may have given him a break. A broken arm. Someone strong will always defeat their enemy and make sure they can't come back and attack again. If someone strong doesn't impose their will, then others will impose their will on her. Or him."

Aila's comments were greeted by silence. Not total silence, since she could still hear the buzz of the crowd around her, but her two friends didn't say anything and she couldn't hear their horses' hoofs anymore. She turned back to see Tere and Lily, mouths open almost identically.

"What?"

"Do you really believe that?" Lily asked. "That having no mercy is what it means to be strong?"

"That's not exactly what I said, but yeah, kind of. My father always told me how I needed to be stronger, to do my own thing. If anyone tried to stop me or impose their will on me, I needed to show them I was stronger than them, through combat if necessary."

"That's utter horseshit," Tere said. He and Lily started their horses walking again and Aila urged Muscade to adopt their stride. "I didn't have any concept of being strong or being a hero when I was young, but I've had a lot of years since then, and I know that strength doesn't mean being mean or vindictive. Knowing what I know now, after all the things I've experienced in my life, I would have done exactly the same thing again with Senod."

"You're just saying that because you know how it turned out," Aila said. "So, you got lucky with that one. You can't tell me you never used your superiority to get things done, despite what it did to others. You left the world without its favorite hero for twenty years. That's not a show of strength, a clear confirmation that no one else could tell you what to do?"

"That's not it at all," Lily answered for Tere. "You heard the story, the horrible things that happened to him. He went to the Grundenwald to get away from his perceived failure and to mourn the woman he loved. It's got nothing to do with strength."

"Everything's got something to do with strength. That's what makes the world go 'round. The strongest always hold all the cards. Why else do you think we're here? To beg for help from someone with strength that we need against the animaru."

"That's ridiculous. It has nothing—"

"Oh, look," Aila interrupted. "We're here."

❦   4   ❦

It had been a day for reminiscing for Tere Chizzit. He hadn't realized how powerful the memories of his first visit to Metrovial were. It had been a time of anger at what had happened to his family, fear over what he would face and whether he would ever find the man responsible, and wonder at the many new experiences he'd had. The library, Senod, even the feeling of walking down the streets of the city amid so many people cast his mind back decades, although the people he'd seen this day were not quite as lively or happy as the remembered ones. Maybe his viewpoint was tinged with his own experiences and misconceptions.

Aila's comments, though, had thrown him into a spin. Did she really believe what she'd been saying? What was her obsession with strength all about?

When Aila had said, "We're here," it hadn't registered in Tere's mind exactly what she was talking about. It took him several seconds to realize that they were indeed in front of the castle gate, and a pair of guards were approaching them.

He dismounted, Aila and Lily doing the same. It was bad form to speak with castle guards from horseback, though many people did it. Tere had known more than a few guards in his life and they constantly complained about it.

"What's your business here?" a young guardsman with bright blue eyes asked. The man hardly flinched when he met Tere's white eyes. He was well-trained to keep his composure.

"We need to see the king," Tere said. "We're emissaries from Sitor-Kanda and carry a letter of introduction from the headmaster, Qydus Okvius."

"The king is not granting audiences at this time. Come back in a week or two, and that may have changed."

"Did you not hear me? I said that we are emissaries from the Hero Academy."

"I heard you. You still will not enter. Turn around and leave."

Tere lifted his foot to step up to get face-to-face with the guard, but Aila put a hand on his shoulder.

"Guardsman...?" she said.

"Argad Solsin, ma'am."

"Guardsman Solsin, please ask your sergeant to come here."

"Sergeant Vilonay is busy with more important matters. He'll tell you the same thing I'm telling you. You will not enter."

"Guardsman Solsin, I will give you exactly five seconds to fetch your sergeant to prevent you from making a mistake that will end your career. Get Dropsy now, or you will rue this day for the rest of your life. One."

Tere looked back and forth from Aila to the guard. He hadn't used the name Aila had used. It sounded like a nick-name. Her voice, too, was different. Imperious, commanding. It seemed to work. Guardsman Solsin stepped quickly over to a small building inside the gate and returned a few minutes later with an older man, one with a sergeant's rank on his uniform.

"What is this?" the man said. "The king is granting no audiences. Don't try my patience or—"

The man stopped talking abruptly. He stood staring straight ahead, mouth open, like he'd seen a spirit. Tere turned and found Aila, standing as tall as her short stature allowed. No, taller than her stature allowed. She'd pushed back her hood and she glared at the soldiers like they were her personal servants, her chin raised and her jaw set.

"I...I'm sorry, Highness," the sergeant said. He slapped the guard on the shoulder. "Get an escort here right now, and someone to take the horses and bring them to the stables. Now, Argad. Now!"

The confused guard ran back toward the little building. Tere traded confused looks with Lily and glanced at Aila, who stared straight ahead at nothing, an irritated look on her face. The sergeant shifted his feet.

Then, men exploded with activity, rushing out of the guardhouse like a kicked anthill. Five soldiers, including Guardsman Solsin, joined the sergeant in forming two rows. Sergeant Vilonay bowed to Aila.

"We will escort you to the palace, Highness. Please, follow me."

The sergeant turned and barked a command, setting the other soldiers in motion. Aila glided along behind them. Her gait looked, of all things, to be the stroll of a noble lady.

Tere looked at Lily again, hoping for some semblance of sanity. "What the hells is going on?" he whispered to her.

"I don't know," she said. "Highness?"

The two followed quickly when Aila looked back toward them and jerked her head toward the palace.

"I hope she knows what she's doing," Tere said. "This has the feeling of something that might land us in a dungeon."

As their escort led them into the palace, Tere had a good view of the reaction of different people they passed. From soldiers to servants, and even a few courtiers, they all reacted like it was the most important procession they'd seen that day. The soldiers saluted, but everyone else—even the nobles—bowed as they passed. Tere had never experienced anything like it.

They marched from the more public halls to fancier, more private areas. The carpet along the center of the wide corridor became plusher and plusher; the tapestries and figurines along the walls took a marked jump in quality and, no doubt, price; and Tere felt the tension mount. He recognized the feeling. It lingered in places of political power. He winced inwardly.

A dungeon? No. Aila might just get them all executed.

In the hall before a large door, one of the famous Clavian Knights stood in full armor, minus his helmet. His sandy blond hair was cropped short, and his blue eyes fixed on Aila like he was a bird of prey and she a nice, fat mouse.

"You're back," he said, his eyes never leaving Aila. "I can't believe it. You're back and you're safe. Thank Vanda."

Aila waved the man aside and for a wonder, he actually stepped to his right. Aila passed by him and through the door the sergeant had opened for her, Tere and Lily following.

Inside the room, heavily padded chairs and couches sat in precise arrangements. Tables along the walls held platters of fruit, breads, and cheeses, along with several pitchers with mugs and glasses.

A woman rose to her feet as they entered.

She wore a long dress of a fine blue material with grey designs that looked something like flower petals throughout. It covered her more thoroughly than most dresses he'd seen noble women wear, though that seemed to be the style in the Great Enclave. The dress couldn't conceal the slender figure of the woman, though it wasn't as revealing as the tight clothing Aila wore, let alone what Lily had on.

The woman was short, even smaller than Aila. He and Lily towered over her, but her attractive, heart-shaped face revealed no intimidation at the sight of them. Her long brown hair was gathered by a gold circlet around her head and flowed down behind her shoulders past her waist.

Her blue eyes were on only Aila as she stepped forward. "Alevia, you're back. My daughter has returned." She wrapped Aila in a hug and, to Tere's surprise, Aila not only allowed it, but put her own arms around the woman.

Tere swung his head around to find Lily as poleaxed as he was, not sure exactly what he should do. He let the women embrace for a moment, then cleared his throat. "Alevia? Aila, what is this about?"

The women released each other and Aila turned to face Tere. There were tears in her eyes.

"Yeah. Uh, I'm sorry, but there are some things I may not have been entirely truthful about. One of them is my name."

"What did he call you?" the older woman said, somehow appearing to look down at Tere though her eyes were at the level of his chest.

"Please, Mother," Aila said. "Tere, Lily, this is my mother, Mora Davenson. Mother, this is Lily Fisher and Tere Chizzit, who was born with a name you might be more familiar with. Erent Caahs."

Mora's mouth dropped open. Tere thought she must be very surprised to gawk like one of the common people. Nobles tended to try to keep themselves from being off-balanced like that. Of course, he found that his mouth had dropped open, too.

"Wait," Lily said. "Davenson? Are you related to the royal family?"

Mora regained her composure. "Related? We *are* the royal family. Myself, my husband the king, and Princess Alevia." She waved toward Aila as she said that last part.

"Princess Alevia?" Tere sputtered.

"Don't make such a big deal of it," Aila said. "I gave all that up when I ran away."

"You did no such thing, Alevia. You are the princess of the Great Enclave, heir to the throne. Fleeing and mucking about in the dirt will not change that." She looked her daughter up and down. "Which reminds me that you should bathe and change into more...appropriate clothing. It simply won't do for you to traipse around dressed thusly." She paused for a moment, then seemed to recall that there were other people present. "You two as well. You will be given rooms. You look to have traveled much and might also desire baths. The royal tailors can clothe you, too, if you should wish it." Her blue eyes fixed on Lily.

"Thank you...your majesty," Tere said. "Rooms and a bath would be appreciated, but we have spare clothes in our saddlebags. "We haven't come for a social call as much as to speak with the king. Your...husband?"

Aila chimed in. "Yes, we must talk to Father. We've come from the Hero Academy and there are important things to discuss. Where is he? Does he know I'm here?"

Mora's face fell, but as she put her hand to Aila's cheek, a slow, sad smile formed on her lips. "Bathe first, then we will go see your father. An hour will make no difference in your discussion." Aila opened her mouth to speak and Tere recognized her posture. She was going to argue. But her mother lifted a finger, her face serious and sad. "Please, Alevia."

Aila's mouth clicked closed. She nodded, then turned to Tere and Lily. "It looks like we'll be bathing first. Fair enough?"

"Fine with me," Tere said. More than anything, he wanted to get Aila away from her mother so he could question her. A princess!

Mora Davenson kissed Aila's cheek, then picked up a bell

from a side table and rang it. "I will have servants show you where to go and to bring your *saddle bags* to you." She wrinkled her nose at the term. "When you have bathed, you will be shown to where you will meet the king."

The door opened and this time, instead of guards, a small group of liveried servants entered.

"Guide the princess's guests to the suites in the west wing and prepare baths for them. Ah, good, I see you have already retrieved their belongings. Carry them to their rooms. Remain at hand to provide anything they desire."

The servants bowed. One, an older man with a dusting of grey through the hair at his temples, addressed Tere and Lily. "If you would follow me, please. I am Maurius Gainet, Chief Steward of the castle. If there is anything you desire or any question you need answered, please ask and I will do my utmost to satisfy you."

He motioned for them to follow him as he exited the room and headed down the hallway. Aila accompanied Tere and Lily as they did as they were requested.

"Princess Alevia?" Lily whispered to Aila.

"Just call me Aila. I'll explain it all after our baths. I'll meet you in Tere's room while we're waiting to be summoned by my mother."

## 5

Aila soaked in the bath for far longer than she really should have. Her rooms remained as they had been when she left five years before, and luxuriating in the bathing chamber that was part of her rooms felt more wonderful than she ever remembered it feeling.

She opted to dress in some of the clothes from her saddlebags instead of one of the number of dresses in her wardrobes. She liked her tight-fitting functional garb and couldn't even think of flitting around the castle in more formal and—in her mother's view—more appropriate clothing. Besides, she liked it that her mother was put off balance by her daughter's sudden reappearance and would press that advantage. It might go so far as to possibly affect her father as well.

Her father. No doubt her mother would have already spoken to him, preparing him for her. That was fine. She had no desire to reignite the arguments of the past. There were more important things. She had a mission and that was the top priority.

For now, though, something else needed to be done. She

bit her lower lip thinking about it. Tere and Lily deserved an explanation. To be honest, all her friends did, but those two were with her at the moment and they had already been clued in. An uncomfortable sensation low in her belly increased the more she thought about it, like she'd eaten spoiled meat.

*Well, Aila*, she thought. *There's nothing for it but to meet it head-on and hope they accept my explanation.*

There was no need for servants or guides. Aila had grown up in the palace and could navigate it with her eyes closed. She headed straight for the suites granted to her friends. They weren't far from her rooms. When she got to the one she was sure had been given to Tere—her mother hadn't missed that he was the former hero Erent Caahs—she nodded at the servant seated on a small chair in the hallway and knocked.

The door opened quickly, revealing Lily's beautiful face. The tall archer wore her familiar clothing and her skin was slightly flushed, freshly scrubbed.

"Aila," Lily said as a greeting.

"Hi, Lily."

Tere was sitting on one of the couches in his sitting room, inspecting the arrows in his quiver. He took out one at a time, ran his fingers over it while examining it intently, then set it aside in one of two piles. The largest collection was those with no damage—at least, that's what Aila hoped—but there were a few in a smaller pile, no doubt ones that needed work. Cracked shaft, damaged fletching, chipped or bent head, any of those problems could affect flight or effectiveness. Aila had seen Tere and Lily perform their inspections more times than she could remember and the familiar task comforted her. At least a little bit.

Tere glanced up at her and set the arrow he was holding in the larger pile. "Has your mother called for us yet?"

"No. I wanted to explain some things before then. And I wanted to apologize."

"Apologize for what?"

That surprised Aila. Had he forgiven her so quickly? "Uh…"

"After all," the archer continued in a conversational tone, "you've probably told us dozens of lies. Which are you apologizing for? Is there anything you've ever told us that's true? It stretches the limit of my mind to sort through all the many ways in which you've misled us."

"Ouch," Lily said. "Tere?"

"No, never mind," he said, clenching and unclenching his fist. "I'm just a little bit sore, disappointed, and insulted. I always knew there was something off about you, from the moment we met. The little lies and awkward moments before you fabricated answers to questions. I was so busy with everything else, so preoccupied with helping Aeden and trying to save the world, I didn't even act on my instincts to look carefully at the magical matrix to see if you were lying or not. I liked you and didn't think hiding personal information would do us any harm."

"And did it?" Aila spat. "Did it, Tere? Or should I say Erent Caahs. I'm not the only one who had secrets. When would you have told us yours if Lily hadn't recognized you for who you were? Even after she did, it took a while for you to come clean about your past. Can you blame me?

"Sure, I could have just woken up one morning and told everyone, 'Hey, you know how I told you I was an orphan and that my parents were killed? Well, I'm actually heir to the throne of the Great Enclave. Sorry about the confusion.' How would that have been, do you think?"

Tere huffed a breath. "Fine! Point taken. Still, do you expect me to take this easily? How can we believe anything else you've told us, Aila? Alevia. We didn't even know your real name."

"I know," Aila said, "and I'm very sorry. Doesn't it count for something that I volunteered for this mission? I knew I'd have to tell you the truth and that it was all for the greater good, but it was so hard. We've been through so much together. I didn't want a stupid thing like who my parents are to ruin that.

"Tere, you of all my friends know me better than my parents ever could. We were in prison together, for Vanda's sake. You saw me at my absolute worst and at my best. None of that was a lie. I didn't have to say a word. Just trying to survive with you and Urun told you what you need to know about me."

"Yeah, well..."

"Tere, give her a break," Lily said. "She probably started off trying to protect herself. Once she found real friendship in you and the others, it would have been really hard to come clean and admit it all. What harm has she done?"

Tere grumbled for a moment, wringing his hands, before he addressed Aila again. "What else? What of all the things we know about you are true and what are false?"

Aila moved the small pile of arrows and sat down next to Tere. She put her hand on his shoulder. "Everything you know about me from traveling with me is true. I'll tell you the whole story and maybe that will help."

"I'm all ears."

"Okay. As you've heard, I was born here, the only child of Joceus Davenson and Mora Davenson, the King and Queen of the Great Enclave. Our family are direct descendants of Thomasinus, Son of Daven, the founder of the Great Enclave. So, yes, I was raised as a princess, with all that entails. I was tutored and educated to be a proper lady—a proper princess—

and I was trained in the things I would need if I eventually took the throne. That included combat, strategy, history, all of that. It's probably no surprise to you, but combat was my favorite.

"It was rough growing up. I had so much weight on my shoulders, it was hard to be a child. As I got into my teenage years, I began to disagree with some of the things my parents said. I felt pressure to be stronger and better than I was. Nothing I did ever seemed to be good enough. It was stifling. I felt like I was being smothered in it all.

"I did as I had been educated to do. I discussed it with my parents. They still treated me like a child, not taking my opinions seriously. At least, that's what it seemed like to me. I finally had enough and ran away. I didn't leave a note—though I wrote later to tell them I was still alive—and I did something that might be considered unforgivable. I took with me precious heirlooms: my vinci. I'd been trained to use them from a young age, but they are artifacts of the Great Enclave and were not mine to take. Anyone else might be given a death sentence for taking those alone.

"My faith in Vanda and his church is as you've seen in my... discussions with Urun and others, including you. Faith in the church is strong in my family and I made it my own when I was young, though I am a bit disillusioned at what I've seen recently.

"The stories about my parents being killed and my adoption by Rortam were expedient ways to explain my skills and some of the other things I made up either previously or on the spot as they arose. Believe it or not, I don't like lying, but how could I travel the world telling people I was a princess? I would have either been abducted to be ransomed, ignored as a crackpot, or rumors could have eventually reached Clavian ears. Do you doubt the King of the Great Enclave would spare no effort to regain his daughter and heir? Even start a war over it?

"I'm very sorry for my deception, but please know that necessity, not maliciousness, made me do it. I know it will be hard to trust me for a while, but I look forward to proving to you and all my friends that I will never do anything to hurt any of you. Now that my big secret is revealed, I won't do anything to try to deceive any of you again. I ask you to give me a chance to prove to you that I care for all of you and want to help. I've finally found something so important to me that I'd risk my life for it. Please don't tell me I can't help."

Tere looked straight ahead of him, toward the wall, though that didn't really make a difference with the way his magical sight worked. For all Aila knew, he might have been staring right into her eyes as she looked at the side of his head.

"That's all reasonable," he finally said. "I can't find anything malicious about what you did, though it does rankle. Maybe I'm madder at myself for trusting you to begin with."

"I..."

"Let me finish, girl. I do think I know you better than your parents do. Facing death with someone can tell you more in a few days than living with someone safely day to day for years. Your bravery and self-sacrifice in that prison in Praesturi is one of the most heroic things I've ever seen. You have it in you to be a great hero, Aila Ven. Or Alevia Davenson. That means a lot to me. We'll call it past and move on from here. Please don't lie to us anymore. It's going to be hard enough for everyone to trust you, especially those who didn't experience what I did with you."

"I feel the same way," Lily said, "not the least reason of which is because Erent Caahs finds it acceptable to call you a heroine. *That* means a lot to *me*. Besides, we girls need to stick together. Far too many heroes are men."

Tension dissipated from Aila's body like she'd been lanced and it flooded out. She reached over and hugged Tere from the side. He squirmed, but she only hugged him tighter. She released him and hugged Lily too, getting a better response. "Thank you. I'll show you I'm not a liar and a thief...okay, I actually am a thief sometimes, but I'll show you I can be truthful."

"See that you do," Tere said. "We have to have trust or this whole thing is going to be a lot harder."

"Speaking of which," Lily said, "the mission should be loads easier with you presenting the Academy's alliance to your father."

"Yeah, it should. I never thought it would be a problem. Despite anything I might have said that sounded negative, my father is honorable and caring. He'll agree that it's his duty to ally the Great Enclave with the Academy to help defend the world. All we have to do is talk to him. I hope my mother isn't trying anything tricky in not letting us talk to him right away. I guess we'll see soon enough."

❧ 6 ☙

When the steward arrived to lead the group to where they would meet Aila's father at last, the trio followed without speaking. Aila wasn't sure why her friends were silent, but for her, she was trying to sort all the things bouncing around in her mind. Why had her mother been so secretive about going to see her father? Why was the mood even within the palace strained? It wasn't quite as recognizable as it had been out in the city, but there was a tension in the palace that was palpable.

"We're heading toward Father's private rooms," Aila said when they turned toward the vast area that housed living quarters for her father and mother.

"Yes, Princess," the steward said.

"Please Maurius, none of this princess business. Call me Aila or, if you must, Alevia."

"That would be inappropriate, Princess Alevia."

She sighed. "Of course it would. Fine then."

They stopped at the door to her father's bedchambers. The steward stepped aside and Aila opened the door herself, nodding at the man. Tere and Lily followed her inside.

After passing through the large sitting room, they entered the actual bedchamber. Aila's mother was there, along with two other people, but Aila had only eyes for the bed itself. Her father lay within it, blankets covering all of him but his face.

"Father?" she said, rushing to the bedside. "What happened? What is this?"

"Peace, Alevia. We will get to that in time. For now, let me look at you." She didn't like how weak his voice sounded.

Mora helped her husband to sit up, propping pillows behind him so he could see his daughter better. While he positioned himself, Aila looked at the other two people nearby.

Before she could greet them, a shape appeared from around the bed. A familiar shape. Aila smiled and knelt down with her arms out.

"Rumbler, old dog. How are you? Catch any squirrels lately in the garden?"

The old hound plowed into Aila's hug, tail wagging behind him. Her heart ached a little that it had been so long since she'd seen the dog. They'd had some nice adventures when she was younger. After petting Rumbler and giving him a few kisses on his grizzled head, she rose and shifted her attention to the other humans.

Sudin Torfan, his bulky form slouching at the side of the bed, looked as he always had, though perhaps a bit heavier. He was on the King's Council and was Joceus Davenson's oldest friend. Of course he would be close. The man dipped his black-haired, shaggy head at Aila and forced a smile.

The other person was also familiar to Aila. Verona Gilcaryn was a graduate of the Hero Academy, and the king's mage. In blue robes reminiscent of the cut some of the masters at Sitor-Kanda wore, she stood regally—perhaps even a little arrogantly—watching everyone. She was more than half a foot taller than Aila herself, and though she had some grey speckling her brown hair, her face appeared much younger than her sixty-two years. After having spent so much time at the Academy, it didn't seem strange to Aila anymore.

"Alevia," Verona said. "It is nice to see you again. We all thought you lost to us."

"No, not yet," Aila said. She had no desire for conversation with these others. She purposely turned her back to the two visitors and faced her father directly. She'd probably get a reprimand for that once things settled down.

"I'll leave you to your family, your majesty," Sudin said, sketching out a bow that looked humorous with his squat figure.

Joceus waved to his friend but locked his eyes onto Aila.

"Alevia, I'm so glad to see you again. Your mother has told me of your companions. I welcome them to my home. Is it true? Do you travel with the hero Erent Caahs?"

Aila could hardly stand the small talk. She gritted her teeth against the urge to yell that everyone stop wasting time with trivialities and address why her father lay weakly in bed.

"I was born with that name," Tere said. "Nowadays, I go by the name Tere Chizzit, your majesty."

"Ah." The king coughed into a hand. "I have found that a name does not mean as much as the way with which someone comports themselves. I am honored to meet you, Tere Chizzit. A hero by any name is worthy of honor. So, too, I am glad to meet you, Lily Fisher, one who no doubt is as accustomed to heroic acts as your companions. Is that not correct, *Aila Ven?*"

As he'd always done, Aila's father had taken control of the conversation and left her wondering what she should say. She did her best.

"It is, Father. I couldn't very well use my true name, could I? How long would it have been until your spies had found me and dragged me home by my boots? As to heroes, my life is awash with them. We will speak of it, maybe, but now I want only to speak of one thing. Why are you abed and what is happening?"

Joceus's eyes twinkled, but they lacked the fire Aila was used to. For the first time, she noticed his gaunt cheeks and the dark circles under his eyes. His hair, usually so thick and vibrant, lay on his head like a dead thing.

"Your father is ill," Verona answered. "From what I can tell, he has been poisoned."

"Poisoned?" Aila said. "Who would poison the king? *How* could he be poisoned?"

"We do not know the how of it. I have used all the knowledge and magic at my disposal to identify and combat it. It does not look good."

"You're a graduate of the Hero Academy. You should be able to heal anything. If not with magical healing, then with alchemy. Why haven't you contacted Master Videric, Master Saikio, or Master Vaeril? I have a message tablet linked to one Headmaster Qydus himself has. I can notify them, and any help the Academy can provide will be here soon. Why have you not asked for aid? How long has he been ill?"

"I'm afraid it's not that easy, Alevia," Verona said, though Aila read interest in her eyes. She must have been wondering how Aila knew the names of the masters of the School of Magical Healing, the School of Mundane Healing, and the School of Alchemy, let alone having a direct line of communication to the headmaster himself. "He has been afflicted thus for nearly two weeks with a poison that is gradually tearing his body down from the inside out. I have not asked for help because no one from the Academy will be able to aid us."

"The Academy is the heart of the most powerful magic and healing elixirs in the world," Aila said. "They can heal anything."

"Oh, if only that were true. I say they cannot aid us because I already know how to heal the king. It is a relatively simple matter, though not an easy one. He has been poisoned with Soulrot poison."

A sharp intake of breath behind her drew Aila's eyes. She blinked at Tere, whose face was twisted in fear.

"What?" Aila asked.

"Soulrot poison," Tere said. "It's a mixture of several rare poisonous ingredients. Once within a victim's system, it's resistant to neutralization and healing. The interaction between the components also provides protection from magical healing or purging. Attempts at healing will often speed up the reaction. There is no cure."

"I am impressed by your knowledge," Verona said, "but it is incomplete. There is one way to neutralize the poison. The extract of an exceptionally rare flower, one that is known to grow in only one place in Dizhelim."

"There we have it, then," Aila said. "We obtain the flower and cure him of the poison."

"The flower grows only in Sintrovis, and no one has seen a fireheart flower in decades. It is believed to be extinct."

"No! I refuse to believe that. Just because no one has reported seeing the flower does not mean it's extinct. Tell me that you've sent people to find some of the flowers."

"We have, Alevia," Mora said. "We have sent three different expeditions into Sintrovis to find the flowers; nearly forty soldiers, herbalists, and trackers. None have returned."

Lily raised her hand to get everyone's attention. "I'm sorry. Sintrovis?"

"It's essentially the center of the Great Enclave," Tere said. "Legend holds that it's the source of the magical power Kebahn the Wise harnessed when he and Thomasinus holed up against the combined might of the Salamusian and the Souveni armies trying to crush them. It is, for all intents and purposes, the most precious area within the Great Enclave."

"More than that," Aila said. "Though Kebahn and my ancestor originally came here looking for a place that was steeped in legends of strange magic, they were never able to penetrate the heavy forest that makes up Sintrovis. Expeditions have tried to explore it, but most never return. The kings haven't made a concerted effort to press through with massive forces because it's a sacred place, the birthplace of our nation. They would not defile it by trampling it with massive numbers of troops."

"That is correct," Verona said. "Unless any of the expedition members return with the flowers, I'm afraid all we can do is try to keep the king strong for as long as possible. Soulrot is always fatal, but perhaps we can lengthen the time he has left."

"Which is why I'm so delighted you have returned, Alevia," the king said. "Now that you're back, I can spend my remaining time transitioning, preparing you to take the throne. Vanda has surely answered my prayers by leading you back here."

"What?" Aila said. "I'm not going to sit by while you die, nor am I going to waste time learning matters of state when I can be doing something to help. I wish I'd known about this before so I could have brought others with me. Still, I have Tere and Lily. We've faced things you wouldn't believe in the last several months. My friends Aeden Tannoch and Marla Shrike are together the Malatirsay and I've seen them, as well as all of my other friends, do miraculous and heroic things. Only we three are here now, but we're no slouches.

"We're going into Sintrovis and finding those flowers. If I have to capture magic that will let me conjure them from thin air, then that's what I'll do. You will not die, Father. I forbid it."

Joceus Davenson chuckled for half a moment before doubling up in pain at the action. He eased himself back to rest against the pillows, his face wan and his eyes slitted. "Oh, Alevia, how I missed you and your affection for the dramatic. I would like to hear more about these friends of yours after I have had a chance to rest. You will not be going to Sintrovis. The kingdom cannot afford to lose you. *I* cannot afford to lose you again."

"I'll speak with you further after you've rested," Aila said. "It will have to be later today, however. Tomorrow morning, I and my friends will be leaving to explore Sintrovis." She shifted her eyes to Tere and Lily, both of whom nodded to her.

Aila leaned in and kissed her father's forehead, then spun on her heel and left the room. Tere and Lily said their farewells and followed after.

The trio hadn't gone more than ten paces down the hall before Mora Davenson and Verona Gilcaryn caught up to them.

"Wait, Alevia," her mother said. "Please."

Aila stopped and turned to meet the two older women.

"Is it true?" Verona said. "The Malatirsay? Has the prophesied hero come at last?"

"Yes," Tere said, "but not like people expected. The masters have recognized Aeden and Marla—who are twins— as the Malatirsay."

"Marla Shrike?"

"Yes, and her twin brother Aeden. They were separated at birth."

"I have heard much about Marla. It was expected that she would be the Malatirsay. The masters have proclaimed they are indeed the prophesied ones?"

"They announced it to the entire Academy," Aila said. "I

was there. They are publishing it to the rest of the world, but it isn't common knowledge yet."

"Then the rumors of dark monsters...?" Verona asked.

"True. We've fought them. A lot of them. It's our main occupation lately. That, and freeing bound magic from Wells of Power."

"Wells of—"

"Enough," Mora said. "None of that matters. What does matter is doing as your father has told you, Alevia. You will prepare yourself to rule the Great Enclave. You will not go against his wishes."

Aila raised her chin and stiffened her stance. "I will do what I think is right. I will not sit idly by as my father dies. He is too young and too strong for that. Instead of spending your time trying to command me to do something, why don't you find out who poisoned him and why. Leave his healing to me, or at least the retrieval of the flowers needed for his healing. I will let my father rest for three hours and then I will speak with him again. Until then, I have other matters to attend to."

She turned and headed back toward Tere's rooms, her two friends a step behind. They had an expedition to plan, and there was no time to waste.

❧ 7 ☙

"Yes, Princess Alevia," Maurius said. "I will have everything ready for you by tomorrow morning."

"Thank you, Maurius," Aila said. "You understand I'm doing this to help my father, don't you?"

"I do. I will turn the task over to others so that you will have your supplies even if your mother or father command me not to aid you. I cannot disobey the king or the queen, no matter that it is for their good."

"You're the same Maurius who used to sneak me sweets as a child. I'm glad."

"And I am glad you have returned, if only briefly. Please be careful. I have a hard enough time helping you without anything untoward in the mix. I would never forgive myself if harm befell you."

"I'll be fine." Aila gestured toward Tere and Lily, both sitting on chairs in Tere's sitting room. "I have these two heroes watching my back."

Maurius nodded. "You are truly Erent Caahs?" the steward asked Tere.

"I was."

"I used to love tales of your adventures. Still do, if I am honest. I told them often to a certain princess who was much too interested in people putting themselves in danger to aid others. It seems I may be somewhat responsible for...ah, certain tendencies in you, Princess Alevia."

Tere chuckled. "As am I, though this particular princess doesn't need anyone to give her reasons for acting like she's invulnerable. That comes naturally, if my experiences with her are any indication."

"True," the steward said. He bowed to the three of them and headed for the door. "I will begin preparations. It would make things easier if you could get your father's approval, even if not your mother's. I do hate to go around the edges of my duty. You are the only one who has ever been able to prompt that in me."

Aila smiled at the steward. "I'll talk with Father a little later. I'll do my best to make him see reason."

The three spent some time discussing their plans to find the flowers. Sintrovis was within the bowl of the Great Enclave, not terribly far away, so they could make it to the edge of the area within a day, a day and a half at most. Once they got there, though, there would be no easy roads to travel, so it was anyone's guess how long it would take them to actually find any fireheart plants.

"There are no maps of the area at all?" Lily asked.

"No," Aila said. "It's far too dangerous for mapping parties to go in and document. Because of the special significance of the place and the magic that's apparent, the kings have never allowed any major expeditions with large complements of guards that might damage the balance of the area. They even declined to allow scholars from the Academy in to study it, afraid of defiling the place. It's an advantage that much of the nation is surrounded by impenetrable mountains. Controlling access is fairly easy."

"So we're going to go there, search from the edges, and move inward no one knows how far until we find the flowers?" Tere asked.

"That's the plan."

"How are we going to know where we're going, or how to get out?"

"We've got the best tracker in Dizhelim with us," Aila said, smiling widely at Tere. "Between your knowledge and experience, as well as your newly enhanced magical sight, your job is to lead us and not let us get lost."

"Great. Just what I need, for the entire mission to be on my shoulders. How do you manage to turn even a simple duty of talking to your father into something that might kill us and affect a whole nation?"

"It's a special talent I have. A habit, really. Better that than for me to become queen of the Great Enclave, though, right?"

"I'd have to agree with you there, though that would make it easier to secure the nation as an ally."

Aila laughed. "Don't worry. I will speak to Father about that also. Before we even leave, I want to make sure he'll help out with the animaru problem. It's why we're here, after all."

"It is. I'm glad you remembered." Tere's eyebrows drew down so he looked like he was glaring at the table in front of his chair. "We should probably send a message to the others. Tell them about what's going on and who you are."

"No. When we leave tomorrow, we can tell them what we're doing, but not a word about my real name. I want to tell them in person, if I can. Sending a message that the headmaster will get the same time as the others seems rude to me. Please, Tere, let me tell them personally."

"She's right, Tere," Lily said. "This isn't something that should be done in a letter, so to speak. It can wait until we're back at the Academy."

"And if we don't make it back?" Tere asked. "What then?"

"Then they'll find out eventually anyway," Aila said, "but it won't matter to us. Let's not even think that way. We'll do this, we'll help my father, we'll get the alliance all set up, then we'll return to the Academy and the others. There is too much for us to do not to be successful."

Tere sighed. "Fine, but we send a message tomorrow to tell them about our mission and the situation with the king."

"Agreed."

Two hours later, Aila led her friends back to the king's rooms. The guards were still posted outside, though the watch had appeared to have changed since earlier. Aila nodded to them and entered to find her father propped up in a sitting position. He was speaking with another familiar figure.

"Father," Aila said. "Conren." She managed to make the second word sound bored. Or disappointed. Maybe a little like an accusation.

The young man bowed to Aila, his armor creaking at the motion. "Princess Alevia, I'm glad to see you again. There wasn't time for us to talk earlier."

"There still isn't," she said. "Tere Chizzit, Lily Fisher, this is Conren Gardner, a friend and sometimes irritant I have known most of my life."

"*Sir* Conren Gardner," the king said. "Conren was knighted almost two years ago. Young for a knight, but you know how dedicated he has always been to his training."

"Hmph," Aila said, and left it at that.

"Alevia, I've rested and am ready to continue our conversation. Please, sit." The king waved toward the chairs lining the sides of the room.

"You can go now, Conren." Aila dragged one of the chairs to the bedside. Tere and Lily imitated her with chairs of their own.

"No," her father said. "Stay, Conren."

Aila frowned at that, but turned a little more to focus directly on her father and break the line of sight to Conren's eyes.

"Father, I and my friends have come from the Academy specifically to talk to you. You've no doubt heard rumors of the dark monsters causing problems in the East. They are the dark creatures of the Prophecy. Animaru. I have fought them, and they are as monstrous as the rumors state. More are coming from their world to invade our own and the time of the Prophecy is at hand. The Dark Days are here.

"My mission was to speak with you to secure an alliance with Sitor-Kanda. The masters and the students have magic, but they are not numerous. Those we have are mighty, but the numbers of the monsters are too great. We will need soldiers, and there are no finer than the Clavian Knights."

"Alevia, you know better than to try to stroke my ego. No doubt the Clavian Knights are the finest heavy cavalry in the world, but it's too much to say they are the best warriors in the world. The Teroshimi, the Shinyin, and especially the Crows, they can match our troops in the right situation."

"Funny you should mention that. My close friend Aeden Tannoch has become the high chieftain of all the Croagh, and all the highlanders are now at the Academy, preparing for the battles with the animaru."

Joceus's eyes grew larger. "All the clans? They came together and are cooperating with these forces the Academy is gathering?"

"They have and they are. Oh, Father, you should see Aeden fight. I've never seen anyone do what he can do. Not even his twin sister, Marla, who is the best student at the Hero Academy. We're all working toward trying to save Dizhelim. We need your help."

"Of course," he said. "We will help as we can. I'll need to

bring it up with the Council. I have excluded myself from the day-to-day workings of the kingdom since I have been ill. Verona and Sudin tell me it's best that way, to preserve my strength for fighting the effects of the poison rather than worrying about other things. I'll rest and call for a special meeting of the Council to discuss it."

"Thank you, Father. I knew you'd help. When we bring the flowers back and you're healed, maybe you can come back with me to the Academy and speak with the masters there yourself."

The king's eyes dropped to his blanket. "Alevia, you can't go do this. You must prepare to take the throne. I don't know how much longer I have. I can feel the poison taking over. I'm getting weaker. I need your strength."

"Strength," she said. "You always told me I needed more strength. I was always too weak for you and for mother. Now you say you need my strength? I tell you, Father, I will use every bit of any strength I have, but I will use it to find the means to cure you. I would have your blessing on my mission, but even if I don't, I will go to Sintrovis."

"I am the king and your father, Alevia. If I tell you that you cannot go, you will not."

"I will. Do you think you can stop me? Could you stop me from leaving before? Could you stop me from staying away? I do not want to kill any of your knights or soldiers, Father, but I will not be kept from this mission." Aila drew her weapons and dropped into a ready stance.

Conren's hand went to his sword hilt as he stepped to widen his stance.

"Ah, the vinci," the king said. "I'm glad you have kept them safe. Would you really use them against my guards?"

"If they try to keep me from helping you, yes. My years away have honed my skills, Father. Not just combat. You cannot hold me here. Conren cannot stop me. I beg that you don't try."

The king's brown eyes, so like those she saw in the mirror when she looked at herself earlier, met hers. They stared for a moment, neither making a move to give in. Then Joceus smiled. "Very well. I am not fond of you going into danger, but I will not force danger upon you by making you an enemy. You may go on your search, but you must return within one week. Promise me. Whether you have found the flowers or not, one week from when you leave, you will be back here in the palace."

Aila looked over at Tere and Lily. The older archer nodded. "Fine. One week."

"And you will take Conren with you."

"What? No. I have no need of a metal-covered brute. We will travel quickly and quietly. There is no room for an armored knight clanking around behind us."

"You will take him. It is one of the stipulations for me agreeing to the mission. He can forgo the plate and wear leather armor." The young man did a double-take at the king. "It's fine, Conren. Your skills are sufficient. Traveling through heavy vegetation with plate armor is not something I would wish on anyone. Believe me, you'll be better off."

Aila still didn't want the man to go with them, but her father grew visibly weaker as the conversation went on. "Fine. He can come, but he has to obey me."

"He will follow you, but you'll not order him about like some servant. If you want to command knights, then you will have to wait until you gain the throne."

Aila gritted her teeth but didn't argue further.

"We'll be leaving in the morning, Father. I won't wake you for our departure. Rest. We'll get back as soon as possible with the flowers so you can be healed. Stay strong."

"You be careful, Alevia," the king said. "I look forward to

hearing about all the adventures you've had since you left us. I hope you won't have too many in search of the fireheart flowers."

Aila hugged her father carefully and kissed his cheek, then said goodnight. Out in the hall, once the door was closed, she turned to Tere and Lily. "I think I need a little training after that, to get rid of some of the pent-up energy. I'm going to head to my favorite training room. You want me to meet you back at Tere's room before dinner?"

"No," Tere said. "We'll go with you. I could use a little exercise, too."

"Fair enough. Let's go. I'll see you later, Conren."

"I'll join you," the knight said. "To make it an even number. Maybe we can get some sparring in."

Aila rolled her eyes and started toward the training room.

8

The Clavian princess led the others to one of the lower levels of the castle. She stopped in front of the heavy wooden door and ran a finger down its surface. It had been five years since she had entered the room. A warm, nostalgic feeling washed over her. Some of her best memories were in this place.

"Aila?" Tere said.

She realized she hadn't moved for too long, her hand still on the door. She cleared her throat. "Sorry. It's been a while since I've been here. Just reliving some memories, that's all."

Aila grabbed a cold torch from the wall and lit it on a lantern, then opened the door and entered the room.

The space wasn't as large as many of the other training rooms on levels above, only about thirty feet by forty, but what had begun as a place for her to get away from others to train by herself had become her favorite haunt. It felt like home, much more so than her rooms far above them.

The others couldn't see the extent of the room, of course, or not anyone but Tere. She touched the torch to the closest wall lamp and a circle of light spread out, revealing a pair of training dummies near the stone wall. She went to the next lamp.

A quick swishing brought Aila's attention to the others. She recognized that sound. As expected, she found Tere with his bow up and an arrow nocked. The man was so fast. His bow had been across his chest, the string on his front and the stave on his back.

"Alevia," a familiar voice said from the still-darkened part of the room.

"Master Olar," she cried, dropping to the ground in a kneeling bow, torch on the floor in front of her.

The man chuckled and stepped into the light. He looked as he always had: old and weathered, of no consequence. Aila wasn't sure exactly how old the man was, but he had to be well into his sixties, perhaps in his seventies. His age, and his appearance, were deceiving, though. The long grey hair tied into a tail behind his head, his craggy face, and his slight stature hid one of the finest warriors Aila had ever seen.

"Alevia, it won't do for the princess of the Great Enclave to bow to an old man of low birth. Please, don't soil your clothing for me. Up, girl."

She obeyed and rushed to her combat master to wrap him in a hug. He wasn't too much taller than her and his whip-thin body felt firm and sinewy in her embrace.

"Were you waiting here for me?" she asked.

"No, of course not. I routinely sit in the dark in an unused training room." He winked, forcing a laugh from her.

"Oh," she said. "Tere, it's fine." She looked back at her friends, but the old archer had already put his arrow back in the quiver.

"I gathered that."

"Everyone, this is my combat master, Olar Zeen." She ran

through the names of her friends, and the master greeted them with the respect he always showed to anyone he met.

"Pardon me for intruding upon your training," he said. "When I heard Alevia had returned, I knew it would only be a matter of time before she came to her old training room. She was the only one to use this place."

"It's so good to see you, Master Olar. You haven't changed a bit since I last saw you."

"Ah, yes. I was old then and I am old now, eh? You, on the other hand, *have* changed in your absence. Your childish face has grown into that of a beautiful woman and your form—" He stepped back and appraised her. "You have continued with your training. That gladdens my heart. There is nothing worse than a student who forgoes training and becomes fat. You are even fitter than when you left. Life out in the world agrees with you."

Aila laughed. "Or maybe you're confusing my leanness for fitness. Meals are harder to come by in the world than here in the castle."

"Don't be modest, girl. I can see it in the way you move. You have a warrior's grace. Difficult, is it? Dangerous?"

"Very. I'll tell you a little about it."

"Later. Do you have them still?"

Aila drew her vinci from their sheaths and held them up for the master's inspection.

"Very good," he said. "You have maintained them well. Have you also grown in skill with them?"

She smirked. "Wanna find out?"

"I would like nothing better." Olar stepped back in the shadows and retrieved a long, slender staff. Aila remembered it well.

"Let me finish lighting the lamps," she said, moving quickly to light another of the wall lamps.

"You need light to fight?" he said. He sounded disappointed.

"Not really." She lit another lamp. "But I want my friends to see this. It's always a treat to watch your skill, even if it means being on the receiving end."

Once the entire room was illuminated, Aila deposited the torch in an empty sconce, then faced Master Olar in the center of the room.

The old man bowed to her as she bowed to him. Without a word or a pause, he lunged in, his staff a blur.

Aila was well familiar with the weapon her master wielded. She'd felt its sting many times, though Olar was controlled enough to hold back the full force of his strikes. Made of solid metal, the weapon wasn't much heavier than a wooden staff of the same length—somewhere between four and five feet. It was thinner than a wooden staff, true, but it was just as strong. Aila wasn't sure what metal it was composed of, but even if it was harder than wood, it was also more flexible than any metal weapon had a right to be. Like spring steel, though with no edge.

Aila sidestepped the downward blow, drawing both vinci and parrying with the one in her left hand. The satisfying ring of metal on metal reverberated in the room. As expected, the staff swung around in a tight circle to come at her again, but she was already spinning out of the way. She tapped it with her other blade to make sure.

"Good," the master said, and sped up his movements.

It had been five years since she had sparred with Olar, and her reflexes were better than ever. Of course, one of the master's favorite tricks was to manipulate an opponent to believe they were doing better than they actually were.

There. Master Olar feinted a low strike with one end of the staff while kicking at mid-height. Aila dodged to the side and slashed with the weapon in her right hand, but kept her left vinci in a checking position just in case...as expected, the other end of the staff zipped down toward her head. Even prepared, she was slightly off balance and the parry she attempted turned out to be more of a block. Her weapon vibrated in her hand so violently, it almost shook itself free. She harnessed the force of the strike and dropped into a roll to gain distance from the attack she knew would follow.

She had forgotten the feel of facing the master's speed. As she came up out of the roll, she immediately had to roll away again to evade a horizontal strike to her head. That was followed up by a low, sweeping attack that she narrowly dodged by diving into a midair somersault.

Master Olar was relentless. Now that she was pressed, he wouldn't let up until he had finished the fight. Aila had been in the situation before. Many times. But she'd learned a thing or two in the years she'd been gone. With the next strike, a downward diagonal slash that morphed into a powerful thrust with the tip of the staff, she did something she hoped would be unexpected.

She stepped into the blow.

The master's eyes widened fractionally, a movement that was equivalent to any other warrior's mouth dropping open. Aila timed her movement perfectly so that the downward strike missed her by a hair's breadth and when the thrust came in, it was awkward because she was so close. The master recovered and rotated to strike her in the face with an elbow. Aila also twisted, displaying her body's profile to the master and jamming her own elbow into his strike to nullify it.

The princess dove at the ground to her right side, rolling and coming up to her feet quickly a few feet away. She threw out her vinci, one after another, controlling them with the chains attached to their hilts. The magic of the weapon allowed her to control the length of the chains and years of practice let her swing them with precision.

Master Olar batted the first vincus away and evaded the second. He was too far to strike at her effectively with the staff, but Aila's opponent was at the perfect distance for her own weapons. She whirled them, arms crossing over her chest to generate momentum, and struck time and again at the master. He calmly dodged or parried the weapons but was unable to close the distance between them. He tried, but each time, Aila would shorten the chain on one of her weapons to cut off any charge he might make.

Aila knew better than to continue with the same methods. The master had more tricks than her and he would eventually exploit any small error in her attack.

She whipped the chains around, maneuvering Master Olar into position. He almost caught her once, lunging in so quickly between the swinging blades, she was barely able to hop back and out of range in time. She swung the right vincus down at his feet and instead of diving as she would have expected from another opponent, the master jumped over the chain weapon like a skipping rope.

That was what Aila had been waiting for. She jerked her left shoulder painfully to snap the vincus on its chain and it wrapped around the master's ankles while he was still in midair and not able to dodge. He landed, somehow still keeping his balance, but the battle was won.

Aila pulled on the chain and realized she had been premature in calling it the end. Master Olar, ankles tied together, still had the strength to resist the pull of the chain. She met the master's eyes and knew from the intense look there that he was about to do something unorthodox. He was going to throw his staff.

In the fraction of a second it took the master to change his grip on his weapon to throw it at her, Aila acted. She whirled her right-hand vincus around, but not to attack. She lengthened the chain considerably so that it touched the master at about its midpoint. The force swept it around and wrapped its length around Olar, squeezing his arms together and keeping the staff within its coils.

Aila lunged in, shouldering the master in the chest, knocking him down. When they landed on the floor, Aila grasped the hilts of her weapons and brought them to the master's throat.

"Ungh," Master Olar said. "You have been training. Well done, Alevia."

She unwrapped the chains from the master and pulled him to his feet.

Master Olar looked Aila up and down, then nodded. "Very well done indeed. It has been many years since I was bested in combat. Many years."

"I know you went easy on me," she said, but the comment made her feel like she was floating anyway. "But yes, I have been working on my skills. I have to. We're fighting thousands of dark monsters from another world."

Aila explained a little bit of what had been happening while the others availed themselves of the training facilities. By the time Aila had caught the master up on what she'd been doing, her friends and Conren wore a sheen of perspiration. Tere and Lily from sparring with their knives, and Conren from his work on a training dummy he'd kept himself busy with.

"Are you ready to meet me in the circle?" Conren asked her.

"Do you think you would fare better than Master Olar?" she answered.

"I don't mean with your magic weapons. How about a wrestling contest? Do you remember how you used to tease me about not being strong enough? You're not the only one who has gotten stronger."

"A wrestling contest? Is this your way of being able to hug me?"

Strangely, the young knight flushed at the question. "Afraid to fight me? Know I'm too strong for you?"

"Never," she said. "Fine. Come on then. No weapons, just us."

They set their weapons aside and walked to the center of the room.

❀   *9*   ❀

Standing face to face so closely with Conren, it struck Aila how tall he had gotten. He was almost the same height as Tere, though not as large all the way around. He'd gained some muscle since she'd seen him last, no doubt, but she remembered their bouts when they were younger. He'd been bigger than her then, too, but she had been victorious in their matches more times than not.

"I'll try not to hurt you," he said and got into a wide stance, arms outstretched.

Aila growled at him and launched herself forward, her hands going to his legs to bring him down.

But he didn't. Whereas she'd always been able to tip his balance with a good, strong lunge and been able to peel his feet from the floor, now it felt like she'd run into a stone wall. The impact of her shoulder on his chest jarred her; had she not had her teeth gritted, they would have clacked together hard enough to crack a tooth. For a moment, she was stunned and had to shake her head to clear her vision.

The time she took to do that was enough for Conren to

grab her shoulders and shove her body aside. Luckily, he let go as he tossed her.

Aila spun in the air, landing on the floor in an awkward roll and coming up onto her feet. Her opponent was still in the same position he had been, feet wide and rooted to the floor, arms back in the ready position.

She rethought her tactics. What had worked before wasn't effective anymore. She mirrored his stance, shuffling around him, trying to think of what to do next.

This time, it was the knight who surged forward, reaching for Aila's legs as she had just done to him. She knew she had no chance of stalling his attack by standing her ground, so she spun as he reached for her, skittering over his back like a monkey to take him down from above and behind.

Again, she met strength that outmatched her own. Though she pulled back on his shoulders while trying to force his knees to bend from behind, his body refused to buckle.

Conren snatched her arms from his shoulders, trapping them, then twisted and let himself fall sideways. Right on top of her.

All the air in Aila's body left in a huff and when she could focus on her surroundings again, Sir Conren bloody Gardner was astride her, his arms pinning her shoulders as he sat on her legs.

"Done?" he asked.

"Done," she wheezed.

He climbed to his feet and held a hand out to her to help her up. She ignored it and scrambled to her feet on her own, still trying to refill her lungs.

"Like I said, I've gotten stronger." He returned to the bench where he'd put his sword belt and strapped it back on.

Aila's face burned with the fire of the sun. For the moment, she couldn't think of anything clever to say. She nodded instead, and returned to retrieve her weapons as well.

The awkward silence stretched for a moment before Tere came to the rescue.

"Isn't it close to dinner time? Your mother won't be happy with us if we keep you from arriving on time."

"You're right," Aila said. "We should probably go back and get ready."

Thankfully, Conren didn't say anything else, only took up his position as if he were guarding the whole group. Master Olar bade them good evening, the shadow of a smile on his face, and offered to put out the lamps in the training room.

"Thank you," Aila said to the master. "I will speak with you again when I return from the mission we'll start tomorrow."

"I shall look forward to it."

The group made it to the dining room on time, for which Aila was thankful. Conren was there, honored with a place at the table. It was not typical for one so young as he, but the king's insistence he travel with Aila and her friends must have had something to do with it.

Others were there as well.

Aila sighed and explained the situation to Tere and Lily. "There are usually a handful of people given the opportunity to dine with the royal family. For the most part, it's nobles or high-ranking military folks. My father always said that it helps to keep in touch with those in his kingdom. I always argued that if he wanted to keep in touch with the people, he ought to invite commoners." She looked around the room at the dozen and a half people who were already seated. "It doesn't look like he took my advice."

Aila and her friends were shown to their places at the head of the table. The king's chair stood empty, but beside it sat her mother. The princess's place was next to Mora, with Tere and Lily on the other side of the table facing them.

Conren sat next to Aila, and sitting next to Tere was an older man in the dress uniform of the Clavian military.

Tere nodded to the man as he sat, reaching for a cup a servant filled with wine before the archer had even brought it to the edge of the table.

"This is Colonel Quinn Watson," the queen said.

"Retired colonel," the man corrected. His head was almost completely bald, his skin saggy, but he sat as straight as always. It looked to Aila that the man had aged twice as many years as it had been since she'd seen him last.

"Of course. You know my daughter, Colonel. These are her friends, Tere Chizzit and Lily Fisher."

"It is a pleasure to meet you," Quinn said with a bow of his head. "It is a joyous even time that the princess has returned. Are you to thank for convincing her to come back home?"

Tere was busy with his wine, so Lily answered. "No. We actually came here on a mission from Sitor-Kanda. Aila...uh, Alevia has been traveling with us for some time, helping to..."

Aila jumped in. "It's fine, Lily. Colonel, we've been occupied in fighting the dark monsters, the animaru, who have invaded Dizhelim."

"Truly? That sounds exciting. And dangerous."

Aila noticed Tere staring at the colonel. She wondered what it was about. Had he seen something in the magical field that tipped him off to some danger?

"Pardon me," the archer said before Aila could think much more of it. "Did you say your name was Quinn Watson?"

"That is correct, sir."

"You were detailed to the desk at headquarters when you were very young? Dealt with bounties and such things?"

The colonel tilted his head and swiveled to face Tere more

squarely. "I did. I had that duty for almost two years before moving to another assignment. Why do you ask?"

Tere smirked. "I met you back then. Briefly. You asked me if I could use my weapons and I told you I could. I also told you to watch for my name. I wonder if you ever heard of me again after that."

The colonel's mouth dropped open. It was the single most pronounced expression Aila had ever seen from the man, and she saw him often as she was growing up. "The slaver...?" he stammered.

"Yes. Ossar Sattis."

"You. It can't be you. You're dead?"

"So I keep being told. *That* man is dead, but I linger on. I don't use my real name anymore. Too much history. It *is* good to see you again, my friend. I hope I didn't disappoint you back then."

The colonel barked a laugh. "I made three silvers. Some of the other guards heard us talking and bet me we'd see a report of your death. I saw something else in you. I bet that we'd be hearing your name soon, and often. If this wine were not free, I would buy you a drink."

"Don't let that stop you," Tere said, holding up his cup. The colonel tapped his own cup to Tere's.

Conren watched the exchange, switching his gaze between Tere and the colonel. His forehead was crinkled in confusion.

"Tere Chizzit is not his real name," Aila told Conren. "You might recognize his real name. He's Erent Caahs."

Conren choked on the water he was drinking, narrowly avoiding spitting it out in a spray. "He's who?"

"You heard me," she said, sipping the wine in her own cup.

Mora Davenson excused herself early. Tere and Lily were speaking animatedly with Colonel Watson and Aila figured it would be a while until they were ready for bed. She excused herself, wanting a few minutes of time with her mother alone. She headed up to her mother's rooms, hoping the woman was there and not visiting the king.

When Aila knocked on the queen's door, a voice from within said, "Come."

"Oh, good. Alevia. I was hoping you would come by to chat." The queen was sitting on a large stuffed chair near the fireplace.

"I have a few things I want to talk about before we leave on our mission tomorrow." Aila sat on a couch in the sitting room and screwed up her courage to address all the things she wanted to talk about.

"Your friends seem to have hit it off with the colonel."

"They're both good with people. Besides, Tere has an amazing amount of history in this part of the world. In all parts, to be honest."

"You believe he's really Erent Caahs resurrected?"

Aila quirked an eyebrow. "Resurrected? No. He is Erent Caahs, without a doubt. He knows things, can do things that eliminate all doubt. I won't explain because it's not my story to tell, but he is the hero everyone always said he was. Even more so, since I have come to know the man behind the legend. He's more human than those cold stories. He's a great man."

"And Lily?"

She smiled at the thought of the tall archer. "She is nearly everything Erent Caahs was, and beautiful besides. Tere seems constantly amazed at her skills."

"At more than her skills, I'd say," the queen said.

"Enough about my friends. That's not what I wanted to talk about."

"Will you tell me why you left?"

"It shouldn't be a mystery, mother. I was stifled, pressed

upon. The constant pressure to become stronger and stronger was relentless and I couldn't stand it anymore."

"You could have talked to me."

"I tried talking to you. Your answer to everything was 'obey your father and everything will be fine.' That was the worst of it, I think. You never stood up to him for yourself, but for some reason I expected you to do so for me. You never did."

"Alevia, you have to understand that your father is a king. He's like a boulder rolling down a hill. You can try to stop him, but that only gets you crushed. It's best to get out of the way and allow him to do as he will."

"No. I've learned a lot in the last few years. One of the things I've learned is that if you give in, it only invites you to continue to do so. Maybe there is a boulder rolling down a hill. Maybe trying to stop it will get you crushed. In that case, you need to push it from the side, divert its course. Discretion and intelligently applied force, that's what's needed, not to give up and allow your life to be mapped out for you."

"Alevia..."

"I resented you for years because you sat idly by while my father pushed and pushed."

"He loves you. He wants you to be the best you can be."

"I know he does, but he's wrong in the way he shows it. I think his obsession with me becoming stronger has more to do with the kingdom and our duty as the ruling family than me as a person. I know it's important. Being a ruler is not a job one does for a handful of hours a day and then leaves until the next work period. Still, I am not a thing, a machine to be tinkered with. I'm a person and I have feelings and thoughts of my own. My life was miserable here. I had to leave."

Her mother moved from the chair she was sitting in to a space next to Aila on the couch and took her hand. "But now you've come to your senses and have returned. Now we can be a family again."

"No, Mother. Can't you see? I'm only here because the Academy needs help from the Great Enclave. Once I find the flowers and father is healed, we will tend to the alliance and I will return to the Academy. I have work to do, important work."

"Nothing is more important than preparing for ruling the kingdom."

"You're wrong. The threat of the animaru is real. They are thousands strong already and they are very difficult to kill. In fact, they can't be killed without magic. More are coming over from their world all the time. We're talking about the end of all things, not problems with ruling one kingdom. You and father have always talked about duty and responsibility. Isn't it a ruler's job not only to the kingdom but to the entire world to preserve life? What's more important, a single throne or the elimination of all of humanity?"

"Alevia, don't believe all the rumors you hear. You can't—"

"Mother! Don't you understand? I have fought the monsters, I have seen how many there are and what they can do. I have seen magic released into the world, power that has been locked away for millennia. I've seen magical creatures that have not existed for thousands of years. I've done things you wouldn't believe if I told you. These are not stories I've heard. I have been living it. One kingdom is not enough. I'm helping to save all of Dizhelim. I thought you would be proud of me."

The queen squeezed Aila's hand. "I am proud of you. I've always tried to do what's needed for you to grow up to be a person the kingdom would be proud to have as a ruler. If I failed to stand up against your father, I'm sorry, but it's not like he abused you or did you any harm."

"No, he didn't do any harm that can be seen. I'm proud of

myself, that I risked leaving home and learning the things I did. My life has been rough, but I have friends to show for it, real friends who would die for me and with whom I am working to save the world. But I need you and Father to understand that my commitment is to the greater population of Dizhelim. I will rule the Enclave, if necessary, many years from now when Father wants to step aside, but for now, I will keep doing my work with the heroes of this world. Nothing you or Father can say or do can stop me."

Mora nodded sadly. "Understood. I still don't want you to go looking for the flowers, though. Your father may have agreed, but I do not."

"Tch. It's out of your hands, Mother. I would go even if Father tried to prevent it. I will find the flowers, he will have his poison purged, and he will sit his throne during this most crucial time in history."

"Alevia, I'm afraid for you. It eases my mind a little bit that Conren will go with you. He loves you and will protect you."

"What? First, my friends will provide more protection than that arrogant ass can. Second, what do you mean he loves me?"

"Oh, Alevia. You're still young yet. Conren has always had affection for you. Several times, he begged your father to allow him to go search for you. Don't confuse his confidence with arrogance. Remember how close you two were when you were growing up."

"We were children. I'm an adult now. He's coming with us because Father wants it, nothing more. When we're done with this mission, I don't care if I ever see him again."

"Don't say that. True, he's not the best choice for a husband. He is a Clavian Knight, but his social status is not high enough for a princess. Still, he will be a loyal friend. He will give his life for you."

"I'm done talking about this. I should get some rest. We leave early tomorrow. The sooner we can get to Sintrovis and get the flowers, the better."

Aila stood and her mother stood with her, dropping her daughter's hand. She reached out and pulled Aila into a hug.

"Please be careful. You are not invincible, no matter what your young mind tells you. Come back safely."

Aila patted her mother's back as she returned the hug. "I will. I'll come back safe and I'll do so with the flowers necessary to heal Father. Trust me in this."

Aila went back to her own room, replaying what she and her mother had talked about. Strength, duty, responsibility, and a childhood crush that could mean problems for her during the mission. After what she'd been through in the last half year, none of that fazed her a bit. She readied herself for bed, planning on enjoying the softness before embarking on who knew how many nights of sleeping on the ground.

It was all for a good reason. No one ever said heroes had comfortable lives.

$$\text{❧ 10 ❧}$$

Aila collected Tere and Lily, and the three had breakfast before leaving the next morning. When they finished and brought their saddle bags out to the entrance to the livery, they found Conren already there.

The knight had changed his plate out for leather armor. He stood next to a packhorse and a warhorse that was obviously the one he would be riding. The chestnut-colored charger looked like it was born to wear the barding that knights' mounts usually sported. Without it, the equine looked more naked than Aila had ever seen a horse appear.

"Good morning," the knight said. "I have our supplies here, more than enough for a week, and I took the liberty of having your mounts saddled. We can leave immediately, if you still insist on this foolish errand."

Just when the young man was starting to impress her, he had to open his stupid mouth with something like his last statement.

"You don't have to go with us." She picked up the reins of her horse and led her to the courtyard.

"Actually, I do. A direct command from the king himself. I

am to be your shield and helper, doing what I can to aid you and putting myself between you and danger."

"Please," she said, rolling her eyes. She mounted as Lily's chuckling reached her ears. "Let's just get going. Tere, it's pretty easy to get to the edge of Sintrovis, but once we're there, we could really use your tracking skills and especially your magical sight."

"I figured," the archer said. He seemed grumpy. Maybe he'd had too much wine the night before and was feeling the effects of it.

The roads within the bowl of the Great Enclave were very good, cut hundreds of years before, traveled and maintained frequently. The way to Sintrovis was virtually clear of other travelers and the party made good time to the edge of the mysterious area. They had more than an hour of daylight left when they set up camp.

"The road just stops?" Lily asked.

"Yes," Aila said. "It's maintained up to this point, but once the edges of Sintrovis are reached, there are no other roads or paths. It's wilderness within. No one knows what Sintrovis holds. We may well be the first ones ever to go into it and come back out alive."

"You are not making a good argument for us to continue," Conren said. "Does it strike no one else as anything but pure hubris to believe we can go in and come out safely where others could not?"

"We're used to doing things no one else has ever been able to do," Tere said. "It's kind of our thing."

Aila laughed and began brushing down her horse.

After setting up camp and scavenging the abundance of deadwood around them, Aila started a fire in a ring of stones. Once it was large enough, she sat back against a boulder and took a good look around.

She'd been to the edge of Sintrovis before, of course. An

adventurous child would not have passed up the opportunity to take a gander at the place of so many legends. If there was one location within the Great Enclave that could be considered sacred, this was it.

The vegetation was wild and thick, trees close together and choked with ferns, grasses, and assorted bushes. Some of the trees twisted, as if they were trying to find a path between and around their neighbors to catch precious sunlight. Even without the afternoon shadows, Sintrovis would be dim and gloomy during the day. It would probably be pitch dark at night, the trees blocking any moonlight or starlight that might otherwise break up the black.

"This as far as you've ever gone in?" Tere said, lowering himself to the ground beside her.

"Yes. I've come here three times, the last of which was a few months before I left the Enclave for good. That time, I was alone. I almost entered, just to see what the trees hide, but even I had enough sense not to do it."

"Unlike now," he said.

She chuckled. "Unlike now. Of course, there are differences. Back then, I didn't have a dying father to help. I also didn't have the world's greatest tracker and hero with me."

"Yeah, lucky you."

"Which me? The one back then or the one now?"

"Yes."

"Anyway," she said, "I figure if there's anyone who can get us through that place, it's you. Lily and I can fight, but we'll need your woodcraft. Thank you for coming along. There's no way I could do this without your help."

"Sure." He scanned the wall of trees ahead of them. "It's kind of pretty, in a chaotic and dangerous way. Reminds me of the Grundenwald."

"The Grundenwald is nothing like Sintrovis," Conren cut in.

"How would you know that?" Tere asked.

"I've seen the Grundenwald. It doesn't look anything like this."

"Conren," Aila said. "Just stop talking."

"It's fine," Tere said. "What part did you see? Did you go into it? How long did you stay?"

Conren stepped over to where Tere and Aila were sitting and straightened up to his full height. "I saw the edge of it near Drugancairn. Of course I didn't go in. That place is dangerous."

"Is it?" Tere asked. Lily drifted over from where she'd been going through her saddlebags, an interested smile on her face.

"Yes. I learned all about it during my geography training."

"I see," Tere said. "All about it. Well, your opinion that it is nothing like this here must be correct then."

"I should say that it is," Conren said with a firm nod.

Aila snorted. The offended look on the knight's face made Aila laugh harder.

"What are you laughing at?" he said, his fair cheeks flushing.

Aila got her glee under control enough to answer. "Tere lived in the Grundenwald for more than twenty years. In the heart of it, not the edges. You know, when he decided to retire from being Erent Caahs and seclude himself. There is not one person in Dizhelim who knows more about the Grundenwald than Tere, not even our friend Urun Chinowa, the priest of Osulin. Who also lived in the forest. You should probably think before you speak, especially around my friends. Every one of them have seen a thousand times more of the world than you have." She didn't add that she'd also seen much more of the world than him.

"My apologies," the young man said. "I meant no offense."

Tere considered the knight for a long moment. "No

offense taken. It's good that you have training and that you utilize the knowledge you've gained to formulate opinions. I suggest you try to present them in not quite so firm a manner, however. Everyone knows different things, and what we may think we know might not be as correct as we believe."

"I can see that. Thank you, sir."

Tere chuckled. "You don't have to call me sir. I'm not a military man. Tere is fine."

"Quite. Thank you, Tere. You were saying before I rudely interrupted you?"

Aila suppressed another laugh. It was definitely going to be interesting with Sir Conren Gardner tagging along.

"Oh, that. I was just saying it reminds me of the Grundenwald, and not just because of the wild vegetation. In my magical sight, I can see all kinds of power within. This is not just a bunch of trees and bushes. There's magic here. What I see here doesn't concern me much, but seeing that these are the edges of Sintrovis, I expect there's more powerful magic within."

Conren wisely kept his mouth shut. Aila did not.

"Do you think it's all like this? Tangled and thick?"

"I doubt it," Tere said. "Most forests have a range of terrain. Hills, flats, heavier trees, meadows, rocks, even caves. There's no telling how far what we see goes. A quarter mile from here, there may be a city in an open space. I doubt it, but you never know. It's one of the things that makes people like to explore such places. We might be standing on the ruins of a city ten thousand years old right now. Who knows?"

"Good thing we're not here to look for ruins," Lily said, finally joining the others and plopping down next to Tere. "Where do you think those flowers grow? In open areas, in the middle of the tangle, on the banks of rivers, where?"

"That, my lovely archer, is a good question," Tere said.

"Aila, do you know anything else about the flowers? I'd never heard of them before Verona mentioned them, so I don't know where they might be growing."

Aila bit her lower lip as she thought. "Not much, only what she told me. They're large, with triangular petals that spread out from a tight cone. They're deep red with yellow flares blossoming out from their origins through the middle of the leaves. The stalks grow to a foot or two in length. That's it. I didn't think to ask her what kind of soil or anything they grow in. Sorry."

"That should be enough. I don't know too many plants that appear anything like that. At least we probably won't bring back the wrong thing."

"Speaking of wrong things," Aila said, turning to Conren. "What is going on in the kingdom lately? Passing through, especially in Metrovial itself, it feels like something is wrong."

"Something wrong?" the knight asked. "Something like its king dying with no heir to take over. That type of something?"

Aila's eyes drilled into his, a flat look on her face.

"Fine," he said. "Sorry. I am a bit out of sorts lately. What exactly are you talking about?"

"The people," Aila said. "They seem disheartened, beaten down. I recognize the look in their eyes; I've seen it in other places I've been. Places where the populace is simmering, the pressure building to civil unrest or even civil war. I've never seen anything like it in the Enclave. What changed? Besides my father being ill, I mean. Am I correct that the news is not widespread about his condition?"

"You are correct. Many, even in the castle, don't know. The Council has declared it something to be closely held. I only know by happenstance, because I have always been close to the king's family. It's being kept secret from as many as possible, even within the military."

"Then I ask you again, what has changed? Why are the people so miserable?"

"I didn't know they were," Conren said, "though I do not engage with them in my daily service. My duty is within the castle. As to changes, I am not sure about what could be happening. I know the King's Council has been running the kingdom for the last few weeks as the king puts forth his entire effort to trying to remain strong."

"What does that mean, 'running the kingdom'?" Tere asked.

"They make decisions that need to be made, ensure the civil departments are functioning, make judgments and enact new laws, things like that."

Aila focused on the last part of his statement. "Enact new laws? Have there been new laws enacted since the Council took over?"

"A few," Conren said. He snapped his fingers. "I do recall hearing something about new taxes that the commoners were not happy about. A silly thing, really. The crown is due taxes, so for commoners to complain about it is ridiculous. All they need do is open their purses wider and their lives will go on unchanged."

Aila's mouth dropped open. "Please tell me you don't actually believe that."

"Believe what? That they should simply pay the tax and continue with their lives? Absolutely. Why grumble about something so simple?"

"Conren, you have no grounding in real life at all, do you? These commoners barely survive as it is. When you hardly earn enough money to feed your family, new taxes can mean that you don't eat. These people are scared their children will starve to death, and you're talking about 'simply paying the tax?' It's because of that attitude that I am ashamed for anyone to call me a noble."

"Well, you're not a noble, are you?" the knight said. "You're a member of the royal family. That's higher than a noble."

"I would request you to remain silent for the rest of this mission, but I'm afraid I have to ask you more questions. Do try not to sound as ignorant as you already have. Who enacted the new tax laws and why?"

Conren puffed up, as if he took offense to what she'd said. He had to answer her, though. As he'd said, she was a member of the royal family, much higher than his noble family. "I am afraid I don't know for sure. Elnaril Leovaris perpetually argues for increasing the crown's income. He probably had something to do with it. He most certainly would have championed the idea, even if it wasn't his to begin with."

"And these curfews I heard some talking about?"

"That was in response to some issues in one of the outlying towns. There was some unrest, it seems. The Council decreed the curfews be put in place for the citizens' protection."

Aila met Tere's eyes briefly. She had almost forgotten what she'd be seeing when she did. His white orbs didn't show any expression, of course, but his raised eyebrow did. She could almost hear his voice. *This is how rebellions start.*

"We need to hurry and get the flowers to my father so he can take back control of the kingdom. If we don't, there may not be enough of a kingdom left for him to rule."

❦  11  ❦

After eating dinner, the travelers settled into chatting about less controversial topics. Aila almost expected someone would tell a story, but that didn't happen. She thought of Raki, of course, and his obsession with each person taking a turn to tell a tale. She wondered where he was and what he was doing.

"Oh," she said out loud before she knew she had spoken.

"What?" Lily asked.

"I was just thinking of Raki and his stories and it reminded me that we were going to send a message about what we're doing. I got so caught up in everything, I forgot. I'll send a message now to let them know."

"Good idea."

Aila retrieved the message tablet and jotted out a short note.

HEY, EVERYONE, IT'S AILA. WE HAVE A LITTLE DETOUR FROM WHAT WE'D PLANNED. WE GOT TO THE PALACE BUT WE'RE OFF HUNTING SOME HEALING FLOWERS BECAUSE THE KING'S BEEN POISONED. WE'RE ABOUT TO SET OFF INTO SINTROVIS TOMORROW.

She figured no one would respond, but surprisingly, another message appeared even as she was putting the tablet away.

HI AILA. WE JUST GOT BACK TO THE ACADEMY A FEW HOURS AGO. EMILIYA STERRIS IS BEING SEEN TO AT THE MEDICA AND WE'RE HAVING A LATE DINNER WITH THE OTHERS. BE CAREFUL, WHATEVER YOU'RE DOING. IT SOUNDS DANGEROUS.

--RAKI

Another message came close on its heels.

SINTROVIS? BE VERY CAREFUL. THAT IS A PLACE OF POWER AND AS FAR AS I KNOW, NO ONE HAS EXPLORED IT AND RETURNED.

--HEADMASTER QYDUS.

"WOW," AILA SAID AFTER SHE'D READ THE MESSAGES ALOUD to the others. "Even the headmaster got involved in the conversation."

"The headmaster of the Academy at Sitor-Kanda?" Conren asked.

"Yep."

"He must know your identity for you to have a direct connection with him like that."

"Nope. He only knows me as Aila Ven. He's taken an interest in our friends and it extends to all of us. He's really very nice, even if he looks a little scary."

Conren mumbled something, but Aila wasn't paying attention. Another message was coming through, and it was longer than the others.

EVON HERE. AEDEN, FAHTIN, AND EVERYONE ELSE SAYS HELLO. WE HAVE SO MUCH TO TELL YOU, BUT I WON'T TAKE

THE TIME TO WRITE ALL ABOUT IT NOW. BE CAREFUL AND COME HOME SAFE. URUN SAYS HE CAN RUSH TO METROVIAL TO HEAL THE KING, IF YOU'D LIKE. IT WOULD SAVE YOU FROM GOING INTO SINTROVIS. I'VE HEARD IT'S AS DANGEROUS AS THE HEADMASTER SAID.

I ALSO WANTED TO TELL YOU THAT MARLA HAS A BIT OF NEWS. SINCE WE'VE RETURNED, SHE HAS FINALIZED THINGS AND COMPLETED HER TESTING AND IS NOW A MASTER OF THE SCHOOL OF ALCHEMY. HOW SHE DOES THAT WHEN SHE HASN'T EVEN BEEN HERE IS A MYSTERY TO ME, BUT I WANTED TO TELL YOU BECAUSE SHE WOULDN'T.

AILA READ THE MESSAGE TO THE OTHERS, THEN ANSWERED and spoke what she was writing as she scratched it into the message tablet.

TELL URUN THANK YOU, BUT VERONA GILCARYN SAYS THAT THE PARTICULAR POISON CANNOT BE HEALED BY MAGIC. SHE SAYS IT MAKES IT WORSE. THE POISON IS CALLED SOULROT.

THE MESSAGE WAS IMMEDIATELY RESPONDED TO.

VERONA IS CORRECT. THE ONLY ANTIDOTE TO SOULROT INVOLVES THE FIREHEART FLOWER. I ASSUME THAT IS WHAT YOU ARE SEARCHING FOR. PLEASE SEND HER MY GREETINGS.
--HEADMASTER QYDUS

"WELL, THERE WE HAVE IT," AILA SAID. "THE HEADMASTER confirms that the poison can only be healed by the flowers. I guess we're on the right track."

"Who are these people?" Conren asked. "How many people can you communicate with from afar like this?"

"They're all our friends," Tere said. "Well, all but the headmaster, though I guess we might be able to count him among our friends. Marla and Evon are students at the Academy. Marla, who apparently added another school mastery to her name, is the finest student the Academy has ever had. She's mastered more than ten schools so far—maybe as many as fifteen, I can't remember—more than anyone in history. She's also half of the Malatirsay."

"The Malatirsay? The hero prophesied in the Song of Prophecy?"

"The same. Did you not believe Aila when she told you we were working to save Dizhelim?"

"I...uh...it's not that. I thought maybe she exaggerated her role. Many could say that they are working toward saving the world, myself included."

"Ah," Tere said. "The difference is that she truly is. We are directly fighting against the dark monsters that are trying to destroy all life. If that is exaggerated at all, it's an under exaggeration."

"Oh."

Conren was quiet for the rest of the evening. Aila wondered if it was embarrassment or intimidation. Either way, she was glad she didn't have to hear his arrogant opinion of anything else before she went to bed. At least he had volunteered for the first watch duty. She had the third, so crawled onto her bedroll early and fell quickly asleep.

The morning came with diffused light and a thin mist that had settled in during the few hours before dawn. The air was crisp but not cold and she enjoyed the silence before the birds and her friends woke from their slumber. It was the kind of morning that made one feel alive, and she was grateful for the opportunity to observe her surroundings coming to life.

After a quick breakfast, the group packed up and discussed what they would do with the horses.

"Leave them here," Tere said. "We can tie them to a rope tether so they can move around to browse the vegetation, but they won't wander off. I don't think anyone will come by. Am I right in assuming that this place is not frequented?"

"It's not," Aila said. "I don't feel right leaving the horses here for several days, though."

"We can't take them into that," Tere said, pointing at the tangled vegetation. "It'll take us longer to try to find a place they can get through, and they may end up twisting an ankle or breaking a leg. Better if we go as quickly and efficiently as we can and get back to them soon."

"I think he's right," Conren said, "though I do not like the idea of leaving my horse. We should have brought someone extra to watch the animals."

"Had I thought of it, I'd have suggested it," Tere said. "It's too late now."

All three of her companions looked at Aila as if waiting for her to make the decision. It was that damned princess thing again.

Aila patted Muscade's cheek. She'd become attached to the cinnamon mare during the time the Academy had let her ride the horse. The thought of something happening to her twisted something inside Aila.

"What do you think, girl? If you go with us, you will be in danger, but if we leave you out here, you might be harmed, too."

The horse didn't answer, only nuzzled Aila's hand and snorted a blast of warm air.

"We'll have to leave them," she finally said. "It's going to be too dangerous to bring them in with us."

"I haven't seen any signs of predators in the area," Tere said helpfully. "They should be safer than they would be in there."

"Beacon is a trained warhorse," Conren said. "He's deadly with his hooves. If something comes after them, he'll be able to protect them. If not, he's smart enough to break the lines and allow them all to run free. The bear and occasional cat in the Enclave won't be able to catch them in the open. They'll be able to run full out on the road."

Aila cocked her head at the knight. "You know, Conren, that was a good idea, bringing someone to watch over the horses."

"Alas, too late to help us, though," the knight said.

"Not necessarily. You could stay with the horses."

He didn't bother answering, only giving her an unimpressed look.

"Come on," Aila said, sighing. "Let's get started. The sooner we go in, the sooner we'll be back out."

Each of the riders said a few words to their horses and Conren and Tere set up the line for the reins to loop around. A creek branched off from a larger stream nearby and crossed the area where the tether was placed, and there was plenty of grass and other plants for the equines to nibble on.

"They'll be fine," Tere said, patting Aila's shoulder.

With a final look at the horses, they began their trek into Sintrovis, Tere in the lead as the tangled growth swallowed them up.

Aila had traveled extensively, especially in the last few months. The experience had made her appreciate having Tere or Urun in the lead when traveling through heavy vegetation. Urun could—in most cases—bend the plants to his will to make their passage easier. Tere couldn't do that, but he had an uncanny knack for selecting the easiest path to tread. Or at least the least strenuous.

Now was no different. The archer identified courses through the plants that Aila didn't think she would have ever found. He did such a good job, she was second-guessing her decision to leave the horses. It was too late to turn back now, though.

Three exhausting hours and there seemed to be no end to the slog they had inflicted on themselves. The wet, sharp scent of crushed leaves tickled Aila's nose and the closeness of the plants kept the air still, almost stifling. When she focused on it, her breathing became more difficult, the humidity and exertion compounding to press in on her. Her head swam and she shifted her thoughts to other things. The mission. Her father. The horses. It helped, a little. Without thinking about it, her breaths came easier, if only because she was too distracted to notice the heavy air.

A crackle from in front of the group drew Aila's eyes. Tere had never made such a noise and Conren—by far the loudest of them—was behind her. The party stopped, each of them, as well as the entire world it seemed, holding their breath.

Another crunch, then two more from different directions, though still in front of them. Tere put his finger to his lips, then swung his bow from where it hung across his chest. Once in hand, he pulled an arrow slowly from his quiver and nocked it. Lily did the same, while Aila slowly drew out her vinci. Conren was cognizant enough to draw his sword slowly and to bring his shield from where it hung on his back to his hand without making too much noise.

The noises continued, leaves shuffling. Something heavy moving, though no broken twigs or branches, strangely. An odd crunching did sound occasionally, though, indicating bare patches in the forest where gravel or other hard materials grated against each other as something moved over them.

No one had spoken yet, as per Tere's gestured command.

The tension continued to build, like a gifted storyteller describing assassins stalking their prey in one of their tales.

When she got the first good look at what was around them, she almost laughed out loud. Were it not for the way the creatures circled them menacingly and moved inward, Aila would have relaxed completely.

From all different directions, strange animals showed themselves. They moved slowly, though that in itself seemed strange to Aila.

They looked like nothing if not very large squirrels. Mastiff sized, but squirrels just the same. Triangular furry heads with their pointed noses, long bodies, and bushy tails that twitched occasionally—they were adorable.

Until the first of the animals got within a few feet of Conren and its face went through a transformation from cute, furry animal to monstrous hunter. Teeth that looked as long as Aila's forearms suddenly made an appearance as the animal's wide mouth bared them. The hissing, screeching sound it made grated on Aila's insides, not only bringing her fear back, but doubling it.

All the monsters lunged at once, and thoughts of anything but trying to stay alive flew from her mind.

The first creature leaped through the air with agility reminiscent of the smaller and cuter versions of them Aila always saw chittering in the trees. It spread its short legs as the fur all over its body stood on end. Somehow, the monster's mouth grew even wider and its dagger teeth homed in on Conren. All Aila could do was watch.

The knight brought his shield up in time to foil the attack, deflecting the animal's body away from him, but the force of the impact seemed to surprise him because he backed up a step to maintain his balance and didn't slash with his sword as he had been trained.

Aila stopped staring just in time to see another of the

creatures running at great speed after her. It launched itself like the other one had just done at Conren. She dove to the side, rolling to her feet awkwardly on the path they'd trampled down as the thing passed by. She took a quick look around her to make sure she wouldn't be attacked from the side, and then repositioned herself with her back near Conren's. They could cover each other's backs, if not their flanks.

Aila brought her vinci up, ready for the next charge by the creature, but even before it could bunch itself to pounce, an arrow punched into its face. Aila waved her thanks over her shoulder to where Tere and Lily were systematically hunting down individual attackers. She had no time to figure out which of the two had helped her.

Three more of the monsters came toward her and Conren. They started chittering, much like small squirrels do to chase you away from their trees, but the sound was deeper because of their size. The noise rumbled into Aila's body and shook her where she stood.

One of the monsters picked her out and dropped into a wider stance. It danced back and forth, a familiar warning ritual amongst its smaller cousins.

"I'd love to leave your territory," she yelled to it, "but you're not giving me any room to do so. I don't care about your home. Go away."

Conren threw her a concerned look, no doubt wondering if she'd gone mad, not only talking to an attacker, but to an animal at that. A flash of grey and brown fur slammed into the knight, but his stance was firmer this time and he rebuffed the attack and slashed out with his sword, laying a cut along the creature's side. It screamed and danced away.

Aila's monster decided it was time to do more than yell at her. It charged in, running faster than a horse, mouth wide open. She barely twisted away in time to avoid the teeth, but it still slammed into her, accelerating her spin. As she was thrown to the ground, she used the momentum to lash out with both of her weapons, cutting into the shoulder and rump of the beast.

She regained her balance before the monster could attack again and she threw out her blades, swinging them with the chains to damage the animal once more, this time near one of its eyes and along its side. It grew frantic, chittering and screeching at her.

Or maybe at its friends. One of the others swung its head around and sped toward her.

Two against one was not a position Aila wanted to be in within the confines of the heavy vegetation. With her vinci still in motion, she pulled on the chains to direct the blades around again, this time toward the newcomer. She didn't try to cut this time, though. Instead, she lengthened the chain as the blades flew, then jerked them backward, hard, at exactly the right time.

The uninjured creature ran right into her movement and the chains wrapped around its front legs. It went two more steps before it realized that the chains had tied the two legs together. It screeched and dropped onto its face and slid along the forest floor, out of control. Even its companion, the one Aila had already hurt, paused to watch in confusion.

Aila leaped aside as the monster locomotive slid to a stop. Before it could react, she picked up the blade ends of the vinci and slashed repeatedly at the monster. When she tore a deep gash into its throat and then managed to punch another of the daggers in its eye, the furry creature twitched a few times and then lay still.

She wasn't sure what was happening with the others in her group, but hopefully they were holding their own. Her top priority at the moment was to unwrap the chains from the dead monster's legs before its friend…

Aila ducked at a flash of movement to her side and the injured creature—thankfully moving more slowly than normal—skimmed her as it passed by. Its claws tore into her, mostly deflected by her armor, but still did some damage to the back of her shoulder, where the protection didn't fully cover her. She cursed and worked to get her weapons free.

The monster had another idea. It hadn't committed completely to the leap and managed to turn immediately to lunge at her. There was no way she'd get the vinci free in time.

The Clavian princess leapt up and back, performing a crooked back flip over the carcass of her downed enemy. She landed awkwardly and slid down its back on her stomach, narrowly avoiding its very alive companion currently trying its best to eat her. It scrambled over the body of its friend more quickly than she had expected with its injuries.

When it did, though, she was ready.

The monster splayed its forelegs out again and opened its mouth so wide it would be able to bite completely through her body with its long teeth. Aila dropped to the ground, huddling close to the dead monster, drew two spare daggers she kept in sheaths on her calves, and punched them upward as the creature's trajectory put it above her. She thrust up with her legs at the same time, hoping the force would be enough to do real damage...without it breaking her arms or any other part of her.

The creature clamored in pain as one dagger was pulled from Aila's hand and the other helped to drag her along with it as it passed. They landed in a tumble and she managed to draw the knife out, then to repeatedly jam it into the creature again and again. She drove the point into its head, ending their combat.

Aila heaved breaths, trying to recuperate while looking around to see if she was about to be bitten through by another creature. From her vantage point, she couldn't see any other dangers close. Conren was busy cutting another of the creatures to pieces, two others dead lying nearby. She couldn't see Tere or Lily, but she heard the slap of strings on forearm guards and the sweet melody of monster carcasses hitting the ground. She dug out the dagger she'd lost—it was wedged in between two of the creature's ribs—and dragged her tired body over to reclaim her vinci.

She'd no sooner untangled the chains from the monster's front legs than another flash of movement brought her into a guard stance. It hadn't been grey or brown, but green. One of the giant squirrel things running through the foliage, maybe?

A sudden, painful prick in her thigh tore a scream from her throat.

"Auuuugggghhh! Vanda, what the hells was that?" The jab itself hadn't felt too painful, but immediately after, the sensation was like molten lava being injected directly into her leg. "Make it stop. Make it stop!" she yelled, slashing out in front of her with her vinci, but not striking anything.

Another flash of green and the same pain and fire sensation afflicted the same leg, only a bit closer to her knee. This time, she saw what did it. A thick vine with a pointed tip floated near her like a snake poised to strike.

She blinked at the sight, wondering if she was losing her mind.

An arrow shaft came out of nowhere and punctured the vine, slamming it into a nearby tree. It quivered like it was trying to get free. Another one rose up from the ground, even more snakelike than the previous one, and slithered closer to Aila.

"Lily," Tere's voice said.

"Got it," she responded. A miniature fireball flew past Aila. It landed several feet away, in a bundle of vines and leaves. A fraction of a second after it punctured what looked a lot like a pile of landscape trimmings, the whole thing exploded with a *pfft*. The two vines that had seemed so intent on getting to Aila went slack.

A loud thump and the unmistakable sound of a sword being plunged into flesh and soil led to several sets of feet stomping toward Aila. Her head was swimming and the fire within her seemed to be moving upward. Toward her heart.

"Aila," Tere said, suddenly right above her. "Are you all right? Did that thing puncture you?"

"Huh," she said dreamily. How did she feel so tired even with her body feeling like it was on fire? "It got me. Twice. It burns, Tere. It burns."

"Does it travel?"

Aila scrunched her eyes, wincing at the pain.

"Aila, does it travel? Is it moving? The fire?"

"Yeah. Up. It's going up my leg. What's going on, Tere?"

Her answer was a string of curses that would make Aeden proud, though she understood each one.

"I don't know what that thing is, but it's probably venomous. Give her water, Conren. Protect her. Don't move from this spot in case there are more of them. Lily, with me. Do you know what draw weed looks like?"

"I...uh, yes. Draw weed."

"Good. Go find it, and anything else that can strengthen her, neutralize poison, or heal. I noticed several varieties of helpful plants earlier, but I didn't want to take the time to pick them. Get what you can and get back here as soon as possible. I don't know how long it'll take the poison to kill her."

## 12

Aila couldn't focus on any one thought. That was probably good because her leg hurt like a thousand stinging wasps, and it was spreading.

"Alevia, drink some water," a voice said from next to her.

"What?"

"Water, drink some water."

"Who?"

"It's me, Conren."

"What did you call me?"

"I…I didn't call you anything, Alevia."

"My name is Aila Ven."

"Uh…Aila, please drink some water."

"I *am* thirsty."

"Here, I'll help you."

A waterskin pressed against her lips and she opened her mouth to allow a dribble of water to go in. "Mmm," she said. "Thank you, Conrad."

"It's Co…oh, never mind."

A mass of red appeared suddenly in front of Aila and she thought for a moment something had caught fire.

"How are you, Aila?"

Was that Lily's voice? "Hi, Lily. It hurts."

"I know. Tere will be back in a moment. We'll fix you up. Just hold on."

More movement and Tere's white eyes and bald head appeared. Aila concentrated on him. He usually had important things to say, if she was remembering correctly.

"What have you got?" Tere said.

"I couldn't find draw weed," Lily answered. "I'm sorry. I did find some featherflex, though. I dug up some roots."

"Pasteroot. Great thinking. Crush it up and add a little water so we can make a salve. I found some catspaw and yellow temani. It'll take me a moment to prepare them."

"I also found some bearded aru," Lily said.

"Fantastic," he told her. "Can you prepare it? We'll need to give her some internally as well as treating the wound sites externally."

Aila was having trouble following what was going on, but Tere and Lily seemed to know what they were doing.

"How can I help?" the other man said. What was his name again?

"Get the armor off her leg so we can see where she was poisoned. We'll need to treat the wound there as well as giving her medicine by mouth."

"Her armor?" the man said.

"Do it, Conren. I don't know how much time we have."

Aila chuckled. Tere didn't even know the man's name. She wondered if Conrad would be mad about it. A tugging at her leg turned her attention there, but she lost focus again when a sharp pain in her hip drew her attention.

"Okay, Aila," Tere said. "Here you go. I want you to swallow this. It's going to be bitter, but it'll help fight the poison. Can you do that for me?"

"Sure, sure," she said, opening her mouth. Tere shoved a

fibrous wad of some kind of plant into her mouth and—had he not pushed her mouth closed, she would have spit it all over him. "Ugh. Dat's fou…" When it became clear the man wasn't going to let her spit, she forced herself to swallow it. She retched, but it stayed down.

"Just a little more. Meanwhile, Lily is going to put more medicine on your leg, all right? It should make the burning feel a little better."

"Dogay," she said with her mouth full of more of the horrible slime Tere was giving her.

A sudden cooling on her leg, like someone had packed snow in their hand and put it on her bare skin, dragged a moan from Aila's lips. It felt soooo good. She swallowed the latest pinch of goo without even thinking about it.

Two more mouthfuls of the rancid goop and Tere was satisfied. Lily had finished putting more of the medicine on her leg, too, and she was feeling much better.

"Will this do it?" Lily asked Tere. "It's not the same poison that we need the fireheart flowers for, is it?"

"I'm not sure what the poison is, but I doubt it. That poison is concocted. This is naturally occurring. What we gave her should do it. We'll know soon because the soporific effect will lessen and she'll regain lucidity. It didn't have long to circulate in her system. If it all works, she should be ready to travel in an hour or two, though she'll probably be tired."

Aila's attention floated and waned as her body reacted to what was going on within her. The burning inside cooled somewhat. Not as much as the ice-cold feeling of the salve that Lily put on Aila's legs, but much more tolerable than the lava-like feeling from before. Even more importantly, the fuzziness in her brain dissipated and her thoughts became crisper. She could actually follow the conversations occurring in between her friends checking on her.

"How...how did you know what to do?" Conren asked Tere.

"Training, experience, a lot of reading. My first mentor stressed that it was as important to know how to heal as how to injure or kill. He taught me about herbs and medicines, as well as tracking, hunting, and fighting. He always said that anyone entering the wilderness should know how to address wounds and such, both in themselves and others."

"I'd never heard that about you," the knight said. "The stories don't mention it."

"Some stories do," Lily said, "though most people don't bother listening. They prefer the fighting."

"Damn stories," Tere spat.

"I paid attention to the times you used your herb lore and wound dressing in your adventures," the female archer said. "It's what made me learn about them. I didn't have the benefit of a teacher, though. I had to learn the hard way: sometimes by trial and error and sometimes with things I read."

"You did a good job. I'll try to teach you if we ever have a minute where we're not running for our lives or chasing after someone or something else."

Lily laughed. "I look forward to it."

"Water?" Aila said, drawing the others' attention. "Can I have some water? My mouth feels like it's full of sand and pond scum."

Conren handed her the water skin and she took a long swallow.

"You're looking better," Tere said. "How do you feel? Besides the horrible taste you probably have in your mouth, I mean. I wouldn't wish having to eat that medicine on anyone, but it's better than the alternative."

"I feel great compared to earlier," Aila said. "Thank you for the help. All of you."

"Your mind isn't fuzzy?" Tere asked. "Some poisons dull the mind until the person is unable to do anything besides wait to die. Judging by the way you were acting and responding earlier, I figure this was one of them. I didn't recognize the plant that attacked you, so I can't be sure."

"My thinking is clearer now, but yeah, I was a bit loopy earlier. Hopefully I didn't embarrass myself."

The old archer smiled at her. "No, you did fine."

Aila took another drink, swished it in her mouth to rinse some of the bitterness away, then swallowed. "Those animals..."

"They're all taken care of," Conren said. "Nasty little monsters."

"Not so little," Lily added.

"What were they?" Aila asked.

"Some kind of giant squirrel monster," Tere said. "I've never heard of anything like them, but the way extinct animals and monsters have been popping up with the magical shifts, who knows? One of our Academy friends might be able to tell us more about them."

"They're not...you don't think they could be...?"

"Trebaxels?" Tere finished for her.

A shiver ran through Aila's body. She didn't think it was because of the poison. "Yeah."

"I don't think so. You probably know more than I do about them, but I think one of the distinguishing features are that they're humanoid. These creatures definitely weren't."

Lily put her hands up. "Wait. Trebaxels? What are you talking about?"

"It's a Clavian legend. It's not a surprise you haven't heard of them. These two should know." Aila and Conren both nodded. "It's one of the few pieces of information I know about Sintrovis. But even growing up here, I doubt Aila and

Conren know much more about the creatures and Sintrovis itself."

"For something so close," Aila said, "it's amazing we don't know anything, but you're right. Other than what we've talked about already—which isn't much—the trebaxel legend is really the only other thing we know about Sintrovis."

"As I thought," Tere said. He turned to Lily. "There was a researcher thousands of years ago. It was during the War of Magic, or just before. We don't even know a name, though we do know it was a man. He was interested in the entire bowl area and specifically in Sintrovis. There had always been rumors and stories about strange things happening nearby. Those with magical abilities could feel something, though I've never heard a fuller description of what that something was. Just a sensation of power.

"In any case, this researcher hovered around near the edges of Sintrovis, trying to make sense of it. He was apparently not the adventurous type. Either that, or he was reasonable and intelligent. Even back then, it was clear that to go within Sintrovis itself was to disappear forever. He spent the better part of a year circling the place, based on his feelings of the power emanating from within. It's because of this that we even have rough limits to the most dangerous part of the region.

"During his studies, he came upon an intact skeleton. It was beyond the limits of Sintrovis, but barely. He couldn't tell what had caused the thing's death—detecting no damage to the bones that would indicate a weapon or attack of any kind —but it was clear the body had not been subject to scavengers.

"The creature had been larger than man-sized, but human-shaped. Its arms were proportionately longer than a man's, its head larger and squarer, and its eye sockets bigger than they should be for the size of its head. Other than that, the bones were similar, though not exact. The researcher couldn't identify what creature it came from. It certainly wasn't human or any of the other races known to exist.

"He left it where it was, never telling anyone else where he'd found it. In his long study of the place, he'd come to respect it as sort of a sacred site, one with its own peculiar magic. He spent much of the rest of his life arguing for keeping the place pristine. The reverence he had for it made him refuse to reveal where he had found the skeleton. In fact, he didn't even let others know he'd found it at all until decades later, at which time he was sure the forest had reclaimed the bones.

"In the report of his finding, he called the creature trebaxel, alluding to its clever, sly nature. Legends grew from the report, of course, and others claimed they'd seen the lanky monsters, but none had the veracity of the original claim. Those who mention the monsters typically assign them as guardians of Sintrovis, the reason no one ever comes out."

"So, we can expect to meet large, human-shaped monsters that will try to kill us to prevent us from going further into the place we have to go to get the flowers we're searching for?" Lily asked.

"Exactly," Tere said.

"Of course. It sounds like another ordinary day for us."

## 13

Aeden Tannoch rubbed his tired eyes, then widened and squinted them to focus on the wall of the common room in the Academy dormitory they called Batido. He shifted on the padded chair and leaned his head from side to side, resulting in a satisfying crack.

"Me, too," Fahtin Achaya said from the chair next to his. "This reading stuff is hard."

The young Croagh chuckled at his adopted sister. "Not everyone is cut out for studying, it turns out. This is probably the wrong place to find others who understand that, though."

Fahtin set aside the book she'd been reading. Studying, actually. She raised her arms toward the ceiling and stretched.

"Have you learned anything interesting yet?" Aeden asked her.

"Sure, lots. Our esteemed prophet really did a good job. He starts by explaining what prophecy is and is not, the history of the gift, and a thousand other things that, although interesting, are doing exactly nothing to help me understand what I'm going through. I thought this book was supposed to teach me how to use my ability, not prepare me for a history test."

"Why don't you just skip to a part that interests you, then?"

"I'm afraid to. What if I skip over something that I need to understand the good stuff later on? What if I miss something like 'whatever you do, don't try this technique unless you prepared yourself by doing this...'? I could hurt or kill myself, not to mention others."

"Good point. I guess you'll have to be patient and try to learn as much as you can."

"What about your book? The Prophet wrote it to guide you as the Malatirsay. Have you learned anything?"

Aeden ran his fingers through his hair. "I have, actually. The Prophet is a fascinating guy. He explains how the vision came upon him, how he was at a loss for what to do with his life. He'd failed to end the War of Magic and he even got depressed enough that he was thinking of taking his own life. When he got the prophecy—in that place we found all the books, by the way—it changed his mind about a lot of things. He dedicated the rest of his life to preparing for it...and for me and Marla. I can almost hear him as I'm reading. I wish I could have met him."

"I think he would be scary," Fahtin said. "He was so powerful and knew so much. How could anyone talk with him? Did he always know what everyone was going to say, what they were going to do?"

"I don't think prophecy works that way."

"I know my abilities don't, but he was Tsosin Ruus. Who even knows what he could do?"

Aeden shrugged. "Maybe that's why he wrote all about its history and what it can and can't do. You probably need to understand that before you can effectively use your ability."

"Tch. Now you sound like Evon. Can't you just let me whine about how hard it is to read for hours at a time?"

Aeden smiled at her. Same old Fahtin. "Sorry. I know it's different than what you're used to, but doing new things helps us to grow and get better. It's the same as exercise or combat in that way."

"Yeah, yeah. Well, if we spend hours upon hours reading what the Prophet has left for us, maybe we'll eventually figure out what we're doing."

The door to the common room opened and Evon came in carrying a stack of books. Right behind him, Khrazhti's blue figure followed, a larger stack in her hands. She closed the door with her foot.

"The stuff we found in that cave is so fantastic," Evon said, his blond head swiveling back and forth from Aeden to Fahtin a few times, but finally settling on the dark-haired Gypta woman. "Uh, what's going on?"

"More books?" Fahtin said. She set hers on the table in front of her.

"Of course," Evon said. "We just found the largest collection of rare and previously unknown books since the founding of the Academy. What's wrong?"

Fahtin crossed her arms under her breasts. "I've been reading forever and I still don't know how to use my visions any better."

Evon set the stack of books he was carrying down on another table and dropped onto a couch near Fahtin's chair. "We've talked about this before. You have to be patient. You have a book from the Great Prophet himself, one written specifically for you. You—"

"To an unknown Gypta," she said.

"Yes, yes. Come on, Fahtin. You know that's how prophecy works. Some things are very clear and detailed and other things—like your name—aren't available. You'll note that he didn't call Aeden or Marla by name, probably didn't even know they were two people. Can't you see how awesome it is that he knew of your existence and your talents three thousand years before you were ever born?"

"I guess."

Evon looked to Aeden, who shrugged. "Like I was saying, you need to have patience. I've seen it many times before in the Academy. Students get excited about learning one thing or another, but they don't have the patience to learn it properly. They either give up or, if it's some type of magic, they end up trying to use it with only half an understanding. A lot of times, they'll hurt themselves or other people."

Fahtin guiltily met Aeden's eyes and he laughed. "She just said something close to that. She knows. She's just feeling frustrated and wants acknowledgment of how hard this stuff is. Maybe we need to go out for a walk instead of staying cooped up in here with the books all day."

"It *is* a nice day out," Evon said. "Oh, but what I was saying before was that there are some fabulous things in these books. Not only are they helping to change our understanding of history, but some of the tomes about magic gives us a glimpse of what we've been missing out on all this time. So much new information."

"Evon Desconse has been allowing me to help him," Khrazhti said. She had already set down her stack of books and was standing and watching the others interact. "I have read some of these and it has granted me understanding into many things I had not thought possible previously."

"She's a natural," Evon said. "So amazing. It's no wonder many of the masters want to talk with her, even study her. I'm not just talking about the ones who are interested in animaru or Aruzhelim, either. She uses magic unlike anyone we've ever seen. It's almost like she is magical herself."

Khrazhti blinked her large glowing eyes at the Academy

graduate. "I still find it difficult to use other types of magic, but I am learning."

"That's great," Aeden said. "It seems we all have some things to learn and some books to read. I've barely cracked open the historical record of the Cridheargla because I've been so busy with the Malatirsay book. Which reminds me, where's Marla? I need to talk to her."

Evon shifted his eyes to the ceiling, almost like he was waiting—hoping—for someone else to answer. When no one did, he said, "She's in a mood lately. I'm not sure why. She just finished off another school, so it seems like she'd be less busy and pressed upon, but no, she's prickly as a wet cat."

"Oh, is everything too much for her?" Fahtin asked. "She does have a lot of things going on. She's still learning magical healing, working on at least two or three other schools, helping the masters coordinate all this stuff with the animaru, she's half the Malatirsay, and more."

"I don't know. Sometimes she gets in a foul mood and I've found the best thing is to leave her alone and wait it out. I've stopped trying to find the reasons, though I'm pretty sure it's not that she has too much going on. I've seen her with more stress than I thought a human could handle and she thrived on it."

"I'll talk with her," Aeden said, "see if I can figure something out. She may be willing to talk to me. The new feeling of having a brother hasn't worn off yet, so she probably won't attack me. Again."

All three of his friends grinned at that, no doubt recalling their first meeting, where Marla did her level best to knock Aeden out cold, if not worse.

"I'm feeling some pressure, too," he continued. "If this book doesn't tell me how to enhance my Raibrech spells, I may not be powerful enough to do what I need to do."

"Any progress on understanding the other clans' Raibrechs and how it all relates?" Evon asked.

"Not much. We're still trying to get a handle on it all. It's so hard when we have to deal with hundreds or thousands of years of history that changed everything. This book and the one that talks about the Croagh might shed some light. Again, it's a matter of time and patience. Hopefully we have the time."

"I can go through the Prophet's journals and mark the passages that refer to the history of the Croagh, if you want. It'll save you from having to read as much."

"That would be great," Aeden said. "It'll let me focus on this guide. So far, Marla has been happy with me keeping it, but she may decide she wants to take it for a time, too. So much to do and so little time until the animaru do something serious."

"We will grow in power and knowledge," Khrazhti said, "and we will defeat them. I will help in whatever way I am capable."

"Thanks. That means a lot to me. Thank you both."

The door opened again, this time so forcefully it slammed against the wall. Marla stomped in, green eyes blazing.

Evon stepped in front of the books as if to protect them from her wrath. "Uh-oh."

❄ 14 ❄

Tere hadn't been kidding. Aila felt like she'd climbed a mountain twice in one day. She recognized that the group was moving more slowly than they should be, but couldn't dredge up the energy to go faster.

"Sorry guys," she said.

"You don't have to be sorry," Lily responded. "Fighting off poison takes a lot of strength, even with the help of herbs. You'll need to take it slow. Only a little while more and we can stop and rest for the day."

"We talked about this. There's no time for us to go slow or to rest. You should probably leave me here and go find the flowers yourselves. Pick me up on the way back out."

"Stop being ridiculous," Tere told her. "You know we'll never leave you. This is the compromise we came up with, since you won't let any of us carry you, so accept it. After some food and a full night's sleep, you'll feel a lot better, I promise."

Aila gritted her teeth. She hated being a liability. If they didn't get the flowers back to her father because she slowed them down, it would be all her fault.

Soon enough, they did stop. They reached an area where the trees were spread out more than they had been and the underbrush even seemed to lessen. It probably had something to do with the trees. She remembered hearing that some trees poisoned the area around them so other things didn't grow. She shrugged. Or maybe it was just coincidence. In any case, she liked moving through the trees much better when she wasn't pushing through thick bushes and nettles. Some of the thorns on the bushes found their way into gaps in her armor, or through her clothes, to prick her. But at least they weren't venomous.

In the morning—the other three took watch duty and let her sleep all the way through—Aila felt like she might actually survive after all. Her body hummed with the special energy that one only felt after recovering from sickness. She wasn't in top shape, but her exhaustion had turned into mild fatigue. There was hope for her future after all.

"Well?" Tere asked as they prepared to get started for the day.

"Yes, you were right. Like always. I do feel better."

"That's what I like to hear. The terrain is cooperating with us, too. This should be easier to move in." He swept his hand out toward the forest that was more friendly than the tangled jungle-like areas they'd been hiking through.

Their ease didn't last long, however. Midmorning, Tere put his hand up to stop the others. The old archer swung his head, scanning the surroundings, but the way his brows were drawn down, something didn't make sense to him. After a few minutes of him searching for something in vain, he motioned them to continue on.

Aila sped up to join him. It wasn't as important for him to be up ahead when the only thing in their path was the trunks of trees. "What was that?" she asked.

"I don't know. Something moved through here, but I only got flashes of the magical traces they left. No real tracks. It's strange."

He stopped them again sometime later, but again, he couldn't pin down what was making him nervous. Aila didn't think she'd ever seen him have problems with his magical sight, except for when he'd lost it completely.

"No," he said when she raised a finger and opened her mouth. "My sight is fine. I think it's something to do with the saturation of magic in the area. There's a lot of it here. A lot. I think maybe it's interfering with me seeing things, like a snowstorm or dust storm would to regular sight."

Aila had noticed as they continued that the ground itself had been changing. Rocks littered the open spaces and they passed a few boulders large enough for a person to hide behind. She'd never been any good at identifying trees, but it seemed like the same mix as before. Between the uneven terrain, the rocks, and the trees, she started to feel pressed in upon. Uncomfortable.

Movement caught her attention and she ducked behind a tree. Something struck the trunk where she'd been standing.

"Take cover," Tere said just as a loud clang sounded from nearby.

Conren was standing in the open, shield up and surveying the surroundings. As Aila watched, a fist-sized rock slammed into his shield again, making another loud clang.

Aila drew her vinci, though she didn't know how they would help her with rocks flying at them. Another stone bounced off the trunk she had taken cover behind, and she squatted and crunched her body down lower.

More rocks pelted the trees and ground around them. One struck Aila a glancing blow on her shoulder, and though her armor mitigated it somewhat, it still hurt. "That one's going to leave a bruise," she said, still trying her best to catch sight of their attackers.

Tere helped her out in that respect. The twang of his bowstring announced the loosed arrow that took down their first enemy. A hair-covered figure slammed to the ground some distance away, an arrow jutting out of its face.

Aila stared at the creature. She wasn't sure if it was an animal, a monster, or a strangely shaped human that was abnormally hairy. It looked a little taller than her, with extended arms, a squarish head, and eyes bigger than seemed natural.

"Trebaxel?" She hadn't been speaking to anyone in particular, but Conren answered as he darted toward her, placing his shield in front of both of them.

"It looks like what the legend says about them, except for the size," he told her. "If all they can do is throw rocks at us, I find it hard to believe no one has ever escaped Sintrovis to tell the tale of meeting them."

"Focus," Tere said. "They're in the trees. I don't know if they can move from tree to tree up there, but if they can, they'll surround us and drop rocks on us."

"There aren't any coming from behind or from the right," Lily said, releasing an arrow, which stuck into a tree twenty-five feet above the ground. A fuzzy shadow poked its head out from behind the trunk and threw a rock with incredible accuracy at the red-haired archer. She ducked behind her own tree to dodge it.

Aila watched as Lily and Tere loosed a few more arrows, taking down two more of the creatures, but missing the others. As much as she could tell, there were probably more than a dozen of the monsters attacking them.

"I have to say, this isn't the most pitched battle I've ever been part of," she said as another rock bounced off Conren's shield. Letting the knight take care of protecting them, she was able to concentrate on observing the movements of the hairy creatures. "They're swinging around, gathering on the left to push us away. They're...they're herding us."

"Yes," Tere said. "I don't like to be told where to go. Besides, if they don't want us to go to our left, I think that's where we need to go. There's something there they don't want us to get to. Maybe the flowers or some treasure?"

"Or their nests," Lily said.

"Maybe. Follow me. We're going to find out."

Tere took off running in a zigzag pattern, threading through the trees toward the area where the bulk of the trebaxel were. The rest of the group followed, running erratically and trying to keep the trees between them and the monsters up high throwing rocks at them. Tere and Lily only shot a few arrows each, making each one count. Still, only a little better than half struck their targets. Those they loosed would be gone forever, so they were conserving them. No telling what they'd face in the future. To do so without arrows would put them at a distinct disadvantage.

"How are they throwing so many?" Aila grumbled as she darted to the side, barely avoiding a piece of stone that would have definitely left a mark. The monsters didn't seem to be running out of things to launch, though they couldn't just bend over and pick up more. The creatures Tere and Lily had taken down didn't have any bags or pouches, so they must have placed a store of the projectiles in advance. She wasn't sure she appreciated that the creatures were so intelligent.

A curse from Conren behind and to the right of Aila grabbed her attention just as the knight stumbled, then tripped and slammed into the ground, shield first. He did an admirable job in rolling and coming to his knees, shield lifted above his head. In that position, he resembled a turtle.

"Are you okay?" she called out to him after taking refuge between two trees growing close together. They were in a dangerous area, with the trebaxel almost directly above them and the two archers several paces ahead.

"Fine," he growled. "A stone bounced and hit my leg. It hurts, but no permanent damage. I think. Go on ahead. I can't cover you with the shield while we run anyway."

She glanced at Tere and Lily, then back at Conren. He was right. There was nothing either of them could do for each other. The best thing was to try to get to whatever safe place Tere was shooting for and hope the knight came through it as well. It was every person for themselves for the moment.

She took off without another word, the attackers quick to target her as soon as she left the safety of the trees she had been hiding behind. She'd trained wearing a helmet before and had never liked it, but she almost wished she had one now. Almost. With the size of some of the rocks and the force with which they were thrown, head armor might not help, even if it were a plate helm of one of the Clavian Knights.

Suddenly, no more rocks came at her. It was almost like she'd passed an invisible line and could no longer be targeted. Tere and Lily waited next to two very large tree trunks, each wider around than both of them.

"They don't seem to want to throw at us now," Tere said, his nocked arrow pointing toward one of the hairy creatures in a tree high off the ground.

It watched Conren, a stone filling its palm. It drew the rock back to throw and Tere drew his bowstring to his cheek. Then, like some signal was given, the creature relaxed. Tere did likewise.

"What?" Aila said, but didn't finish her question when Lily gestured toward Conren. The knight limp-ran toward them, apparently having passed whatever line caused the trebaxel to call off their attack. "Oh. That's just strange."

"Come on," Tere said, eyeing the knight. "Let's get a little farther away. Those things seem content to stay where they're at. Are you good for another few dozen yards?"

"I'm fine," Conren said, wincing each time he planted the leg that had apparently been hit.

They found a group of trees close enough to each other to form a kind of fort the four were just able to fit into.

"They seemed like they were on guard duty," Tere said. "Once we passed their post, they suddenly lost interest. Either that, or there's something worse here that they didn't want to deal with."

"That was the strangest behavior I've ever seen in an animal," Lily said. "They're smart enough to throw rocks at us, and smart enough to stockpile the stones, but they didn't really gang up on us or come down from the trees to attack us up close."

"They wanted to scare us away," Tere said. "It's obvious they wanted us to go back or to our right. They're not what I expected trebaxel to be."

"What does that mean?" Aila asked.

"They're smaller than I thought they'd be, for one. Another thing is for a place where no one comes out alive, they seemed happy for us to turn around and leave. With that behavior, there should be a lot more people who have seen them and reported it."

Lily shrugged and readjusted her quiver. "There were those other creatures. And plants like the one that got Aila. I do agree that they acted differently than I thought they would, though."

"One more thing," Tere said. "It's hard for me to distinguish them from the surroundings. I told you this place is flooded with magic. It seems to be the same magic that those creatures have. It's like they hide in it. Not purposely, I think, but it does interfere with me tracking them in the magical matrix. Like they're part of the landscape. If there are more things like that, we might be able to be ambushed, something that usually isn't likely with my abilities."

"Wonderful," Aila said. "We bring a hero with magic eyes and this place reveals that it can pull the wool over them."

## 15

"How's the leg?" Aila asked Conren as the group passed more slowly over the forest floor than they had previously.

"It hurts like a hard sparring session with Master Olar. How's your energy level?"

"I'm tired again, but not much more than I would be after running around dodging rocks normally."

"What about your shoulder?" the knight asked.

Aila hadn't said anything about the rock that had hit her, but Conren may have seen it. "It's sore. I'm sure I've got a nice bruise there, but I've had bruises before."

He nodded and they continued following Tere without speaking further, which suited Aila. She was too tired for conversation anyway. She'd just wanted to make sure Conren wasn't going to drop to the ground or die or anything else inconvenient.

Tere stopped and Aila came to a halt, wondering when they would set up camp. She stared at her feet, the same thing she'd been doing since they got away from those monsters, but the silence from her companions brought her head up to see what was going on. Tere, Lily, and Conren were all staring straight ahead. She looked in the direction they were and her eyes grew larger.

The vegetation had thinned even more after they'd left the trebaxels and visibility had increased. Through the tree trunks, the land erupted into a series of strangely shaped boulders. If she squinted and tilted her head, it almost looked like a legitimate wall of dull tan stone spreading across her field of view.

The more she stared, the more it didn't look like anything that could occur naturally. The flattish sides and how they stacked together almost made it look like...

"A maze," Tere said, the first words anyone had uttered in several minutes as they gawked at the stone shapes in front of them.

Aila was going to argue, but then she saw what he was referring to. The way the stone was arranged did seem to be evidence of some type of intelligence. She couldn't tell how far they went because the trees obscured her vision to the sides. In the section directly in front of her, she picked out three openings about twice the width of a normal doorway.

"There's no way this is naturally occurring," Aila said.

"Who's to say what's natural in Sintrovis," Tere said. "This place is saturated with magic. Such things can happen where there is a lot of magic, even without any kind of intelligence directing it."

Her head snapped toward him. That sounded too much like what she'd been thinking. "Do you think it happened by itself?"

"Who knows. Even if it did, there are probably a lot of great locations in there where animals or monsters would desire to make a den. If not, monsters may be stationed at locations to prevent anyone from going through."

"Can we go around it?" Lily asked.

"We'll have to get closer before I can answer that. I think the more important question right now is, do we *want* to go around it?"

"We're here for the flowers," Aila said. "If the chances of finding them are better inside that thing, then we go through. If you think they'll grow better outside, then we can try to go around."

"Those are my thoughts, too," Tere said. "What do you say we get a little closer before we decide? It might be good to rest, too. We're not in the best condition to meet more monsters right now."

"I'm not sure we'll be in good condition to meet monsters until we get back to Metrovial and rest for a week," Aila said.

It turned out that the stone obstacles stretched as far as they could see to the left and right.

"We can choose one of the two directions and walk until we are able to go around it," Tere said, "but there's no guarantee we'd be able to do so. It might run into a mountain or off a cliff, or it could even keep going for miles and miles. There's really no telling unless we take a direction and commit to it. Or we can choose to go through one of these openings."

"So we've a choice to waste time trying to circumnavigate or to waste time braving an unknown stone structure that appears uncannily like a maze and seems to indicate some intelligent design," Conren said.

"Exactly."

The knight looked to Aila. He closed his eyes briefly and shook his head. "Enough, Alevia. We are putting ourselves at risk for no good reason. Are you not satisfied? Come, let us return to the castle so you can utilize the time he has left so the king may pass on the knowledge you need to take the crown."

Aila wanted nothing more than to punch the arrogant knight in the face, but she chose to ignore him completely. Instead, she turned to Tere and Lily. "We go into the maze."

"Fair enough," Tere said.

Aila was happy, at least, that he didn't argue with her. He didn't seem to prefer one choice over the other anyway.

"Thank you, Tere. Lily. I appreciate your support."

Conren stomped off about a dozen paces away from the others, grumbling to himself.

"He's just trying to protect you and do what he thinks is best for the kingdom," Tere said.

"For my entire life people have told me they only want to do what's right for me and the kingdom. I've found that often, that translates as wanting to do what they think is better for the kingdom *and themselves*. I do want what is best for the kingdom, though I want to help my father even more. Luckily, in this case, the two are the same. Finding the flowers that can heal my father and allow him to continue ruling the Enclave is truly the best thing. I'd make a horrible queen."

"I don't believe that," Tere said.

"And I don't think you believe it either, Aila," Lily added. "I think you'd do a good job."

"I thank you for the vote of confidence," Aila said, "but my top priority is still to help my father not die. I honestly don't know if Conren's problem is not caring about my father enough as a person, failing to believe anyone else's opinion matters, or if he thinks he'll somehow gain from it if I do become queen."

"I think he's thinking mostly of your safety, Aila," Lily said. "I've noticed how he looks at you. He cares, a lot. I can understand him wanting you to be safe."

"Well, I'm no porcelain doll that needs to be looked after

and put in a case for my own protection." She raised her voice, glancing over at the sulking knight. "If he really cared, he'd listen to what I'm saying." Dropping it again, she continued. "He can't go around thinking I'm his to protect and to guide. If I do become a queen, I'll not be one who is led around by a ring in her nose. Maybe he's too stupid to see that."

Tere and Lily had traveled with Aila enough that they didn't pursue the topic, which she appreciated. The last thing she wanted to do was to argue with her friends. There were more important things to be about.

They made camp and rested up, as Tere had suggested. After a strangely quiet night spent in an unprotected area near the mysterious stone maze, they chose the closest opening in the walls of the maze and headed in. For better or worse.

Up close, the stone walls of the maze were even more intricate than Aila had realized from farther out. They weren't carved into shapes, nor were they fitted like a fortress wall. The monolithic stones, taken individually, appeared to have occurred naturally. No marks of any kind of cutting or sizing marred their surfaces, only the uneven bumps, cracks and other features that could be seen on any stone in the wild. The uncanny part was that the huge objects fitted together so perfectly to create a larger whole: a maze.

In her travels, Aila had chanced upon a curious group of people near one of the villages in the southern part of Promistala. They made a sport of climbing on boulders, as well as on larger faces of cliffs. She had watched their death-defying activities for nearly a solid day before she'd asked what they were doing—and more importantly, why. They explained that it was fun. She'd balked when they proposed showing her how, but finally took them up on the offer.

It *had* actually been fun. The small boulders she'd scaled, barely higher than she was tall, were nothing like what the villagers climbed with nothing but their fingers, soft shoes, and sometimes bare feet. The experience greatly improved her skill in scaling more conventional obstacles, and it gave her an appreciation of what the climbers called *features* of a rock. As a course of habit, she noticed such things as she traveled. It went beyond distinguishing worked stone from natural stone. Each feature, whether it be a bump or a hole or a crack that one could jam an entire fist into, not only made the surface of a rock unique, but it allowed a clever and experienced climber to perform feats that at times seemed magical.

So Aila recognized that the boulders surrounding her were not shaped, nor had they probably been moved. As far as she could tell, they had always been in their places, as if they'd grown up from the very ground.

The thought sparked a shiver that ran the length of her body.

"What other than a god could manipulate so much stone?" she whispered, awestruck at the display. "What has that power?"

"Did you say something?" Lily asked.

Aila startled. "Oh. No, nothing. Just thinking aloud." She realized she'd been standing just inside the opening to the maze, running her eyes over the surface of the walls while her friends entered it.

It wasn't only the natural look of the stone that piqued her interest. The passageway—it resembled a hallway far too much for her liking—was fifteen or so feet wide. It only went about ten paces before it ran into another wall of stone, but it opened both left and right.

Plants grew within the maze, another thing that surprised her. For some reason, she never thought of mazes as having things grow within it. Except hedge mazes, of course, like those in large gardens in noble estates. They were *made* of growing things, as the name implied, but what she was seeing was different.

"Not high enough," Tere muttered.

"What's not?" Aila asked.

"The plants. The height of the stones vary, though the lowest is about a dozen feet up. The plants aren't high enough to climb on to get on top of the wall. I can see trees poking up over the tops of some of the walls, so maybe we can use those to climb up, if we can get to them. If we can get on top of the wall, we can look around and see where we need to go. If we can all get on top of the walls, we can actually travel along the edges of the stones and bypass going all the way around obstacles."

"Oh, that's a good idea."

"It's simple enough," Conren said. "Between us, we should be able to stand on others' shoulders so one of us can get to the top of the wall."

Aila eyed the rocks, measuring the heights of her friends. As the smallest, she'd be the one to climb the ladder of people standing on each other's shoulders to get to the top. She scanned the walls of the passageway she was in, and saw that it wouldn't work.

"Won't work," Tere said.

"And why not?" the knight asked as if his intelligence was being called into question.

"Don't you see the shapes of the walls?" Tere said. "They slope outward, creating a type of overhang on each. In addition, they're rounded. Even if the lightest of us were to climb up, she wouldn't be able to grab hold of an edge to pull herself up, since there *is* no edge, and not with the overhang."

"Are you so sure?" Conren said. "I seem to recall Alevia scurrying up trees and walls like a monkey when we were younger. I can only imagine that she has maintained her skill, or maybe improved it."

"I have gotten better," Aila said, "but Tere's right. I can't see anything to use as a handhold."

"Will you admit defeat without trying?"

Aila gritted her teeth. She was about to tell the knight what he could do with his idea, but decided that it would be better to go along with it and try. Once he saw it wouldn't work, maybe he would shut his mouth for a time.

They tried in three different places to do what Conren had suggested. She climbed up the backs of first Tere and Conren—both of them just an inch short of being six feet tall —and then Tere and Lily, the redhead just a bit less giant than the two men. It was no good. Even when she was able to scramble up them, with or without kicking or scraping them, the outward slope of the rock was too great for her to climb up. The one attempt at using all three of her taller companions resulted in bodies crumpled into a pile at the base of the stone wall.

"I admit the defeat of my idea," Conren said as the three dusted themselves off while Aila stood back and chortled at the sight.

When the party reached the first larger area in the maze, an hour or so after they'd given up on climbing the walls, they saw some of the trees Tere had spotted earlier.

"They are almost exactly the distance they need to be in order to be completely unusable in jumping to the wall," the archer said after a long whistle. "Whoever or whatever designed this really did a good job. Even the strongest and most acrobatic people I've known couldn't quite make the leap from those trees onto the top of the wall. It's as if they were planted—or allowed to grow—in a place where they would entice others to try, if they were daring, but to no benefit."

"The good news is that the trees are still climbable," Aila said. "Even if we can't jump on top of the walls from them, we can get a look at the maze from above. That should help to find which way to go."

"Are you volunteering?" he asked. "You *are* the resident scurrying monkey."

## 16

Aila glared at Conren as she chose a tree at the edge of the little bunch near the center of the open space in the maze. There had to be thirty feet or more from wall to wall and the group of trees consisted of maybe a dozen that were—as Tere pointed out—located nearly dead center in the area. They were all of similar height, so she selected one of those on the edge at random.

Conren wasn't fazed by the glower. He gave her a thumbs up and said, "Careful, Alevia. You're not a child any longer. You will heal more slowly from injuries."

What in Vanda's name was he talking about now? She shook her head and methodically climbed the tree she'd selected. Calling her an old maid?

When she was more than twenty feet in the air, Aila looked out between the leaves of the tree and scanned the maze. Something at around the level of her throat dropped into the pit of her stomach.

"It goes on for miles," she shouted down to the others. "I'm not sure if this is the way we'll end up going, but aside from some large open spaces like this one, it's all a jumble of passages. There are a lot of trees and vegetation I can see from here, but they obscure my view of other things."

"Can you see anything that looks like an end?" Tere asked, his hands cupped around his mouth so his voice went farther. "Or a center?"

"No. I can only see a wedge of what's out there, though, maybe a little less than a quarter. These other trees get in the way. I'll have to come down and climb up the others to get a better look."

The three on the ground discussed it for a moment, then Tere yelled back up. "If you've seen all you can, come on down."

She scrambled down like the monkey they'd been calling her and dropped to the ground among them.

"I'm assuming you weren't able to get much information, aside from seeing how large it is?" Tere asked.

"Sorry. I could have tried to memorize which way we should aim toward, but with the trees blocking my view and not knowing exactly where we want to go, I'd have needed to map the whole thing out on paper. Even then, it might not make a difference. I can check the other sides on trees around the edges of this bunch."

"Do you think it's worth the effort?" Lily asked.

"Truthfully? No. Unless I saw something distinguishable from everything else and then I could somehow map how to get to it even though some of the maze is hidden by trees, I can't see it doing much for us."

"It's fine," Tere said. "We're going to have to do it the old-fashioned way: trial and error. It's not the best thing when you're on a time limit like we are, but it's the best we can do right now."

Aila took a drink from her waterskin and sighed. She hated puzzles like this. They always made her feel like a mouse in an experiment. One of the old scholars in the castle used to create mazes and entice mice to navigate them to find treats or food. Old Alzore swore that the nasty little beasts were able to learn and solve the maze better after going through it once. Aila had always been skeptical.

If only there were pieces of cheese to help her and her friends find where they needed to go.

"Does anyone else think it's strange that there's a maze like this in the middle of an area that has always been too magical for anyone else to explore, or at least to explore and then get out of alive? Do you think maybe there actually might be mages or other people or something else living in here that don't want others to know about them?"

The lack of answers didn't make Aila feel any better about the situation.

With nothing clever left to do, the group chose their path at random, with input from Tere about how the magical matrix felt. He could detect, it seemed, some fluctuations in the magic within the maze, barely distinguishable, but different enough from the background that it might help them to keep track of where they were heading and, even more important, how they could get out. It wouldn't do for them to find the flowers and then get lost in the maze, either never returning or getting back too late to save Aila's father. Though she knew the seven-day time limit was imposed by her father, a comment by Verona before they'd left indicated that the king wouldn't last too much longer than that.

They'd already burned three days. There were only four left. If they didn't find the flowers soon, they might not get back to the castle in time.

"Hold," Tere said as they tried another passageway, this one with a nice carpet of grass on the ground and scattered shrubs to break up the seemingly endless path they needed to tread. "A group of...something came through here recently."

"Can you be more specific?" Lily asked.

"No, not really. My magical sight is still overwhelmed by the ambient magic in the area, so I have to use mundane tracking techniques. Whatever is moving through here is pretty good at not leaving a trail, but I've spotted a few traces of their passage. Be on your guard. This maze is an excellent place to ambush four visitors ignorant of the local area."

Within two turns, Aila had already lost her sense of direction completely.

"Uh-oh," she said.

Tere chuckled. "Lost your way already? Don't worry about it. I didn't expect you to remember the part of the maze you could see from the tree. I've had to do something like that before and it's easy to lose direction. Even for me."

"I thought you never lost your sense of direction," Lily said.

"I don't, not when I can use my magical sight. That's not much good here, but I still know which way we're heading from experience. I think I've taught my body to keep track of it without me thinking about it."

"Really? So which way are we heading?"

"Right now? We're all facing east by northeast. I figure the next chance we get to head to our left, we should do that."

Aila scratched her head. "Why?"

"Because that will put us in a more northerly direction. Sintrovis is slightly west of north from Metrovial, so I figure due north, or slightly to the west of that, will get us to the center of the area no one knows about. If you want us to go in another direction, tell me."

"No, it's not that. I thought maybe we'd wander around until we can find the center of the maze.'

"Uh, no," Tere said. "That's a good way to get completely lost, never find the center, and end up starving to death or dying of thirst. I like my way better."

"Don't you adventurer types draw symbols on rocks and caves so that you can go back the way you came in?" Conren asked.

Aila thought Tere might take offense to the question. She felt insulted for him after the knight's sweeping generalizations. The archer shrugged.

"I didn't bring chalk and I don't want to take the time to search for rocks that might leave marks. As long as I know which way we're going—and which way we've gone—we won't get lost and we'll be able to find our way back. I'm not saying we won't be killed by monsters, but we won't die because we're lost. As long as *I* don't get killed by monsters."

Aila didn't care for the comment about being killed by monsters, but she did appreciate his assurance he'd lead them out when they were ready.

As they navigated the maze, the unlikelihood and marvelous structure of the walls became less impressive. Not because they weren't as perfectly put together as they were in the edge of the maze, but because Aila grew accustomed to the stone edifices arranged so efficiently.

Or it could have been because she started noticing the things *within* the maze instead of the structure of the maze itself.

In each section they passed through, whether it was a long, straight corridor or the larger sections that she thought of as rooms, she noticed something. She knew she should be concentrating on where they were going and how they'd find the flowers, but an idea struck her and her mind couldn't shake loose the concept.

"Do you guys notice anything about the terrain in the maze?" she asked, wondering if her mind was bored and making up things to think about or if there was really something to what she'd figured out.

"What, that it's like normal outside stuff, like plants and

things," Lily said, "instead of seeming like they're inside passageways?"

Aila walked around a small bush growing up from the ground in front of her. "That's almost what I was thinking. Imagine what we can see here in front of us, especially when we're in one of the large rooms. In your imagination, remove the walls."

"That would make it a lot easier to navigate," Tere said.

She shot the archer a frigid look. "Very funny. Really, though. If you ignore the walls, this area is like any other section of the forest we have been passing through, but maybe with fewer trees. I mean, if someone were to drop a series of walls onto an already-existing forest, it would look a lot like this, don't you think?"

Lily looked around as they reached another of the wider areas. Tere didn't move his head, but then again, he didn't need to with the way his sight worked. Conren's head remained rigidly facing forward, but his eyes jerked around, looking for what she'd talked about. She suppressed a smile.

"You know," the tall, red-haired archer said, "you're right. When you really look at it, it doesn't look so much like the plants and grass and stuff is growing in between the wall, but that they were growing and the walls intruded on their space. All except the one feature that the tall trees are far enough away from the walls to keep us from jumping between them. But so what? It's a matter of perspective, right? Does it make a difference?"

"Maybe not," Aila admitted. "I thought it was weird. There has to be magic involved, right? Could something like this exist without..." Aila trailed off as she noticed something ahead and off to the side, near the left wall of the wide area. Though Tere was in front, Aila drifted toward the left. She sidestepped a few small trees, then threaded her way through some bushes to stand before what she'd seen and—when she got close enough—heard.

The others came over to find her staring down as she tried to make sense of what was in front of her.

"It's a...stream?" Lily said.

"Spring," Tere corrected, but after taking a closer look, he amended what he'd said. "A spring fed stream."

A narrow ribbon of flowing water burbled past them. Water flowed through a channel it had carved in the rock itself. That wasn't the strange part, though. Upstream, they reached a hole in the ground from which the water flowed. Downstream, it disappeared into another. In between the stream rushed happily by, clear as glass.

It bubbled up like a spring, but the way the water emptied into the other hole was something Aila had never seen. It must have been an underground river that happened to surface in a perfect location to provide drinking water, then dipped back down to its subterranean streambed to continue on its way.

Tere got on his hands and knees and put his face down near the water. He dipped a hand in it and his eyebrows jumped upward. "That's really cold." He splashed some on his head and sighed. It wasn't a hot day, but it was warm enough that a little water on the face would feel nice.

"Let's take a break here for half an hour or so. I'm going to drink a little bit and see if it does anything to me. It looks very clean."

He dipped his cupped hands in, then gulped down some of the water. While they waited to see if anything detrimental happened to him, the others splashed water on their faces, washed their hands and arms, or even put feet into the chilly stream. Of course, Conren gave Aila a disappointed look when she took her boots and socks off to soak her feet, but that was his problem. The cool water refreshed her like nothing had since they'd entered Sintrovis. At least she did it downstream from where the others were.

Tere felt no ill effects from the water, so after combining what each person had left into two of the waterskins, they filled the emptied skins with water from the stream.

"That will take care of not dying of thirst," Tere said. "If there is as much vegetation as you said, Aila, we may not have to worry about starving, either. There may be vegetables or berries within the maze."

"That's good news," Aila said, "but remember, we're on a time constraint. If we run out of food and need to forage, we're already too late to help my father."

"Point taken," Tere said.

When they started off again, Aila couldn't help it. She scanned the plants for recognizable food. She was no expert at foraging, but she'd spotted edible things before in their travels. At least, she thought they were edible. It was only because of her scrutiny of the surroundings that she saw the fireheart flowers.

## ❧ 17 ❧

Tere led the group, Lily following on his heels. Aila was third, with Conren behind and to her right. There was no real need for them to be in a single file, but it was comfortable, and they'd settled into it. Aila's head swung back and forth, examining the plants they passed and searching for anything else that might be interesting. True, they were there only to find the flowers to heal her father, but she was curious about a place that no one had ever entered and then departed safely.

As they passed a thick tangle of bushes and grasses, she happened to look back behind her left shoulder. She wasn't looking at Conren, who was on the other side of her, and she wasn't really checking for threats. She couldn't explain why she looked back at that particular moment. She just did.

A little splash of color caught her eye and she stopped walking. She leaned toward the bushes to search for what she'd seen. There. A little bit of red and yellow barely visible through the vegetation. She didn't explain to the others, wanting to make sure she was actually seeing something significant first. Conren made a sound that was an awful lot like what parents make when their child is acting up. She ignored him.

By the time the others stopped—no doubt due to Conren's "A*lev*ia," said with such exasperation, the others turned to see what was wrong—Aila was on her hands and knees reaching for the bit of color she'd seen.

"Alevia," Conren said again, this time speaking directly to her and not using her name as a curse. "Don't reach into a bush like that. You don't know what kind of dangerous animal might be—" He cut off whatever he was going to say when she held up her hand. In it was a scrap of a soft, thin petal of deep crimson and a slash of yellow that turned to a sliver of orange before it melted into the red.

"Is that...?" Tere said, racing up to her. She handed it over to him and he turned it over in his hands. "That's fireheart. It has to be. You found them, Aila. You found them!"

She'd put her attention back on the bush as he inspected the scrap of flower petal, and she moved the shrub back and forth to see better into the main mass of the plants. "Not so fast. I don't see any whole flowers, though there are some other remnants."

After several minutes of searching, she came up with about half a dozen other fragments, three of them with obvious teeth marks and one that had a portion of the little green base of the flower where it attached to the stem.

"Something likes the taste of these," she said. "With how the teeth are arranged and their size, it looks like something with mouths at least as big as ours." She realized how she'd worded it and raised a finger to Tere, who was already opening his mouth to say something. "Don't you dare." Tere swallowed what he was going to say and Lily laughed.

The old archer held the tattered petals in one palm. "This isn't enough to make an antidote for the poison for a grown man."

Aila wasn't going to allow her finding to be a source of sadness. "Don't you see, though? You have proof in your hand that the flowers do grow here. Not this bush; these were obviously dropped. But if something is eating them, then there has to be a decent supply, right? The maze is big. If some grew near here, they have to be in other places in the maze, or even outside of it. We know what we're trying to do is possible. It's a good thing."

Lily stepped over to Aila and patted her on the shoulder. "I agree. It should give us hope, energize us."

Tere frowned at the scraps in his hand. "You're correct. We're on the right track. We'll find them. Let's get going. We have a lot of daylight still today."

"We should go back," Conren said, stomping down on the satisfied feeling Aila had convinced herself to experience.

"Go back where?" she asked the knight.

"We should take the pieces of the flowers and go back to Metrovial. We're running out of time. As it is, we will barely make it back in time, and that's if nothing has happened to our horses. We should be thankful we found these and take them to Verona."

"Conren, I understand your concern," Tere said, "but these small parts of the flowers won't cure the poison."

"You don't know that."

"I do know that. I'm a more experienced herbalist than most town apothecaries. I am telling you for a fact that these scraps, even if they were fresh when we brought them back, will not be potent enough to heal anyone bigger than a toddler. You don't understand dose and the effects of body mass, but I do. If we return to Metrovial with these, we will watch the king die."

"I do not think you have the expertise you think you do. If we go now, we'll get back in time for Verona to use them. She graduated from the Hero Academy. She will make them work. If we continue in this gods-forsaken maze, we will get back too late and the king with die anyway. Better a small chance than no chance."

"You have no say in it, Conren," Aila said. She stood at her full height, back straight and fists clenched. "You are with us because Father forced you upon us. We agree that the right thing is to go on." She raised her eyebrows at Tere and Lily and they both nodded. "If you want to go back, feel free. We'll not stop you from doing what you want to do. Not everyone has the strength of character needed to risk themselves for others. There's no shame in it."

The knight's blue eyes blazed, as Aila had known they would. It may have been petty to poke at his pride in such a way, but she was good and tired of him constantly putting stumbling blocks in their path.

"We're going forward," she continued. "Do what you think you should do. Perhaps we'll see you back at the castle. Come on, Tere, Lily. We're using up daylight."

The three started walking and Conren stood right where he was, his body shaking. Aila wasn't sure if it was in rage or embarrassment, but she glanced back twice and found him still in exactly the same spot. She let out a breath. That was the end of that.

Tere took a turn in the maze and the other two followed. After they were walking in the new direction, Lily glanced back at Aila. The shorter woman shrugged and the archer gave her a sympathetic look.

A few minutes later, the heavy thumps of the knight's boots cycling at a faster tempo than the feet of the other three caught up to them. Aila glanced back and saw Conren steadily catching up to them. When he'd taken his place in line, she gave him a smile, which he met with a neutral expression with his mouth in a straight line. He'd get over it. She was kind of glad he'd come around. Her father would scold her if she had gotten his favorite young knight lost or killed.

All four kept an eye out for more of the flowers as they went. A lot of the bushes looked the same and Aila wondered if only some of them bore the flowers while others were sterile. She hadn't seen any evidence that the flowers had come from the bush she'd found them under, so they couldn't even be sure that had been the right type of plant. They would find them. They had to.

A sound from ahead of her grabbed Aila's attention as they entered one of the wider sections. Tere grunted and darted out of the way just as a palm-sized rock flew through the space he had just been in. It bounced on the ground and had Aila not been looking at the time, it would have hit her. She was able to shuffle to the side to avoid it, and it passed the group without hurting anyone.

"More," Tere said. "On the walls."

Several more stones came at Aila. She moved back to a section of wall that would cover her at least a little, but found Conren lunging in front of her, his shield up to deflect the missiles coming at them. The clanging as she huddled behind the shield was loud enough for her to need to cover her ears.

Tere and Lily loosed a few arrows, though they were being careful only to use one when it was sure to take one of the attackers out.

"We can't do this," Tere said. "Even if we hit one for every arrow we shoot, we'll end up with no arrows, and their supply of stones seems endless." He ducked behind a small tree with a trunk not even as wide as he was. Lily was likewise taking cover behind two other trees that had grown into each other, forming a bit of a wider obstruction.

"What do you suggest?" Aila yelled at him over the sound of the rocks hitting the shield.

"We either go back or we go forward and try to find

better cover or a way up onto the walls. They had to have gotten up there somehow. If we can find it and fight them close up—or at least where I can be assured I can get my arrows back after I put the shafts into them—we may survive this."

Aila only thought for a moment about it. "We can't go back. If you can find a path to push forward, I'd prefer that."

"Fine. Follow me. This might hurt."

That was an understatement. Aila had felt one of those rocks striking her. Luckily, it had hit her armor, so it didn't break anything, but if one of those hefty stones thrown with the force the trebaxels were generating hit someone's head, it would be all over. She was betting Conren wished he had his plate armor, though even his normal helmet might not soften the blunt damage of one of the projectiles enough to save him. At least he had a shield, which benefited Aila, too. Tere and Lily were more vulnerable.

She shook her head. It was no time to second-guess the decision. They did have to move forward. Going back would mean her father dying, and she wasn't ready to accept that. She prayed to Vanda that they'd find shelter or a way to get to the creatures to fight face-to-face.

"Go," Tere shouted and sprinted from his hiding place. It took several seconds for the attackers to react and adjust their aim toward him, but he ran quickly, changing directions often, and ended up behind another tree deeper into the middle of the large area. He settled behind it, a bigger trunk than he'd been behind before.

Lily did almost as impressive a job as Tere and soon, she was hunkered down at what seemed to be the edge of the trebaxels' range, or at least their range of accuracy. A few stones flew toward her, but the distance worked in her favor and most wouldn't have hit her even if she were in the open.

Aila watched for a few seconds. True, the creatures

couldn't hit Lily at the moment, but she could see others running around the edges of the walls, moving to get into a better position to attack her. Where were they climbing onto the walls?

Aila and Conren didn't move as quickly or gracefully as the two archers had. The knight kept his shield up to protect them and he kept stumbling, trying to make sure he covered Aila as the pair ran. Eventually, they made it to the center of the area as well. Just as they did, rocks started coming from the other walls. They'd taken too long.

"Again," Tere said, loosing the rare arrow and taking one of the creatures in the eye as it popped up to throw a rock. The force of the attack unbalanced it and it fell backward, presumably into another corridor or open area in the maze. While the archer took off running, Aila wondered if they'd find the thing's body in their travels. She hadn't yet seen one up close.

Of course, to find it, they'd have to survive the current attack.

$$\text{❧}\quad 18 \quad \text{❧}$$

For Aila, the whole world consisted of short sprints from cover to cover. When there were obstacles to hide behind at all. Some of the bushes and tall grasses that grew within the center of the large area they were in were worse than no cover at all.

Once, Aila directed Conren into one of the tangled parts. Immediately, she realized they should have followed Tere's and Lily's paths more closely. Suddenly, they weren't able to move as quickly as before, but the leaves and blades of grass did nothing to stop the stones thrown at them from getting through to strike them.

They were lucky, really. Aila took a rock to the left thigh and on the right side of her chest. Conren—trying to protect Aila—was hit at least three times that Aila saw, once in the right shoulder and twice on his legs. They huddled beneath the shield when they finally made it to a tree that gave them at least some protection on one side.

"Are you all right?" the knight asked her.

She felt guilty that where she led them resulted in both of them being struck, and she felt doubly bad because the first thing he said was to check to make sure she was fine. "It hurts like Percipius's wrath, but I got hit in muscles and...uh, other padded places. I don't think any bones are broken or anything. How are you?"

"I am"— he paused while he moved his leg and rolled his shoulder as best he could from the crouched position—"in some measure of agony. I will never underestimate the value of thrown stones as a weapon again."

Her nervous energy came out in a maniacal chuckle.

They followed the archers more carefully after that, but still, the place they were trapped in seemed like it was five times as long as the sixty feet or so it really was.

All four of the travelers were bundled up behind the last of the significant trees before the section they were in ended. Less than twenty feet separated them from the opening that emptied into another hallway. Or, at least, it was a section that was significantly narrower than the one they were in, and it had few small trees that would provide a barrier to flying rocks.

"What now?" Tere asked. "I can't see anything we can hide behind up farther. The only positive thing I can say about going into the narrower section is that, for some reason, the trebaxels aren't posted on the walls up ahead."

"That doesn't make any sense," Lily said, darting her head back behind one of the trees when a rock came too close. "They seem like they've been pretty smart so far. They haven't jumped down to engage us, knowing they have the advantage from up there. You'd think some of them would move up and start throwing their rocks at us if we try to make a run for it. They'd be throwing at us head-on with nothing for us to hide behind."

"There's too much about them we don't know," Tere said. "I don't even know how they keep up their supply of rocks. They have to have large stockpiles or have a lot of other trebaxels in the background hauling them up for the throwers. If we're going to go forward, we should probably do it before they decide to take advantage of what you just described."

"Going back is even less an option now than it was before," Aila said. "We're more tired, we'd have to backtrack through the entire section, and we still need to go forward. What are the chances that when we get to the narrow area, we'll be able to outrun them or find something to take cover behind?"

Conren watched the other three, listening to what they said, but he didn't offer any comments about it.

"The chances may be slightly better than if we tried to go back," Tere said. "Or maybe worse. I can't see any cover ahead. We'll basically be putting our lives at risk on the chance there's something up there around the corner. I realize it's your father's life in the balance, as well as the rest of Dizhelim if we can't get some help fighting the animaru, but we have to think about our lives as well.

"It's up to you, Aila. From what I see, we're pretty screwed whatever we do. It might be different if this background magic wasn't affecting my magical sight so much, but it is. Decide. I'm with you."

"Me, too," Lily said, trying at a smile, but failing as another stone hit the tree right next to her head. "Damn, those things can throw rocks. Their accuracy is amazing."

Again, Aila noticed that Conren didn't comment. She'd worry about why later. For now, it was time for a decision and, despite her better judgment, the others had left it to her.

"Let's make a run for it and pray there's a nice big boulder or something to hide behind up there."

Tere nodded, scanned the narrowing section, and repositioned himself so he could take off at a run.

"Stay to the left, as close to the wall as you can. The way it slightly curves, it ought to block some of the rocks they throw. From the left side, at least. There are still some on the walls on the right. Everyone ready?" A round of nods. Conren adjusted the grip on his shield. His face looked...determined. "Right. Let's lead them off, Lily. Aila, you and Conren follow as closely as possible this time. Any gap will give them another second or two to aim at you. We don't want that. Lily, ready, go!"

The two archers took off at a speed Aila found difficult to believe for such tall people, not to mention that Tere had more than thirty years on Aila's age. She and Conren were only a step behind as the group started a run for their lives.

Aila and Conren performed a tricky dance as they neared the narrowing of the passage, trying to foil the monsters' aim. The trebaxels didn't race along the tops of the walls to keep up with the humans, instead staying where they were. This had the happy effect of the projectiles coming at them from behind, with none flying at them from the front. Conren slowed down a little and swung in behind Aila, but his speed faltered until she figured out that he was trying to shield her from behind. Their awkward ballet resulted in two rocks hitting Aila in her rump—though how that happened with Conren directly behind her she didn't know—and several exclamations from the knight as he apparently was struck as well.

They kept running, though it was awkward and slower than Aila would've liked. Tere and Lily had opened up a wider gap ahead of the two slower runners, and they looked like they could continue their pace for the rest of the day.

Then the sound of stones striking the ground and walls around them stopped. It was so sudden, Aila's head turned to look back over her shoulder without her consent, making her stumble and almost fall. They slowed down enough to regain her balance, though Conren looked at her like he was about ready to pick her up with his free arm and continue on, carrying her like a child.

Aila waved the knight away and slowed even more, until she finally stopped completely. Her mouth dropped open, and not just because she was trying to catch her breath.

The trebaxels weren't throwing rocks anymore. At all. Even stranger, they weren't moving. Several dozen of the hairy monsters stood on the tops of the walls, watching the humans, but they weren't doing anything aggressive, nor were they coming after them.

"Tere," Aila shouted. "Lily. Stop." She had to yell it twice more before the pair saw Aila and Conren, who had halted to protect her, standing in the middle of the passageway.

"Are you mad?" Tere yelled back, though he did stop. "Come on, before they swarm you."

Aila pointed at the motionless attackers, most of them with rocks still in their hands. She walked toward Tere and Lily at a pace more appropriate for strolling in a park in the afternoon than dealing with dead-shot monsters holding projectiles.

They came together thirty feet into the narrow passage.

"They stopped as soon as we got in here," she said. "They don't look like they're going to follow, either. I think we're just out of range. Do they look disappointed to you? They kind of look disappointed to me."

"Disappointed?" Lily asked, eyeing the furry figures warily.

"Yeah. They're obviously not supposed to leave their area. There's no other explanation for it. They don't look like they're afraid of anything in here. To me, it seems like they're sad they didn't get us before we left the place they're guarding."

"That's ridiculous," Conren said.

Tere put up a hand. "No, not really. They do actually look

like they're disappointed. They're even smarter than I thought if they're assigned a particular area and they understand they're not supposed to go beyond it. Now that I look carefully, they do look like soldiers who have failed in their duty and are not looking forward to their superiors finding out. Do you realize what this means?"

"That we might actually survive?" Aila asked.

"Sure, that too. What I was thinking was that it means if we run into more of these rock-throwing sentries, we can outrun them. We don't have to worry about trying to fight them if we can get by and they stay in their own place."

"I think you make it sound too simple," Conren said.

"Oh? How so?"

The knight took the shield off his arm, set it against the wall, and clenched and unclenched his left fist. "Let's say you're correct and they're like soldiers who have specific orders and are very obedient. All it will take is for their superiors to give them new orders. Maybe something like, *chase after the humans and attack them until they're dead?* If that happens, which it will if we keep going forward because conceivably the place we want to go will have higher-ranked officer monsters, now we have troops behind us as well as in front. We're surrounded."

Aila suddenly felt sick to her stomach. Conren was right. They might just be in a worse position than they were before.

"If you carry the supposition further," the knight said, "if these creatures are actually as intelligent as you may think, they might have stopped throwing rocks so we would jump to the conclusion they're not supposed to follow us out of their area. It could all be a ruse. A trap. They could be playing with us. I hardly think that Sintrovis would hold its secrets for thousands of years based only on a few score of rock-throwing apes. There must be more to it."

Tere rubbed the side of his face, considering what Conren

had said. After some thought, he answered. "You might be right. We could have just put ourselves into their control, or their trap. That's some solid analysis."

"I have been trained in tactics since I was a boy. Being a knight is not just riding around and swinging a sword."

"Fair enough. Good job. It gives us more to think about. For now, at least, we're not being attacked, so why don't we continue on and see if we can make that situation last. Keep thinking, Conren. I like it that you're not giving us only negative comments anymore, but are analyzing things and communicating what you figure out."

Tere turned and headed down the passage. Aila caught the look of confusion on Conren's face. Maybe he was used to people not considering his opinions since he was still much younger than the other knights he interacted with. In any case, the expression on his face was worth remembering. It reminded her of the boy she used to know. Her friend. Before he became the self-absorbed and arrogant man he seemed to be now.

"Thanks for the help," she told him. "Sorry I tripped you up and was such a burden."

She watched his confused expression deepen and his cheeks color. She fixed that one firmly in her mind, too, as she walked briskly toward the archers, hiding her smile.

"Is this really necessary?" Marla grumbled at her twin brother.

"Necessary? No, I don't think so. I think it would be good to find out once and for all if the Raibrech the way I do it is unique to me or if it's a Malatirsay thing, though."

"A Malatirsay thing," she said flatly. She wasn't in the mood for any of this.

"Yeah. I would think that it's something both of us could do in our role of Malatirsay, but it could be something only I can do because of being trained by the Croagh and then learning the Song from the Gypta. Aren't you curious if you can use the Song as a source of power?"

"No," she said. "I have dozens of spells I can cast because of my training in the Academy. Not to minimize the Raibrech or anything, but the spells in it seem kind of weak to me."

"Not the enhanced spells," Aeden said. "The ones I've learned to enhance are pretty powerful."

"You've only enhanced a few of them. The rest are maybe a little more powerful than what every highland warrior can cast. It seems like a lot of work to learn spells that can't even do the damage of most of the ones I already know."

Aeden looked into Marla's eyes. "Are you whining? Do I sense a tantrum coming on?"

Laughter from the other side of her brother reminded Marla that she and Aeden weren't alone in the little corner of one of the practice fields they'd made their own for the time being. Evon was the source of laughter, but Fahtin was also there, a smile on her face. Insufferable. Didn't they have anything better to do?

"Look," she said. "I haven't been in a good mood lately. Too many things are pressing in on me. If you think I'm whining about it, maybe we should do this another time. Or not at all." She realized her voice had been rising with each word she said and cleared her throat, as if that would erase it all.

Aeden continued looking at her with those piercing blue eyes of his. She wondered why she got green and he got blue. He'd told her that it had been the same with her parents, with her father's eyes being blue and her mother's green. He didn't speak now, only kept looking at her. The bubbling lava of her anger started to flare up again. Why was he wasting her time like this?

Aeden reached out and pulled her into a hug, surprising her so much she didn't even try to defend herself. She stood there, tense, while he embraced her.

"I'm sorry things are rough for you right now," he said softly enough so that the other two couldn't hear him. "We don't have to do this. There's so much I don't know about this whole Malatirsay thing. I'm finding some stuff out as I read through the book the Prophet left us, but I feel like if we can just get more information, things might go better for us, and easier. I also want to share it with you. My sister. Talk to me. Tell me what the problem is. We can do that instead of me trying to teach you the Raibrech."

At his words, she finally relaxed enough to hug him back. She didn't know why things were so hard for her lately. She'd been under tension before—her whole life was one series of crises after another—but everything stoked the fire of her anger so easily recently.

She looked over Aeden's shoulder toward the south. That was another thing. She didn't know what it was, but she felt something from that direction. It was such a fleeting thing, she wasn't even sure if it was real, but at times like the present moment, it seemed there was something she needed to do. In that direction.

"I'm sorry," she told him. "Let's do what you wanted to do. Maybe it'll distract me and make me less moody." He released her and stepped back, giving her a significant look. She laughed. "No, it is not time for my moon cycle, so don't be an idiot and ask. Not everything in a woman's life hinges on that. Gods, I should know better than to use the word *moody* when talking to a man."

Aeden put his hands up to ward her off. "I didn't say anything."

She eyed him for a moment but decided to let him off the hook. When she heard another chuckle, she had no doubt it was Evon. That one did not deserve her leniency.

"I just thought of something," she said. "Fahtin is Gypta, through whom the magic of the Song flows more powerfully, according to what you told me you read in Tsosin Ruus's book. Also, Evon knows some Dantogyptain. How about if we're going to do this, all three of us will try to learn. That will tell you if it's just a *Malatirsay thing*, an *Aeden thing*, or something related to the language or other magical blood-lines. Plus, Evon can already use magic, so it's an even better test."

She'd said it loud enough that the other two must have heard her clearly. Right away, Fahtin started making excuses.

"I have enough to deal with trying to learn what's in the book the Prophet left for me. The visions and the magical protection are plenty for me."

"Come on, Fahtin," Evon said. "It'll be fun, and we'll be helping Aeden and Marla out. Aren't you curious if your Gypta blood will allow you to cast spells like Aeden does? Think of what that could mean. Your family—all Gypta—might be able to use it to protect themselves from the animaru. Wouldn't that make you feel more comfortable about their safety?"

Fahtin bit her bottom lip. Damn, but the girl was beautiful. Marla couldn't blame Evon for losing his thought process when Fahtin looked at him.

"Okay. We can try it. To help out Aeden and Marla."

"Great," Aeden said. "Come on over here. I'll need to teach you the movements. The words won't be hard; there are only three of them. It could be better if you knew the whole quatrain for the spell—it seems to help make the spell more powerful when I think of the words in the context of the Song—but the motions and the three words will tell us if you can cast the Raibrech spells."

Evon and Fahtin joined Marla, and Aeden stepped out in front of the three.

"It's fairly simple," Aeden said, "but I'll tell you right now that you have to be precise with the hand and body positions. I'll correct you several times. Keep your mind open, watch carefully when I demonstrate, and try not to get frustrated. I won't even bother with teaching you the words until you've got the motions down. It may take more than the time we've got right now."

Marla groaned inwardly. Why? Why did she have to agree to the ridiculous thing? She had dozens of things she needed to get done. There wasn't time to spend hours just to see if they could even manage to cast one of the weak spells. She closed her eyes for a moment and took in a breath, trying to keep her anger at bay.

"You all right, Marla?" Aeden asked.

She plastered a smile onto her face and pointed it at him. "Yep. Just getting my mindset right."

He raised an eyebrow at her but didn't push the issue. Instead, he took up a stance in front of them, feet parallel and greater than shoulder width, toes pointed forward.

"This is the basic stance to get us started. Go ahead and get into it now."

Evon and Marla easily put their feet where they were supposed to be, which was to be expected. They'd had training in combat, so stances weren't anything new to them. Fahtin, on the other hand, needed a little correction.

"Bend your knees and make sure your feet are parallel," Aeden said. "It might not seem that it matters, but it does. The stance gives us a firm foundation to allow the magic to flow."

The Gypta girl grumbled, but quickly learned how to position herself.

"Now, watch me a couple of times, then I'll have you do it one at a time to make sure you're doing the motions correctly."

Aeden swung his arms out to the sides and then up, palms facing the sky, like he was lifting two objects in his hands. When his hands made their arc, he bent his wrists so his palms faced downward and followed with his elbows, like he was pushing a large ball down into a lake he was standing in with both hands. He then rotated his wrists so his palms faced up and moved them together toward his heart. Finally, he rotated his wrists again and pushed down as he had done before. He repeated it three times.

"Now you," he said, pointing at Marla. She was familiar with much of the movement from her meditation and mind magic training. She performed it in front of her brother and he adjusted the angle of her wrists a little. "I'm not just being picky. It really does make a lot of difference. You'll see."

Marla didn't tell him what she thought of whether he was picky or not.

Evon went next and needed a few more corrections than Marla did, but he seemed to pick it up quickly. When Fahtin tried, Aeden had to work with her for more than ten minutes to get her to remember the correct motions and hand placements.

"Good," he said. "The words are simple enough. They mean last, and dawn, and ringing out. The name of this spell, by the way, is Dawn's Warning. It's the first spell in the Raibrech and corresponds to the first quatrain in the Song of Prophecy. The words of power are *Fantim, Lishant,* and *Stuta.* I'll demonstrate the spell now."

He did so, taking up the stance he'd taught them, then moving his arms as they'd just learned. The words came out with a particular rhythm, one that Marla found strange. Not the tempo of normal speech, but not precisely musical, either. The last one he emphasized as he pushed his hands down the final time. A bright flash of light erupted from him.

"That's the basic spell. The light is peculiar—it can not only be used as a signal, but it will blind those hostile to the caster. Somehow, the magic knows who is an ally and protects them. This spell was the first I ever enhanced. I did it without knowing what I was doing during the night when the animaru attacked the caravan." Fahtin gasped. "You remember that one, huh?"

"Very clearly," she said.

"What was that rhythm you said the words to?" Marla

asked. "It almost sounded like you were singing them, but I don't recognize it well enough to duplicate it."

"Oh, that. I can't help but to sing the words because I always think of the context of the song whenever I use Dant-ogyptain. I wasn't taught that when I learned the Raibrech with the clan, though, and no other Croagh I've talked with has any particular rhythm with which they use the words. Saying them while you're going through the motions is enough. The final word should be pronounced as you finish the movements, but other than that, it can be as fast or slow as you like. Maybe with practice, you'll be able to change the way the spell reacts. I can do that, but let's not get ahead of ourselves.

"Evon, you can go first this time. First, go through the motions so I can make sure you're doing them correctly. After that, we'll do it with the words."

"Uh," the Academy graduate said. "What would happen if I did the motions incorrectly while pronouncing the words?"

Aeden smirked. "That's a good question. The answer is: it depends. No one I know of understands the magic at such a minute level as to know the result of each type of error. It could simply fail to bring forth the magic or it could have different effects. I've heard tales of young Croagh during the Trial of Magic casting incorrectly and hurting themselves or others. One caused another trainee's clothes to burst into flame. Best to do the motions correctly so we don't have to deal with unexpected results."

Over the next hour and a half, Aeden worked first with Evon, then with Marla, and finally with Fahtin. Though Evon performed the movements correctly and pronounced the words better than the two women, he wasn't able to generate so much as a glimmer. After five attempted castings with correct form, Aeden had Evon stop.

Marla still thought the whole thing was ridiculous, but she

went along with it. After a couple of tries and some corrections from Aeden, she created a small flare of light that was wholly underwhelming.

"I suppose that could be seen as a confirmation of your Croagh blood," Aeden said. The male warriors in his clan had outnumbered the female, but both trained together when they were young. It was never a matter of one being chosen over the other. There were just fewer females born into Clan Tannoch, for some reason. Aeden told them he wasn't sure if it was the same for the other clans.

Fahtin had the most trouble getting to the point where she did the motions correctly. She focused on them so carefully, she flubbed the words three times before she finally got both the words and the motions correct. Marla watched with trepidation, wondering if her clothes were going to catch fire.

Aeden squinted his eyes at Fahtin and watched her intently as she repeated her casting. The way Marla's twin tilted his head, he was still confused about something.

"Come here," he said to Fahtin, putting his hand out for her to take. He led her to a shady spot underneath a large tree. "Okay, try it again."

Fahtin stared at him like she was trying to figure out if he was playing a joke on her, but settled into her stance and prepared to cast anyway. She did so, and as she pronounced the last word of power, Marla picked out a bit of light, as if someone with a mirror was reflecting weak sunlight onto Fahtin.

"Was that...?" Marla asked.

"I think so," Aeden answered excitedly. "Fahtin, do it again. This time, really focus on your movements and on the words. Make them part of you, feel them."

"I don't know what that means, but fine," she said. "I did feel something that last time, though it was the same as the couple of times before that."

She repeated the casting. All three of her friends watched closely as she did so. This time, whether it was because it was stronger or just because Marla knew what she was watching for, the little flash of light was unmistakable.

"You did it!" Evon said. "You made light. I saw it. Fantastic."

Fahtin beamed at him, her cheeks glowing rosy. "I definitely felt some kind of magic," she said.

"Great job, Fahtin," Aeden said. "I guess the Gypta blood allows you to use the Raibrech. Even Evon, who can cast other types of magic, couldn't seem to use it. Interesting."

"That's fine," Evon said. "I'm glad I could help you work out how the magic can be used. Maybe we'll figure it out eventually."

Marla smiled and nodded in support of Fahtin, but her mind was elsewhere. So, those with Gypta blood could use the magic. That still didn't make it worth using such weak magic. She hoped, at least, that Aeden was finished with her. She was glad she could help him with his experiment, but frankly, she didn't have time for trivial spells.

She glanced toward the south again and began working out in her head how she was going to attack the long list of things she needed to get done.

❦ 20 ❦

After the revelation that the trebaxels wouldn't go beyond certain limits to chase intruders, Aila and the others engaged in several sessions of sprinting past groups of the rock-throwing protectors to get beyond their domains. It worked well enough, in the end, though there were some painful results in the short term. After hours of sprinting and catching their breath, only to have to race more stones farther on their path, the four travelers sat in the midst of some of the larger trees that could only be found in wider areas of the maze.

"I think the majority of my body is black and blue," Aila said. "Even the parts that aren't so tired, they might as well be bruised. It hurts to walk."

Tere shrugged. "At least we have found a method that works, even if it's painful. We didn't waste any more arrows, and we've crossed through more of the maze. At a faster pace, at that. There's no telling how big it is, but if we can keep it up, we might actually be able to do what we came here for. If we keep going. We're losing the fight against time."

"The king gave us a week," Conren said.

"True, but we're past the halfway point right now, and we still haven't found the flowers. We need to get them and figure out how to get all the way back out again—even faster than we made it in—or we won't be able to get back in time. If at all possible, we keep going until the light fails. After we get the flowers, we can even travel in the dark. There will be little sleep for us in the next few days."

"Plus, we have to get back through all the groups of trebaxels we've passed to get here," Lily added.

Tere blew out a breath. "Right. So, rest up for a few minutes, chew a few of these white fennel leaves I found to dull the pain and soreness, and prepare to push on ahead."

They did as Tere said and found the maze changing as they tried to find its center. More of the areas were wider, with fewer of the narrow hallways. The vegetation altered as well, shrubs they hadn't seen before making an appearance and the familiar trees being replaced by slenderer types with silvery bark. It looked even more like a forest that happened to have walls thrusting up occasionally rather than rooms or halls that had plants growing in them.

The party entered another large area, taking a right turn at the solid stone wall they encountered. A strange sound reached them through the dense undergrowth. It sounded like screaming or screeching. As Aila stopped all movement— and even her breathing—to hear better, she picked out another noise accompanying it. The unmistakable sound of blows being struck on flesh.

Tere scanned the area for ambushers, but did so as he crouch-ran toward the sound. Aila's heart quickened not only at the unexpected distraction, but also at Tere's hero sense that made him go to investigate without pause, though he was still wise and careful in the manner he did it.

After traversing a wild tangle that rivaled any forest they'd ever been in, the group stopped just before a small clearing and gaped at what they saw.

Four trebaxels were engaged in a vicious, pitched battle. Among themselves. Three of them were savagely beating the other one, the victim smaller than the three. Another two lay motionless on the ground at their feet.

The creatures were not using the stones they had been throwing at the humans, but all wielded tree branches. Their technique at swinging them was crude, but there was no doubt how effective the blows were. She winced as the weapon used by the one defender cracked across one of the attacker's shoulders, resulting in a scream as the struck trebaxel dropped its weapon from an arm that it was unable to move properly, hanging limply and twitching weakly.

Despite the injury, the injured trebaxel swung its other arm, hand balled into a fist, and staggered its opponent with a punch to the side of the face. This put the lone defender off balance. It hadn't looked too steady to begin with.

For a moment, the humans stared at what was happening. Aila ran all her observations through her mind, trying to come up with a reasonable explanation for what she was seeing. In the end, the simple fact that the smallest of the creatures was being attacked by all the others brought her to a decision. Without thinking further on it, she drew her vinci and raced into the clearing, already swinging one of the weapons on its chain to strike out from a distance.

Conren's muffled curse followed her, but Aila ignored it. She had a special dislike of bullies, and especially those who preyed on those smaller of stature. She hardly expected monsters to act with honor, but several larger trebaxel against the one smaller? Not something she was going to sit idly by and watch.

Once her vincus built up its momentum, she launched it at

the closest creature. It held its weapon back, looking for an opportunity to land a blow without hitting its companions. Aila's blade slashed the trebaxel's back deeply and it howled at the unexpected attack. It turned toward her with hatred in its eyes.

Then one of those eyes punctured as an arrow entered it.

Aila controlled her weapon and plucked the blade from the air by its handle, silently thanking Tere or Lily for the assistance.

The archers weren't done, though. Just as one of the remaining two creatures struck the smaller one across the back with its branch, two more arrows zipped in and ended the conflict in a fraction of a second. One arrow lodged in a throat and the other in another trebaxel's eye, but both were sufficient to drop the creatures to the ground.

As if it had used all its strength just to stand, the smaller trebaxel stumbled and then dropped to the ground itself. It pushed against the ground to rise, but fell back again in the attempt. When it spied Aila moving cautiously toward it, it chittered frantically and scrambled to escape. It didn't have the strength to do so, and eventually it lay there, panting, fear and panic in its wide eyes.

"I'm not going to hurt you," Aila said in as soothing a voice as she could. "Don't be afraid. I want to help you."

Stomping footsteps sounded behind her and Aila turned just in time to see Conren charging toward her, drawing his sword as he went. Aila waved at him to slow down because he was scaring the creature, but his eyes were locked on the downed trebaxel.

"Stop, Conren," she hissed.

He ignored her. With his sword free of the scabbard, he was almost close enough to strike at the creature.

Aila jumped to her feet, putting herself squarely in Conren's path. His sword, already starting an arc toward the creature, wavered as he tried to redirect it.

She did it for him.

She met his blade with both of hers. With a clang and a powerful twist, she slammed her vinci into the sword so forcefully that it upset the knight's balance. Once the sword passed, Aila rotated her hips back the other way and slammed her elbow hard into his jaw. She was afraid she might have broken it.

The force was devastating. Conren's feet continued to move forward as his head and torso moved backward from her blow. He slammed to the ground on his back with a whoof of air being knocked from him and he made a strangled groaning sound.

"If you so much as crawl toward this creature," she spat at him, "I will cut your throat. Do you understand me?"

He didn't answer.

Aila wanted to scream at him, but was afraid she'd scare the creature. Instead, she lowered her voice and hissed, "Do. You. Understand. Me?"

"Yes," he said, one hand probing his jaw.

Aila noticed Tere and Lily and glanced at them. Tere lifted his chin to her and she understood that he was offering to watch over Conren. She turned back to the trebaxel, who was looking at her with slightly less fear now. It almost seemed to be analyzing what it had just seen, trying to come to some conclusion.

"Now, little one," she said, though the creature was almost the same size as her. Compared to the others they'd seen, though, it was obviously a runt. "Let's see what we can do to help you. Do you want something to drink?"

She slowly drew out the water skin from her pack as the creature's eyes followed every movement. She held it out for the trebaxel, but it didn't seem to know what she wanted. She tilted it to her mouth and took a drink, then poured a few drips onto the ground so it could see what she was doing.

When she held it out again, the creature tentatively moved its own arm out to take it, though it winced in pain as it did so. It inspected the container for a moment, then imitated Aila's movements and tipped it to its mouth. More water than was necessary poured out, sloshing over its mouth, but it did drink some.

Aila smiled at it, though she wasn't sure if showing her teeth was the correct thing to do with the creature. It took one more drink, doing better to control it this time, before it held the skin out so Aila could take it.

They did the same type of dance when Aila offered the trebaxel some dried meat. It took the meat and smelled it, and then handed it back immediately despite Aila having first taken a bite herself.

"I don't think they're carnivores," Lily said. "Look at its teeth. They're not very sharp, mostly rounded. I think they probably eat plants." The redhead brought out some dried fruit from her pack, caught the creature's attention, and took a small bite, then held it out.

This time, after the trebaxel brought the food to its nose, it took a nibble. Aila almost laughed as the creature's expression changed from wariness to interest, to what she thought was pleasure. It took another bite and Aila was sure she hadn't misinterpreted the look. It popped the rest of the fruit into its mouth, then visibly relaxed. It seemed that maybe Lily's gift had earned them a little of its trust.

While Lily and Tere took turns handing the trebaxel pieces of food, Conren pulled himself up into a sitting position, rubbing his jaw and opening and closing his mouth.

"Sorry about that," Aila said. "I did tell you to stop."

"You attacked me," he said.

"I did not. I defended the poor, defenseless creature you were trying to cut into two pieces. If you hadn't charged it so violently, I wouldn't have stepped in your way to stop you."

He glared at her as he put two fingers in his mouth, running them between his teeth and gums. They came out with blood on them. "What are you doing? You choose a worthless monster over your companions?"

"When my companions act like monsters, yes. You saw what happened. This poor guy was attacked by the bigger ones. If there's one thing I can't abide, it's anyone being picked on because they're smaller. For Vanda's sake, it was five against one."

"You don't know that. The other two could have been on that one's side."

"I doubt that very much. Even if they were, it was three against one when we arrived, all of them nearly twice the size of this one."

Conren spat on the ground next to him. It was red-tinged, but there were no teeth in it. "That one might be a criminal or it could have gone against the community in some way. It might have been simple punishment we saw, justice being served for a crime."

"It's possible. If so, I'll take a chance that I might have done the wrong thing. Considering that the community has single-mindedly attacked and tried to kill us from the moment we set foot in Sintrovis, pardon me if I don't consider going against them a valid reason for them ganging up on him."

"It's *him* now, is it?"

"Yes, it is."

"All that time away from home, all your travels and adventures, it was all for nothing. You're still weak."

She blinked at him and the change of topic. "Weak? I just dropped you on your self-righteous ass."

"I didn't expect you to attack me. It would be different if I was ready for you, or have you forgotten our wrestling match before we left Metrovial? Anyway, it doesn't matter.

Showing mercy to an enemy just because they disagree with other enemies is weakness. A strong—and wise—warrior will finish off an enemy so they can't be attacked by surprise later on. It's the biggest mistake we've made here, and we've made plenty of others. All those monsters waiting for us, ready for us, in case we survive to find the flowers and then try to get back out. Your actions with this ape are the same thing: weakness."

Aila found that both her hands were gripping the hilts of her vinci and she purposely relaxed them. What was it about Sir Conren Gardner that aggravated her so? Or was it something about herself? Hadn't she said almost the exact same words to Tere a handful of days ago? "I'm done talking with you for now. Maybe when you learn to stop spouting stupid platitudes fed to you by old bloodthirsty soldiers, we'll have something to talk about." Her mouth twisted and she felt like she needed to spit herself.

She turned away from him to find Tere, Lily, and the beaten trebaxel looking at her. They all had the same expression on their faces, one that said they were just waiting for her and Conren to start screaming. Or fighting. She couldn't help it, she laughed at the mirrored faces, one hairier than the others.

"Aila, what do you plan on doing with...this," Tere said, gesturing toward the trebaxel.

For some reason, referring to the creature as *it* or *this* irritated her. Or, at least, it increased her current irritation. She addressed the trebaxel. "That's not going to do. We're going to need a name for you. Do you have a name, something others call you?"

The creature tilted its head at her. It was such a human mannerism, it made Aila wonder how much he understood. It didn't offer a name, or any other sound. She wasn't even sure trebaxels communicated verbally.

"Well, if you aren't going to help, I'll have to come up with a name. How about...Scrapper. You seem pretty gritty and able to handle yourself, taking on all those bigger guys by yourself. How about it? Can I call you Scrapper?" Again, the way he focused on Aila, she felt he understood at least a little. "I'm Aila." She patted her chest. "Aila."

"You're wasting your time," Conren said.

Aila growled in her throat, but didn't bother addressing the knight directly. She patted her chest again. "Aila. Scrapper?" The trebaxel blinked at her. "Me. Aila. Who is Scrapper?"

Slowly, one furry hand rose and tapped the trebaxel's chest.

"Right!" Aila said. "Me, Aila. You, Scrapper." She tapped Lily's shoulder. "Lily." Then she did the same with Tere. "Tere. Aila, Lily, Tere."

Scrapper gave her a self-satisfied look, then leaned his head so he could see around Aila to Conren. Aila marveled that he understood so much so quickly.

"Oh, that's Conren," she said, though several other names almost escaped her lips.

"While this is fascinating," Tere said, "my question remains unanswered. What are your plans for *Scrapper*?"

"Isn't it obvious? We have to help him. He's coming with us."

Conren groaned and let his body drop back to lie flat on the ground.

Though the others weren't as enthusiastic as Aila about adopting their new acquaintance, it didn't curb her eagerness for aiding the trebaxel. As they headed out again, Tere in the lead, Aila managed to get Scrapper comfortable enough with her to drape one of his arms over her shoulders as she walked alongside him, supporting his weakened body.

The fur covering the trebaxel was softer than it looked, though it was an odd sensation with the two of them so close. She could feel the taut, wiry muscle of his body shift as they walked, and she could tell when she accidentally put pressure on an area where he had been injured by his sudden, jerky movement.

Scrapper made no sound, other than some sharp breaths when his injuries were aggravated. He dutifully placed one hairy foot in front of the other and allowed her to help him. It didn't take long until he was exhausted, though, his battle and injuries catching up to him. Soon enough, Aila was very nearly carrying the little trebaxel. Luckily, they were close to the same size, so she managed it, though with difficulty.

Lily dropped back as the pair got slower and slower. "You're going to exhaust yourself, Aila. Even now, you'll never outrun any of the attacking trebaxel. Let me help."

The archer tried to help support Scrapper from the other side, but the difference in Aila's and Lily's heights was too great. It ended up being so awkward, the trio stopped.

"Scrapper?" Lily said softly. The trebaxel turned his head to her. "Can I carry you?" He didn't seem to understand, so Lily reached out to Aila, swept her arms under the shorter woman's legs, and picked her up. Scrapper's eyes went wide.

"No, Lily," Aila said. "Put me down. Let's try something else. Let me climb onto your back."

Lily bent over and Aila got on her back, legs around her waist and arms around her torso, just below her neck. Lily hooked her arms under Aila's knees and held her there. It was awkward with the quiver and backpack in place, but they managed it.

"Scrapper?" Aila asked as Lily let her get down.

Lily bent over again and Scrapper seemed to understand what they wanted him to do. He carefully climbed onto Lily's back, as if he would harm her if he wasn't careful, and soon he was resting as Aila had been a moment before.

They started out again, Aila thankful to the archer as she stretched out her own back and shoulders that had tightened painfully.

"His fur kind of tickles," Lily said. "It's softer than I thought it would be, too."

"I know," Aila said. "Maybe he brushes it or something."

Despite their best efforts, Aila and her friends were not able to find the flowers before the sun went down. Tere paused them in a mid-sized area surrounded by twelve-foot-high stone walls while he went ahead and scouted where they needed to go.

Aila watched Scrapper drink from a water skin she'd

handed him. The trebaxel didn't look any worse than when they'd found him, but he didn't look any better, either. During the time they'd traveled since he had joined them, Tere and Lily took most of the duty for carrying him around, but Aila helped also. Because it was so nearly her size, she tired more quickly than the other two. Everything always seemed to come back to strength.

Conren had been quiet most of the time, probably still smarting from her knocking him on his ass. She felt a little bad about it, but he was bigger and stronger than her, and talking hadn't kept him from trying to kill Scrapper, so what was she supposed to have done? There hadn't been time for her to try several methods to keep his sword—which had been in motion to strike the trebaxel at the time—from doing irreparable damage.

It was fine. She could handle the guilt it if meant the arrogant knight would stop criticizing everything the other three said and did.

She glanced over at the blond-haired man. They had been inseparable when they were children, before the class distinction had made a difference to them. Truthfully, it still didn't make a difference to Aila. One thing she'd learned in her travels, and especially in dealing with nobles, was that the chance of someone's birth had little to do with their value as a person. More important was how they were raised and trained as they grew up.

The distinction between Conren and her was sharp. He'd fully embraced the system in effect in the Great Enclave and she hadn't. He became a knight and enjoyed the trappings of that title. She had run from her royal responsibilities. What if her father did die? She didn't want to be queen. Queens couldn't travel the world and help fight monsters, at least not personally. A queen would have people for that so she could sit safely—and boredly—at home. Best not to think about all that, not the least reason for which she refused to allow her father to die. Wasn't that why she was out here to begin with?

Tere appeared in the midst of them so suddenly, Conren fumbled with his sword as he tried to jump to his feet and ended up stumbling before he realized it was the archer.

"There's nothing much for a half mile or so," Tere said. "A few hallways and a couple of bigger areas. I did come upon some of the trebaxel after that, though. There were half a dozen or so sitting around for some reason. What they do still confuses me. Too bad we can't get Scrapper here to tell us what it's all about."

At the mention of his name, the little creature looked at Tere and his mouth twitched into what Aila thought might be the trebaxel equivalent of a smile. Or she could have been imagining it or reading into it what she wanted.

"Should we go?" Aila asked. "You can lead us in the dark. We should be able to take six of them without too much trouble. Hells, you can probably take all six from the dark before they even have time to react. Your vision still works in the dark, right?"

"It does," he said. "It's only the part of my vision that tracks the signatures in the magical matrix, allowing me to see magic and follow trails, that is affected by the ambient magic. It's like being in fog or in a dust storm. I can see, though the distance isn't as great and fine details like magical signatures aren't as visible. Also, unfortunately, it's the same thing that allows me to predict the movements of my targets to hit them even when they're moving.

"As for continuing on tonight, no, I don't think we should. I'm not sure what they're doing there and for all I know, the next area over has thirty of forty of them, or more. I'd rather have everyone's eyes to notice if we're about to be attacked. Here, we know we have a distance between us and them."

"If they don't move," Lily said.

"Correct. If they don't move. We'll keep watch, of course, but I'd rather not move unless it's light out. I know that puts us behind schedule. If you have sound reasons to go against my suggestion, I'm open to hearing them."

Aila glanced at Conren, expecting him to object, but he'd settled back into his seated position and was staring at his hands.

"I trust you," she said. "You've done this kind of thing a long time. We'll have to try to make the time up where we can."

"Still you insist upon this fool's errand?" Conren asked, rising to his feet. So much for him remaining quiet. "We should be on the way back right now, yet you commit us to more searching while we are in possession of some of the flowers we came here to find."

"We've talked about this before, Conren," Aila snapped. "The scraps of flowers aren't enough to help Father. If we go back, it won't save him. All we can do is go forward and then do everything we can to make it to him in time with a suffi-cient number of the flowers."

"You don't see," he said. "Your father *will* die. Your duty is to spend as much time with him as you can so you can do a better job in ruling the kingdom. It is clear you do not desire the throne, but it is yours. Instead of doing as your responsibilities dictate, you go on one last adventure, playing out the hero from the stories we used to love as children."

Aila's mouth dropped open. She didn't even know where to start. She finally decided the most important thing she could tell him. "Go."

"Pardon me?"

"Go. Pick up your things and leave. It's probably a good thing I'm not queen yet, because for saying that about my father, I'd have you stripped of your knighthood and thrown into a cell. I don't want to look at you anymore. You disgust me. Go. Leave us and pray that I never see you again."

"Aila?" Tere said. Lily shared his shocked look. "You know if you send him away, he'll be dead long before he gets out of Sintrovis. There are dozens of trebaxel between us and the horses."

"Maybe it's fitting. He seems to know everything, including who will live and die. Perhaps he can use his amazing knowledge to survive."

Conren stood there, stricken, his face rigid, eyes wide. "My duty is to protect you. I was charged—"

"Your duty is to do what I say," she hissed. "If you are so sure the king is dead, then your loyalty and duty is to me. You will not question your queen. Do as I command. I have no further use for you."

"Alevia, please. I'm sorry. I misspoke. It is not easy for me to think of my sovereign's life hanging by a thread, no more than it is for me to see you charging into danger time and again. Danger I am not sufficiently qualified to protect you from. I...my tongue and my frustration got the better of me. Please, let me accompany you. It is all I have left."

Aila opened her mouth, but found Lily's hand on her shoulder. The statuesque archer didn't say anything, but her eyes held caution. She needed to think before answering the knight.

She took a breath, then another. "We are all frustrated and scared. Maybe not scared of the danger, but definitely of the consequences of our search. You say I am playing out fantasies from the hero stories we loved as children. More often than not, which hero were those stories about?"

Conren mumbled something.

"Louder," she said.

"Erent Caahs. Most of them were about Erent Caahs."

"Exactly. If there was one hero you would take for this

most important mission, who would it be? You don't have to answer; I'll do it for you. We have that hero with us. This is no cry for attention, no wanderlust or thrill-seeking. My friend, the hero who was called Erent Caahs, and his protégé, the hero once called Phoenixarrow and now simply called Lily Fisher, are with us. Where I lack, maybe they can make up for it. I would name you a valiant hero among us, but at every step you have done nothing but argue and try to change our minds about this mission.

"I will tell you this one more time, Sir Conren Gardner. You may accompany us and aid us and share in our fate. However, I will not hear another word about going back until we have the flowers to save my father's life. If you accompany us, you will be part of this party and you will act as a knight should, not as a spoiled-rotten child who demands his own way. You may take my conditions and continue on with us, or you will leave and do as you desire. I will release you from your duty.

"Before your decision I tell you this: if you decide you cannot act as a knight should and you leave us, there will be consequences. If I survive to return to Metrovial, in success or—Vanda forbid it—failure, I will see to it that you are stripped of your knighthood and banished from the Enclave forever. If you survive to return. Now is the time for you to determine if you are truly a noble knight at heart or if you are still a little boy playing with a wooden sword. Decide."

Conren immediately dropped to his knees and put his hand on the hilt of his sword. "Please forgive me, Princess Alevia. I want nothing more than for you to be safe. Allow me to continue with you and I will comport myself as befitting a Clavian Knight."

"Very well," she said. "Let's forget what has passed and move on from here. We have enough to deal with considering the danger ahead without wasting precious energy on arguments. Oh, stand up. You're just being melodramatic."

❧ 22 ❧

Fahtin caught herself biting her fingernail and forced herself to drop her hand to her side before Evon saw it.

"I don't know about all this," she told the blond Academy graduate. "I have enough trouble trying to figure out what the Prophet's book is trying to tell me and Aeden trying to see if I can do the magic of the Song without subjecting myself to being studied by the masters. I knew helping Aeden and Marla save the world would be hard, but it's getting ridiculous."

Evon gave her that smile he so often wore for her. She was beginning to think it was the same type of expression a parent made when their child said something silly and cute. She cocked an eyebrow at him.

"Master Isegrith is in charge of the School of Fundamental Magic. She has studied all kinds of magic for decades. If anyone can help you figure out your magical immunity—or whatever it is—she's right up there at the top of the list."

Fahtin had met Isegrith Palus several times, but she didn't know the master well. The woman seemed to be a stickler for rules and etiquette, and people like that made Fahtin nervous. It was people like that who usually caused problems for Gypta.

"I'm not even sure it happens all the time," she said. "It's just mainly those two times. Maybe that's all there is, like something that can be used up and now it's been exhausted. I think I should ignore it and pretend those things never happened."

"What? Why would you do that? Aren't you interested in a type of magic you might have? I've never heard of a natural immunity to spells like that."

Fahtin raised her hand to her mouth again before realizing she was about to put another fingernail between her teeth. "Don't you understand? I don't want to count on this 'immunity.' If I do, then maybe when I really need it, it won't save me. It's better if I expect any magic thrown at me to hurt me so I don't get sloppy."

Evon laughed. "That sounds like something Aeden would say." He got a pensive look on his face. "No, it sounds like a translation of something Aeden would have said. He's all for learning about anything that can help him in combat or to go against the animaru."

"The point is that I don't feel like being poked and prodded, and worse, being questioned like I'm some kind of criminal. We Gypta are sensitive to that kind of thing."

"Let's talk with Master Isegrith. If it looks like she wants to interrogate you, we can cut it short and that'll be the end of it. I'll be right there with you."

That was something at least. She did always feel better when Evon was helping her. He knew so much about everything, but he didn't come off as a know-it-all. Not that most of the Academy students did, but *some* did act a little too proud of the things they'd learned.

The pair arrived at Master Isegrith's office on time for

their appointment. She invited them in when they knocked, and they took up seats on the other side of the master's desk. It was, as Fahtin would have expected, spotless, with her pens and ink bottle in precise arrangement, a tidy stack of papers in one corner, a cup of tea, and three books stacked exactly one on top of the other on another corner. Fahtin couldn't help but to notice how much open space there was on the surface. Didn't that defy the reason for a desk's existence?

"Evon told me you have been exhibiting an interesting ability to negate—or at least withstand—magic that has been cast at you. That's a fascinating power to have."

"It was only a couple of times. I'm not sure if it will happen every time magic is cast at me."

"Well, that is easy enough to determine," the master said.

Fahtin's belly trembled a little. So there it was. The master did plan on hurling harmful spells at her to test her so-called ability.

"When did this occur for the first time?"

The Gypta barely had to think about it. "It was when we were being chased by Falxen assassins and they finally caught up to us. We chose a location and prepared to fight them. I ducked out of cover to throw a knife, and one of the assassins threw a lightning bolt at me before I could go back behind the rock I'd been using as a hiding place."

"A...lightning bolt? Do you mean he cast some spell that flashed like lightning?"

Fahtin raised an eyebrow, then looked over at Evon. Had she been unclear or was the master trying to minimize what had happened?

"Several of the Falxen could cast spells. From what Jia and Lily told us, there were at least two in the group that came after us who had learned their magic from the Academy, including the one who cast the magic at me. He was called Boltshadow, though I don't know what his real name was. He cast actual lightning bolts. Jia told me she'd seen him kill people with one lightning strike before."

"Truly?" the master asked. "I was not aware there were Blades who had previously been Academy students."

"It was news to all of us," Evon said. "The things Jia and Lily know about the organization are fascinating. It's on my list to compile it all and create a book of all the information, but there are so many other interesting things that need to be recorded first..."

Leave it to Evon to get carried away with all the things he wanted to write down. Master Isegrith scribbled something on a sheet of paper and while she was not looking at the two of them, Evon winked at Fahtin. Had that been an act to distract the master for her, to keep the pressure off Fahtin?

"Right. So, Boltshadow cast a lightning bolt at you. What then?"

"It struck me in the middle of the chest and threw me back a dozen feet, out of the sight of the others. They thought I was dead. When the battle was done, they checked on me and found me unharmed. Oh, maybe that's not correct. I was a little bruised from being thrown to the ground and I had a big hole burned in the center of my shirt, but there were no marks on my skin from the lightning and it didn't do any damage to me."

"I see. What did it feel like when you were struck? Did you feel the tingle of electricity or magic?"

"I...uh, I can't really remember. I don't think I felt anything like that. It was more like someone pushed me *really* hard. I lost track of the whole world, like when someone shoves you down when you're not looking and your eyes and mind try to catch up to what's happening."

Master Isegrith tapped her pen on her lips. "You never tested this ability in any way?"

"No. With the visions starting and animaru and assassins

trying to kill me, trying to study something was the last thing on my mind."

"Hmph."

"Master Isegrith," Evon broke in, "I did discuss it with her and I had plans to—"

"To record the information in a book?" the master asked with a wry smile.

"Uh, yes. I find it difficult to keep up with the things happening when I am around Aeden, Marla, and Fahtin. Animaru, Dantogyptain, magical shifts, mythological creatures come again, Wells of Power, a millennia-old cache of the Prophet's reference works, even magical time travel. It really deserves a team of scribes and scholars. I do what I can, usually in the order dictated by their direct applicability to our survival." He gave the master an unsteady smile.

"Just so," she said. "I understand. I appreciate your contribution not only to the Malatirsay's work, but also to adding to the body of knowledge of this institution. Especially for the great work in locating and transporting Tsosin Ruus's secret cache of information, you should be commended." She turned to Fahtin. "That goes for you as well, Fahtin. As someone not trained at the Academy, it must be more fearsome than even Evon here finds it. I will do what I can to help you learn more of this ability, if you would like. You are under no obligation, however. Any time you want to stop or don't feel you have time, simply say the word and we will postpone our study until you want to resume. Or you can choose never to resume. It's up to you. I am here to help."

Fahtin let out a breath. "Thank you, Master. That makes me feel a lot better. I thought I was going to have to stand around while you threw harmful magic at me."

The master's eyebrows climbed her forehead. "Oh, you will, if you want to continue. There's no better way I can think of to test your ability." Fahtin must have shown her surprise and nervousness in her expression because the master laughed. "It won't be as bad as all that. We'll start with simple, weak spells, the equivalent to a flick on your arm, and go from there. No need to worry."

"That makes me feel better," Fahtin said. "I never know if I'm going to get a vision or if I'm going to go off with the others on some mission or another. It's been difficult to adjust to all this."

"For all of us, child. We are living in the Dark Days prophesied thousands of years ago, the time for which the Academy itself was built. In a very real sense, my duty to the Academy and to the Malatirsay also requires me to aid you in any way I can. The Prophet wrote a book specifically for you, I understand. That carries at least as much weight as the charter for this school. Incidentally, I've been told that you have developed a sensitivity to magic that allows you to feel the effects of the shifts that have been happening, much like the students here also have?"

"Yes. Sometimes, the shifts from the Wells of Power make me feel dizzy and weak. The random shifts never did that, though I don't think we've had one of those for a while, so it may just be that I'm more sensitive now than I was then."

"Interesting."

"That reminds me, Master Isegrith," Evon said. "We recently figured out there were more than one or two of the Wells of Power. Do you know anything about them? From before a few days ago, I mean. None of the records from the Prophet say anything remotely about them. Could it be that he didn't know or was the information too sensitive to share?"

The master took a sip of her tea. "I had never heard anything of the like before the information was presented in the meeting with Master Qydus and your group. If there is no reference to them in the Prophet's works—even in the book he wrote specifically for the Malatirsay—I would have to conclude that he had no knowledge of them. It's quite a mystery, something I would very much like to know the explanation for. But we are straying off-topic. Fahtin, would you like to start?"

The Gypta swallowed, then nodded. "We can get started."

"Splendid. Let's go to one of the training rooms. They have wards to prevent magic from leaking out during casting and they will also prevent others from bothering us. Come." She got up and swept through the door, Evon and Fahtin following.

The training room the master had chosen was only a few doors down the hallway. To Fahtin, it looked like a classroom, except with only a couple of training dummies and four chairs instead of being filled with the common chairs and desks like the lecture classrooms she'd seen. One of the magical chalk boards took up the majority of one wall, but other than that, there was only open space.

"We will first test you with a handful of minor spells. So as to keep preconceived notions from affecting the results, I would ask you to close your eyes when I cast, only focusing on what you can feel. Be precise when describing what happens to you so we can record it accurately. Can you do that?"

"Yes, Master."

"Good. Evon, please take a seat and do not speak or in any other way distract Fahtin."

Evon sat down in the closest chair and the master walked to the other side of the room.

"Please close your eyes. I will tell you when I am casting. Open your mind and pay close attention to all your senses. Are you ready?"

"I am," Fahtin said.

"I am casting now."

Fahtin heard a slight buzz, as if a fly was a few feet from her head. She also felt the unmistakable tingle of magic. She said as much.

"You felt the magic tingling through you?" the master asked.

"No. It's the same thing I feel when I concentrate and someone close is casting."

"Tell me if this feels the same."

"Both the buzz and the tingling are the same," Fahtin said.

"Interesting. That time, I cast the spell at the training dummy. Let us continue."

Several more times, the master told Fahtin she was casting. Each time, she felt the general sensation of magic being used, but no ill effects on her personally. The sounds differed, from buzzes and zips to sloshes and clacks, but none of them caused anything that seemed like she was being struck.

"The last two tingled more than the other ones," Fahtin told the master when she was finally able to open her eyes again.

"That is good. The last two spells were more powerful. Still no pushes, pinches, pricks, or pain of any kind?"

"No, Master."

"Fascinating. We have been at it for more than an hour. I find that after that amount of time, students' focus often fades, so we'll stop for now. I think we can say with some amount of certitude that your ability or immunity, at least for lower-level spells, is not random. It worked each time and I expect it will continue to do so. Next time, when you have an hour or two to spare, I will use stronger spells and begin to rotate through different types to see if you are susceptible to one or more elements or categories of spell."

"Thank you, Master Isegrith," Fahtin said. "I'll have to see when I will be able to do it in the next few days. I'll need to check with the headmaster or Aeden and Marla if they have something they need from me."

"No rush. Schedule it with me when you are able."

On the way back to Batido, Evon asked Fahtin what she thought about the session. "So? It wasn't as bad as you imagined it, was it?"

"No. It was fine. It's strange. Was she really casting spells at me?"

"Definitely. I watched as several offensive spells struck you and disappeared. Interestingly, though, when she cast a light globe spell at you, it stuck to you and didn't go out. I think that means that only harmful spells are negated. I'm going to ask Master Isegrith next time to cast some beneficial spells to see if your ability can distinguish between them and harmful spells. If, for example, someone casts a spell to let you breathe water, it wouldn't be good if your ability negated it."

"Water breathing? They can do that?"

"Of course. It's a fairly simple elemental spell."

"We definitely need to test that one out."

They arrived at Batido just as Aeden and Khrazhti were coming out of the door.

"Hi, you two," Fahtin said. "What are you up to?"

"Going to the clans," Aeden said. "When I'm here at the Academy, I have to do my thing as high chieftain. When I'm gone, Greimich acts as the Tannoch clan chief and Seoras helps out with anything they might need me for. The clans are getting antsy about trying to take the Cridheargla back, so I need to go and calm them down."

"That sounds like fun," Fahtin said. "You sure you don't want to bring Marla with you? Maybe she can beat them into submission again."

"Ha," Aeden said. "She'd have her hands full with the clan

chiefs. They're not simple Trebhin warriors. I'll keep it in mind, though. See you in a couple of hours?"

"Sure," Fahtin said. "I need to read more of the book the Prophet made for me. I'll be falling asleep in an hour or two, so you can tell me all about the clans and help me stay awake."

❧  23  ❧

Morning brought Tere, shaking Aila's shoulder. He'd been on the last watch, so he apparently decided if he wasn't going to sleep, no one was.

"It's still dark," she whined.

"The sky is lightening. By the time we pack up and eat something, it'll be light and we'll be ready to go. We don't have any time to waste."

She growled, but cut it short when her stomach answered with a rumble. As if it weren't bad enough that he was right, her body had to betray her too? "Okay, okay. I'm getting up."

She took a look on the other side of her as she sat up. Sure enough, Scrapper was there, eyes open and curious. He probably didn't have anyone pushing *him* awake in the morning. She thought twice about that, though. It seemed the trebaxels were military—if not militant—so she wouldn't be surprised if there was something akin to a drill sergeant chittering at them to wake up in the morning to wage war against everything else in existence. Or maybe she was just bitter because she wanted to sleep. She gave even odds to each.

"Are you ready to go out looking for flowers this morning?" she asked the trebaxel. He didn't answer, of course, but his eyebrows—or at least the ridges over his eyes—did rise a little bit. "You know, flowers. Fireheart flowers. It's why we're here. They can cure my father so he doesn't die."

Scrapper kept eye contact the entire time. Aila wasn't sure how much he understood, if anything. It could be like what people said about dogs and cats: they understood tone more than what was actually said. It did give her an idea, though.

"Here, I'll show you." She fished out a few of the fireheart flower scraps from her pack and held them out in her palm.

The response was undeniable. Scrapper's large dark eyes got nearly twice their normal size. He reached out as if he was going to snatch them from Aila's hand, but pulled his arm back just before he actually touched them.

"You recognize these?" she asked him. "Here. Go ahead and take them. It's what we're looking for." She extended her arm to its full length toward him, flowers there for the taking.

The trebaxel slowly reached and picked up the flower scraps from her hand. He brought them to his eyes and inspected them, then lowered them a little so he could sniff them.

"Do you like those? Do you know where we can find them? We need more, but the whole flowers, not just chewed on petals."

He tilted his head at her in confusion but held the flower parts out for her to take back.

"It's fine." She held her hand up, palm toward him. "You can have them if you want. You seem to like them."

He moved his hand closer to her, to which she made a pushing gesture with her own hand to communicate she wouldn't take them back. He pulled his hand in and watched her. She smiled and nodded. Maybe he understood what a smile was, because he relaxed and didn't try to push the flowers back to her. He considered them, sitting in his palm, then looked back to her. He made a motion similar to the one she had used when trying to tell him the food she was offering him was edible. It looked like he...

"Yes," she nodded. "Go ahead. You eat these, right? Those teeth marks are from your kind. You can have them."

He seemed to understand because he brought them reverently to his mouth and took them in his teeth, then chewed and swallowed them.

"Did he just eat those flowers we found?" Lily asked. Aila jumped. She hadn't heard the woman. How could someone so big move so silently?

"Just a few of the scraps. I think the trebaxel eat them."

"Yeah, but he did it so reverently. We've seen him eat before and he was more careful and methodical about it this time. Like it was a treasured treat. Or something sacred."

"Or a medicine," Tere piped in. "I'm betting they know it has healing properties, though gods know what they are. They're rare enough that even the Academy doesn't know everything it can do, according to Verona. I wonder if it does different things for the trebaxels. Kind of makes you wonder what it could do if a human ate the flowers instead of preparing it and using it in medicine."

"I wish we could communicate better," Aila said. "He obviously knows the flowers. Maybe he could tell us where they grow." She turned back to Scrapper. "Do you know where to find them? Can you show us where they grow?"

Scrapper scratched his head. Aila wasn't sure if that was a common expression for confusion or ignorance like it was with humans or if the trebaxel had fleas or a simple itch. She shrugged and hoped that he would let them know if they got close to some of the plants that grew the flowers.

Tere led them to an intersecting passage as soon as they set out.

"Straight ahead is the small group I saw. I went for a short distance left and right and crossed another intersection like this in both directions. I didn't go far enough to see if there were passages crossing this one again after those. I'm thinking as we get farther in, the maze is adopting more of a grid structure. That wouldn't occur naturally, but I think we can agree this maze is not natural. If we have a choice, I'd rather take a passage that doesn't have trebaxel guarding it, but we also can't search all day for an unguarded area. I'm thinking they probably all lead to the same place."

"How about we check out two intersections in each direction," Lily said. "If we find one that's not guarded, we'll take it. If not, we'll go back to the one with the fewest guards or the superior location for us to break through them. We should be able to do that relatively quickly if the intersections are close."

"My thoughts exactly," Tere said. "Great archers think alike."

Lily's husky laugh sounded good. Somehow, it relieved some of the stress of the situation. A little, anyway.

"Sounds good to me," Aila said. "Lead on. I'll take the first shift at carrying Scrapper. Sorry you've been having to help me, but he's close to the same height and weight as me and I'm not strong enough to carry him all day long."

"It's not a problem," Lily said, handing some more dried fruit and cheese to the trebaxel. "He's one of us now. I'm sure he'd help carry one of us if we were injured."

"Do you think so?" Aila said.

"Don't you?" The red-haired archer looked into Scrapper's face. "You'd help us if we needed it, wouldn't you?" Her voice was soft, not quite so honey-smooth as if she were talking to a pet, but definitely different than speaking normally. The trebaxel reacted by handing a piece of fruit to Lily and mimicking eating with his other hand. "Why thank you," she said, popping it in her mouth. "See. My point is proven."

Aila found her mouth in the widest smile she'd worn so far on the trip into Sintrovis. She'd always liked Lily, but her affection for the tough archer had just doubled. Lily flashed her teeth back at Aila and even Scrapper joined in with his toothy expression.

"Okay, enough," Tere said. "For Surus's sake. Can we all bond and play around later? We've got some flowers to find. After we figure out how to get farther into this maze."

The four went into motion, in a strange hybrid of scouting and full-party searching. Starting with the left passage, they easily covered the distance to the next intersection within ten minutes, at which point Tere had the others stay put.

"It'll go easier if I scout ahead to see if there are any trebaxel there guarding the way. It shouldn't take long. Stay here and I'll be back in a few minutes."

"I'll go with you," Lily offered. "I'm good at scouting."

Tere shook his head. "You are good at scouting, but I need you here in case some patrol or something comes upon you. If I get spotted, I'll be able to run back here before fighting. Be ready in case I am. We'll need to all fight together if we're attacked."

Lily acquiesced and Tere disappeared down the intersecting passageway. As promised, he returned in a handful of minutes.

"Eighteen. They're in loose ranks, like a whole guard unit."

They pressed on through the passage until the next intersection and Tere scouted the area to the right. This one had more than twenty-five trebaxels.

"As we agreed, let's go back and check the first two intersections the other way," he said.

They did as he said, Lily taking over with Scrapper duty. Aila still felt bad about the others having to help, and not only because they had to carry the trebaxel. It could actually put them at risk because of the awkward way Scrapper clung to them, covering up the quivers on their backs. If they were suddenly attacked, they would drop the trebaxel before pulling arrows out, but that delay might get them hurt or killed.

Her eyes darted even more frantically than they had been, wanting to make sure that if there was an ambush, she'd give her friends back the few seconds they lost because of carrying their injured companion.

They passed the intersection they started with and repeated Tere's scouting with the next one. That area had fifteen of the trebaxel guards. The final spur to the left of the passage held fourteen.

"It looks like the best bet is the one where we started," Tere told them. "There were only six there when I checked last night. I'm not sure we'll find a way farther into the maze without guards. We don't have time to look for a better option."

Back at where they started the morning, Aila mentally kicked herself for the time they'd lost. It hadn't been more than two hours, but every minute could mean her father's life. They were rapidly getting to the point where even if they found the flowers—when; *when* they found the flowers—they might not be able to make it back to the castle in time.

But there was another issue to deal with. First they had to find the flowers.

"What about Scrapper?" Lily asked. She's set the trebaxel down on the ground while they discussed their plans.

The creature's condition didn't seem to be deteriorating, but neither had there been enough time for him to heal since they found him. He could move, slowly, shuffling for short distances without support, but he was shaky and looked as if he'd fall at any moment.

"I'll go and look up ahead to make sure it's still only the six. We won't be able to run through them like we've done before. We'll need to take them out fast and then pass. We can't let any of them escape or they may sound an alarm or something, and we'll have dozens of the creatures all over us."

No one looked to like the plan. It was one thing to kill a person or another intelligent creature when it was actively trying to kill you. It was quite another to attack them and kill them without provocation.

Aila voiced what had been on her mind since they found Scrapper. She pointed to him. "How do you think he'll react to seeing his friends killed?"

"I've been wondering about that, too," Tere said. "Was it a rogue group that attacked him or is he an outcast? Even if the others attack him, how would you feel to see some in your community killed in front of your eyes? We'll have to wait and see, I think. With such a small group, Lily and I should be able to handle them long before we're in melee range. Maybe you and Conren can watch Scrapper for signs he might turn on us?"

Aila's chest ached at hearing that. Something similar had popped into her mind, but hearing it solidified verbally like that made it worse to think about.

"Okay." She looked Conren in the eyes. "Only take action if he tries to attack us, and then only take the minimum effort to incapacitate him. He's weak, so we should be able to hold him back."

The knight nodded.

Aila didn't like the disappointed look on Scrapper's face. She wasn't sure how much he understood, but he'd apparently caught the group's mood. *Please don't turn on us*, she sent to him mentally. *Don't make us fight with you.*

## 24

Tere came back from scouting ahead with a look on his face Aila recognized. The furrowed brow, the firm set of his jaw and the slight tilt of his head didn't bode well.

"There are nine of them now," he said. "It's only three more than before, but it could mean other things. What, I don't know, but I think we need to be careful even with so few. It'll be tougher to get all of them if they decide to scatter and warn other trebaxels."

"Is there anything else we can do?" Lily asked.

"Not really. We need to get by them. I think it might be a good idea to be ready for all of us to fight, though." He glanced at Aila uncertainly. "I think we should leave Scrapper here and come back for him after we take care of the guards. You and Conren should be ready to fight, and Lily and I have to have free use of our arrows."

Scrapper twitched his head up from where he was sitting on the ground when Tere mentioned his name. He definitely recognized it as the name they gave him.

"Give me a minute," Aila said, "to explain to him. Then

we can go." She knelt on the ground next to the trebaxel. "Scrapper, we have to go...uh, do something. I want you to stay here, just for a few minutes. We'll do what we need to do and come back for you, then we'll continue. Okay?"

The trebaxel nodded his head, recognizing at least the *okay* and her intonation to represent a question.

"All right. Let's go, Tere."

The other three headed toward where the nine trebaxels waited. Aila gave Scrapper a smile and started to follow. He emitted a lonely sound that spiked right through Aila's heart. She kept walking, determined not to let her sympathy for his misunderstanding affect her. He mewled other sounds, each sounding sadder than the last. She finally turned around to see him half-dragging himself after her, a look of such anguish on his face there was no way she could leave him.

"Shit. Tere, new plan," she said to the retreating archer. "He's coming with us. I can't let him think we're abandoning him. If nothing else, his cries will alert the other trebaxels. I can set him down to fight."

Tere frowned through his mustache at it, but he didn't argue, either. For a wonder, Conren didn't say anything. She didn't even get an impression of an eye roll from the back of his head. He was still smarting from the tongue-lashing she'd given him.

She quickly helped Scrapper onto her back and followed her friends. Scrapper gently stroked her hair as they went.

The narrow path—really a trail through some grasses between the two stone walls of the hallway—widened as the walls spread out into a larger area. Scrapper made a humming noise just before Aila saw the sentries. Was that a warning? If so, for her or for the guards?

The passage was only maybe twenty feet wide when Aila spotted the trebaxels guarding the passage. She recognized what Tere had described before. The creatures were in a loose formation three of them across and three deep. Aila wondered if they stayed that way all day every day or if it was something special since outsiders were in the maze.

It also brought up questions about how the trebaxels knew the humans were in the maze. Did the whole area sense them or had some of the creatures they raced past notified some kind of central authority? If the latter, then why hadn't the humans been hunted down instead of sentries being set up? It seemed a lot of work on the off-chance the intruders would wander into one of their guard posts.

Then again, isn't that exactly what they were doing?

"It's fine," she whispered to the little trebaxel and set him down on the ground. "We have to get through them. Stay here. We'll be in sight."

Scrapper emitted what Aila would take as an affirmation. She gripped her vinci and prepared for a fight.

Tere and Lily had gone to either side, using some of the shrubs there as cover. Regardless of what else the creatures ahead of them could do, it didn't seem that they had better hearing or senses than humans. That was good, at least.

With some unheard signal, two arrows zipped into the midst of the trebaxel guards, taking one on the right side of the formation in the eye and in a nearly identical location on the left. Before the bodies hit the ground, two more dropped.

The monsters reacted immediately, their gazes locked onto where Tere's and Lily's movements identified them. Three of the five ran at Tere while two picked up the familiar stones and hurled them at Lily. Conren stood between the trebaxel and Aila, glancing back nervously to make sure she was safe.

No, that wasn't right. His eyes skipped right over Aila. He was looking at Scrapper, waiting to see if the little trebaxel would take the side of the other furry creatures and attack the humans. Aila felt a little foolish that she'd been focusing on the battle and not on the potential threat behind her.

The two stone-throwers were very accurate. Two heavy rocks the size of Aila's fist passed through the space Lily vacated hurriedly, diving to the side so abruptly she was unable to loose the arrow she had nocked. As she came to her feet, the trebaxel reoriented on her and almost caught her with their missiles again, ruining her shot one more time.

Meanwhile, Tere calmly and smoothly released two arrows before the three creatures reached him. Their bodies skidded to a halt while the third reached melee range, its thick branch weapon already swinging to crush the human's head.

In a movement to be expected from the most famous of contemporary heroes, Tere dropped his bow and drew his long knife in one motion, ducking under the trebaxel's strike and cutting into its torso as he spun out of the way. The other knife was suddenly in his hand and it arced down diagonally to cut into the creature's back. It screamed in rage and pain until Tere circled his knife around again and slashed its throat. The archer spun out of the way as he did so, avoiding the spray of blood the attack caused.

In an instant, he had his bow off the ground, an arrow nocked, drawn, and loosed. Aila didn't think it was humanly possible to do all three in a fraction of a second without pausing to sight the target, but as so often was the case, the hero defied all expectations. The arrow flew true, punching into the chest of one of the rock-throwing trebaxels. A second later, the other dropped to an arrow from Lily, who needed only a pause in the double projectiles flying at her to sneak in a shot.

Both archers had new arrows on their strings and moved forward as one toward where the trebaxels had been standing guard mere moments before. While they scouted for any they might have missed, Aila turned to see what Scrapper was doing.

He was sitting right where he had been before all the action started. His dark orange eyes swung up to hers and for a moment, and the intelligence she saw there sent a shiver through her. For a face that wasn't human, the wrinkles and folds in his furry skin communicated exceptionally the sadness and—at the same time—understanding of the necessity of what had just happened.

They froze like that, looking into each other's eyes, until Conren spoke.

"Is everything well?" he asked her.

"Huh?" The sudden sound shocked her out of the trance she'd been in. "Oh, yes. Everything is fine."

The knight gave her a quizzical look and then turned his head to watch Tere and Lily returning to them.

"That was all of them," Tere said. "They didn't run to warn the others."

"I saw that," Aila said.

"How did he take it?" Lily asked, not using Scrapper's name.

"Fine. He looks sad, but I think he understands. They're not his friends, but they're not enemies either. At least, that's what it seems like."

"Sorry, but we need to get going," Tere said. "We need to find those flowers."

Aila let Scrapper climb onto her back again and then passed through the area that had briefly been a battlefield. The sight of the twisted bodies, fur matted with blood, caused bile to bubble up onto her throat. It was strange. She rarely had that kind of reaction to humans dying, and never to animaru or monsters dying. The literal weight on her shoulders was the reason. Any one of those could have been

Scrapper. The thought made her sadder than she cared to admit.

The introspection flew out of her head as the group passed through the area the trebaxels had been guarding. Gone were the forested places in between the stone walls. From where they stood, the terrain looked more like desert than forest. Vegetation was suddenly scrub brush and twisted, prickly trees. They could see for more than a hundred yards, a feat they'd not been able to accomplish with the vegetation choking the areas they'd been passing through.

Nothing obscured the stone obstructions that described the room they were in. There was still no ceiling and the sun, not yet at its peak, shone down with more intensity than she remembered at any other time during their mission.

"That should make travel quicker," she said.

"At least until something spots us," Tere said. "I wonder if it's only this area within the walls we can see that's like this or if the rest of the maze is desert-like. Either way, we need to be careful. There's no cover for us. It's a kill zone. While the throwers on the walls won't have a chance of reaching us, they can send ground troops to intercept us."

Aila gave the archer a quizzical look. "You sound like you're talking about soldiers, some kind of military force whose area we're trying to infiltrate."

"That's what this is. The groups stationed in certain areas, guards arranged in ranks. What else could it be? Sintrovis isn't just some area with dangers that kill visitors. What we've seen shows there's a lot more to it. It's like the place is organized to prevent anyone from getting in and then, if they do, to keep them from leaving alive. You have to face it. It's already too late for us to be allowed to leave. The whole of Sintrovis will try to keep us from leaving with the information on what we saw, let alone flowers that the world has barely any knowledge of. Come on. We still have things to do.

Keep your eyes open. I don't like this, even less without the full use of my magical sight."

It didn't take long to make it to the other side of the desert chamber. Tere led them unerringly in the direction they'd been traveling, and they passed through into another desert-like place, then another. The narrow passageways connecting the open areas were shorter and the rooms were bigger. They continued to switch off carrying Scrapper; the trebaxel, for his part, didn't react in any way to the terrain change.

Their injured companion was riding on Tere's shoulders when Aila squinted and put her hand over her eyes to shade them from the sun. She'd caught a flash of color amid the muted shades of brown, grey, and pale green. She swung her head. It had to be...

"There!" she said aloud. "Does anyone else see the reds and yellows over in that direction?" She pointed off to the right of where they'd been heading.

Lily imitated Aila's pose, hand up and eyes squinting. "I see it. Those colors. It looks like—"

"Fireheart flowers," Aila said. "A whole bunch of them. To me, it looks like a huge flower bed. Let's go. That's our goal, right there. Get as many flowers as we can and leave as fast as we can. We can still make it in time to save my father."

## 25

The little party headed toward the flowers with urgent steps. Aila took her usual place in line, behind Tere and Lily and ahead of Conren, who seemed to think it his job to protect them from behind. As they pressed toward their destination, she scanned the terrain that looked so barren compared to all they'd passed through in Sintrovis before.

It was her diligent searching that caught movement from behind one of the smaller rock formations. Boulders and pieces of stone—darker grey than the stone walls—lay scattered about in the desert-like terrain.

"There's something stirring to the left," she shouted. "It's moving fast."

Tere set Scrapper down and turned toward a group of trebaxels racing toward them. They loped easily, but the speed was something Aila knew the humans couldn't match, even if they were sprinting for their lives. There was no way she could ever keep up a pace like that for more than a hundred yards or so.

They were going to have to fight.

As the group moved to meet the oncoming monsters, Aila took the opportunity to examine the rest of their surroundings. If another group came at them from a different direction, they'd be in big trouble. Luckily, she didn't spot any other enemies.

While she'd been looking, the group of trebaxels had gotten much closer. There were a dozen of them, but it was even worse than that. The closer the creatures came, the more apparent it was that these were not the same trebaxels they'd been fighting and running from.

These were bigger. Much bigger. Before, they'd discussed how the skeleton found by the Academy researcher all those centuries ago was abnormally large. Compared to this group, the opposite would be true. What had been recorded and assumed for the trebaxels *under*estimated their size. That ancient trebaxel would be a runt in this collection.

The charging monsters finally got close enough for Tere and Lily to start thinning them out with arrows. The creatures' gait seemed erratic, at least as much as it could be with their smooth, efficient motions. She couldn't reconcile the contradiction. Their heads bobbed strangely, spoiling the aim of the archers. Only one in two arrows they released resulted in a kill. Damn whatever magic was affecting Tere's ability to detect where his targets *would* be. In a very short time, the trebaxels were within range for melee fighting, with three of them dead and two more injured.

The attackers were even bigger than they'd seemed from a distance. At close range, Aila had to crane her neck to see their furry faces, similar to Scrapper's but for the size. They had to be twice as tall as her and probably outweighed her four to one.

Two of them slammed into Conren's shield, nearly knocking the knight off his feet. He stayed upright, but was pushed back so strongly he wasn't able to bring his sword to bear. The two trebaxels tried to pummel him with their blunt weapons, but he managed to keep his shield in place to block blows that probably could have broken bones.

Aila darted in to help Conren while Tere and Lily loosed one more arrow each before ditching their bows for their long knives. The two heroes slipped through the mass of attacking monsters, cutting them as the creatures' eyes widened and tried to follow the fluid movements of the archers.

Once the forward momentum of the charging trebaxels in front of Conren was arrested, Aila stepped off to the side and flung her vinci at the monsters from several paces away. As the furry arms tried to utilize brute force to bring the knight down, they accumulated cuts from Aila's darting blades.

One of the creatures, after a particularly deep cut to its side, gave up on Conren and turned to attack Aila. That was the last action it took. The knight, blocking a blow from the other trebaxel, landed a powerful slash that cut halfway through the monster's neck. It lingered on its feet for a moment before stumbling off and falling to the ground to finish its dying.

Conren proved to be a match for the remaining trebaxel attacking him, so Aila turned her attention to her other companions. Tere and Lily danced between four other attackers, having finished off the others, either with their last arrows or with their knives. The trebaxels were fast and strong, but they were all offense and no defense. As long as the archers could evade their blows, the humans' victory was a foregone conclusion.

Another flash of dark fur caught Aila's eye and she realized there was another trebaxel still alive. One that was heading toward Scrapper. Aila's new companion had its face set in a grim visage but, if anything, the look of disgust and hate on the attacking trebaxel was even worse. She wondered what it was that made the community dislike Scrapper so much.

The attacking monster was still a few paces from her injured friend, but it was moving quickly. Aila whirled her vinci to gain the momentum needed to attack.

The vinci whipped around in large swooping arcs, gaining speed before slashing at the trebaxel. Accuracy was key with the weapons. If Aila released the chains a little too much, the blades would cut deeply, but the momentum would be arrested. Too short and the slashes would harry the enemy, but not do significant damage. If the accuracy was even worse, the blades could miss the target completely or could slam into it, striking with the hilt or guard and only doing slight blunt damage.

But Aila had practiced with the weapons for many years and had mastered the distancing required to use them effectively. Both the blades struck the trebaxel and parted flesh, one on its right shoulder and the other across its back.

The monster screamed and halted its attack for a moment, shifting its attention, which is what Aila had intended. What she hadn't expected was that the trebaxel could turn and change its direction so quickly that it closed the distance between it and her before she could retract the vinci.

The club the thing wielded—a rough, twisted branch nearly as thick as Aila's leg—hurtled toward her and she had to dive out of the way and completely abandon calling in her swinging weapons to catch them. She evaded the blow, but the vinci struck the ground and came to rest after skipping over it.

The follow-up kick, though off-balance and inefficient, wasn't so easy to dodge while Aila was already in motion. It caught her with a glancing contact that shot pain through her hip and spun her wildly to the ground. The crazed monster didn't stop. It chased after her once it regained its balance.

Aila scrambled to her feet and pulled back on the chains of her vinci. The blades skittered over the dry ground until they reached her. She fumbled with the one in her left hand, but managed to wrap her fingers around the hilt just as the trebaxel swung its massive club at her again.

This time, she wasn't in mid-roll and she smoothly side-stepped to her right. The wind of the passing club showed her how closely she'd judged it, but as the wood slammed into the ground where she'd been, her thousands of hours of practice paid off. She lashed out with a backhanded slice with her left hand, then twisted to use her momentum to land a more powerful right-handed blow. The first strike took the creature high on the chest, but the second did more damage, cutting deeply into the lower neck and bouncing off the collarbone. It wasn't a fatal wound, but the trebaxel was bleeding heavily. All she had to do was to evade it and place another cut or two and she might survive the encounter.

The monster recovered from its failed strike and the force of Aila's attacks rapidly, turning to swing the club horizontally at the tiny human that was causing it so much trouble. With no other option since she was so close, Aila dropped to her belly on the ground, narrowly avoiding the club. While she was down, she slammed her blade into the monster's foot, then rolled away to avoid the blow she knew was coming.

As expected, the creature howled and redirected its weapon to slam it straight down onto Aila. Or, at least, where she had been. The tip of the club grazed Aila's back as she rolled away. If she'd delayed another fraction of a second, the monster would have crushed her spine.

Aila came back onto her feet. The trebaxel had slowed, the blood loss finally catching up to it. As it stumbled toward her, she wondered why Conren hadn't jumped in yet to protect her. She despised the thought as soon as it came to mind, but she'd been off balance and barely escaping injury for the entire fight. She just wanted it to end.

The end came more quickly than expected. With a last surge of strength and speed, the trebaxel charged in with the predictable downward strike. Aila dodged left this time and as the monster's arm came down, Aila slashed it with her blade. She circled around the attacker, which had lost its balance. She shredded the skin on its back with three fast attacks. It turned to face her, and she finished the job she had started before, slashing its throat with one blade and punching the other through its eye. The monster fell, nearly pulling her down with it until her knife tore free with a wet, slushing sound. Her attacker twitched a few times, then stopped.

Aila expelled a breath and looked around. Conren was a few steps away, already slowing down from his sprint to aid her. Tere and Lily had finished their grisly work, as well, and were picking up their bows and retrieving what arrows they could salvage. Scrapper stared at Aila, apparently unharmed.

"Everyone okay?" she asked while looking at the little trebaxel. Grunts of affirmation came from the humans, but she only had eyes for her furry companion. She wasn't sure exactly what she was looking for, but all she found was those sympathetic orange eyes.

"Well," Tere said, rolling his left shoulder, "this group wasn't like the other sentries. They chased us down. Maybe they're responsible for protecting the flowers. Speaking of which, let's get the damn things and get out of here. If these trebaxels get much bigger, we're going to have a *very* rough day."

$\frac{1}{2}$ 26 $\frac{1}{2}$

"So," Aila said, "you noticed the last batch were a lot bigger too, huh?"

"It didn't escape my keen powers of observation," Tere answered. "Tch."

"Do you really think they get bigger the farther we go into the maze? These were even larger than the assumed size based on the skeleton that researcher found."

"I'd rather *not* think about it, if you don't mind. I want to get to those flowers, gather as many as we can, and leave fast enough that no one will ever know we were here." He glanced around at the trebaxel corpses all around them. "Well, except for this mess. No helping that."

Aila bent over so Scrapper could get on her back. A sigh escaped her lips at the thought of hauling the little trebaxel all the way over to the flowers, still some distance away. At least he wasn't as big as the other ones, though. She'd never have been able to carry him around.

"I'll take a turn," Conren said.

She turned to look at him and found him considering her. "What?"

"I'll take a turn carrying him. You three have been doing all the work. It's about time I helped out."

Aila squinted at him. "Why? What changed?"

"I just want to help, Alevia. You're obviously tired and it's too much of a risk for Tere and Lily to have access to their quivers restricted. I'm strong and even with Scrapper on my back, I can use my shield well enough to allow him time to hop off if we get into battle. It'll slow me being able to use my sword, but that's not as important as my shield is."

"He makes a good point," Tere chimed in.

"He does," she admitted. "Great. Thank you. It'll help."

Scrapper's face didn't give her confidence that the trebaxel agreed with her. Since Conren had tried to kill him, he'd glared at the knight whenever he came into the furry creature's sight.

"Scrapper," she said softly. "Conren has offered to carry you so I can rest and so Tere and Lily can fight better if any more danger is ahead. He's helping you. Will you let him?"

The little trebaxel shifted his eyes from Aila to Conren, then back again. His expression was inscrutable, but Aila thought she saw at least a hint of acceptance within his eyes. Sad, resigned acceptance.

Conren bent over to make it easier for Scrapper to climb onto his back. The trebaxel did so, slowly, eyeing Aila the whole time. Was that a *this better not turn out badly* look he was giving her? She wished she could communicate better with their injured companion.

Once Conren and Scrapper were settled, Tere took his position in front and led them toward the flowers.

Aila studied the terrain even more closely than she had before. If another of those roving groups of trebaxels were going to attack them again, she vowed she'd notice them as quickly—or more so—than before. They couldn't afford the time and the risk of a pitched, prolonged battle with the monsters. The best way would be to whittle down their numbers before they got within range to attack face-to-face.

The ten or fifteen minutes it took to reach their destination seemed like an eternity. The distance wasn't great, but they had to clamber up an earthen embankment and rocks to get there. The last thirty yards included a lip of rock that slanted gradually upward toward the flowers. They were hidden until the group was standing in front of what they'd been chasing for more than half a week.

The problem was, what they had found was not what they'd been chasing for more than half a week.

What they found was a stone face with assorted splotches of color on its surface. Reds, yellow, greens, even small spaces of white and an area less than the width of Aila's hand that was blue. All of it was lichen or some other plant life that adhered to the stone.

"Sons of—" Tere started, but was interrupted by Lily.

"Trap!" she said. "They're coming for us. Get ready."

Aila looked back the way they had come. Several groups of large, furred creatures loped toward them. The movements were all too familiar.

"There have to be at least five or six dozen trebaxels coming at us," she said aloud, wincing at so blatantly stating the obvious. Her friends could see the attackers coming as well as she could.

Tere rubbed a hand over the imitation flowers as Conren set Scrapper down near the wall a few feet away. The knight moved his arms around to loosen them up, gripped his shield tightly, and drew his sword.

"It doesn't look good," Conren said.

"No," Tere agreed. "Lily, it might be a good time to use those fire arrows you're so proud of. If you can make them explode in a group of them, it'll help. A lot."

"Way ahead of you," she said, already fitting one of the red-fletched arrows to her bowstring.

Aila's breathing labored as she swung her head to look at each of her friends. It was her mission and now it would be her fault that the world lost the great hero Erent Caahs, not to mention Lily, who would become famous in her own right. Damn her and her big, stupid, stubborn plans.

Luckily, the path up to the lip of rock they stood on was only so wide. It would allow five or six of the creatures to come up at a time, but at least it was something. If they were fast and piled the bodies up quickly, they might be able to hold on long enough to decimate the force coming against them. Of course, there was no telling how many groups were on their way. For all she knew, it could be the entire trebaxel population charging them.

"It was an honor," she said, raising her vinci. "I'm sorry I led you into this."

"Don't, Aila," Tere said. "No talking like that. Don't start the negative thinking just yet. I've been in worse situations."

Against all common sense, she laughed. "I suppose maybe you have. Any suggestions on what I should do?"

"Don't die," he said. His first arrow took the fastest of the trebaxels in the face. That was one thing about the monsters running at them bunched in groups: they couldn't move side to side like when they were spaced out.

Scrapper was making a whining, chittering noise, but Aila ignored him. There was still a little time until the first of the attackers reached a distance where they could attack—none of them seemed to be carrying rocks to throw—but she had to watch to decide when to launch her vinci at the creatures.

A flash of red zipped past Aila's vision and slammed into another of the trebaxels. Half a second after it impaled the creature's chest, it exploded, blasting parts of the monster in all directions and damaging those surrounding it. Several went down, and others tripped over the bodies—or body *parts*—of their companions. If they ever got out of this alive, Aila was going to kiss Marla right on the lips for giving Lily those magical explodey arrows.

A furry hand gripped Aila's arm and she almost slashed at it until she realized it belonged to Scrapper. The little trebaxel was chittering excitedly as it tugged on her arm. She tried to shake his hand off so it wouldn't affect her ability to fight, but his grip was surprisingly strong. He pulled her toward the wall.

"What, Scrapper? I can't really deal with you right now. I'm trying to keep from dying."

Again, his rapid-paced trills spilled out toward her.

"Alevia, they're almost here. We could use your help."

Aila finally extricated her arm from the trebaxel's grip. "I'm sorry, Scrapper. I know you're scared; I'm scared, too. I have to help my friends, though. We might survive this, but not if I don't help. Stay back here near the wall and maybe they won't see you or get to you. Sorry, buddy."

She stepped up near Conren, a pace ahead of the two archers and far enough away that he could use his sword effectively. They would need to shoot arrows for as long as they could, so she and the knight would have to be on the front line. Suddenly her vinci didn't seem to be such ideal weapons. Some kind of magic, self-reloading cannon would be ideal.

She nodded to Conren and he returned the gesture. Any moment now.

The corpses Tere and Lily were creating were actually having an effect. Especially Lily's fire arrows—when they exploded and threw bodies and knocked others down—made the trebaxels stumble as they tried to gain the slight rise on which the humans were making their last stand. The creatures' insane drive to get at the intruders kept them from taking the climb a bit slower.

The lead creature stumbled into Conren's shield while Aila's swinging vinci cut at others that had almost reached her. The two cut off some of the attackers from getting to Tere and Lily, and the archers paid their companions back by dropping several more trebaxels in the front.

Scrapper's incessant chittering finally stopped, so abruptly that Aila feared one of the bigger monsters had gotten through to him. She chanced a look behind her to check on the little trebaxel and a spike of panic shot through her.

Scrapper was nowhere to be seen.

"Scrapper!" she yelled, almost losing control of the chains her weapons were swinging on.

The injured trebaxel's furry head popped out from the wall, his high-pitched keening doing nothing to explain to Aila how in Abyssum he had materialized from the stone like that.

One of the big trebaxels slipped through the others' guards and swung at Aila with its club. She evaded the blow—knowing well enough not to try to parry or, Vanda forbid, block—and shortened the chains on her vinci enough to swing them at close range like a flail. They bit into the monster and upset its balance and composure enough for her to snatch the hilts of her weapons from the air and jam them into its head in one motion. She stepped over the falling body and prepared for the next one.

Conren intercepted it and there was a slight gap before the next clambered over the growing pile of dead trebaxels to get to the humans. Aila took the opportunity to step closer to the wall and see what was going on with Scrapper.

The little trebaxel was still halfway into the wall, but from her new angle, she realized that he was in a small opening camouflaged by the shadows and the design they thought were flowers. It was big enough for Tere and Lily to get through, even big enough for a trebaxel to easily pass, but probably not more than one at a time.

"Can we get out that way?" she shouted at Scrapper, then realized how ridiculous it was to be asking him. She turned back to the battle in time to narrowly avoid another trebaxel that Conren clipped with his sword to protect her. "Everyone, Scrapper found a way out. It's restricted, but it looks like we can all fit through there. The monsters won't be able to fit more than one or two at a time. If we can get in, it'll act like a choke point."

Tere didn't bother looking at her. He took the time to sling his bow over his chest and draw his knives. The attackers were intelligent enough to know that they'd better take out the archers first, especially Lily with her fire arrows. "Go," he said. "Conren, go after her. We'll bring up the rear."

The knight had other ideas, though. "No. You two go after. I'll follow at a retreat. If we time it right, I can back into the passage and keep them off us with my shield."

"Fine," Tere said. "Do it, Aila. Now. We're not going to last much...aughh!"

Aila recognized Tere's experience in the simple fact he wasn't going to argue with Conren about the effectiveness of them all going first. She would follow his example, even though he'd just taken a glancing blow on his left arm from one of the trebaxel clubs. She darted after Scrapper, hoping that the archer's arm wasn't broken. He was still a dynamo with his knives, but him having only one arm to fight with would give them a severe disadvantage. If anyone could use a bow with one hand, it was Tere, but she'd rather he not have to.

Tere tried to wait for Lily to follow Aila first, but she

stepped toward the trebaxels, in front of him, and kicked him back behind her while she slashed at the oncoming monsters. She had her bow across her chest as well, though Aila hadn't seen when she'd positioned it.

"Damn stubborn woman," Tere spat as he ran the few steps into the passage where Aila and Scrapper already were. The Clavian princess and the injured trebaxel went deeper into the passage, but Tere waited a dozen feet in, taking his bow in hand and launching a few arrows to aid Lily. He muttered curses at the pain it caused his arm, but he was able to loose several shafts.

Lily made the passage opening, leaving only Conren against the entirety of the mass of trebaxels. Tere moved a few steps farther into the passage and Lily threw herself to her knees while pulling her bow over her head, then turning so she could support the knight as well.

Conren kept his composure, backing toward the opening while somehow holding off half a dozen huge club-wielding trebaxels. It was mainly his shield, but a few tried to get around his right side to attack from the side or behind him, and his flashing blade kept them wary enough not to charge. Before they realized they should have risked the cuts to bring him down, his back was to the open space of the passage, shield held up as a barrier to their further advance.

The staccato clangs of club on shield made Aila wonder how the knight's arm felt at the moment. There was some padding on the protective device, but having huge monsters beat at him with all their strength couldn't have been fun.

Tere shot a few more arrows, able to get around the shield because of his height, but Lily stayed put and waited for Conren to reach them.

"What now?" Conren said, panting from his exertion.

"Now we run as fast as we can backwards and hope they

don't figure out a way to get around us and trap us in here. Oh, and that there isn't already a large group of them waiting for us, wherever this leads."

The knight shook his head, spraying drops of sweat from his hair. "Wonderful."

Aila helped Scrapper shuffle through the passage he'd found. The walls were close enough that the trebaxel could use them for support, but Aila's shoulder was more convenient and she needed to keep an eye out for what was in front of them anyway. If it was left to Scrapper, they'd only get rapid chittering as a warning. Not good.

"How are you holding up, Conren?" she called back over her shoulder.

"Shield still up. None passing. Following us," he said, speaking in fractional sentences. That worried her a bit. If he was so tired he wasn't speaking properly, they needed to do something before he dropped from exhaustion.

The walls sloped away, making the space between twice as wide as it had been. The space settled into its new width, not growing or shrinking for as far as she could see. Granted, that was only forty or fifty feet because the walls drifted left, but still.

"It gets a little wider here," she told the others. Tere and

Lily had been merely walking along with Conren as he backed up, unable to do much.

Tere looked past Aila to see the configuration of their path. "Let's stop for a moment. I have an idea. How about we stay at the edge of where it widens. Lily and I can pepper them with arrows, maybe even close off the passage a little. I've been wary of using too many because there was no way for me to retrieve them. In this situation, though, I think we might be able to get some of them back after I use them to kill a few of those creatures."

"Don't you have some spares in your pack?" Lily asked.

"I do, but even if I take them out and put them in the quiver—which I'll do when we get ready to do this—I won't fill it up. At this rate, I may not have enough to fight our way out of here."

"Yeah," she said. "Me, too."

"Like I was saying," Tere continued, "if you can keep them bottled up, Conren, we can take a bunch out, either with arrows or even with knives. It may be enough to make them go away."

"Do you really think so?" Aila asked.

"It's not likely, but I can hope. Poor Conren can't keep this up all day."

He had a point there. Aila wasn't sure it was the only plan they could come up with, but it was worth a shot, so to speak. "Let's do it. If Conren thinks it's a good idea."

"I'm willing to try anything at this point," the knight said. "I'm almost at my limit. The shield feels like it weighs a hundred pounds."

Aila had no part in the plan, so she stood back with Scrapper and watched Tere coordinate it. Conren inched backward until he braced at the edge of where the tunnel widened out. The archers would arrange themselves on the sides.

"I'll take the right side and you the left," Tere told Lily.

"Uh, no," she said.

"No?"

"No."

"And why not?"

"Because your left arm is injured, Mr. Hero. You don't need to be aggravating it. The right side will get more action because there's more room there to get by Conren's sword. The left side will have fewer opportunities because his shield will reach almost to the wall. Besides, you're taller than me, so you'd have an easier time getting arrows around or over the shield."

"Fair points," Tere said, and took his place on the left. Lily shot Aila a wink and then positioned herself on the right side, just behind the knight.

"Ready?" Tere said. Conren nodded. "Back up one step."

As soon as Conren did so, the trebaxels surged forward, pushing at the one in the front of the line. As a reward for being first, Lily put an arrow in its left eye. It dropped to the ground and the next one was pushed ahead. This one ran right into Conren's sword, but the abdominal wound wouldn't have killed it quickly enough, so another of Lily's arrows sped things up a bit.

In a matter of a few minutes, the pile of trebaxel corpses was almost as high as Conren was tall. That's when something that none of the humans had anticipated occurred. One of the trebaxels climbed up the bodies of its companions and leaped over the knight's shield. In fact, it leaped completely over Conren and landed near Tere. He dropped his bow to cut it with his knives, but Aila had been watching carefully, her weapons in her hands. Before the trebaxel landed fully, she cut so savagely at its neck with both blades that she nearly cut through.

"Shit," Tere shouted. "I'm an idiot. Of course this was

going to happen. I'm not thinking. Conren, back up another couple of steps. It's going to be harder to hold, but it's not *that* much wider."

Conren did as Tere commanded, but it soon became clear that the trebaxels were not going to turn around and walk away. With the extra space, it wasn't only Conren that was getting tired. Tere and Lily had to keep up with two and sometimes three of the monsters attacking at a time. There was no way they were going to be able to keep this up.

Aila turned to tell Scrapper to continue on in the path. He began to shuffle away. As she brought her attention back to the area in front of her three friends, she noticed something.

"Lily, do you have more fire arrows left?"

"Yeah." The archer was frantically cutting down the monsters as they came, easier by the fact that they were restricted by Conren's presence. "Why?"

"Up and to the right. Do you think you can manage to hit it with two or three in close succession?"

The redhead's gorgeous face lit up. "Consider it done. You'll have to take up the slack here, though."

"Gladly." Aila slipped in front of Lily smoothly and worked her vinci in conjunction with Conren's sword to keep the trebaxels at bay.

Lily pulled a red-fletched arrow from her quiver, nocked it, drew it back to her cheek, and launched it with blinding speed. Before the first had even hit, her hand blurred again and a second shaft was speeding after the first one. She paused for half a second, then repeated the process with one more precious fire arrow.

The first struck a large outcropping of rock twelve or thirteen feet above the ground, shaking the whole area as it exploded on impact. The second struck the rock first and the explosion came a fraction of a second later. The third somehow struck exactly on a small crack that had grown with the first two arrows. When it exploded, a huge chunk of stone nearly the size of a small carriage blew away from the wall and came down on the hapless trebaxels underneath, crushing them and blocking off the passageway.

Ten or a dozen of the monsters were trapped with the humans, but those odds were much better than they'd faced for some time. With the prey trapped, Tere and Lily launched arrow after arrow until the only movement ahead of them was of injured and dying trebaxels. Tere stepped forward to harvest the arrows they'd lent to the monsters, finishing any that needed finishing with his knives, while Lily watched for any clever enough to lie down and play dead. Within a few minutes of hard climbing over piles of corpses, there were no creatures alive to play dead and Tere had a handful of arrows to be cleaned of blood and inspected for damage.

"I'm not sure if that will hold them for more than a short time," he said. "They may try to climb over it. How about we make ourselves scarce?"

No one disagreed.

The tattered and beaten heroes kept a slow pace through the new stone maze they found themselves in, a much simpler one than they'd traveled through lately. Aila helped Scrapper in the lead as they shuffled through the twists and turns of what she imagined as a water-carved path through the stone. There were no other intersections or outlets, and when their passage narrowed again to allow only one person to pass comfortably, the tension heightened until it was palpable.

As far as Aila knew, the only real concern so far as injuries was Tere's arm. He could use it still, but sometimes when she looked back, she caught him with a grimace on his face. When he spotted her, his expression immediately turned to the neutral hero face the archer normally wore.

Conren seemed to be limping a little bit, favoring his left

leg, but that could be soreness. Even Lily dragged. What must Aila look like?

More than anything, she wished for the narrow confines of the passageway to open up. Failure in the mission was one thing, but to die of thirst or starvation because they trapped themselves in a dead-end? That was not the way she would choose to go. She tried to cheer up by telling herself that surely the trebaxels would clear the obstacle the humans put in place eventually and they would come hunting. Chances were they'd be killed quickly in their weakened, trapped state. How was that for a pep talk?

"What?" Lily asked. It took a moment for Aila to realize the archer was talking to her.

"Huh?" she responded intelligently. So tired.

"You said something, but I couldn't quite catch it."

"I did? Sorry. I think I was mumbling incoherently. Just thinking about the sticky situation we're in, trying to work things out in my head."

Lily laughed. It was a half-hearted thing. "You let me know what you come up with. My grand plan consists of putting one foot in front of the other until something happens. I suppose I lack creativity."

"You're fine," Aila said. "Your plan sounds..." She had stepped around the turn in the passage and caught sight of the first open area since they'd made their daring, scary escape.

"I think maybe we made it to the middle of the maze," Tere said. "Though it's a really big middle."

The wall to the left and right of the little passageway they'd been following stretched off as far as Aila could see. There were breaks in it, no doubt leading to other paths into the center of the maze. If that was what they were in.

Ahead of them lay an open plain with grasses, ferns, and

other low-lying vegetation. Abruptly after that, though, every space as far as could be seen exploded with growth.

It wasn't like the forest they'd gone through. If there was one word to describe the mélange in front of them, it would be *jungle*. There were places on Promistala that had jungles, though Aila had never visited them. She'd seen drawings, though, in some of the books she read as a child. Jungles were marvelous places of beauty and wonder.

They were also supposed to be as deadly as any other type of terrain. Deadlier, maybe.

True, one would probably never die of thirst in a jungle, but you could easily die of sickness from the water within, or from the many dangerous creatures that made the water and the trees their home. Still, it looked fantastic to Aila.

"Huh," Tere said. "I'd have never thought there'd be a jungle here. I wonder how that works out with the climate."

Humid air oozed from somewhere near Aila where they stood a few dozen feet outside the jungle's border. It was like a little piece of the dank environment flowed out of the center to give visitors a taste of what to expect before they committed themselves to entering.

The trees defied any experience she'd had. They were huge and twisted and each had a character all its own, even though she could only identify maybe half a dozen general types. All of them had moss or some type of vine or creeper adorning them; many had both. Even the sounds coming from within were unfamiliar. Hoots, coughs, and assorted calls of birds and probably other things reached out and tickled Aila's ears.

"It's amazing," she said.

"It is," Tere agreed. "Any other time, I would wholeheartedly support wandering around and exploring, or even standing here and observing and appreciating the jungle. However, we do have a job to do. Now that we're in the middle, maybe we can get to the middle's middle. My magical sight is still overwhelmed, so I'm no help there, though I can make sure we're going in the same direction even if we have to go around to bypass difficult areas."

"I don't think we'll need to rely on that," Conren said.

Aila whirled on him. Was he trying to start a fight again? She'd thought he was finally settling in as a member of the group. "What?"

Conren didn't answer, only pointed.

Aila turned her eyes to follow his finger. Lily let out an "Oooh."

Then she saw it. Within the lush vegetation, lighter colored objects poked out. The more she looked, the more of the objects she saw. No, not objects. Object. It finally registered that she was looking at the top of a wall poking out of the upper reaches of the canopy. Not a natural stone wall like the one that hemmed them in for the entire trip, but a *built* wall. She could see the irregularity of the shapes making it up now, bits and pieces of the picture revealing themselves through small gaps in the green. Monstrous blocks of light tan-colored stones stacked on top of each other.

"How high must that be for us to see it over the tops of the trees?" she asked.

"Really high," Tere said. "What do you say we go find out? Conren's right. No need to worry about going in a specific direction if we have that to use as a landmark. I'm betting that's in the middle of Sintrovis, and if we agree that important things might be in the middle, I say we go there."

"Are you saying just because it's the middle, the flowers we're looking for are growing there?" Lily asked.

"Not really. Just a hunch, though. This place obviously has some strong magic within it. I don't know what it's for, but if the magic emanates from something, it would be in the middle, radiating out equally in a huge circle. The more magic, the more likely it is that magic flowers grow, eh?"

"I guess I can't argue with that," Lily said. "I hope you know what to do in a jungle, because I've never been to one. Everything I hear is that they're really dangerous. Tiny bugs that are so poisonous they can kill you, strange animals that drop from trees or come up from out of the water to try to eat you, things like that."

"All true," Tere said. "I've been to a couple of jungles. They're beautiful, but not great for your health. If you're not careful."

"Two?" Lily said. "There are only three jungles in Dizhelim!"

"Untrue, or possibly untrue. There are only three jungles on Promistala. There may be jungles on other parts of Dizhelim. I don't think anyone really knows what's out in the ocean. I'm sure there's land out there somewhere, but we'll leave that discussion for another time. Right now, we need to survive the *fourth* jungle in Promistala."

❈   28   ❈

Aeden held up the tent flap and ducked inside. Within, the man he was looking for sat on a low chair, hands on his head. They looked suspiciously like they were about to tear some of the brown hair from the scalp.

"That bad, huh?" Aeden said, and blue eyes flashed up at the high chieftain. Aeden put his hands up as if to ward off any attack the man might make and was instead treated to a smile he remembered all too well from their time as boys training to be warriors.

"Codaghan's balls, Aeden, I'm glad you're here."

Aeden clasped forearms with Greimich and nodded to Cat, who was standing at a table that held three pitchers and half a dozen cups.

"Hi, Cat. Have you been keeping him sane? We've not time for him to crumble under the weight of being a clan chief."

The stunning brown-haired woman gave Aeden a little wave.

"Hello, Aeden. I've been keeping him as sane as he's ever

been, which isn't to say that he wasn't always a little loose in the head."

"Aye, he'd have to be more than half-cracked to have spent so much time with me when we were younger, I suppose. I'm glad of it, though. There's no one else in all the clan I'd rather have as acting clan chief."

"There are only three people in the clan, Aeden," Greimich mock-growled. "Marla's even busier than you, which leaves exactly one person to take up the slack while you're gallivanting all over the world. Me."

"That doesn't belie the truth of what I said, now does it?" Aeden said, giving his friend a wide grin.

"Ale, wine, or water, Aeden?" Cat asked.

"Ale, I think. Thank you, Cat."

She poured from one of the pitchers and brought Aeden the cup, along with a cup she'd already poured for Greimich.

"Really, though," Aeden asked, "is it bad? How are things going? I do hate to put all this on you, Greimich, but there are some things I have to do. Malatirsay things."

"Aye, I know." Aeden's boyhood friend took a drink from his cup. "It's fine. I know you're not trying to avoid your duties as clan chief or high chieftain, though I could under-stand if you were. Dealing with clan chiefs is not a pleasure. I wonder why anyone would want to be a chief."

Aeden chuckled. "Some for the glory and power of it, some out of their sense of duty, and maybe some because they're not smart enough to get out of it."

"And which are you?"

"I..." He took another drink. "Have the distinct honor of being born into it and the unfortunate privilege of believing in my duty to the clans and to the world. It's unfortunate that the Malatirsay responsibilities interfere with my commitment to the clans. Again, I apologize for dragging you into it. Know that I appreciate it greatly and that I believe you're doing as fine a job—or better, probably—than I could do."

It was Greimich's turn for humor. He snorted. "You've no reason to stroke my ego. The truth has always been good enough for me. I honestly don't know how you keep a leash on the huge heads on the clan chiefs. How they all fit in the meeting tent, I'll never know."

"The secret is to challenge them all to fight to the death," Aeden said. "And then to kill one of them." The hint of the smile he had on his face dropped off and he set his drink down on another table. "Well, there's a thought to crush all humor. So, tell me what's been happening. I'm not sure how long I'll be here in the Academy before they send me off somewhere else. Anything I can help with?"

"Send you off?" Greimich said. "You're the bloody Malatirsay." He raised a finger. "Or half the Malatirsay. I know, I know. Still, you and your twin are the heroes prophesied thousands of years ago. Who can send you off running on errands?"

"It's not quite like that, but also, the masters know a lot more about what's going on. I rely on their knowledge and their magic. Yes, I can choose to say no to them, but each time something needs to be done, I can't find fault in them— or my friends—wanting me to go."

"I understand. Well, to answer your question, I—"

Someone knocked on the tent pole outside. Aeden looked to Greimich, his eyebrows raised. Greimich shrugged.

"Come," Aeden said.

Seoras Corcan poked his red and white speckled head into the tent. "One of my men spotted you trying to sneak in here. I thought I'd say hello. Are you two...talking about anything I shouldn't hear?"

"Only his many complaints about the Corcan clan chief. You can hear them if you like."

Seoras's face split into a grin and he brought the rest of his body into the tent and put it in front of Aeden for a hug. "How long are you back here this time?"

"Not sure," Aeden said. "I never know. I'm sorry for all the trouble I'm causing by not being here. I've missed talking to you."

Seoras waved the comment away. "It's no harder than it normally is. You know that if there's a chance for an argument with all the clans together, it's going to happen with or without the high chieftain patrolling the camp."

"Is it that bad, then?"

The Corcan clan chief looked toward Greimich and Cat with a disbelieving look. "Have you struck him in the head, Greimich? He doesn't seem to understand clear Ruthrin."

Aeden glared at the man. "Oh, is that what you're speaking? With that muddy accent, I thought you were speaking Chorain."

Seoras slapped Aeden on the shoulder and stepped over to the table to pour himself something to drink. He waved Cat away, who had sat down just before he arrived but was rising to pour for him. "Thanks, Cat, but I am capable of pouring a cup of ale. You do too much already. Sit down and watch the three fools."

"Two fools and high chieftain," Aeden mumbled, to which Seoras chortled.

"No, things aren't all that bad, but the clans are getting restless," the clan chief said. "Alpin grumbles about it in the meetings with the chiefs, but surprisingly, he doesn't say anything against what we decide in those meetings. You told us we needed to stay put and so that's what we'll do."

"Who, exactly, is getting restless in the clans?" Aeden asked.

"Padraig doesn't have a problem speaking out against staying here, whether in the meetings or out in the camps,"

Greimich said. "He gives support to the warriors from most of the clans who are bored and missing the Cridheargla."

Seoras took a drink and nodded. "It's hard to take for some. Having to flee our home was bad enough, but now to sit here, not even inside the Academy, waiting to be told what to do. That's not the Croagh way."

"I understand that," Aeden said. "I'm afraid that some of them think we're going right off to take back the highlands, even though I've made it clear there are other things that need to happen first. Things like beating the animaru so they don't simply flood back into our homes and take the whole area back from us. The Croagh scare the animaru. We're the only group who can harm them, aside from the students and masters at the Academy. If they can isolate us and throw thousands of attackers at us, we could cease to exist."

"I know. I've told them. The clan chiefs understand. Even Padraig, I think, though he always seems to think he knows better. The fact is, though, that warriors can only sit around for so long before they start to feel like they're not true warriors after all."

"In times of peace between the clans, warriors never had a problem with training and living their lives."

"True, but in times of peace with the other clans, they hadn't had their homes taken from them, either."

Aeden ran his fingers through his hair. "Right. What'd you have me do, then? I can't let them go back and try to take the highlands. It'd be the end of us."

Seoras sat in one of the chairs and tapped his finger on the side of his cup. "I don't know. Is there someplace they can go to fight? Are there places that need good warriors to, I don't know, squash dissention or rebellion?"

"No. There are places where people are deciding to join the animaru, but we can't waste our time and effort attacking other humans. It's the animaru we need to fight. We're hoping the people who think it's a good idea to try to make a deal with the monsters come to their senses without us having to go kill them."

"What about small groups of the monsters. If they spread out from their main encampments—Kruzekstan and Artuyeska, right?—we could go and wipe them out."

"I don't know, Seoras. I'll ask Master Qydus what he thinks. I'm wary of attacking the edges of where they've expanded right now. I think once we engage in open battle, the war will well and truly start. Better to take the time to gather our resources while small magically specialized groups like me and my friends try to prevent them from being able to bring more animaru over from their world. We'll need to follow the strategy set out by...oh, that's it!"

"What?" Greimich asked.

"Master Goren. He's the Master of the School of Military Strategy. He's designing the strategy for the war, essentially the supreme commander for the war against the animaru. He's in the beginning stages of figuring out how to separate the students and the graduates, as well as nations that have committed troops to the cause. He's told me before that he'd love to talk about strategy and tactics, not to mention the Croagh's individual combat techniques.

"I can talk to him, offer him some Croagh, maybe even a clan chief or two, to help him with the strategy. Also, warriors can be selected to help train soldiers. We live and breathe combat and are second to none in skirmishes, and up in the top few groups in the world for larger battles."

"That will appeal to the egos of those who are selected," Seoras said, "but it's still a small number of us."

"Aye, but maybe we can rotate to increase the numbers involved. The second thing I was thinking about can help, too, though it won't be accepted as readily. The Croagh are the best individual warriors in the world. I'd bet good money on it. However, they're not the best soldiers. In large scale wars like this, there is a lot we can learn. We're working on getting the Clavian Knights to join us and we already have Shinyan as an ally. In order for us to work together, we'll need a common footing, people who understand many or all of the groups that will be coming together. We need some Croagh to learn, help Master Goren to mold the troops into an army that can fight together, and to teach all the Croagh warriors what to do."

"Hmmm," Seoras said. "It might be enough. There will be opportunities for those who want to do more than sit around and wait. For those who only want to complain about everything, this will help to put them in the minority. There will be enough work to do that most won't listen to whining. There's no better way to get highlanders interested than to tell them they can learn how to kill better, and to show others how much they already know."

"Exactly. I'll go and talk to Master Goren right now. If he is open to it, which I think he will be, we'll have a meeting with the clan chiefs and see what they think. How's that sound?"

Seoras scratched his chin. "Don't think it's too easy, though. Expect many to scoff at the idea they can be taught anything by non-Croagh."

"Better some complain than all."

"It sounds like we have a lot of work to do," Greimich said. "Which is good because busy warriors are happy warriors, right?"

Aeden was already working out how he'd approach Master Goren. "We'll soon see."

## 29

The jungle in the center of Sintrovis was as strange a place as Aila had ever been. Even the air was different. Heavy, like she had to work to pull it into her lungs. She'd been covered in a soaking wet blanket one time as a child, hiding from her friends in a game they probably shouldn't have been playing during a summer rainstorm. Breathing through that blanket had felt the same as the open air in this jungle. If being crowded by trees and vines and assorted big-leafed plants could be considered open air.

Tere did his thing, treading a path that made for the easiest travel. *How did he do that?* She tried to predict which way he'd go, but the tangle looked the same in all directions. Yet, that they were moving ahead at anything greater than a snail's pace was proof the archer knew what he was about.

Movement drew Aila's eye.

A snake, as big around as she was and six times as long as her body, slithered across and around a massive branch above them. It had greens, browns, and black mixed into a perfect pattern for camouflage. If it hadn't been moving, she never would have seen it.

"They're not very fast," Tere said. Of course he'd seen the animal. "What you have to worry about is them dropping on you as you pass underneath. They can weigh hundreds of pounds and once they're on top of you, they wrap themselves around you and squeeze. I saw one do that to a man once. We couldn't cut it up fast enough to save him. As we attacked, we could hear individual bones being crushed. The popping sounds, mixed with his screams—at least until he ran out of air and the snake's body covered his face—replayed in my nightmares for days after that. Not a pretty way to go."

Aila gulped and checked on the snake again to make sure it wasn't directly above her.

"The smaller ones, faster ones," Tere continued, "tend to be venomous to compete with the rest of the animals in the jungle. I haven't seen any here yet, but they often live in places like this. They're harder to spot than the big ones. Walk carefully in the path I'm picking out and you should be okay. They don't go out of their way to attack bigger things, but if they feel challenged or are surprised, they'll strike you faster than you can react."

"What a lovely place," Aila said. She heard Lily's chuckle up ahead of her. Scrapper, on Lily's back, made a sound that could have been a trebaxel laugh.

The injured trebaxel suddenly stiffened and chittered softly but urgently. Aila was about to say something, to ask him what was wrong, but Tere had apparently already figured it out.

"There's something coming. Several somethings. Everyone drop to the ground and don't move."

All four of the humans hit the ground immediately. Scrapper, motivated by some instinct, had already ceased all movement and his vocal warning. They waited, Aila nestled in the damp foliage. She was already wet all the way through her clothes to her skin, just from the air, so it wasn't any more of an inconvenience. Not unless one of those snakes Tere had been talking about decided to slither onto them while they weren't moving. If that happened, she couldn't guarantee she wouldn't jump up screaming even before it bit her. Several more beads of sweat popped from her forehead and dribbled down the side of her face at that thought. Perspiration didn't evaporate in this place.

Then she heard it. Or felt it. A soft thumping against her prone body muffled by the soft detritus. It increased until she could separate the vibration running through her body and the noise of something passing through the underbrush. More than one something. It grew louder and louder until she was sure whatever it was would run right into them—over them.

A dozen paces away, bounding through the vegetation as if it weren't even there, were at least a score of large, furry bodies carrying the familiar branches they used as weapons. Aila could easily see them to identify what they were because these *were even bigger* than the trebaxels that had come at them before they escaped through the narrow passage.

They didn't look around, for which she was thankful. They ran and jumped quickly and efficiently, following a single creature in the lead. She couldn't tell the difference between any of them, but then again, she didn't have time to compare facial features. Nor would she want to. She could recognize Scrapper, but part of that was probably his size.

Within seconds, the group had zipped past them without noticing the humans hiding so close by. She thanked Vanda that they didn't seem to have a keen sense of smell. There, in the middle of the jungle without good mobility, the fatigued humans would be slaughtered handily by such a large group. Aila let out a breath and found herself shaking, her heart fluttering, as she strove to fill her lungs with the heavy air again.

They waited for five more minutes after the last sound of the trebaxels faded, then Tere stood up.

"I don't know if that's a patrol or if they were in a hurry to get somewhere, but it was too close in any case. Let's keep our ears open and for Surus's sake, take any warning Scrapper gives as an alarm and hit the ground. We can only hope that if we run into more, they won't trample right over the top of us."

Aila looked back and met Conren's wide eyes. He tilted his head with a look that told her he was as shaken as she was about their proximity to the trebaxels. She forced a smile, but it didn't seem to help. It probably looked like a grimace anyway.

Twice more they had close calls with trebaxels, but they were never detected. Maybe word of their making it to the jungle hadn't come through or maybe they were actually searching for the humans, though they didn't swing their heads in search or pause to scan the surroundings. All the time they traveled, Aila studied the tops of the trees. When she caught glimpses of a piece of the manufactured wall they were heading for, it was always directly in front of them.

After what seemed to be many hours, but probably was only one, Tere pushed his way through the edge of the jungle and into another more open space.

In front of them, relatively unobscured by plants, was the wall. As she'd glimpsed, it was built with massive blocks of tan-colored stone. Sandstone, maybe? Aila couldn't tell how thick the blocks were, but they had to be at least ten feet tall each. There were at least twenty layers.

She inspected those closest to her. The wear at the edges, as well as vines that had affixed themselves to certain sections, indicated it was old. Very old. Strangely, many places were naked stone, the plants not wanting—or not being able to—adhere to them. It had to be some kind of magic. What else could it be?

"I think we're at the true center now," Lily said.

"It's about damn time," Tere grumbled. For some reason, that brought a smile to Lily's face.

Off to their left, an obvious opening beckoned. It was the only one in sight.

Tere scanned the entire visible length of the wall, and the uncluttered area around it. "I'm guessing we need to go in. I hope this is a garden, because we're running out of places to look for the flowers."

"It looks like a stadium," Conren said.

At first, Aila thought that was ridiculous, but then she noticed that the wall wasn't straight. As it ran off to either side, it curved. If it continued in that way, what they were seeing was a huge circular wall. There was no telling what was inside it, but she could see the similarity to the grand stadiums some cities—like Metrovial—had for jousting matches and tournaments.

"You're right," she told him. "But why would there be a stadium in the middle of a jungle in the middle of Sintrovis?"

"Magical duels were all the rage before the War of Magic," Tere said. "I'm guessing this place was built at that time. Or before."

"That would make it more than three thousand years old," Aila said.

"Yep."

"A three-thousand-year-old magical tournament stadium? Oh, I'm sure there's no danger in us going in there."

Tere shrugged. "Not much more than going into Sintrovis to begin with, I reckon. Let's do this. We're behind schedule and if we don't find flowers inside this wall, there's nothing for us to do but to try to get out alive."

The thought of all they'd done and still failing to even find the flowers, let alone get them back to her father made Aila frantic. If they didn't find what they were looking for, there had better be a lot of trebaxels in the stadium because she was going to need to kill large quantities to expel the anger and frustration she'd feel.

"Come on," she growled. "Vanda help anyone or anything that stands in my way when we're so close." She started off in a straight line toward the opening, her surprised friends scrambling to keep her pace.

It occurred to Aila before she reached the breach in the wall that she was being ridiculous. She was in a wide-open space, marching up to the only passage they could see through the wall, and they were totally visible from any part of the edge of the jungle. She was putting her friends at risk because of her anger. Because she was throwing a tantrum, and not even for any good reason.

She slowed and allowed the others to reach the split in the wall at the same time. It was a legitimate opening, the size of a large gate, with an arch ten feet above the ground. The type of space that would have had a nice door or a grate that could be swung open to admit people.

"Sorry," she said over her shoulder. "I'm calm now."

"Glad to hear it," Tere said.

"I was also thinking about it, and this had to have been built before the War of Magic. No way someone could build this while my ancestors were in the bowl made up by the mountains. They'd have seen someone doing construction in the sacred place no one went to."

"That's a good point," Lily said.

They stepped through the opening and Aila's eyes could barely take it all in. She'd been surprised so many times in the last few days, but apparently the world had at least one more revelation for her.

She had taken the idea of the place being a stadium in

stride, not believing it nor disbelieving it. She owed Conren an apology.

The wall was not simply a wall. Along the inside of the curved walls were tiers that looked much too coincidental not to be made for seats and spectators. Of course, there were none of those at the moment. Rubble, vines that had crept inside, and dust lay in their place. None of that could dispel the feeling of grandeur the space must have demonstrated in its prime.

Within the field of the stadium, more vast than any five such areas she'd ever seen or heard of, were assorted plants and grasses, though not nearly as many as there should have been with the open sky above.

"Do you think there's a catacomb system underneath, with a stone block floor?" Conren asked. "Maybe that's why there aren't any trees growing in here."

"Maybe," Tere said. "Could be magic, too, though if it was meant to keep all plants from growing, it's getting weaker."

Aila walked toward the center of the area, unimpeded by the random stones and low plants present. A small bunching of sizeable boulders lay off to her right, but she paid them no mind. Something deep within her told her it wasn't smart to traverse the space, considering anyone or anything anywhere within the walls could see her as she did so. She ignored the warning.

Along one edge of the field, near the wall, she spotted a splash of color. Excitement spiked within her, but she tamped it down. Though the colors were green, yellow, and red, she recalled the last time she'd seen such things and how it almost cost them their lives. Still, she had to check.

"Alevia?" Conren said, but she ignored him, too.

Halfway to the wall, she could tell this was not another illusion made by patterns on stone. Some of the shapes moved with the slight breeze. The green leaves and stems, the vibrant yellow and red flowers, they danced with each other. They were real.

She set one foot forward in preparation to run toward them when Scrapper began to chitter madly. It was sort of like the sounds he'd made when the groups of trebaxels surprised them, but different, too. Looking back, she saw the little creature hop off Tere's back and lie down on his belly, face pointed into the thin grass.

The boulders slowly unfolded. Grey stone, unlike the tan stone of which the wall was made, straightened and revealed itself to be the curved back of a creature as big as three of the largest trebaxels they'd seen so far. Its furry head swiveled to peer at Aila, who was closest to it.

It opened its mouth, showing teeth that she had no doubt could punch through her entire body, and, in a more powerful version of the language of the trebaxels, roared at them.

## 30

The last of the Council members arrived in the meeting room, their slightly faded appearance making it clear that the final attendee was using a meeting stone, if the fact that she suddenly materialized didn't. The straggler was Thalia this time. It was usually either her or Cara.

Alloria fought the urge to shake her head. Sometimes things were too predictable. But then, that made it easier to know what someone would do in a particular circumstance, allowing her to foresee their actions and manipulate them more effectively.

Her father had trained her to watch for such predictability, and to utilize it. So much of leading the Dark Council involved steering people. Goading, cajoling, threatening, rewarding, she used all these methods. Whatever she had to do to carry on the mission of the Council, so she would do. This meeting was a perfect example of that.

"Thank you all for coming...promptly." She purposely didn't look Thalia's way. The point was made better if she didn't. "First, I would like an update from Evindia and Amatia on our progress regarding finding these magic wells we recently learned about."

"Wells of Power," Ren Kenata corrected. "Pardon, Vituma. Our spies at the Academy tell us the masters are calling them Wells of Power."

Alloria's jaw tightened briefly. "Of course. Wells of Power. So, what have we learned about them? Where can we find the next one?"

Amatia glanced at Evindia, who was looking at the seeress. Amatia gave a small shrug and fielded the question. "I have had no visions of wells. In fact, I have had no visions at all since we were tasked with finding them. I am sorry, but my gift does not function so. In the past, when I have forced visions—whether purposely or simply because I created tension in myself because of my desire for certain information—I have had similar dry periods. I am trying to readjust my energies so that the visions come naturally. My hope is that once they do, I will receive something valuable for our search."

Alloria knew a little bit about the *tension* Amatia was speaking about. She felt it herself. If their seeress didn't find where one of these wells were before the Academy minions, they would never get to one in time. Part of her wanted to scold Amatia, tell her she needed to perform, but she was aware enough how the woman's abilities worked to realize it would make things worse.

Instead, she said not what she wanted, but what she needed. "I understand. Yes, by all means, center yourself and once you regain your balance, perhaps you will have visions that will aid us." She turned to Evindia. "What of you? Have any of the group causing so much trouble left the Academy to go on another of their journeys? It seems that lately, whenever they do, they find another of the wells."

"None have left since the archers and that small woman

departed along with the boy, one of the masters, the former Falxen, and the priest. The second group has returned, but the one including the hero...uh, the man who formerly went by the name Erent Caahs, hasn't returned yet."

Alloria's middle jumped as it was stated so plainly. Gods, they were fighting against Erent Caahs. An older and more beat-up version of the hero, but the renowned hero all the same. Even in a family of the Vituma of the Dark Council, she had thrilled at stories of the man's exploits when she was a child. She wondered if she could ever explain the mission of the Council well enough to convince him to join their side.

Probably not.

"Continue to watch," she told Evindia. "Between Amatia's visions and your spies, we will get to one of these wells sooner or later. I would rather we find one without having to follow the Academy stooges. I do not relish the thought of combat with them unnecessarily. Better to go and seize a well and its magic without having to battle for it and take it away from someone else.

"Very well. There is something else we need to discuss. I would like to do so now. We can consider whatever other activities you have in progress after that. What has been missing up to this point is the thing that will give us a sense of legitimacy in the world's eyes. It's time we start building an army of our own."

Several of the others whispered to those next to them, as expected. When Gareth Briggs opened his mouth, Alloria had to keep the smile from her face. She knew what he'd say, almost word-for-word.

"Are you sure that's wise at this point?" the handsome man asked. "I haven't reported yet on what the church is doing, and armies take so much work, not to mention money. Should we be saddling ourselves with the burden of having to pay soldiers' salaries?"

Alloria did her best impression of someone considering something she just heard, pausing for the requisite amount of time with a thoughtful look on her face. "Do you have another idea as to when would be good to gather our troops in earnest? How would you handle it if I put you in charge of the army we require to withstand not only the church, but the animaru and the nations banding together to fight them?"

"I would be a poor choice for the leader of our forces," he said. "I'm more of a logistics man, myself. The Council has money, no doubt, but I hardly think the appropriate place to spend it is on drinking money for soldiers at this point in the timeline."

"So you have no thought to when, if not now?" Alloria clarified.

"I cannot predict when it would be appropriate. I think the time is not yet here, however."

"I appreciate your comments, but I disagree with you, Gareth. You are doing an admirable job in the tasks I've assigned you, but as you say, military matters are not your forte. Now is the time to begin building our army so that when events dictate that we have strength of arms, we will be ready. To that end, we need someone to deal with the mercenaries and to recruit regular soldiers, though of course we cannot simply tell them they will be serving the Dark Council.

"The Council member we need must understand war and warriors and be able to select key officers to train and command soldiers as we gain them. Thritur Nyhus, you will do this."

Others besides Gareth Briggs reacted with wide-eyed surprise. The large man she had named was one of them. His mouth moved silently underneath his mass of facial hair. Alloria had never seen him so thoroughly poleaxed.

The massive man finally got control over his ability for speech and spoke. "Me, Vituma?"

"Yes," Evindia Elkien said. "Him?"

Of the entire council, only Isbal Deyne looked unsurprised that Alloria chose the barbarian member of the Council. Yoniko Takesi's face held something else as well. Disappointment.

Thritur was perpetually underestimated in anything except for pure combat by the other members of the Council. He spoke seldom in meetings, and when he did, he used few words, cutting straight to his thoughts, regardless of whether or not it would insult or offend the others. Alloria knew what most of the others thought: Thritur was good to have at your side when violence broke out, but you couldn't carry on an intelligent conversation with him.

But Alloria paid more attention than most, and she suspected even she hadn't come to understand all of the man's complexities and competencies.

"You, Thritur," she told him.

He stroked the head of his favorite weapon, his battle axe, as if to comfort himself. It wasn't common for items to appear along with the Council members when they used the meeting stones, but he must have had a firm grip on it when he activated the stone.

"You know war better than most, and you have an ability to cut through unimportant details to get to the heart of things. Your directness will serve us well in dealing with soldiers and especially mercenaries."

"I will do as I am told," he rumbled. "But I am shit with strategy. Battle is simple for me. Hit the enemy over and over until he is dead."

The Vituma laughed. "Don't be so modest, Thritur. I know you have a better grasp of how to wage war than that, but I understand your reluctance. I said that you would be in charge of recruiting and building our army. I did not say you would be responsible for strategy.

"For that task, I have selected Yoniko."

The Teroshimi woman sat up straighter—not that her posture wasn't nearly perfect to begin with—and nodded. "Thank you, Vituma."

Ren Kenata's mouth twitched into a smile that was quickly wiped away. Interesting. Why did the decision make him happy? Perhaps a Teroshimi honor thing?

"You have had great generals and warlords in your family for generations," Alloria told Yoniko. "You have proven that the ability has not skipped past you. You will work with Thritur. Cooperate, but if it comes down to a contest of authority, you will make the decisions about where our forces go and what they'll do, whereas Thritur will determine how the army is organized and trained. I trust that there will not be major issues with this?"

"None," Thritur said. "I respect Yoniko's knowledge and abilities. She will act with honor and not out of pride. We will work fine together."

"That is my sentiment, too," Yoniko said, bowing her head toward the barbarian. "The southern tribes are not famous for warfare for nothing."

"Good," Alloria said. "Begin immediately. Speak with Hane about the funds necessary."

The secretary and accountant for the council nodded. Hane Bryce looked like nothing if not a clerk, from his hair parted on the left and combed across his head to the coat with several pens in its pockets and constant ink stains on his hands. Alloria trusted him implicitly and thought very highly of his ability with finances and records.

"Now," she said, "let's discuss anything and everything you are working on to further our cause. Gareth, we can start with you and move around the table from there. Impress me with your reports."

Gareth Briggs cleared his throat.

"My efforts are bearing fruit, both in Arania as well as in the Great Enclave. A little more time and a hefty dose of more extraordinary effort on my part and I think you will all be very pleased at what I've accomplished. The plans are..."

Alloria listened with half an ear. So much to do in such a short time. At least she had set them on the path to having their own army, and plans were in the works that could mitigate some of their major obstacles. Knowledge was power, but it didn't hurt to have a few thousand swords to back up that knowledge.

The sound of the huge trebaxel's roar pushed on Aila like a physical force. Like a storm wind. She stepped her right leg back and bent her knees to keep her balance as her hands flew to her ears to keep her eardrums from bursting.

Within that roar, she recognized certain patterns that were undoubtedly speech components in the trebaxel tongue. She'd heard them—though much, much quieter—in the chittering Scrapper engaged in. It sounded more dangerous coming from a forty- or fifty-foot-tall monster.

"Aila!" Tere's voice barely passed for sound as the big creature's monologue died out. "The flowers. Go get the flowers. We'll keep it busy."

Already, Tere and Lily were peppering the monster with arrows while Conren stepped forward to a position in front of them, shield up. As if it would help against something so massive.

She could see Tere's point, though. Without the flowers, their trip would have been for naught. The smart thing was to grab them and then run as fast and as far as possible, especially in something like a narrow passage where the beast could not get at them.

Clarity gripped her mind and allowed her to shake loose the effects of the panic she had already started to succumb to. Right. The flowers! With a wary look at the huge, furry creature, she took off running exactly in the opposite direction from the thing. Her plan was to get out of its range and out of its attention, then swing back around to where the flowers were, stuff handfuls of them in her pack, and then...well, she'd figure out how to flee for her life, along with her friends, after that. First things first.

The king trebaxel—or whatever it was—eyed her, but shifted its attention to the people who were launching sharp projectiles at it. One came dangerously close to its eye, and it apparently reprioritized things to take care of that threat first. Aila was in the clear.

She ran like she'd never run before. She ran like a massive monster was chasing her. If she wasn't so freaked out, she would have thought the irony was funny. Legs burning, she finally made it through her circuitous route to her destination.

It was true. No illusion of shapes on rocks here. Dozens of bushes of mid-sized green leaves on robust stalks led to flowers that, even in her time of stress, made her pause to gape at their beauty. She'd thought she knew what they looked like from the scraps they'd found, but those had only been pale representations of the growing, living flowers.

From each of the main branches split off sub-branches, and on each of those was at least one bud or flower. Their structure reminded Aila of roses, and the fireheart flowers were certainly as beautiful as any rose she'd ever seen. They expanded up from little green cups as big around as her thumb and the petals swept out into goblet-shaped flowers as big across as her spread hand. Some were yellow with red shooting up through them, while others were red with yellow laced through, different shades of those colors, as well as oranges dancing in a gradient along their lengths and widths. A few contained swirls of the colors as well.

And the smell. She'd read enough poetry about the scent of a rose, suffered through the clichés of their intoxicating aromas and how they metaphorically represented everything from true love to sex to life's journey. None of that compared to the euphoric aroma of the fireheart flowers. She could tell that different bushes had slightly different smells, though surrounded by the flowers, it was difficult to distinguish if those of the same colors and designs smelled the same. All of them together, though, made her head swim, even more than her heavy breathing from sprinting to them would account for.

She shook her head violently. Standing here, waxing poetic, literally enjoying smelling the flowers. What the hells was wrong with her?

According to Verona, it was the flowers that they needed for her father, but she also had learned enough from Tere to know that most medicinal plants could be used for many purposes. The roots for some things, the stalks for another, the flowers for something different. She would most likely never have the opportunity to get more of the flowers again. Without thinking about it too much, she tore whole plants from the soil. Small ones, true, but whole. She beat the roots against the ground to shake off most of the dirt and unceremoniously stuffed them into her pack. She knew she was going to damage them, but having a whole backpack full of damaged plants was better than not having them at all.

It didn't take long to fill up the space available from the food she no longer had. In all, there had to be at least thirty flowers and more than half that many whole plants. When she picked up her pack to swing it onto her back, she considered that she may have made a mistake and overloaded it. But if she had to lug around a heavy pack, even running for her life, to not only save her father but possibly advance herbal medicine lore to aid others, she'd do it. As for taking too much of what was available, she'd hardly made a dent in the total number of plants arrayed before her.

Aila turned to see that the big trebaxel was completely focused on her friends. Tere and Lily moved around, loosing arrows while keeping their distance. The monster swatted at them but wasn't able to catch one before arrows from the other archer grabbed its attention and lured it after the newest threat.

Conren stood by, all but ignored by their enemy. Scrapper was still where he had dropped to the ground, face down, his shaking visible even from where Aila was. She ran directly for Conren and Scrapper.

The big trebaxel had gone mostly silent. It occasionally screamed at an arrow that struck it in a painful place, but for the most part, it didn't sustain a lot of damage for each shaft. The small injuries might pile up—it was bleeding from many places—but all they needed to do was to keep it from grabbing them as they ran out of the stadium, then to a more defensible position. They weren't going to kill the thing.

Then she heard it. Chittering, screeching, echoing sounds that were too much like what she'd heard the past several days. Looking up from the battle on the floor of the stadium, Aila's legs went weak and she stumbled, almost falling. On the different tiers of the arena, hundreds of furry figures bounced and bellowed. Grey fur, brown, tan, a multitude of shades in tones of dirt and stone surrounded the humans in every direction.

Apparently, the trebaxels liked their entertainment with a bit of bloodshed.

She brought herself to a complete stop beside Conren.

"Tere, Lily, I've got them. Let's go. If we can get out of the stadium, maybe we can make it back to that passage, or another place they can't get to us."

She knew it sounded stupid. There was no way they'd avoid not only the big trebaxel, but the countless others in the tiers above. But what could they do? It was either that or stay and be killed where they stood. Better to run.

"Go," Tere said. "Don't wait. We'll keep them busy. If we can get out, we will, but the most important thing is those flowers get back to the city."

"No," she shouted back, but he'd already turned to evade the trebaxel again, launching two arrows in rapid succession, one going into the monster's cheek and the other cutting its head right next to its left eye. If only Tere had his full magical sight so he could track the potential trajectory of his shots...

"Alevia," Conren said from beside her. "You have to do it. Don't make our sacrifice worthless. Get out. I'll stop them from coming for you."

She laughed, a frantic, hoarse thing. "It's too strong. They're too strong, the monsters. I'll never make it."

"*You* have to. You have to be stronger. Go."

Aila blinked away tears from her eyes. When had she started crying? With no other alternative, she did as she was told and ran for the entrance they had come through. They were right. What could she do with her small weapons against the giant monster facing them? Even Conren's shield and sword wouldn't last long. She hated herself more with each step, but she understood their directions. The important thing was for her father to live. Without that, the Enclave would fail, and probably the whole world with it when the Academy didn't get the soldiers they needed. They needed the Clavian Knights not only to fight, but to provide an example to other nations. Without that, there might not be any other allies.

Aila Ven leaned forward, pumped her arms, and ran as fast as she could to escape the stadium.

She got exactly as far as twenty paces from the opening and slid to a halt.

There, in the doorway, the only way out of the slaughterhouse that she was in, were at least fifty of the biggest trebaxels, all of them with their signature clubs.

She was trapped.

❧ 32 ❧

Aeden blew out a breath and dropped heavily into the chair in his room in Batido. He'd had dinner with the others in the common room, but he hadn't remained there like most of them had. It wasn't that he didn't enjoy time with his friends; he did. The sense of family and closeness with those he'd been through danger and adventure with was unmatched by anything besides the bond he'd experienced with Greimich and the different type of connection and love with his adopted Gypta family.

It wasn't that he didn't want to spend time with them. It was that he had so much to do. So much.

The masters had been keeping him busy. Headmaster Qydus had strongly urged him to avail himself of some of the magical training at the Academy. Others begged for his time in talking about the Raibrech. Still others wanted to hear everything he knew and had experienced with the Song and the special way he used it. That wasn't even mentioning his work with the clans and helping to coordinate the interface between them and Master Goren to achieve the idea he'd explained to Seoras and Greimich.

Pulled in so many directions, sometimes he wanted to run away into the forest and just breathe. Or train. His daily exercises sometimes seemed the only thing that kept him sane, especially on the days when Khrazhti joined him. Early in the morning, performing martial training with her, it seemed they were in a pocket of peace untouched by the turmoil in the Academy, let alone the world.

But he had other things he needed to do, primary among which was to accept the tutelage of the man who had started it all. He'd read some of the book Tsosin Ruus had left him, but his guilt at not doing more with it beat on him. How could he sit around and tell stories and chat with his friends when the undeniable treasure of the book written specifically for him sat in his room?

True, it was written for him *and* Marla, but she was letting him go through it first. She had even more going on in her life, including working to finalize mastery in several other schools. So here he was, finally seizing a few moments for himself to delve into the Prophet's message from three thousand years ago. The thought made Aeden shiver.

He gingerly opened the hefty tome to the page marked by a ribbon he'd inserted to save his place. Though ancient, the book was in the same condition as it was when it was first bound together, solely due to Tsosin Ruus's magic specifically cast on the book as well as attached to the secret cache in which they had found it.

A slow smile crept onto his face. The thought that an outcast Croagh boy had before him what amounted to a very long personal letter from the most important mage to have ever lived was overwhelming and humbling at the same time. He had to make sure he didn't fail in his assigned task. Literally the entire world was at stake.

Aeden ran a finger down the edge of the page. He'd never read a book like this one before. It was warm and genuine, personal yet profound. Thinking of it as a letter from a friend wasn't too much a fancy. The style was easy to read, though maybe not so easy to understand sometimes. How long had it taken the Prophet to write it? The penmanship was nearly perfect, very few smudges and no places he'd seen so far where something was crossed out. Tsosin Ruus had written it with his own hand, bound it himself, and left it to help Aeden save the world.

Enough of his musings, though. He flipped back a page so he could recall where in the commentary he was. Then he began to read.

It wasn't as simple as that, though. Wrestling with the millennia-old book was more of a battle than simply reading. To start, it was in Alaqotim. Not the language that scholars and mages used in the modern day, but closer to what Khrazhti spoke. He'd place the language in which the book was written as just short of halfway between contemporary and classical Alaqotim.

Several of the masters offered to translate the book for him, but Aeden had declined. When he brought it up, Marla told him that accepting the help would make the process of assimilating the information faster, but it might also introduce some inaccuracies. Not that the translator would make mistakes, but the unique context in which each word resided dictated its meaning to some extent. Alaqotim was a complex language and translation could be tricky. Aeden's sister told him that although he would not as easily be able to translate the text, his connection with the magic of the Song—Tsosin Ruus's magic mingled with the universal power of prophecy— would allow him to intuit the correct meaning.

*Of course,* she had said with a wink, *the book could be so straightforward that there are no tricky translations and then you'd be wasting your time by doing it yourself.*

That had left him wondering if tackling the project

himself was an appropriate use of his time. With the first paragraph, however, he did feel a connection, a gentle buzzing surrounding him and the book. At that point, he knew he had made the correct choice, even if it might slow down his progress.

After all, the book was titled *For the Malatirsay*. How much clearer could the Prophet's intent be?

Aeden only read a few sentences before he found himself flipping back to the foreword of the book. He'd read it many times already, and had it essentially memorized. The thrill of reading it never faded, however, so he didn't fight his desire to start his study session with the familiar words.

*I have labored long and hard to do what I may to prepare for your coming. Please allow me to take this opportunity to thank you for your heroism, for your sacrifice, and simply for your existence. I know not how it must feel to know your birth was awaited for some time. How much time, I also do not know, but my feeling is that it has been centuries, perhaps millennia, since I passed from the mortal realm. I understand a tiny fraction of what it is to be swept up in great events of the world and I am grateful for the small part I have been able to play to aid you in what way I can.*

*Let me be clear from the first. Though I was the recipient of the prophecy, I claim no possession of it. Rather, I would say that the song itself possessed me. I was fortunate and blessed enough to be the vessel through which it was transferred to Dizhelim. Everything I have done in support has been what I feel I owed to somehow justify the privilege I have been afforded. I am sure you understand to what I refer.*

*Even now, toward the end of my life, I have gained acclaim, the greater part of which is because of the prophecy itself. In the way of history, I can assume that years, decades, and centuries from my time, I am either famous for my contributions, or I am infamous because of the claims of my detractors. I pray that you will understand that neither of these is the true story. I am a man, nothing more. Tsosin*

*Ruus is simply a mage who has found fortune and disaster in his life, but one who always strove to do what he thought was right.*

*With these things in mind, you must understand that I do not know all. Yes, the prophecy came through me, and I had many visions in conjunction with it, but I am fallible. It is a great feat to ferret out details of events centuries hence and in that respect, I am no greater than the lowest street charlatan claiming sacred knowledge of all things. Should some of what I have written here, or in any other place, be incorrect, please be gentle in your thoughts of me. I did the best I could.*

*One must understand the way prophecy works, how visions may be prophecy, simple foreseeings, even scryings. Where I know for sure what something means, I will state so in these pages. Other things I may have misinterpreted completely. There are many moving parts to the mechanism of the universe, and I have had the opportunity to glimpse a small number of them. There are great mysteries, even involving the prophecy and its fulfillment, that I have missed, I am sure. I can only apologize for my lack.*

*I beg your pardon for my casual style in this tome. I felt it better to organize it and execute it as a letter to a friend I have never had the privilege to meet rather than a treatise on magical studies. It may, perhaps, be easier to read. With no idea if you are a great scholar or a simple man like myself trying to do what the world requires of you, I hope the manner in which this book is written agrees with you.*

*How I long to be able to actually speak with you, brave Malatir-say, but alas, time cannot be defied no matter how fervently one yearns for it to be. Again, my thanks for your service to Dizhelim. I wish I could have done more for you, but I find myself unable to meet my own expectations. Please take solace in this, for I am sure you have felt like emotions, and perhaps are doing so even now. Read, then, and benefit from what you can, ignore what is not valuable, and most of all, share your knowledge, feelings, and fears with good friends and family, for those are what will strengthen you and make you victorious in the end.*

. . .

As always, reading what the Prophet had written sent a shiver up Aeden's spine. Tsosin Ruus, undoubtedly the most important person who had ever lived, sounded like someone he would really enjoy having tea and chatting with. If a man like that could claim he hadn't done enough—not with penning the most important prophecy ever, not with all his inventions and research, not with creating the great Academy—how could Aeden be sorry that he felt inadequate for the tasks he'd been given? He had a group of masters, an entire school, and even a book written by the Prophet personally to him to help with what he had to do. What did Tsosin Ruus have?

Good friends, the family he chose. No wonder he gave Aeden the advice to stick close to his friends. From what the Croagh understood, everything else was against the Prophet, even his blood relatives. It staggered Aeden to think about it.

Flipping back to the page he had translated the last time he studied, Aeden arranged the book of blank pages Evon had given him, moved his ink bottle a few inches to the right, and took a breath. His mind was in the right condition now. It was time to learn more of what the Great Prophet had written for him.

Aila slid to a stop before reaching the gate and the dozens of waiting trebaxels. She backed away toward her friends, thankful the gate guards didn't follow her. Apparently, it was the big trebaxel's job to kill the humans. How great for them.

Conren glanced over at her when she reached him. He flicked his eyes toward the gate, then back to her. "No way out?"

"No. At least the masses of trebaxels seem like they're fine with watching us be torn apart by their leader rather than doing the job themselves."

Tere and Lily, their quivers significantly less full than they were the last time Aila looked, joined her and Conren. Strangely, the monster they were fighting paused to watch them.

"We can't get out," she told the archers. "They blocked the gate and they're all over the tiers, so even if we could get up there, we couldn't climb over the wall."

"We fight, then," Tere said. "There's nothing else we can

do. There doesn't seem to be any kind of negotiation possible."

"That thing is too strong," Conren pointed out. "How can we fight something like that?"

"There's more than one kind of strength; otherwise, the one who can lift the most would always win. I've proven countless times that doesn't happen."

"Yes, but...oh, fine. Arguing will make no difference. Maybe if we take down the big one, it will scare the others away." The knight stretched his neck to each side, a popping sound coming from it. "It's not like a Clavian Knight is going to cower and wait for an enemy to end him."

"That's the spirit," Aila said. She dropped her pack next to Scrapper, who was still face-down on the ground.

"The flowers," Lily said, pointing at Aila's discarded pack.

Aila shrugged. "They'll be waiting there after we take care of this big gorilla. The weight will only slow me down."

The others deposited their packs on the ground near hers.

The huge trebaxel had finished watching them and plucking out arrows from assorted places on its body. It glared at them, glanced briefly at Scrapper's prone form, and roared at them again. It deepened its stance, like it was getting ready for something, probably a charge.

"See you on the other side?" Aila said.

"Definitely," Lily said. She felt around the fletching of the arrows left in her quiver. There were four of the red ones Aila could see and they apparently felt different, because the red-haired archer paused when her hand found each one. "Four," she whispered.

"Make 'em count, girl," Tere said.

The trebaxel started at them at an easy lope, building speed as it went. With the size of the thing, it wouldn't take too many steps until it reached them.

Three of the humans scattered. Sir Conren Gardner hefted his shield and ran directly at the monster.

"Conren, no," Aila screamed. She got a wink in response.

Aila and Lily peeled off to the right, while Tere went left. By the time the knight and the trebaxel were to meet, Aila already had her vinci circling so fast they were whirring. She lengthened the chains on them and jerked them at the precise time needed, causing them to arc sharply and slash at the trebaxel's face. Meanwhile, arrows flew from two bows in a similar trajectory.

Just before the beast and Conren would slam into each other, one of Aila's blades cut above the big left eye of the creature. A few inches lower and the vincus might have taken the eye, but the sudden sting and blood was enough for the trebaxel to jerk its head by reflex.

Which changed its running trajectory. Just enough.

Conren did a masterful job in spinning and redirecting the glancing contact with the monster. The slight impact didn't affect the trebaxel at all, but it buffeted the knight and spun him off to the side, knocking him to the ground in a roll. He regained his feet quickly and seemed no worse for wear, while the monster slid to a halt, looking around in confusion.

Aila let out a breath and focused on directing her blades. The vinci were a versatile weapon, useful in close range all the way out to fairly long range. The motion of the weapons when she let the chains grow long could be erratic and was difficult to manage. Nearly twenty feet from the monster, she needed every bit of skill and concentration to keep the blades under control, especially when she used both at the same time. One strange bounce or deflection and she might cut into herself. That was never a good thing.

"The eyes," Tere said. "We need to get the eyes."

Aila's first thought was to spit out a sarcastic response,

but she let it go. She could be witty and abrasive later. For now, their lives depended on their teamwork.

"Distraction coming up," Lily said. "Not sure what it'll do, but get ready." Her arm blurred and a flash of red left her bow, growing in size and intensity as it sped through the air.

Aila spun, harnessing her own momentum and feeding it to her spinning blades. At precisely the moment Lily's arrow struck the trebaxel in the chest and exploded, the vinci laid down two deep cuts in the left side of the monster's face. She'd missed the eye by more than two feet.

She spat curses at the monster, her weapons, and life in general, but mostly at herself.

What her attack—and Lily's—had done, though, was to open up the right side of the trebaxel, now that it had turned around to search for Conren again. A perfectly placed arrow loosed by Tere punched into the creature's right eye. It screamed in frustration and pain, swatting at the site of impact and blinking both eyes rapidly. The motions apparently dislodged the arrow, or maybe pushed it all the way in, but the damage was done. Tears mixed with a gush of other fluids and a gel-like substance from the eye.

It wasn't clear if the eye had been blinded, not until Conren sprinted around to the right side of the creature and took a risk by charging it. The other three paused for a moment, Aila's weapons spinning around her but not seeking out the monster, and the two archers holding nocked arrows. It was long enough for Conren to slash wildly at the trebaxel's leg, placing a long red line along the thick, furry hide.

The monster swung its head around, but didn't seem to spot the knight until it turned enough so its left eye could find him.

"Right eye blind," Tere pointed out. "Get the other one and we can put this thing down. Eventually." The last word was a lot softer than the others and Aila didn't think they were meant to hear it.

The trebaxel caught sight of Conren with its good eye and swung a long arm out so fast, the knight couldn't react more than bracing his shield with both arms. The limb slammed into him with a thud much deeper than the normal clang Aila was used to hearing. It launched him through the air. He sailed for a good twenty feet before landing and rolling on the sparse grasses of the stadium floor. He didn't move after that.

"Conren!" she screamed. "No!" Her vinci wobbled a bit in their flight, but she got them back under control. She needed to focus, to work with Tere and Lily to take the creature down. Once they did that, she'd see to the knight. Not before.

The thousands of hours of training with her weapons guided her body as she twisted, directing the chains to the ideal trajectory and speed. As the big monster turned toward her and Lily, Aila made the slight adjustments with her hands and wrists to flick the ends of the blades. Instead of slashing, the angles would cut deeper. Hopefully deep enough to deliver some real pain, if not serious damage.

Aila had guided the blades to the back of the creature's right leg, timed perfectly so that when it faced them, the vinci could swing around and cut with greater leverage. One then the other gashed the monster just above the knee. They struck almost simultaneously, one a fraction of a second after the other, cutting exactly where the first one had, but deeper. She hoped it was deep enough.

A roar of pain tore from the monster's throat, louder and more frantic than any they'd heard before.

But it didn't fall. All that work, and still it didn't fall.

Arrows pelted it again, most of them centering on its face, seeking its one good eye. It moved erratically, though, and without Tere's magical sight, the target was too difficult to reach. So far.

Aila tugged her weapons, correcting their spin and whirling them back under control. The monster came at her and Lily, limping but not crippled as she had hoped. *Nothing to do but keep trying*, she told herself, and danced to the side to swing her chain weapons with more force.

Lily used another of her fire arrows, exploding it near where Aila had cut, but the angle was wrong and though it blew a chunk out of the front of the leg, it too didn't cause quite the havoc Aila had been hoping for.

Finally, Aila was in position to attack again. The shallow cuts she could place quickly weren't going to do in this battle. Only the deeper cuts, over and over again in the same place, would do significant damage. She let fly with her vinci again, using the same tactic as before, overshooting the creature's leg and tugging back on the chains to cause the blades to arc back to where she wanted them to go.

She aimed for the exact same spot with both. The weapons were not quite as precise this time, perhaps fatigue affecting her performance. The first was an inch or two off from the previous cuts, but it still slashed deeper than the current wound. The second blade hit where she wanted it to go with a little tweak of her shoulder as she pulled back on the chain.

The vinci cut into the muscle, maybe into the tendon, too, and the monster's leg collapsed, pitching it to the ground.

The limping gait it had been using wasn't as fast as its normal speed, so the stumble didn't force it to roll or slide, but it did stop it for a moment as it tried to figure out why its leg wasn't working. Aila's friends took the opportunity to loose several arrows at the creature as it swung its head around, looking for what had caused it to fall.

It wasn't clear whose arrows struck the remaining eye first, but in a blink, as Aila shortened the chains on her weapons and observed the monster, three shafts punctured the orb.

The trebaxel's screams were now punctuated with heavy gasps as it fought with its panic at not being able to see when it was surrounded by enemies. Aila caught her vinci to rest her arms for a moment as Tere and Lily both ceased shooting arrows.

With its leg hamstrung and both eyes blinded, Aila wondered if they could escape, but the smaller trebaxels still had them trapped at the entrance. She raised her blades, ready to start them swinging again, when another screech from the monster and a flash of motion grabbed her attention with the effectiveness of a strong hand gripping her neck.

Dented shield held at an awkward angle, Sir Conren Gardner methodically cut at the trebaxel's face as it crawled along the ground toward where it had last seen Aila and Lily.

The trebaxels on the different tiers of the stadium were much quieter than they had been before, and Aila darted her eyes at them, more than half expecting the monsters to swarm the grounds and attack her and her friends. They didn't. They only peered intently at what was happening with their massive leader.

Conren moved woodenly as he tried to strike the big trebaxel from as many different directions as he could. The monster swung, almost connecting with the knight, who had dropped to the ground after his latest swing of the sword. He'd only be able to keep that up for so long. Eventually, the injured creature would overcome its panic and start thinking more clearly. Then it would start hunting the humans more intelligently, the closest first. Conren.

"Keep it busy, Conren," she yelled as she swung her vinci to generate the momentum needed for strikes that could injure the monster's tough hide. Tere and Lily, having finished their job of delivering critical strikes, harried the beast with their remaining arrows, but it was too big and its hide too thick for them to deliver a kill shot. Arrows landed on its neck and face, but the distance through its skin into vital areas was too far for the relatively tiny shafts to reach them.

Unfortunately, the only thing Aila and her friends could do was to whittle the monster down, try to keep it from making attacks that could kill the humans instantly, and hope that blood loss and accumulated injuries would eventually bring it down. It was a horrible way to go, a long and painful process. Bile bubbled up in Aila's throat. She killed when necessary, but this, this seemed unnecessarily cruel. She would end it quickly if she could, but it wasn't something she had the power to do. Not yet, anyway.

The process devolved into Conren cutting into the monster when he could, Aila helping from afar by slicing at wherever she could land slashes with her vinci, and the two archers almost lazily picking their targets and grouping arrows in whatever important locations they could. For now, that meant drilling the shafts into the back of the trebaxel's good leg.

The multiple injuries finally added up to a failure in the other leg of the monster. With both unable to bear weight, the once majestic and terrifying creature mewled piteously as it dragged itself with its arms, still crawling toward Aila. Lily had moved a distance away to find a better angle for her arrows, but the monster still came directly toward where she and Aila had been. Where Aila still was.

Blood matted the monster's fur, and it heaved wheezing, gasping breaths that sounded like ten blacksmith bellows all in concert. Still, it moved onward inexorably, though more slowly than before.

As if it sensed the futility of its actions, the trebaxel finally stopped its forward movement. It half curled and partially sat, panting breaths rattling in its massive chest. The smaller versions of the creature all around the stadium had grown completely silent, adding to the eerie sound of their dying leader. Not one of the other furred creatures moved, all sitting or standing stone still, watching the spectacle unfold.

The trebaxel brought its massive head around and with its ruined eyes, looked right at Aila. It couldn't see her, but she felt like it knew she was there. Did it blame her for its condition? She had damaged it, true, but so had her friends. Why was it so fixed on her?

A wave of sadness washed through her, threatening to overwhelm her. This creature, possibly hundreds or thousands of years old, the guardian of Sintrovis, didn't have long in the world. Aila couldn't feel complete sympathy for the monster, but it was only doing what instinct told it, after all. For it to die in such pain and ignominy affected her more than it probably should have.

The fireheart flowers. They'd found the remnants of some, mostly eaten. Was it a coincidence that a large garden of the flowers grew here, where the creature seemed to live? Could they bring it back from the brink of death? There were plenty left, even for a creature the size of the one in front of her. There was no real reason for it to have to die. She was so sick of everything always resulting in death.

Conren still stood, though shakily, next to the monster. His breaths were heaving as well, though more from exhaustion than injury, Aila thought. She let her vinci slow and then finally stop their swing and drop to the ground while she stared wide-eyed at the knight lifting his sword as high as he could to wind up for a massive strike. He'd dropped his shield and held the hilt in both hands. He planned to finish the creature, no doubt, with a final terrible thrust. Tere and Lily, forming up the corners of a square surrounding the creature with Conren and Aila, watched, arrows nocked but not drawn. Waiting for the end.

"Stop!" Aila yelled. "Conren, stop. Put your sword down."

At first, what she'd said didn't seem to register with the

knight. He threw out his chest while drawing in a great breath, then, after reaching the apex of his preparation, began to bring it down on the trebaxel, its neck exposed in its twisted, almost fetal position.

"Sir Conren Gardner, you will stand down immediately!"

The air of command seemed to get through and the knight stopped. His sweat and blood-streaked face turned to Aila. For a moment, the two locked eyes. Then Conren drove the point of his sword into the ground and knelt before it in a show of obeisance.

Aila let out the breath she'd been holding. With a thought, she drew her vinci back to herself, the chains magically shrinking until the hilts hit her hands. She ran and stumbled, heading just past Conren to where Scrapper was still on his face. Where Aila had dropped her pack. She didn't know if what she was doing would help, but something deep inside her told her it was right. Pack in hand, she stepped up to the dying monster.

The trebaxel leader cocked its head, as if hearing—or sensing—her coming near. When she reached in the pack and drew out a handful of whole fireheart flower plants, its nostrils flared at the scent.

"Aila?" Tere said. His voice, in a normal speaking volume, was easily heard in the silent stadium.

Aila felt tears tracking down her cheeks as she held the flowers out to the monster. There was a very good chance it would use its last bit of strength to crush her, and she would join it in death. She was suddenly fine with that. If she wasn't going to get the flowers back to her father, she might as well go, too. There was no way they'd survive if all the trebaxels attacked. Maybe showing a little kindness could buy them a chance.

But that wasn't the whole reason. She felt it, somewhere deep, that the creature before her was important. More important than her, even. If it died—thinking the flowers would heal it was a slim chance—at least it would know kindness before it went, after the torture of being whittled down like it had been.

A huge furry hand, shaking with effort, gently and surprisingly precisely, plucked the flowers from her hands and brought them to its mouth. In one swallow, they were gone. Aila wasn't sure if it was a trick of her imagination or not, but she fancied that its breathing eased at least a bit.

A jolt passed through Aila as the monster, which could have crushed her with one finger, adjusted its massive body. It groaned as it stretched its legs out, then hissed, moving its arms and twisting its trunk.

Dipping its head, the leader of the trebaxel laid flat on the ground, face in what was left of the blood-soaked grass.

In exactly the position Scrapper had taken and maintained for the entire battle.

"What...?" she said, but stopped when Tere's laugh rang out across the stadium.

"Surus's sweaty ass," Tere said. "It's submitting to you. More, it's showing respect—no reverence—for you. Some of the more intelligent animals on Dizhelim do similar things."

"Does...does that mean it's going to survive?" she asked. "Does it mean we won't be attacked by the others?"

"I have no idea. Gods, Toras Geint would have loved to see this, even if it was the last thing he'd ever seen."

The trebaxel wasn't finished yet, it seemed. It raised its head, as if it could actually see Aila with its ruined eyes. It reached up to its mouth and grunted as it snapped a section of one of its fangs off, nearly as big as Aila's forearm. Pinched in between a thumb and finger, the monster held it out to Aila. She took it without really thinking what she was doing.

The yellowed piece of tooth was rougher than she'd have expected. Deposits that looked like stone had built up on it over many years, allowing her to hold it easily though it was still wet with saliva.

"Uh...thank you?" she said, not sure herself if it was a question.

The trebaxel dipped its head again, putting its forehead against the ground. With a moan that sounded a lot like an old woman sitting down after being on her feet for hours, the trebaxel's body slumped.

The four humans stared at the monster they had fought. Scrapper, moving for the first time since he had dropped to the ground, lifted his head to join them in their silent vigil.

The trebaxel's body burst alight and exploded into different colored flashes so abruptly that Aila gasped. It only lasted a few seconds, and what had been a monster a few dozen feet long condensed into a gemstone of a familiar design.

$$\maltese \quad 35 \quad \maltese$$

Aila Ven stared at the gem the size of her palm floating in the air in front of her with no visible means of support. She'd seen multi-faceted glowing gemstones like that before. They had also materialized from a lightshow after some great danger had passed.

She found herself bobbing her head slightly in time with the gentle motions of the gem. This one was green. A deep, forest green, darker than any emerald she'd ever seen. Instead of light entering it and diffusing, however, it generated its own light, a soft glow that drew a sigh from her.

"It's all you, Aila," Tere said.

"I'd make it quick if I were you," Lily added. "No telling how long those trebaxel in the stadium will stay still. We did just kill their boss."

Conren's head swiveled back and forth from Aila to the gem, his mouth slack. He looked horrible, his face bruised and dried blood caking his lips and dribbling down his cheeks from some injury on his scalp. "Alevia...what are they talking about? What is that? Where did the monster go?"

She had to replay what Tere and Lily had said. They

hadn't made any sense until Conren spoke, shaking her from her dream-like condition. "Oh," she said, more to herself than the others. She scanned the stadium floor and finally found what she hadn't seen before. In the shaded alcove near where the massive trebaxel had been doing its boulder impersonation, a low stone wall circled a hole in the ground. It looked old, weathered, and yet perfect all at the same time.

She pointed to it and Conren followed the line of her finger until he spotted it as well.

"That wasn't there before."

"No," she said. "That's kind of what they do." She blinked, then slapped her palm to her own cheek. The sound made the stalwart knight jump. "You're right, Lily. We don't have much time." She stalked up to the gem, plucked it out of the air, and headed for the well and the indentation on its wall that she knew would be a perfect fit for the cool stone in her hand. "If you will, we're short a few fireheart flower plants. Grab some for me?"

Tere and Lily jogged over to scoop up their packs, then to the flower garden while Conren stared dumbly at everything and Scrapper gazed reverently at Aila. There was going to need to be some explanation soon, but at the moment, releasing the magic of the well and getting the flowers back to Aila's father were top priority.

If they could.

Despite the hurry, Aila paused for a moment in front of the well. She'd seen two of them released before, but standing in front of the ancient source of magic with the gem in her hand was a completely different thing. Her limbs trembled, her belly quivered, and even her breathing grew shaky. Who was she to have this honor, something the great heroes and scholars of history hadn't been given a chance to do?

She almost asked Tere to place the gem, or Lily. Maybe even Scrapper, who was more intimately tied into this place and this power than the rest of them. When she finally decided to do what needed to be done, it wasn't in any way that she thought she was worthy. It was simply the fastest way to be finished so she and the others could try to escape Sintrovis without being killed and bring the flowers to her father. She looked back at her friends. Tere and Lily had stopped to watch, both of them smiling. The hero who had been named Erent Caahs nodded toward the well. Conren still looked dazed.

Aila reached toward the indentation in the wall and released the stone when she felt it being tugged from her hand. It seated in the wall with a click.

Then, nothing.

Had she done something wrong? Had the well decided she was not worthy to place the gem? She looked into Tere's white eyes, her stomach sinking. His smile didn't slip an inch.

Light exploded out of the well, scaring Aila so much she jumped back and landed on her backside. As with the other wells she'd seen, the motes of light, thousands of bright little stars of all colors zipped upward, then, like a flock of precise and speedy birds, swept around the entire stadium, circling the inside starting at the top and funneling down almost to ground level. Once the cluster was barely higher than Aila could have touched it—had she been standing—the mass of flares shot straight up and exploded into the most fantastic fireworks display she'd ever seen.

It was even more beautiful than the others she'd witnessed, so many different shades of green mixed in with a lesser range of reds, yellow, blues, and handfuls of colors she didn't think she'd ever seen before. From the center of the explosion, a solid shape floated to the ground. She got to her feet, ran to snatch it up, and wasn't surprised at all to find a stone with symbols on its face. They didn't look carved, but as if they actually formed with the rock itself, faintly glowing but rapidly dimming in her hand until there was only the smooth lines of the design with a faint glow of pale green light within the center.

AILA BROUGHT THE STONE TO HER CHEST AND HELD IT there for a moment. She would think about it more later. For now, they had a mission to complete.

"Right. It's time we get out of here. If we can make it out quickly—and alive—we might be in time to save my father. Tere, Lily, you have more plants?"

"Got 'em," Tere said, closing up his pack and putting it on his back.

"Conren, are you well enough to run?"

The knight's eyes were still on the space where the lights had disappeared. He blinked at Aila repeatedly, almost as if his brain was chugging through what it had seen and trying to understand it. He nodded numbly. "I...yes." He straightened and winced from some injury or another as he did. "Yes, I'm ready."

"Good. I think maybe the other trebaxels are in shock as well. Let's leave before they decide they want to get revenge for us killing their leader."

All four headed for the entrance to the stadium. When

Aila reached where Scrapper was, she found him on his feet, his eyes unfocused.

"Scrapper?" she said. "If you think you're safe here, you can stay, but we have to go. If you want to come with us, you can do that, too." She held a hand out to the little trebaxel and his eyes fixed on it. His half grimace, half smile crept onto his face and he reached out for her. Aila was relieved that he was coherent. She'd been afraid that the trauma of what had happened had damaged him somehow.

The group jogged to the entrance only to be met with the same gathering of trebaxel that had been there before. They didn't attack immediately, but neither did they seem amenable to letting the humans pass.

"The tooth," Tere said. "Show them the tooth. Maybe the big one gave it to you as a trophy of your victory over him."

Aila pulled the piece of tooth from her pack and held it up. Sure enough, as the trebaxels caught sight of it, they all dropped to their faces on the ground, like Scrapper had done with the bigger monster. Like the leader had done at the end. She wasn't going to argue. They had a full day to make up.

Once outside the stadium, the group stopped. Aila looked out at the empty area between the stadium and the surrounding forest and realized she had no idea where they were in relation to how they had gotten there.

"Tere," she said meekly. "Please tell me you know how to get out of here, or at least find some familiar trail or something."

"The magic has settled down a little bit," he said, "so the interference with my magical sight isn't quite as bad as before. I can probably pick up glimpses of the trail we used to get here, though I don't think that's the best way to go."

"No? Why?"

"We came through that narrow passage, remember? If we go back that way, we'll have to figure out a way to get around that collapsed section we made to escape the trebaxels. That could take some time, if we could even do it. I know roughly the direction where we left the horses. If we head toward that, I think that'll probably be the fastest way out. If what you just did with the tooth lets us get through the trebaxels. It could have worked because they saw us defeat their leader and the tooth reminded them. Will it work with ones who weren't here and don't know what happened?"

"Good question," she said. "I guess we'll find out. Lead us where we need to go. We're in your hands."

"Come on, then. If we hardly sleep for the next couple of days, I think we can still make it. It's not going to be easy or fun."

The archer turned to his left and started walking quickly toward the forest. Aila bent down to let Scrapper onto her back and straightened with a huff of effort. "Not that I look forward to it or anything, but shouldn't you be running, or at least jogging?"

Tere shook his head. "No. We have a long way to go. If we go any faster than a brisk walk, there's no way we'll have the energy to make it all the way. As it is, we're starting a lot closer to exhaustion than I'd like. Trust me. I've traveled long distances my entire life, many times in a critical rush. Follow my lead and I'll get us there."

"We trust you," Lily said. Tere flashed her a smile and headed for the trees.

They'd only been in the jungle for an hour before one of the roaming bands of trebaxels came upon them. Upon seeing the humans, they charged.

## 36

L ily had taken over the burden of carrying Scrapper, for which Aila was thankful, for more reasons than her fatigue. It allowed her to swing the pack off her back and thrust her hand into it when the trebaxel patrol came at them. What happened next would set the tone for their entire trip out of Sintrovis. Or it might end that trip altogether.

Aila pulled out the piece of the monstrous trebaxel's tooth and held it up in front of her, toward where the group of creatures was sprinting at her. She prayed that it wasn't only a reminder to those that had been present that the humans had defeated the leader.

The closest trebaxel was little more than ten paces from them, tearing through the vines and plants, when it caught sight of what Aila held up. It slammed its heels into the vegetation and skidded to a halt. The others with it did so at almost the same time. Then, as one, they dropped to the ground, faces hidden in the plants. Their bodies heaved from the exertion, but not one of them looked up or made a sound other than their breathing.

Aila blew out a breath of her own. "Thank Vanda. It looks like the tooth is a recognizable symbol. Let's go, Tere."

The archer did as she asked, leading them toward a location only known to his sense of direction. Aila looked back several times to see if the trebaxels came after them, but within half a dozen paces, the vegetation swallowed them up and she didn't see them again.

So it went with every group of the creatures they saw. The larger ones patrolling, the mid-sized trebaxels in ranks guarding a particular room or passage, and the smaller variety manning the walls with their supply of stones for throwing. Aila's upraised piece of tooth was a talisman affording them respect and, more importantly, free passage.

Daylight turned to dusk and then to night, and Aila found herself unable to even react to simple things like recovering from her foot stubbing on a rock in her way. After the fourth time she picked herself up off the ground, Tere called a halt. Even he had slowed and their other two companions were in as bad a shape as Aila, Conren probably more so. The knight and Lily had been taking more turns at hauling Scrapper around and though they didn't complain, it was clear they were exhausted.

"We need to rest," Tere said. He raised a hand to forestall Aila's argument, which she'd already opened her mouth to make. "Trust me. We're all too fatigued to travel efficiently. It's dangerous. Even without the trebaxel attacking, there are other hazards. Remember the plants? We need to be aware, or we'll lose everything we've gained by moving too quickly. Just a few hours and we'll continue."

"How can we all rest?" Aila whined. And it was a whine. She was at her lowest point and didn't even care if she sounded petulant. It was her father's life they were talking about. "Who's going to keep watch?"

"We're going to have to trust Scrapper with that. He's the

most rested of us all. We'll have to rely on him making some noise if danger comes near."

Aila didn't like the idea, but she didn't have a better one. It *was* as bad as Tere said. The battles had taken so much out of them, and with the constant lack of sleep on top of it, she could see herself walking off a cliff or into a monster's mouth without even realizing it. She'd been catching glimpses of stranger creatures and shapes for the last several hours in the dark. If she was hallucinating, it was bad. Maybe as bad as if the monsters were real.

She tried to kneel in front of Scrapper, but both knees slammed into the ground, which was thankfully soft. Her legs didn't have the strength even to do a proper job of lowering herself. "Scrapper, we need to rest. Will you keep watch? Stay alert and tell us if danger comes close. We're too tired to continue. Will you do that, look out for something that wants to attack us?"

Scrapper did as he usually did, focusing on Aila's face and, especially, her mouth as she spoke to him. Aila wasn't sure how much he understood, but he made a good show of listening. As soon as she finished speaking, the little trebaxel set his mouth, lifted his chin, and swiveled his head to scan the surroundings.

It was good enough for Aila. She picked up his hand and stroked it. "Thank you. We'll rest for a couple of hours." She didn't bother finding a place to get comfortable. She dropped her pack, then plopped her head onto it like a pillow. The pervasive scent of the fireheart flowers wafted from within it, sweet and slightly spicy, with an added hint of crushed grass. It was the last thing she remembered as the world swirled around in the darkness of her closed eyelids.

"Aila, time to go," Tere said, jostling her. "Aila."

Aila's eyes snapped open to see a shadowy Tere move over to Conren to wake him. The sky looked lighter than when she'd laid down. Dawn must be no further than an hour or so away. "How long?" she called out to the archer.

"A little over two hours. Enough to survive, but not nearly enough to feel well rested."

He was right about that. She felt like someone had put a drug in her wine, without even having the benefit of drinking wine. She'd always feared that. The thought of being helpless so that anyone could do anything they wanted to her made her shiver.

The ill thoughts flew out of her head when she noticed that her pack had been opened. She must have rolled off it during her rest, because it was a few feet away from her. One look at Scrapper told her why it was open.

"Scrapper, did you take my flowers?"

The trebaxel looked down at his hands, which held the stalks of one of the fireheart flower plants. By the Vandictae's word, if he had eaten all her hard-gained plants...

She flipped the cover of her pack and rummaged around in it. It was still full of the plants. If the little trebaxel had taken any, it had only been one or two. He handed her the stalks and roots of the plant he was holding, a guilty look on his face. Maybe he'd only eaten a few of the flowers.

Aila accepted the offering and put it into her pack with the other plants. As she closed it up, she leaned forward to take a good look at Scrapper. He looked...better. Healthier, not quite so beaten down as he had. Compared to how he'd looked the last couple of days, he appeared to have had rest and food and lots of water. Yet he'd been awake and on watch. She tilted her head at the creature.

Scrapper, misunderstanding her posture, stood and backed a few steps away from her. He wasn't limping as pronouncedly as he had been.

"Scrapper," she said. "Do the flowers heal you? Do they make your injuries better?"

He looked at her quizzically, expectantly. She chuckled. The poor thing probably thought he was in trouble and that Aila was mad at him.

"It's fine. If the flowers are medicine for you, I can't blame you for taking a few. We have enough. I'm happy it made you feel better. Can you walk on your own now? Are you still in pain?"

Scrapper recognized that her tone wasn't an angry one, and he gave a little hop. He had to be feeling better if he could do that. He hadn't even been able to walk normally before.

"What's going on?" Conren said, eyeing the trebaxel.

"He ate a couple of the flowers. I think they healed him. It's no wonder they're so rare. They must be the most prized possessions of the trebaxels."

"He ate..."

"Only a couple of flowers. It's not a problem. I think he might even be able to walk without us carrying him now. Well worth what he took."

"I guess," the knight said.

Tere ostensibly led them toward where they'd left the horses as the sun came up. They couldn't see it, of course, from within the maze they'd traveled during the first part of their journey into Sintrovis, the part with the seemingly unending rooms and passages and high walls with the trebaxels posted around to keep them from passing.

They finally reached the end of the stone walls—or the beginning of them, depending on perspective. Either way, when Aila looked at the opening of the labyrinth over her shoulder as they left it, a sadness settled over her. She thought of the huge trebaxel, and though it may not have even been a real, living creature, its death seemed a tragedy. The others had agreed the guardians they'd faced were probably pure manifestations of magic that took on the appearance of intelligence, but they weren't truly alive. She wondered at that. If something lived and breathed and acted with its own will, what difference did it make if they spontaneously came to be or if they were born? The church had a view on that, but she pushed it from her mind. If she wanted to feel sad for the creature's loss, then she would, damn it. It had certainly demonstrated real pain and suffering.

"We're almost there," Tere said. "Be careful and mindful as we go through this last part. Remember the plants we ran into. We'll take another rest before we get to the horses, just to make sure we're aware as we go through the dangerous forest. We make it to the horses by midnight and we should be able to get back to Metrovial in time."

*Another rest?* Aila thought. *We can push through*. Then she remembered not so long ago when she couldn't even manage walking and thinking at the same time. If she went through the forest like that, it would be easy to walk right into some vicious beast or person-eating plants. Holding the tooth up wouldn't help them in that situation. She decided it was best to keep her internal complaints within herself. Tere knew much more than she did about traveling and heroing and probably everything else. She nodded, mostly to herself, but Tere spotted it and jerked his chin at her with a smile.

Luckily they didn't stumble into any other kinds of monsters. That was mostly Tere's doing. Even as it began to get dark, he had no trouble leading them on a hazard-free path, as long as they followed him carefully. After it got fully dark, they rested again, Scrapper watching over them. The little Trebaxel was tired also because he'd walked most of the day, but he took up a guard position without being asked and waved for the humans to lie down and sleep.

"Thanks, buddy," Aila said. Scrapper straightened, looking more regal than she'd seen him since they met.

When Tere woke everyone—the man had an uncanny

internal clock, as eerie as Jia's—they donned their packs and continued. At maybe an hour before midnight, they broke from the forest into a more civilized place. The moonlight seemed almost bright after the murky confines of the heavy vegetation. It was hard to tell for sure, but Aila thought she recognized the area. It was where they'd left the horses. Which was no surprise considering Tere's talents.

The problem was, their horses were nowhere to be seen.

❦  37  ❦

"**N**o!" Aila wailed. "No, no, no. We hurried and made it in time. We still could have made it back. All for nothing because someone stole our horses, or they escaped." She found herself on her knees, but didn't remember dropping.

"Alevia," Conren said from beside her. "Please." He put out a hand to help her up, but she petulantly slapped it away. Didn't he understand? Her father was going to die, even after all they'd suffered and sacrificed, just because she couldn't trust her kingdom to be honest enough to leave other peoples' horses alone.

Lily bent to bring her face close to Aila's. "Hey, it's okay. Don't take it so hard."

"Don't take it so hard? How would you feel if after all this, your father was going to die because of some stupid little twist of fate?"

Tere stepped up. "Let me try. Aila, get to your feet. We have traveling to do."

"How, Tere? How are we going to walk all the way back to the castle in time? We're exhausted and even if we weren't, it's too far and it'll take too long."

"You're going to quit, then? Just give up?"

"I..." Guilt stabbed her brain and heart, opening holes in the haze in her mind. Of course she wasn't going to give up. They were so close. They could do it. "No. Come on, let's go. We have work to do." She got up and stalked off toward where she was fairly sure the road was.

"Uh, Aila," Tere said. "Don't you want to take the horses?"

"What?"

"The horses. You know, hairy, four-legged, tail, mane, all that? They're over here."

Aila stopped and turned around, goggling at Tere. "They're...over...where?"

"They're this way. I checked on them while you were throwing your tantrum. They're restless, but they're fine."

"Oh." The sunburst that burned under the skin in her cheeks rivaled any of the fire arrows Lily had launched during their journey.

Once the problem with her sense of direction was resolved, the group mounted and after walking to the road, took off at a canter. Scrapper sat in the saddle in front of Aila, with her arms holding the reins on either side of him to prevent him from falling off. Though he had climbed up on the beast tentatively, he settled in quickly, stroking Muscade's mane and chittering quietly to himself.

During the ride back to the castle, Aila slipped in and out of awareness, sometimes snapping her head up as it started to loll. The fear of falling out of the saddle and breaking her neck by striking the ground at an awkward angle kept her just barely cognizant of what was going on.

The sky lightened and the sun came up ahead and slightly to the left of them. There was no way they'd get lost. The road they were on went directly to Metrovial. When they passed through the smaller towns and then farms, Aila grew excited. They were going to make it after all.

The castle came into view and Aila dug her heels into Muscade's flanks. She felt bad as she did it, since the mare had been keeping a pace between a trot and a canter for far too long, but she'd be able to rest soon enough. Just a little more...

Aila's addled brain was aware enough to stop her from leaping from the saddle while the horse was still in motion like she normally did. In her exhausted condition, she'd probably hit the cobbles and break a leg. Instead, she pulled Muscade to a stop and dropped to the ground, nearly kicking Scrapper in the face as she did so. She put her hands out to help the trebaxel down, then took off at a wobbling run into the front doors of the castle proper.

Some of the guards brought their weapons up when they saw Scrapper, but Aila yelled out, "He's with me. Do not lay hands on him or impede him in any way." Though it should have been sufficient, Conren had to bodily nudge at least two separate guards aside as they intended to do something anyway. The knight growled a warning and there were no further attempts.

Aila made it up the stairs to her father's room, not even noticing if the others followed her. She had enough of the flowers in her pack to do the job, as long as she could get them to Verona quickly enough. She burst in the door to find her father's still form on his bed, her mother in a seat next to it, and several people in what appeared to be a shouting match.

"There is still time," the silk-clad Elnaril Leovaris said. Aila always expected the man to be fingering the thin mustache on his lip, like all the villains in plays did. He, more than any one person on the King's Council, argued and fought with the king on nearly every issue. "Do not put him in his grave yet."

Sudin Torfan raised and then pushed his hands down. "Quietly, Elnaril, or are you trying to wake the dead in the tombs beneath the castle?" The heavy man wore much more sensible clothes, or at least more common ones. Loose pants and tunic of good quality and cut, though not silk. "I am merely trying to keep continuity with the crown. It's clear that—"

The three jumped when Aila slammed the door open so hard it hit the wall. Sudin's and Elnaril's eyes went wide with surprise, the latter reaching for a sword that was not on his belt.

Verona, however had a different reaction. "Aila. You...did you...?"

Aila swung the pack from her shoulders and opened it with trembling fingers. She reached inside and pulled out a handful of fireheart flower plants, their reds, yellows, and oranges in sharp contrast with the grey and dark blue rugs in the room.

"Gods," the Academy graduate said. "It's not too late." She grabbed them from Aila's hand without even a *beg your pardon* and took off running, no doubt toward her laboratory. It showed how troubled she was; the woman was usually the perfect picture of etiquette.

The shock of Aila's appearance—and those of her friends behind her—fading, Sudin licked his lips then gave her a weak smile. "You went into Sintrovis?"

"We did," Aila said.

"And you came out safely with some of the flowers?"

"Yes."

"Will they be enough, do you think? Medicines are tricky and a partial dose might only prolong things, not correct them."

Aila fixed her father's lifelong friend with a flat look. Why was he speaking like that, especially in front of her father and mother? He must have been very distressed, watching his friend and king die. "We have four backpacks full of flowers, plants, and roots. More than enough. Verona will do what she needs to do." As she glanced at her friends, she noticed Tere was missing. "Tere?"

Lily stepped up to her. "He told me he's going to go and help Verona, if she'll let him. He's a good herbalist and even if it's just boiling water, he said it might speed things up."

"Bless that man," Aila said, pressure building up behind her eyes. She was so tired, control of her emotions was a tenuous thing.

Elnaril did stroke his mustache then, a nervous gesture and not at all ominous. "Is there anything we can do to help?"

"Verona will take care of it. If you can keep from screaming in front of my father, you can wait here with us until she brings the antidote."

"Don't you think we should clear the room?" Elnaril asked, "allow your father some peace and quiet while he waits?"

"No, I don't. If you would like to leave, feel free. I will be here until he is healthy enough to leave his bed, no matter how long that takes." Aila stepped up to the bed and finally got a good look at her father. He looked worse than when they'd left, paler and more drawn. If it weren't for the rattling breath and his chest slowly rising and falling, she would have thought he was dead. She lifted his hand and kissed it.

"You did it, Aila," her mother said, her voice breaking in the middle as tears freshened the half-dried glistening tracks on her face. "You did what no one has ever done before, went into Sintrovis and came out alive."

"*We* did," she said. "To the very center. I'll tell you all about it when I'm not so...tired. I'll tell you and Father both."

Her mother wrapped her arms around Aila and sobbed into her shoulder. After a few seconds, her breath caught and she jerked her head up, releasing her daughter. Aila looked up to see what had caused the reaction and found her mother staring at Scrapper.

"What is that...thing? Guards, destroy that beast."

Aila's vinci were in her hands immediately as she moved—more quickly than she thought she could manage with how tired she was—to stand in front of Scrapper. Lily's long knives were in her hands as she stepped into the doorway to block the guards from entering the room.

"Stand down!" Conren shouted, drawing his sword. He turned to the queen. "Highness, please do not do this. This creature is friendly and helped us within Sintrovis. He is the reason we were able to find the flowers and to escape alive. I will not allow him to be harmed, even if it means disobeying the throne."

Aila glanced back at her mother. "We'll explain later. For now, if anyone tries to hurt Scrapper, I will kill him or her, whoever it may be. Don't make me kill our own guards, mother. Or council members. Do not."

The queen's eyes, still glimmering with tears, opened wider as her mouth dropped open. "Alevia?"

"I mean it, Mother. This is no game. Call the guards off or you will risk both them and me. Do not test me."

Aila's mother blinked, but then waved a hand. "Guards, take your positions. Do not attack. It's fine."

The two guardsmen snapped salutes to the queen, though their faces showed confusion. They resumed their positions at the wall, on either side of the door.

Aila scanned the room, her gaze stopping on Elnaril and Sudin, then she replaced her weapons in their sheaths. Her left knee trembled and she almost fell, catching herself on the bed. Conren whisked a chair to her and guided her into it. She gave him a grateful smile.

"Now," Aila said. "We wait."

## 38

While they waited for Verona to come back with the antidote for her father, Aila leaned to put her head on the edge of the bed. Within seconds, the swirling, dizzy feeling of plunging into sleep threatened to take her over. She jerked her head up to keep from losing consciousness.

"Alevia, darling," her mother said next to her, "it's fine. Let yourself get some sleep. You look like you haven't gotten any in days."

"Not yet. I need to be awake when Verona comes back with the medicine. Once I go to sleep, I don't think I'll wake up for at least a full day."

She sat up straighter, stretching out her lower back and twisting from side to side to loosen her muscles, which were settling into soreness from her frantic flight over the last day and a half. Lily and Conren sat in chairs at the edge of the room and Scrapper was on the floor near Aila, on the opposite side from her mother, napping.

"Where are Elnaril and Sudin?" she asked.

Her mother cocked her head at Aila. "They left a little while ago. They said goodbye to you."

"I must have already been half asleep."

"They said they had things to check on but would be back later, when Verona gave your father the antidote."

That made sense. The governance of the kingdom had essentially been on hold while her father was ill. Other than those new mandates that had her concerned, anyway. It made sense that the two men would be trying to cobble together some sort of structure to keep things running.

Aila's pack was on the floor near Scrapper. She looked at it, wondering if the trebaxel had eaten any more of her flowers. Surprisingly, lying on the floor near Scrapper, only his head protruding from under the bed, was Rumbler. The old hound seemed to be comfortable with the trebaxel. Even as she watched, Scrapper's furry hand went out and scratched the dog behind his ears. A soft thump from under the bed made Aila smile. That tail must be going at a rapid pace against the floor to make that noise.

"While you were...indisposed," her mother said, "Rumbler came over to sniff your monster. They became fast friends, it seems. I look forward to you telling me what that thing is and what it is doing in the king's room."

"He is not an *it*, Mother. He is a friend, which should be good enough until I tell both my parents the full story."

"Oh, very well."

Aila's eyes went back to the pack. How long had it been since they freed the other well? The stone she found, the one with the Cogiscro writing, was a lump in her pocket. She could feel it now that she concentrated on it.

"The tablet," she said suddenly. Scrapper's eyes opened and his head snapped up. "Sorry. I need to..." She dug through her pack and pulled out the message tablet, which at some point she'd taken from Tere and kept. Sure enough, there were messages there.

We just felt another magical shift. It didn't seem random. Tere, was that you guys?
--Marla

I'll second that. I felt something, too. Did you find another well?
--Aeden

Are you there? Tere? Aila? Lily? Are you all right? Talk to us. What's going on?
--Marla

You're starting to scare us. It's been over a day since the magical shift. Where are you? Please, write something, even a word or two.
--Marla

"Oh no," Aila said. She read the messages to Lily. "I'll answer them right now. I should have thought about the tablet before. They must be worried sick." She pulled the stylus from the side of the tablet and began to write.

I'm so sorry, everyone. Yes, we found a well. I have another one of those fancy Cogiscro stones for you, Marla. We weren't able to message earlier. After we

FOUGHT AN ARMY OF TREBAXELS AND THEIR FORTY-FOOT-TALL LEADER, WE HAD TO GET THE FLOWERS TO SAVE MY FATHER AND THEN ESCAPE SINTROVIS WITHOUT DYING TO MAKE IT BACK TO THE CASTLE IN TIME FOR VERONA TO MAKE THE ANTIDOTE.

WE HAVEN'T REALLY SLEPT FOR A COUPLE OF DAYS, BUT WE'RE SAFE. VERONA SHOULD HAVE THE ANTIDOTE ANYTIME NOW, SO IT MAY BE A WHILE BEFORE YOU GET THE FULL STORY. WE KIND OF HAVE A LOT TO TELL, INCLUDING SOME INFORMATION ABOUT CREATURES NO ONE HAS EVER RECORDED SEEING ALIVE. THAT LAST PART IS FOR YOU, EVON. I'M GUESSING YOU KNOW WHAT TREBAXELS ARE.

ONCE THE KING IS SAFE, WE'LL LET YOU KNOW WHEN WE CAN RETURN TO THE ACADEMY. WE MISS YOU.

--AILA


SHE READ OUT WHAT SHE HAD WRITTEN, MAINLY FOR LILY'S benefit and set the message tablet on the bed before rubbing her eyes. A few seconds later, the tablet flashed that there were incoming messages.


TREBAXELS? YOU ACTUALLY SAW TREBAXELS. I AM OFFICIALLY SCHEDULING SOME OF YOUR TIME WHEN YOU RETURN SO I CAN DOCUMENT EVERYTHING YOU CAN TELL US ABOUT THEM.

ALSO, DID YOU SAY SOMETHING ABOUT THE KING NOT BEING SAFE? WHAT'S GOING ON?

--EVON


AILA LAUGHED FOR THE FIRST TIME IN SHE DIDN'T KNOW how long. She read Evon's message, bringing a smile to Lily's face, too, though Aila's mother and Conren didn't see what was so funny. "Just wait until he realizes one of them is coming home with us." Scrapper lifted his head to her again and she patted the top of his head. "Evon is going to love meeting you, my friend." She reread her first message and sighed. She should have known better than to write it in haste while she was so exhausted. "Well, now is as good a time as any, I guess." She took up the stylus to respond.

YEAH, THE KING HAS BEEN POISONED. I KNOW IT'S CONFUSING BUT LET ME MAKE IT EASIER. THE KING OF THE GREAT ENCLAVE, JOCEUS DAVENSON, IS MY FATHER. LIKE MANY OTHER THINGS, I'LL HAVE TO EXPLAIN MORE LATER. GIVE ME SOME TIME AND I'LL ANSWER ALL YOUR QUESTIONS.

THOUGH SHE THOUGHT ANOTHER MESSAGE WOULD FOLLOW immediately, it didn't. She waited, but nothing appeared, so Aila shrugged and put it down on the bed again. After several minutes of trying to explain to her mother how none of her friends knew her real name—something Aila didn't see how she missed when they were in the castle before—the tablet indicated another message.

SO, YOU'RE A PRINCESS? A REAL, LIVE PRINCESS? IT FIGURES. COME HOME SAFE SO I CAN MAKE FUN OF YOU. FAHTIN SAYS SHE'S IN, TOO.

--JIA

. . .

AILA READ THE MESSAGE TO LILY, A FEW TEARS LEAKING from her much too emotional eyes. She wondered how she had ever done without such a marvelous magical means of communication, and how she had ever survived without such friends.

The door opened and Verona swept in, Tere right on her heels. Of all things the archer looked...worried. He closed the door again, shutting out the two guards waiting outside.

"Thank you for your assistance," Verona said, her blue eyes flashing. "That was...strange."

"I agree," Tere said, taking up a position next to Lily's chair and placing a hand on her shoulder. She put her own hand on top of it and smiled up at him.

"What's strange?" Lily asked.

Tere ran his other hand over his forehead. "While Verona was making the antidote, six soldiers came into her laboratory. They said they were there to help her. She told them it wasn't necessary and to leave. They looked at me and in my magical sight, I caught undercurrents of their desire to force the issue. It wasn't clear if they meant violence, but when I nocked one of my few arrows left and stared at them, they seemed to lose their nerve and reluctantly left. I locked the door, but I half-expected them to be waiting for us when we came out. They were gone, though."

Verona moved to the head of the bed as she spoke over her shoulder. "I didn't recognize any of them. I know there are new soldiers, but for none of them to be familiar is extraordinary, especially if they have a posting at the castle."

"Strange indeed," Conren said. "I will see what I can find out once things settle down."

"Thank you, Conren," she said. That would be a great help. She turned to the king and dribbled some of the liquid from a vial into his mouth. After she'd gotten about a fifth of the quantity in him, she held the glass container out to Aila. "Alevia, if you would help me?"

"Of course." Aila got to her feet and went around to the other side of the bed.

"I will be using magical healing on him. Please dribble more of the antidote into his mouth, just as you just saw me do. Between the magical healing and the neutralization of the poison, the king should get stronger. The more strength, the more easily he will be able to take more of the antidote. It is critical we build up his ability to fight."

"Ready," she said.

Verona's slender fingers made gestures that Aila took as those used for casting. Meanwhile, the daughter dutifully fed her father more of the potion. They continued for several minutes, until more than half the antidote had been given to the king.

Verona paused to tilt the king's head to get a better look at him. He already looked stronger than he had before, not quite so wan. His eyelids flicked as if they wanted to open but weren't quite able to yet.

"Good," Verona said. "It's working. Just a little bit more." She went back to casting and Aila gave her father more of the liquid.

Finally, the king's eyes opened slowly. They focused on Aila's and his tired face stretched into a smile. "Alevia?"

"Don't speak yet, your highness," Verona said. "Use your strength to drink the rest of the antidote. We've a way to go yet."

He opened his mouth and watched as Aila tilted the vial to his lips. She was able to do it at a faster rate than before, the king almost sucking it out of the bottle. With each second, between the antidote and Verona's spell, he was better able to drink it down. When the vial was empty, Aila set it to the side and took up his hand. His other was already clasping the queen's.

A few more minutes of Verona's magic, and the Academy graduate stopped her gestures and the words of power she'd been chanting. She slumped slightly for a moment, but then straightened back to her normal perfect posture.

"It is done. I can sense no trace of the poison left in your body. I have helped to strengthen and heal you where I could, but now you need food, water, and restful sleep. I would think you will be up and about—in moderation—in a few days." Her stern expression left no doubt that she would enforce that moderation.

Aila huffed out a breath like she'd been holding it for a week, and more tears flooded her eyes. Damn emotions. She needed to get some rest herself or she'd be weeping like one of the weak court ladies who'd never fought a battle in their lives.

"It is to you—and your friends—that I owe my miraculous recovery?" the king asked her.

"It's to Verona you owe that," Aila said, "but yes, we were successful in finding the flowers. I promise to tell you all about it once you've had more rest. And we've had some ourselves. We're happy we could help out."

Joceus Davenson narrowed his eyes at his daughter. "You truly will go to any length to avoid taking over the governance of the kingdom, won't you?"

Aila laughed and threw her arms around him. "You know me too well."

Verona stepped aside while the queen took her turn in hugging the king.

"Thank you, Verona," he said, putting his arms weakly around his wife. "You are a magnificent friend and ally, as always." The woman bowed her head to him.

The door opened again, this time with less urgency, and

Elnaril Leovaris stepped through the opening. He saw the king, awake and lucid, and dropped to his knees. "My king, you have regained your health."

"Get up, Elnaril. You argue fiercely with me every chance you get, and it does not become you to go to your knees."

The man did so, then joined the others crowding around the king's bed. "It is miraculous. I've been told that the poison you were afflicted with is incurable, yet here you are, brought back from death's very door."

"I have, but I still have some more to heal. Please continue your good work. No doubt you and the rest of the Council have been taking up the slack from my unfortunate absence."

"We have been doing what we can. I will alert the other Council members that you are on the mend. They will be ecstatic to hear it."

"Thank you. I will want to meet with them tomorrow afternoon. I have been ordered to remain in my sickbed for the time being, so I ask they come here to see me."

"Of course, Highness. I will handle it."

"Elnaril?"

"Yes, your majesty."

"I appreciate your etiquette while I convalesce, but I expect you to fight just as powerfully as you always do once I am back in fighting form."

The man's pointed face jerked into a smile. "Of course, your majesty. I would have it no other way."

Elnaril left the room, leaving only Aila's friends, her mother, Verona, and Conren Gardner. The king took a deep breath and a smile crept to his face. "Vanda's strong right arm, it feels good to be able to breathe without pain, even if I'm not as hearty as I'd like to be. Where's Rumbler? Don't tell me that old hound has abandoned me in my time of need."

"He's under the bed, Father," Aila said. "He's been playing host for a friend I brought back from Sintrovis."

The dog wriggled out from under the bed, licking Scrapper once on the face before putting his paws up on the blankets to greet the king. While he petted the dog, Joceus eyed Scrapper.

Verona, who had been too occupied with saving the king to notice the furry creature at the foot of the bed, started. "Is that a...baby trebaxel?"

Aila gave the woman a tired smile. "We have some things to tell you all. You're not going to believe most of it."

## 39

"Then the huge trebaxel exploded into lights and gave us the stone for the well," Aila said. "I put it where it was supposed to go in the wall around the well and we had the firework show that happens every time we unlock the magic from a well. When it was done sending all its magic out into the world, it left us another Cogiscro stone."

Aila's mother and father stared blankly at her with near identical faces, mouths open. Verona handled it more professionally.

"Cogiscro?" the Academy graduate asked.

"Yeah," Aila said. "The wells always leave a stone with Cogiscro script on it. We think it's the name of the well. Marla can read it, so she's keeping track of what they all say from the wells we've found so far. I'll give this one to her when we get back to the Academy."

"Marla Shrike?"

"Yep. She knows that symbol language."

"Of course she does. May I see it?"

"Sure." Aila took the stone from her pocket and handed it over.

"I studied Cogiscro when I was at the Academy," Verona said, running her fingers over the stone. "Not many did. It's considered dead, though the schools of artifice still use the symbols for enchantments sometimes. Ah, Sintrovis."

"What about it?" Aila asked.

"That's what the stone says. Sintrovis."

Tere barked a laugh and Aila frowned. "That's not as dramatic or exciting as I would have expected."

Verona chuckled and handed the stone back. "Why would the stone say anything else? You said the—wells?—left a stone with their name."

"I thought it would be, I don't know, more mysterious than that. More powerful, maybe?"

"Do you know what Sintrovis means?"

Aila barely refrained from rolling her eyes. "Of course. Everyone who grew up in the Enclave does. It means *center of strength*."

"Which, I believe, is a perfect name for the well. I didn't know what it was earlier, but I felt the magic rush into the world. I thought it was another one of those strange magical shifts we've been having, but it...felt like strength to me. I'd say somehow whoever named the place in ancient times felt the power or an affinity for strength-related magic. They gave the place a name they thought fit, and they turned out to be right. There is still so much I don't know or understand about what's going on."

"You and us and all the masters at the Academy," Aila said. "It's a work in progress."

"Alevia," the king said. "Will you tell us what happened after you freed the magic from the well? I sense we're coming to the end of the story, but I would like to hear it, if you can manage it before you curl up and go to sleep. I am tired, but you look exhausted. I would have you sleep soon."

"We *are* pretty tired. Let me give you the short version of how we got out of there and made it here in time for Verona to make your antidote."

Aila—with help from the others—finished their story without leaving out too many details. Satisfied that she'd told them enough to sate their curiosity for the time being, she took her father's advice and went to her room to sleep. She was so tired, she didn't even think about taking a bath first, even though she was certain she didn't smell as a lady should, let alone a princess.

After sleeping for a solid twelve hours, taking the long-delayed bath, and eating enough for several people her size, Aila escorted Tere and Lily back to her father's room. Her mother greeted her with a hug, as did her father, though he was still in bed. The queen had changed clothes as well and from the look of her, had gotten some sleep herself.

Scrapper, who had followed her around and curled up on the floor of her room to sleep, moved easily. The rest and the fireheart flowers he had eaten helped him recover. The little trebaxel greeted Rumbler with a few soft chitters and some pets, which started the hound's tail swinging so fast Aila could hear it cut through the air.

"Do you feel better?" her father asked. "I understand you slept well and have eaten and bathed."

"I feel much better than yesterday," she said. "It'll take me a few more days of regular sleep and eating to get back to top form, but the traveling from here to the Academy won't be hard and we can stay in inns, so it'll be fine."

"To the Academy?" he asked. "Alevia, you just returned. We haven't had any time to catch up, nor for you to learn what you need to know about ruling the kingdom. Other than what you were taught when you were younger."

"Father, you're fine now. You'll continue to rule for decades. There's no reason for me to rush. Besides, what I'm doing is important. We're working toward saving all of Dizhelim, not just the Enclave."

The king inspected his hands for a moment, his mouth in a straight line. "I do know it's important, but so is family. You've been away for years and now you'll leave again?"

"This time I won't be hiding," she said. "I can stop by when we're near and I can write. You can write, too. I'll be living at the Academy when I'm not out on missions. Speaking of which, the reason I came here was to discuss you committing Clavian forces to the defense of Dizhelim, making an alliance with the Academy to fight the animaru."

"Of course," he said. "I would have pledged support even if it weren't you who brought the message to me. I have heard enough about what is going on in the world to join the cause to protect not only the Enclave, but all nations. I will sign the documents you brought and have my scribes make copies within the day."

"Thank you."

Aila's mother wasn't going to let go so easily, though. "Alevia, why do you insist on standing at the front lines of this conflict? A wise ruler or general performs her actions from behind the lines of her soldiers. Doing what you plan is too risky. You are too—"

"Weak?" Aila asked. "Is that it, Mother? I'm not strong enough to fight, to do what I know is right? My friends, all of us, do our part, which includes fighting the animaru. We even have a young man, a teenager, who stands with us and battles with the monsters. No one calls him weak, yet you have always thought me so."

"No, please. That's not it. I don't think you weak. I only..."

"If not weak, at least not strong. For years, I have fought

with that, wondering if I lacked strength, if I was capable of doing heroic things. Even going into Sintrovis, your words to me repeated in my head. In the center of strength, I felt keenly my lack of strength."

"You are strong," Conren Gardner said, entering the room dressed in his crisp uniform. "Stronger than me."

The queen turned to the newcomer. "Stronger than...?"

"In Sintrovis, Alevia was the one who held us together. When I acted unwisely, putting our companions at risk, she disarmed me and knocked me to the ground until I realized my error. Despite all the dangers and injuries, she fought until the end. I thought I knew strength before, but I was mistaken. Our journey has impressed upon me that there is strength other than that of the arms. On all accounts, the princess is one of the strongest people I have ever known. It nearly makes me pity these animaru that they will do battle with her."

Aila's mother was speechless. Her father smiled at his daughter. Aila silently wished the heat in her cheeks would disappear.

"I am glad to hear you say that, Sir Conren, because I have a new charge for you, a new assignment. Henceforth, you will accompany my daughter on all these missions she undertakes for the masters of the Academy and the alliance they are forming. You should consider this not only a privilege, but the most serious posting you have ever received."

Conren snapped to attention and saluted the king. "I do consider it as such, your majesty. Thank you for your trust in me."

"Do your duty, and that will be more than enough for me."

"Your majesty, about that issue that was discussed earlier...Verona tells me that she has done as you asked. She...uh, is sorry that it turned out as the Council had feared."

"You may speak in front of my daughter and her friends," the king said. "No need to be vague."

"Yes, your majesty. Sudin has in fact fled, taking along more than a dozen soldiers, including those who confronted Verona and Tere in her laboratory. The Council has reversed the laws he enacted on your behalf during your...difficulties."

Aila whirled toward her father. "What? Is he saying what I think he's saying?"

The king sighed. "It is. We had a meeting while you still slept. Apparently, Sudin orchestrated the entire thing. He had Altor create the poison, though he didn't tell our resident Council scholar and part-time alchemist who it was for. When Altor found out, essentially the same time everyone else realized I'd been poisoned, he was too scared to tell anyone. At least, that is what he currently tells us. We have him in a cell, but Sudin took the opportunity of the distraction of your return and my healing to leave."

"Sudin? But he's your oldest and closest friend. How could he do such a thing? I'd have suspected Elnaril, who dislikes everything you say and do."

"Sometimes life doesn't spin out as you would like, or expect. Sudin already had in place plans for what to do when I died. He was counting on you not making it back from Sintrovis, but if you did, he would have tried to eliminate you, too, no doubt. It saddens me, but if he's caught, our friendship will not stay his execution. He has proven a traitor not only to me, but to the entire Great Enclave."

Compared to the happiness of her father's regained health and the success of her mission, Sudin's betrayal made her feel like she'd swallowed a palm-sized stone whole and it had lodged at the opening to her stomach.

"Enough of such things for now," the king said. "Conren, please have Verona attend me at her earliest convenience.

Until then, I would like to hear more about my daughter and what she has been doing for the last several years, especially most recently, when she seems to have joined a very exclusive group of heroes of the world. I would hear the tale from her own mouth before the books and songs are written."

❧ 40 ❧

ila stayed at the castle for three more days, resting up and catching up on family time. Tere contacted Senod and made dinner arrangements to visit with him. When Tere showed up with a Clavian Knight and the princess of the kingdom herself, not to mention the up-and-coming heroine with the flame-red hair, the former thief handled it with such professionalism, Tere slapped the man on the back and congratulated him.

The documents outlining the alliance between the Great Enclave and the Hero Academy were signed and copied, the originals provided to Aila in rigid leather tubes to protect them.

Finally, the time to leave came and the group gathered for one final meal. The king's recovery was nearly complete, and he had no trouble attending the dinner in one of the smaller dining rooms set within the part of the castle where the royal family lived.

It all passed in a whirlwind for Aila, who didn't quite get used to others calling her by her real name. In the blink of an eye, it was time for them to get on their horses, go to

Gemsport, and take the ferry back to the western docks on Munsahtiz. From there, it was a short ride until the walls of the Academy greeted them.

The homecoming wasn't as extravagant as their farewell in Metrovial, but that was fine with Aila. She'd had about enough of state affairs and formal celebrations. A simple meal with her friends in Batido's common room suited her, even if half her friends teased her about being a princess and many of them pressed questions on her for the details of her story.

Raki seemed like he'd grown. Not in physical height, but there was something more solid about the boy, like he'd filled out, and something deeper. Gone was the goofy, shy impression she had of him. He seemed almost heroic, if a teenager could be so. At least until he begged her multiple times to tell her stories for the daily story time. Some things wouldn't ever change, she thought. Nor would she want them to.

As she had expected, Evon was jittery with excitement at seeing Scrapper. The young Academy graduate spent almost the entire evening talking to the trebaxel. The way he did it, not as if he was trying to communicate with an animal but as if he was trying to come to some common ground with a foreign visitor, generated a ball of warmth in Aila's chest.

"Master Qydus would like to meet with everyone tomorrow," Aeden said. "Mostly it's going to be about you lot and your mission to the Great Enclave, but he said there's some news, too. We've been having meetings every few days to keep up with the things happening around the world. It's heating up."

After a good night's sleep in her own bed—Scrapper shared her room though he was going to be given one of his own next to hers, and Conren had been given the one on the other side of her—she joined the others in the headmaster's meeting room.

Watching the headmaster interact with Scrapper was even

better than watching Evon do it. Master Qydus had a way of speaking few words, but with such perfect intonation, in what sounded like some flavor of Alaqotim, the little trebaxel came alive. He chittered and pronounced long strings of sounds that Aila hadn't heard, all while the headmaster nodded and kept his attention firmly nailed to the furry creature.

When there was a break in the conversation between the two, Master Qydus cleared his throat and addressed the others present. "Very well. I will continue my conversation with our new friend later." He nodded toward Scrapper, who leaned back in his chair to emulate the others around the table. "We are all here, so we should get started. First, some introductions."

The headmaster introduced the masters present: Yxna, Isegrith, and Chesaren Golurn, an absolute bear of a man who filled his seat with his massive frame, causing it to creak every time he moved. He was the Master of the College of Woodcraft, but the headmaster explained that the school's purview also included flora and fauna. Chesaren waved a hairy arm at everyone and the great shaggy beard on his face shifted to show a glint of his white teeth as his eyes crinkled slightly.

Master Qydus introduced Aila and all her friends, more as a formality. He also introduced Scrapper, who comically raised a hand in acknowledgment as he'd seen the others do. And he identified Conren also, not differentiating him in any way from the rest of them and, of course, using his proper title as a Clavian Knight.

"Now that we all know each other, I think we should start with a complete account of your mission. Aila, Tere, Lily, please satisfy our curiosity."

The three did as asked, and after the comments Aila knew would be coming, ones about answering further questions on

Sintrovis or access to Scrapper, they moved on to things that Aila hadn't known.

"With the alliance with the Great Enclave, brokered by our own Princess Alevia Davenson, also known as Aila Ven, we are building our forces in preparation for the war," the headmaster said, giving Aila a wink at her title. "Aeden can give us a summary of what situation the Croagh clans are in as well. Master Goren is working on the strategy for the campaign, with the help of others.

"I want to report also on a decision by the masters, one we do not take lightly. In two days' time, we will proclaim across Dizhelim that we are calling back all graduates of the Sitor-Kanda Academy. What we face is unprecedented in history, and we will need every person who has magical skills and training from this institution."

"You...you're calling them back?" Marla asked. "Everyone?"

"We are." He looked right at Aila. "Though special dispensation is being made for Verona Gilcaryn, seeing that she is posted with our new ally."

"What will happen with those who are now Falxen or the ones who are opening portals for the animaru, or those who work with the Dark Council?" Evon said.

"We would not expect them to return, child," Master Isegrith said. "We have no way to force those we seek to come. We can only mandate that they do so and hope that most do."

"It could open the door for our enemies to come back within the walls," Aeden said. "We've faced enough former Academy students to know there's a risk."

The Master of the School of Fundamental Magic nodded. "It is possible. We will sound the call and watch carefully. Any who would take advantage to infiltrate our ranks would most likely do so without the summons in any case. We stand to regain many fine warriors and mages, something we cannot overlook."

"As I said," the headmaster pointed out, "the call will be made. We have discussed the positives and negatives thoroughly. The decision will not change now. More than ever, we need all the expertise, experience, and skill that is the result of the training of this Academy. It may not affect any of you or your work, but it may also. We merely wanted to keep you apprised of what will occur."

The meeting lasted for several hours, and by the time it was finished, Aila felt as if half the energy in her body had been sucked out. Finally leaving the administration area, she let out a breath, only to hear clipped words from behind her.

"I don't care," Marla said to Evon. "It's not something you have a say in. Mind your own business."

"I'm sorry, Marla. I just wanted to—"

"I don't have the time or energy for this," she said, cutting him off. "I have things to do."

The red-haired star of the Academy stomped off, leaving the whole group watching her in shock.

"What was that about?" Fahtin asked Evon.

The young man looked shaken and a little pale. "Nothing. It's...she's been having a rough time lately. I think the tension of everything that's going on is getting to her. She'll be fine when she cools off. I've had to watch every word I've said to her the last couple of weeks."

"I've noticed she's been wound up tight, too," Aeden said. "I'll go talk to her."

"Please don't," Evon said. "I've basically grown up with her. It's best to let her calm down when she's at this point. Usually, I can catch her before it escalates and we can talk it out, but when she's at this point, it's better—safer—to let her be."

Aeden didn't look convinced. Aila thought he would go after her anyway. He closed his eyes and shook his head slowly. "Okay. If you say so, I'll leave her alone. Codaghan knows the Croagh are not known for talking their feelings out. I only know about it because of the Gypta."

Fahtin crossed her arms under her breasts and gave Aeden a wide smile.

"Still," Aeden continued, "I'm worried about Marla. You've seen her like this before, Evon?"

"Maybe not quite as bad as right now, but there is a lot going on. Give her a little time to cool down and then—"

Evon had turned his attention from Aeden to the path they were on. His mouth stayed open, though his words had cut off. Aila turned to see what he was staring at.

A young woman was coming toward them, gliding down the path as smoothly as water flowing over a round rock. She wore long boots that reached to her lower thigh, and her toned upper legs were bare until the shorts she wore below a tight blouse with loose sleeves. Slung across her chest was a strap holding—of all things—a lute. Her sandy blonde hair floated freely loose around her thin, attractive features on the gentle breeze, and poking through were sharply pointed ears.

Aila found herself staring with her mouth open as well. A quick look around, almost painful because it meant her eyes leaving the woman, found everyone else similarly enraptured. Even Tere, with his white eyes opened wider than normal.

"Saria?" Evon whispered and the woman, who hadn't bothered to give her attention to them, looked up. Her eyes were a color Aila had never seen on a person, a soft lavender.

The woman blinked, her expression neutral, until her eyes narrowed the slightest bit and she broke into a smile. "Evon? Evon Desconse." She quickened her steps to reach them and stopped in front of the group. "My, you've grown since I saw you last."

"Saria, how? Why?" Evon shook his head, his blond hair looking, if anything, more stylish from the effort. "Oh, sorry. Uh, Saria Gilwenys, these are my friends." He named them off and each gave a wave or a nod to her. "Aeden, Fahtin, Aila, Jia, Tere, Lily, Raki, Urun, and Khrazhti. Oh, and Scrapper. Everyone, this is Saria. She graduated around five years ago and went out into the world to seek her fortune."

Saria acknowledged each of them, pausing as she looked at Tere and stopping altogether when she beheld Khrazhti. "It's nice to meet you all. Where are Marla and Skril, Evon? Once, I would never have thought of you being anywhere without at least one of them." She smiled wryly, as if sharing a secret joke with Evon.

The flush that was so familiar on Evon's face deepened and his eyes grew sad. "Skril is...was killed by Quentin Duzen, who was working with the animaru—the dark creatures that are invading Dizhelim." He cleared his throat, his eyes misty. "You just missed Marla. What are you doing back, Saria? You said you wouldn't return."

"Things change," she said. "So, they are actually animaru. From the Prophecy? With what has been happening, I decided I would offer my services to the masters, if they had use for me. I'm on the way to talk to the headmaster now. Still Master Qydus, I presume?"

"Yes. We just had a meeting with him. Talk with us before you go off on some mission? We'll be at Batido." He shook his head again. "Oh, I mean Southwest Dormitory Twelve. The masters have given it to my friends for their use. We've named it Batido, which—"

"—means second home in Dantogyptain. Yes, I know. Perhaps in honor of your Gypta friend, there?" She nodded toward Fahtin and winked.

"Right. I forgot that you studied Dantogyptain."

"I did. I will find you after the masters are through with

me. Tell Marla I can't wait to see her. She was the darling of the Academy even when I was here, and I understand she's even more so now."

"You have no idea," Evon told her. "We'll explain it all later, if the masters don't do it for us."

"I look forward to it. It was nice meeting you all, albeit briefly. Hopefully we can remedy our cropped encounter later."

She glided past them toward the administration building, all eyes following her. Aila thought she might look good in an outfit like Saria's. She wished she could look *that* good.

"Wow," Urun said. "That woman oozed magic. And other things."

Evon barked a laugh. "Just like when she was here. Saria Gilwenys always had a group of people following her, both male and female."

Fahtin adopted an expression of disinterest, though Aila recognized it as meaning anything but. Apparently, Evon had become better at interpreting such things because he hurried on in his explanation.

"She's one of the astridae." He seemed to think that explained everything satisfactorily and ended the conversation.

"Astridae?" Tere said. "I thought they were all killed before and during the War of Magic."

"Most of them were. There are very few left, none of pure blood. Saria is not a pure-blooded astri, but she still has the internal magic of her ancestors, if weaker."

"The astridae were beloved of Mellaine," Urun said, "as well as of other gods like Migae. I can see why."

Fahtin outright frowned at Urun this time.

"To make things worse, Saria has an amazing skill with songs. You noticed the lute? She can do magic with her voice that made her one of the top students when she was here. She sort of took Marla under her wing when we were younger, gave her an older person to look up to. Marla will be thrilled she's back. Maybe it'll be enough to break her out of her mood. Anyway, we can all talk with her later. I, for one, would like to know what she's been up to for the last four or more years."

❧ 41 ❧

Back at Batido, Fahtin Achaya decided to take a few minutes to think about what she'd heard during their meeting with the masters and to let her mind dwell on some of the passages she had read in the book the Prophet had left for her. She was having a more difficult time working through the book because her Alaqotim was horrible compared to Aeden's. Evon had been helping her, but it was slow going.

She wondered if she should let him translate the whole thing for her so she could read it in a few days, but so far she'd been stubbornly holding onto wanting to go through it and learn it all herself, like Aeden was doing. The thought of Evon's nervous excitement and eagerness about unlocking the secrets of the book made her smile, but so far he had been able to restrain his enthusiasm and let her do what she wanted.

Fahtin was uncharacteristically tired for having only sat through a meeting and she wondered if she was getting sick. She'd been taking it easy since she came back from finding Tsosin Ruus's secret cache of books, but still, she lacked energy. A nap would help her perk up, she thought, and she settled onto her pillow, looking up at the wooden beams above her.

Like the simple act of lying down had been a signal, everything went black for a moment and she got the sensation of motion instantly transporting her somewhere else.

Her vision came back suddenly, as if she'd had a blindfold on and it was torn off. She stood, not on any kind of solid object she could see, but in the sky itself, overlooking all of Dizhelim.

Panic struck her and she muffled a scream at the thought of falling thousands of feet to the ground. She was above even the Heaven's Teeth mountains, so surely she would die falling all that distance.

But she wasn't falling. Instead, she was staying right where she was, as if she were standing on an invisible platform high above everything. Several long minutes passed until her galloping heart was beating normally and her breathing had slowed to a more reasonable rate. Only then did she search her surroundings for what she was there to see.

Below her—far below her—was the long shape of Munsahtiz Island, nestled in the blue of the Kanton Sea and sitting so close to the mainland to the east that it looked as if two little fingers touched the edge of the territory south of Ebenrau. Somewhere down there, within the tiny shapes of buildings and grounds cut out from the thick forest on the north part of the island, was where her body rested. There was nothing exciting to see from this far up. It was all too small to pick up details.

A flash caught her eye from the far southeast. In the way of dreams and visions, she directed her sight toward the light. Her vision zoomed in and she found that she could see what looked like a thunderstorm, but with abnormally colored lightning. The image of a round stone with symbols carved in it appeared in her mind within the vision that was also in her mind. After the dizziness passed from thinking about it, she focused on the stone. She'd seen such things before. Several times. It was another Cogiscro stone. With a flexing of her will, she burned the design into her memory.

When she finished, the stone vanished, to be replaced by another scene for her to observe. She felt a rushing sensation, wind across her body as she flew across the land, then the water, to another portion of land that seemed as big as the entire continent of Promistala. For some inexplicable reason, a feeling told her that Aeden should be there. Was *required* to be there. Not with her, watching, but on the land below and ahead of her. She was not permitted to look back from whence she came for some reason, her *eyes* forced onto what was happening in front of her.

A great clash of magical power erupted before her, like two gigantic waves crashing into each other, but instead of water, they were made of pure magic. Light and sound threatened to overwhelm her as she tried to figure out if she was witnessing some future or past battle between great forces.

All suddenly went quiet and there was a sensation of many multitudes of eyes watching. Not her, but the space in front of her, where the most violent of the magic had been. A plant sprang into being, growing even as she watched. It developed a flower which bloomed within seconds. Next to it, a tree went through the same process, from seedling to a towering monarch of wood in a handful of seconds. Following that, several beasts generated from thin air, growing and becoming hale even as she watched.

Finally, another shape manifested itself as it coalesced. This one was unmistakably human, or at least one of the humanoid races. Once fully formed, the woman—it was definitely identifiable as female in its lack of any type of clothing —dropped to her knees and bowed her head in obeisance to what was undoubtedly the wielder of the power Fahtin had witnessed earlier.

A strong suction pulled the Gypta back to where she had started, hovering above the Academy. She recognized heat emanating from the south, as if she was standing at an eastern window at midmorning. It warmed until she feared getting a sunburn, yet she couldn't move away from it. She searched, but wasn't able to locate exactly where the heat was coming from. She only knew that it was powerful enough to burn up the world, if given the right circumstances.

The warmth faded and a powerful flash of light appeared to the west. Fahtin put a hand up to shield her eyes from its intensity. As she tried to find any details she could about it, it dimmed rapidly, accompanied by an immense sense of loss and sadness. When it dimmed and finally winked out completely, she found herself weeping helplessly, though she didn't have eyes that could generate tears in this place.

Fahtin's body jerked into motion and she realized she was falling. No, not falling, but speeding downward. Though the instinct to panic flared, something inside reassured her that she was safe. Moving closer to the Academy below, she saw one more jumble of lights, consisting of many different colors. They were far to the northwest and for some reason, they encouraged her. The comfortable feeling of those yellows, reds, greens, and blues would have made her smile, had she had a mouth.

Watching the world grow larger was exhilarating. She recognized Batido before she plummeted through its roof and into her room, returning to her slumbering body. She landed with a muffled thump and lay there, waiting for the feelings of nausea to come.

They didn't, or at least not as strongly as usual. Fahtin did feel out of sorts, but it passed quickly and she swung her feet off the bed. Taking a few deep breaths, she walked to the door, opened it, and headed downstairs to the common room where she could even at distance hear her friends talking.

Evon was the first to spot her, a smile coming to his face and then disappearing. He jumped to his feet and met her at the bottom of the stairs. "Are you all right? Did something happen?"

"Visions," she said, stepping gingerly over to the table to sit down. Evon hovered over her after handing her a cup of water. She tilted her mouth upward in the barest crack of smile and took a drink. All conversation had stopped and all eyes were on her. "I'm fine. I didn't even feel as nauseous this time. Maybe I'm getting the hang of it."

"Are you up to telling us about it?" Aeden asked, watching her face carefully.

"That's why I came down," she said. She described what she'd seen as everyone listened silently. When she was done, the questions began.

"You said southeast," Evon said. "Was it Squalls Landing?"

"No. it was farther south."

Evon gave her a quizzical look. "Horizon?"

"More southeast."

"Fahtin, both of those cities are on the coast. There isn't anything more southeast."

She gave him a level look. "I didn't say it was on Promistala."

"Are you talking about crossing the Aesculun Ocean?" Tere asked. "Since the gods left, the only real ocean travel people can make safely is to Teroshi, and even that is risky. No one goes south, not and survive to tell about it."

"I'm only telling you what I saw. With the Cogiscro stone, I think my vision means that there's another well to the south. I don't know what the other things I saw have to do with it, the animals and plants."

"The Cradle of Life," Urun said. The others turned to

him. "Osulin told me about it. It's the place where the life created by Surus was first put on Dizhelim. That has to be it."

"Most scholars believe that to be a metaphor, that life was literally placed all over the surface of Dizhelim," Evon said.

"Osulin disagrees. Sorry, Evon, but I'm going to believe an immortal, thousands-year-old goddess over you. No offense."

"We better talk to the masters about this," Aeden said. "It sounds like we're about to get busy again."

# EPILOGUE

"You called for me, Your Eminency?" Lerus Costanti asked as he entered the personal office of the leader of the Church of Vanda.

"I did. Please, close the door and sit." Lucio Sanctus watched his High Itera as the man did as he asked. The Patr Pruma discussed most important things with all three of his High Itera in attendance, but some things were best kept close.

Lerus was a good enough servant of the church. A little wild at times, too impulsive for some tasks, but his personality allowed him to do well with certain types of missions for the Patr.

His large frame, more than half a foot taller than the diminutive Lucio's five feet and four inches, was better suited to a tavern tough or a street thug than to a man of the only true god, but it truly took all kinds of people for the church to function. Even if they really should cut their long black hair to a more reasonable length.

Lerus waited patiently as the Patr Pruma observed him. It didn't escape the man's notice when Lucio's eyes stopped on his hair, his own eyes flaring the slightest bit. It was an old and familiar complaint.

"Have you any more news of the dash through our border guards?" Best for Lucio to start off small and get to the bigger discussions later.

"No, Patr. There didn't seem to be any harm in it. Three people simply wanting to cross into Clavian territory without submitting to questioning. They didn't seem to be up to any mischief."

"I see. It is troubling for godless ones to balk at the church's activities to keep them safe. I like it not."

"I understand. I will tell you the moment anything comes of it, but I don't see a conspiracy in a few people running past a blockade."

"Of course, of course. Speaking of the Enclave, what word on our spies there? Is the king dead? You reported last that the princess had returned. Is she in power now and, if so, what does that mean for our plans?"

Lerus fidgeted in his seat and swept some of his hair from in front of his blue eyes. "The king has recovered. The last communication I got from our spy within the court said the court healer was able to revive the king, but that is all. I've received no further word from them. Something must have happened. Perhaps the spy was found?"

"That is not good news. I have no ill will toward Joceus Davenson, but his death would have made some things easier. He has thus far withstood any pressure I have tried to put upon him to create a formal alliance between us. Continue to try to reach your spy and, if possible, insert another or elevate another already in place. As our closest neighbor, it would be advantageous to start with the Great Enclave as we begin to gather...allies."

"Yes, Patr."

"There is something else I wanted to speak with you

about. It has come to my attention that a certain resource which had been thought lost has now been found again. I would like for you to obtain this resource for me."

"Of course. I and my servants are here to aid in bringing glory and victory to the church. Is this something that must be liberated from someone else's possession?"

Lucio managed to keep the smile from his lips. Of the three High Itera, Lerus had the most unconventional—and loosest—interpretation of acceptable actions. The man understood that at times, certain things that would normally be frowned on by the church might be necessary to obtain the greater good. The Vandictae condemned theft, though there were examples of pious men dancing on the line, or even stomping on it altogether, to achieve something more important than strict obedience to every little tenet.

"No, Lerus. It is not something another has. Rather, what we speak about is itself a person. I want you to gather your finest operatives. This person may prove troublesome to obtain, though doing so is of the utmost importance. Let me explain what I want you to do..."

# HERO'S STRENGTH GLOSSARY

Following is a list of unfamiliar terms. Included are brief descriptions of the words as well as pronunciation. For the most part, pronunciation is depicted using common words or sounds in English, not IPA phonetic characters. Please note that the diphthong *ai* has the sound like the English word *Aye*. The *zh* sound, very common in the language Alaqotim, is listed as being equivalent to *sh,* but in reality, it is spoken with more of a buzz, such as *szh*. Other pronunciations should be intuitive.

**Abhincstagna** (*ab·HEENK·STAG·nah*) – a lake in ancient Ascesh that reportedly had magical properties. The great dragon Tero made his home near the lake.

**Abyssum** (*a·BIS·um*) – the world of the dead, Percipius's realm.

**Acolyte** – a current Hero Academy student who has mastered at least one school, but not three or more.

**Adept** – a Hero Academy student who has mastered at least three schools and continues to study at the Academy.

**Aeden Tannoch** (AY·*den* TAN·*ahkh*) – a man born to and

trained by a highland clan, raised by the Gypta, and able to utilize the magic of the ancient Song of Prophecy.

**Aeid Hesson** (*AY·id*) – former Master of the School of prophecy at the Hero Academy. He was murdered in his office at the Academy.

**Aesculus** (*AY·skyoo·lus*) – the god of water and the seas.

**Agypten** (*a·GIP·ten*) – an ancient nation, no longer in existence. It was from this nation the Gypta originated.

**Ahred Chimlain** (*AH·red CHIM·lane*) – noted scholar of the first century of the third age

**Aila Ven** (*AI·la ven*) – a woman of small stature who joins the party and lends her skills in stealth and combat to their cause.

**Ailgid** (*ILE·jid*) – one of the five highland clans of the Cridheargla, the clan Greimich Tannoch's wife came from.

**Ailred Kelzumin** (*ILE·red kel·ZOO min*) – the Master of the School of Water Magic at the Hero Academy.

**Alain** (*a·LAYN*) – the god of language. The ancient language of magic, Alaqotim, is named after him.

**Alaqotim** (*ah·la·KOTE·eem*) – the ancient language of magic. It is not spoken currently by any but those who practice magic.

**Aletris Meslar** (*ah·LET·ris MES·lar*) – the personal clerk and assistant to Headmaster Qydus Okvius, of the Hero Academy.

**Aliten** (*AL·it·ten*) – a type of animaru that is humanoid but has wings and can fly.

**Alloria Yurgen** (*ah·LORE·ee·ah YURE·gen*) – the leader (Vituma) of the Dark Council. She is the 102nd leader since the Council's creation.

**Alpin Trebhin** (*AL·pin TREH·vin*) – the Croagh warrior who was chosen as the chief for the Trebhin clan after the previous chief was killed in the Death Oath ritual combat.

**Altor Vondus** (*al·TORE   VON·dus*) – one of Joceus Davenson's advisors, an alchemist and scholar

**Alvaspirtu** (*al·vah·SPEER·too*) – a large river that runs from the Heaven's Teeth mountains to the Kanton Sea. The Gwenore River splits from it and travels al the way down to the Aesculun Ocean.

**Alzore** (*al·ZORE*) – an old scholar Aila Ven used to know when she was a child

**Amatia** (*ah·MAH·tee·ah*) – a member of the Dark Council, a seeress.

**Ander Tosselnam** – one of the three High Itera of the Church of Vanda.

**Animaru** (*ah·nee·MAR·oo*) – dark creatures from the world Aruzhelim. The name means "dark creatures" or "dark animals."

**Aquilius Gavros** (*ah·KWIL·ee·us GAV·roze*) – the Dark Prophet; he lived in the Age of Magic, during the time of the War of Magic.

**Arania** (*ah·RAH·nee·ah*) – a kingdom in the western part of the continent of Promistala, south and east of Shinyan. A thing of Arania is called Aranir.

**Arba** – an essentially extinct race of magical people whose ancestors were directly created by Mellaine out of the stuff of the forest and her magical tears. They had a special connection to nature and could use magic directly from the natural world.

**Arcus** (*ARK·us*) – the god of blacksmithing and devices.

**Arcusheim** (*AHR·coo·shime*) – a large city on the southern shore of the Kanton Sea, the capital of the nation of Sutania and the home of Erent Caahs before he left to travel the world.

**Argad Solsin** (*AR·gad   SOLE·sin*) – the guard at the entrance to the castle in the Great Enclave when Aila, Tere, and Lily visit

**Arto Deniselo** (*AHR·toe  day·NEE·say·low*) – a dueling master in the Aranian city of Vis Bena who taught Erent Caahs how to drastically improve his combat abilities.

**Aruna** (pl. Arunai) (*ah·ROON·ah; ah·roo·NIE*) – a citizen of the tribal nation of Campastra. Originally, the name was pejorative, referring to the color of their skin, but they embraced it and it became the legitimate name for the people in Campastra.

**Aruzhelim** (*ah·ROO·shel·eem*) – the world from which the animaru come. The name means "dark world," "dark universe," or "dark dimension." Aruzhelim is a planet physically removed from Dizhelim.

**Ascesh** (*AY·sesh*) – the northernmost continent in Dizhelim. Thousands of years ago, it included what is now Teroshi.

**Asfrid Finndottir** (*ASS·frid  fin·DOT·teer*) – the Master of the School of Cryptology at the Hero Academy.

**Assector Pruma** (*ah·SEC tor  PROO·mah*) – roughly "first student" in Alaqotim. This is the student aid to a master in one of the schools at the Hero Academy. There can be only one per school and this person conducts research, helps to teach classes, and assists the master in any other necessary task.

**Aubron Benevise** (*AW·brun  ben·uh·VEES*) – the Master of History and Literature at the Hero Academy.

**Auxein** (*awk·ZAY·in*) – an aide to the master and the First Student (Assector Pruma) at the Hero Academy. For larger schools, there may be more than one. In some schools there may not be any.

**Awresea** (*aw·reh·SAY·uh*) – a kingdom that no longer exists, the home of Tazi Ermenko who taunted the god Fyorio and was destroyed. The fiery, desolate location where the kingdom was is now known as Fyrefall.

**Ayize Fudu** (*aye·EEZ FOO·doo*) – a Hero Academy adept, one of Quentin Duzen's associates.

**Barda Sirusel** (*BAR·duh   seer·oo·SELL*) – the boy who tried to bully Marla when she was a child.

**Batido** (*bah TEE·doe*) – what Aeden's friends call their dormitory, from the Dantogyptain words for *second home*.

**Beldroth Zinrora** (*BEL·droth  zin·ROR uh*) – the Master of the School of Dark Magic at the Hero Academy.

**Bhagant** (*bog·AHNT*) – the shortened form of the name for the Song of Prophecy, in the language Dantogyptain.

**Bhavisyaganant** (*bah·VIS·ya·gahn·ahnt*) – The full name for the Song of Prophecy in Dantogyptain. It means "the song of foretelling of the end," loosely translated.

**Biuri** (*bee·OOR·ee*) – small, quick animaru that recall the appearance and movements of rodents. They are useful as spies because of their small size and quickness.

**Blennus** (*blen·oos*) – Dannel Powfrey's horse.

**Brace** – the term used by the Falxen for a group of assassins ("blades").

**Braitharlan** (*brah·EE·thar·lan*) – the buddy assigned in the clan training to become a warrior. It means "blade brother" in Chorain.

**Brausprech** (*BROW·sprekh*) – a small town on the northwest edge of the Grundenwald forest, in the nation of Rhaltzheim. It is the hometown of Urun Chinowa.

**Brenain Kanda** (*bren·AY·in  KAHN·duh*) – a mythological heroine who stole magic from the god Migae.

**Bridgeguard** – the small community, barely more than a guardpost, on the mainland end of the northern bridge to Munsahtiz

**Broken Reach** – a rugged, unforgiving land to the southeast of the Grundenwald. There are ruins of old fortifications there.

**Campastra** (cam·PAHS·trah) – a tribal nation in the southwestern portion of the continent of Promistala

**Cara Moore** – a member of the Dark Council.

**Catriona (Ailgid) Tannoch** (CAT·ree·own·ah ILE·jid) – the wife of Greimich Tannoch. She is originally from the Ailgid clan, but now has taken the last name Tannoch.

**Ceti** *(SET·ee)* – a higher level type of animaru, appearing aquatic with small tentacles, even though there is no water in Aruzhelim. They are very intelligent and have magical aptitude. Some of them are accomplished with weapons as well.

**Chorain** *(KHAW·rin)* – the ancestral language of the highland clans of the Cridheargla.

**Clavian Knights** *(CLAY·vee·en)* – the fighting force of the Grand Enclave, the finest heavy cavalry in Dizhelim.

**Codaghan** *(COD·ah·ghan)* – the god of war.

**Cogiscro** *(coe·JEE·scroe)* – an ancient system of runic writing that was used in magic spells. The symbols are phonetic and are arranged in a circular pattern.

**Colechna** *(co·LECK·nah)* – one of the higher levels of animaru. They appear to be at least part snake, typically highly intelligent as well as skilled with weapons. They are usually in the upper ranks of the command structure. Their agility and flexibility makes them dangerous enemies in combat. A few can use magic, but most are strictly melee fighters.

**Corcan** – one of the five highland clans of the Cridheargla.

**Cridheargla** *(cree·ARG·la)* – the lands of the highland clans. The word is a contraction of Crionna Crodhearg Fiacla in Chorain.

**Crionna Crodhearg Fiacla** *(cree·OWN·na CROW·arg FEE·cla)* ) – the land of the highland clans. It means "old blood-red teeth" in Chorain, referring to the hills and mountains that abound in the area and the warlike nature of its people. The term is typically shortened to Cridheargla.

**Croagh Aet Brech** *(CROWGH ET BREKH)* – the name of the highland clans in Chorain. It means, roughly, "blood warriors." The clans sometimes refer to themselves simply as Croagh, from which their nickname "crows" sprang, foreigners not pronouncing their language correctly.

**Daana Vaskova** (*DAHN·ah    vas·COVE    ah*) – a prophetess and author who lived at the end of the Age of Magic. She wrote many children's tales, the majority of which had hidden meanings and prophecies.

**Daibhidh Trebhin** (*DAY·vid TREH·vin*) – the clan chief of the Trebhin clan when Aeden went to meet with the other clans of Croagh.

**Dannel Powfrey** – a self-proclaimed scholar from the Hero Academy who meets Aeden on his journey.

**Danta** (*DAHN·ta*) – the goddess of music and song. The language Dantogyptain is named after her.

**Dantogyptain** (*DAHN·toe·gip·TAY·in*) – the ancestral language of the Gypta people.

**Daodh Gnath** (*DOWGH  GHRAY*) – the Croagh Ritual of Death, the cutting off of someone from the clans. The name means simply "death ceremony."

**Daphne** – one of the tavern maids at the Wolfen's Rest inn in Dartford.

**Darkcaller** – one of the Falxen sent to kill Khrazhti and her companions. A former student at Sitor-Kanda, her specialty is dark magic.

**Dark Council** – a mysterious group of thirteen people who are trying to manipulate events in Dizhelim.

**Dartford** – a small town on the mainland near the north bridge to the island of Munsahtiz.

**Darun Achaya** (*dah·ROON    ah·CHAI·ah*) – father of Fahtin, head of the family of Gypta that adopts Aeden.

**Denore Felas** (*den·OR  FEHL·ahss*) – a great mage in the Age of Magic, the best friend of Tsosin Ruus.

**Desid** (*DAY·sid*) – a type of animaru. They're nearly mindless, only able to follow simple commands, but they are fairly strong and tireless. They are about five feet tall with thick, clawed fingers useful for digging. They have the mentality of a young child.

**Dizhelim** (*DEESH·ay·leem*) – the world in which the story happens. The name means "center universe" in the ancient magical language Alaqotim.

**Dmirgan** (*DMEER·gen*) – a town in Kruzekstan, where a young Erent Caahs killed a man he thought was a murderer

**Dob** – a small arba boy whose father was killed in the battle where Urun and the others first met the arba in the Mellafond.

**Dreigan** (*DRAY·gun*) – a mythical beast, a reptile that resembles a monstrous snake with four legs attached to its sides like a lizard. The slightly smaller cousin to the mythical dragons.

**Drugancairn** (*DROO·gan·cayrn*) – a small town on the southwest edge of the Grundenwald Forest.

**Dubhghall Trebhin** (*DOO·gall   TREH·vin*) – one of the representatives of the Trebhin clan who went to fetch Aeden to come back and talk to the clan chiefs. He is abrasive and impolite.

**Ebenrau** (*EBB·en·ra·oo*) – the capital city of Rhaltzheim, one of the seven great cities in Dizhelim

**Elnaril Leovaris** (*el·NAHR·ill   lay·oh VAHR·iss*) – one of Joceus Davenson's advisors, one who routinely argues with the king

**Emiliya Sterris** (*eh·MEEL·ee yah   STARE·iss*) – the Academy operative who went missing nera the Shadowed Pinnacles.

**Emora** (*ay·MORE·ah*) – the term of endearment Tsosin Ruus used for Iowyn Selen. It means *my love* in Alaqotim.

**Encalo** (pl. encali) (*en·CAW·lo*) – four-armed, squat, powerful humanoids. There are few in Dizhelim, mostly in the western portion of the continent Promistala.

**Epradotirum** (*EP·rah·doe·TEER um*) – an extremely powerful entity who lives in another plane of existence, touching the mortal plane when, every few centuries, he is hungry. Aeden and some of his friends met the Epra while running from assassins near Satta Sarak.

**Erent Caahs** (*AIR·ent CAWS*) – the most famous of the contemporary heroes. He disappeared twenty years before the story takes place, and is suspected to be dead, though his body was never found.

**Erfinchen** (*air·FEEN·chen*) – animaru that are shapeshifters. Though not intelligent and powerful enough to be leaders among the animaru, they are often at higher levels, though not in command of others. They typically perform special missions and are truly the closest thing to assassins the animaru have. A very few can use some magic.

**Esiyae Yellynn** (*ess·SEE·yay YELL·in*) – the Master of the School of Air Magic at the Hero Academy.

**Espirion** (*es·PEER·ee·on*) – the god of plans and schemes. From his name comes the terms espionage and spy.

**Eutychus Naevius** (*YOO·tik·us NAY·vee us*) – a renowned mathematician in ancient times. One of his principles, the third theorem of alternating magical series, was the key Marla used to decrypt Ren Kenata's letters.

**Evindia Elkien** (*eh·VIN·dee ah EL·kee·en*) – a member of the Dark Council.

**Evon Desconse** – a graduate of the famed Hero Academy and best friend to Marla Shrike.

**Exulmucri** (*EX·ool·MOO·cree*) – an ancient game of strategy, thought to be the first of its kind. It was also the first game to use dice.

**Fahtin Achaya** (*FAH·teen ah·CHAI·ah*) – a young Gypta girl in the family that adopted Aeden. She and Aeden grew as close as brother and sister in the four years he spent with the family.

**Falxen** (*FAL·ksen*) – an assassin organization, twelve of whom go after Aeden and his friends. The members are commonly referred to as "Blades."

**Featherblade** – one of the Falxen sent to kill Khrazhti and her companions. He is the leader of the brace and his skill with a sword is supreme.

**Fireshard** – one of the Falxen sent to kill Khrazhti and her companions. She wields fire magic.

**Forgren** (*FORE·gren*) – a type of animaru that is tireless and single-minded. They are able to memorize long messages and repeat them exactly, so they make good messengers. They have no common sense and almost no problem-solving skills

**Formivestu** (*form·ee·VES·too*) – the insect creatures that attacked Tere's group when they were on their way to Sitor-Kanda. They look like giant ants with human faces and were thought to be extinct.

**Fyorio** (*fee·YORE·ee·oh*) – the god of fire and light, from whose name comes the word *fyre*, spelled *fire* in modern times.

**Fyrefall** – a desolate and dangerous land in the south central part of Promistala, full of hot pools, geysers, and other signs of volcanic activity.

**Gareth Briggs** – a member of the Dark Council.

**Gemsport** – the largest port city in the Great Enclave, on the southwestern shore of the Kanton Sea.

**Gentason** (*jen·TAY·sun*) – an ancient nation, enemy of Salamus. It no longer exists.

**Gneisprumay** (*gNAYS·proo·may*) – first (or most important) enemy. The name for the Malatirsay in the animaru dialect of Alaqotim.

**Godan Chul** (*GO·dahn CHOOL*) – an ancient mythological race of spirit beings, created accidentally from the magic of the God of Magic, Migae. The name means, roughly "spirit's whisper."

**Goren Adnan** – the Master of the School of Military Strategy at the Hero Academy.

**Graduate** (at the Hero Academy) – a student of the Hero Academy who is either an adept or a viro/vira. That is, anyone who has mastered at least three schools at the Academy and is either still studying there or has left the school.

**Great Enclave** – a nation to the west of the Kanton Sea and the Hero Academy.

**Greimich Tannoch** (*GREY·mikh   TAN·ahkh*) – Aeden's close friend, his braitharlan, during his training with the clans.

**Grundenwald Forest** (*GROON·den·vahld*) – the enormous forest in the northeastern part of the main continent of Promistala. It is said to be the home of magic and beasts beyond belief.

**Gulra** (pl. gulrae) (*GUL·rah; GUL·ray*) – an animaru that walks on four legs and resembles a large, twisted dog. These are used for tracking, using their keen sense of smell like a hound.

**Gwenore River** – a large river that splits off from the Alvaspirtu and travels south, through Satta Sarak and all the way to the Aesculun Ocean

**Gyerju** (*gyare·JOO*) – a village in southern Shinyan where Jia Toun's father was born and grew up.

**Gypta** (*GIP·tah*) – the traveling people, a nomadic group that lives in wagons, homes on wheels, and move about, never settling down into towns or villages.

**Hamrath** – a small town on the coast of the eastern part of the Kanton Sea, just north of the bridge from the mainland to Munsahtiz Island.

**Hane Bryce** – a member of the Dark Council.

**Heaven's Teeth** – the range of mountains to the east of the Kanton sea, in between that body of water and the Grundenwald Forest.

**Heronorus** (*hare·ON·or·us*) – the god of honor.

**Honor's Peak** – the mountain bordering the Shinyan capital city of Tongqi, home of the Chamber of the Trial of Honor.

**Ianthra** (*ee·ANTH·rah*) – the Goddess of Love and Beauty.

**Ianthra's Breasts** (*ee·ANTH·rah*) – a mountain range between Arcusheim in Sutania and Satta Sarak. Even though there are three peaks, the two that dominate were named for the physical attributes of the Goddess of Love and Beauty, Ianthra.

**Iaurium** (*ee·OUR·ee·um*) – a port city in Arania, on the western shore of the Kanton Sea.

**Iowyn Selen** (*EE·o·win  SELL·en*) – a great mage in the Age of Magic, the love of Tsosin Ruus's life.

**Iracundamel** (*EER·ah·COON·dah·mel*) – the ancient name for the well of power at the center of the Mellafond swamp. The name means, roughly, *nature's wrath* or *Mellaine's wrath*.

**Iryna Vorona** (*ee·REEN·ah  voe·rone·ah*) – Master of the School of Interrogation and Coercion at the Hero Academy.

**Isbal Deyne** (*ISS·bahl  DANE*) – a member of the Dark Council.

**Isegrith Palas** (*ISS·eh·grith  PAL·us*) – the Master of Fundamental Magic at the Hero Academy.

**Itera** (*ee·TARE·ah*) – high level functionaries in the Vandan Church. They are essentially the second level from the top, though the High Itera, the top three of their number, are above the rest, just below the Patr Pruma.

**Jarnorun** (*jar·NOR·un*) – an animaru lord, one of Kirraloth's two main commanders.

**Jehira Sinde** (*jay·HEER·ah  SINDH*) – Raki's grandmother (nani) and soothsayer for the family of Gypta that adopts Aeden.

**Jessam (Dropsy) Vilonay** (*JESS·am  VILL·oh·nay*) – the sergeant on duty at the gate when Aila, Tere, and Lily got to the castle in Metrovial. His nickname, Dropsy, was given him during training when he couldn't seem to keep hold of his sword in sparring. He worked diligently to become one of the finest swordsmen in the army.

**Jhanda Dalavi** (*JON·dah  dah·LAHV·ee*) – the Head Scrivener at the Hero Academy. He is in charge of the small army of scribes who make copies of books and who create many of the records necessary for the functioning of the school.

**Jia Toun** (*JEE·ah  TOON*) – an expert thief and assassin who was formerly the Falxen named Shadeglide. She uses her real name now that she has joined Aeden's group of friends and allies.

**Jintu Devexo** (*JEEN·too  day·VEX·oh*) – the high chieftain of the Arunai during the time of the false Malatirsay.

**Joceus Davenson** (*joe·SEE·us  DAA·ven·sun*) – the current king of the Great Enclave, a direct descendent of Thomasinus, Son of Daven, who was the first king of the Great Enclave.

**Josef** – the owner of the Wolfen's Rest inn in Dartford, a friend of Marla Shrike.

**Juinsai** (*joo·een·SIE*) – a village in Arania, in the borderlands south of Shinyan, where Jia Toun grew up.

**Jusha Terlix** (*JOO·shah  TER·liks*) – the Master of the School of Mental Magic at the Hero Academy.

**Kaeso Hiberus** (*KAY·sew  hi·BEER·us*) – the author of the holy book of the Church of Vanda, the Vindictae. He claims to be the prophet of Vanda and that he was given the information directly from the god at the end of the Age of Magic.

**Kaila** (*KY·lah*) – the young encalo girl who Erent Caahs met when he was a boy, searching for his family's killer. He helped her to rescue her caravan.

**Kanton Sea** (*KAN·tahn*) – an inland sea in which the island of Munsahtiz, home of the Hero Academy, sits.

**Katar Trisric** (*ka·TAHR   TRISS·rik*) – one of Joceus Davenson's advisors

**Kebahn Faitar** (Kebahn the Wise) (*kay·BAWN   FYE·tahr*) – the advisor and friend to Thomasinus; the one who actually came up with the idea to gather all the scattered people and make a stand at the site of what is now the Great Enclave.

**Khrazhti** (*KHRASH·tee*) – the former High Priestess to the dark god S'ru and former leader of the animaru forces on Dizhelim. At the discovery that her god was untrue, she has become an ally and friend to Aeden.

**Kirraloth** (*KEER·uh·loth*) – an animaru high lord, given the command of all animaru on Dizhelim after Suuksis failed to turn or destroy Khrazhti.

**Kruzekstan** (*KROO·zek·stahn*) – a small nation due south of the highland clan lands of Cridheargla.

**Kryzt** (*KRIZT*) – a type of animaru with spikes all over it, shaped roughly like a wolf but with a longer tail. It has sharp claws and teeth.

**Leafburrow** – a village in Rhaltzheim, north of Arcusheim off the River Road, the location of a bandit ambush where Erent Caahs demonstrated his special spinning arrow technique.

**Leaf Talker** – the historical name for an arba community's leader.

**Lela Ganeva** (*LEE·lah·gahn·AY·vah*) – the woman Erent Caahs fell in love with.

**Lerus Costanti** (*lehr·OOS   coe·STAN·tee*) – one of the three High Itera of the Church of Vanda.

**Lesnum** (*LESS·num*) – large, hairy, beastlike animaru.

These sometimes walk around on two feet, but more commonly use all four limbs. They are strong and fast and intelligent enough to be used as sergeants, commanding groups of seren and other low-level animaru.

**Lex** – Evon's horse, a chestnut stallion

**Lilianor** (Lili) Caahs (*LI·lee·ah·nore   CAWS*) – Erent Cahhs's little sister; she was murdered when she was eleven years old.

**Liluth Olaxidor** (*LIL·uth   oh·LAX·ih·door*) – the Master of the School of Firearms at the Hero Academy.

**Lily Fisher** – an archer of supreme skill who was formerly the Falxen assassin named Phoenixarrow. She uses her real name now that she has joined Aeden's group of friends and allies.

**Lis** (*LEES*) – a minor deity who battled the sun, nearly killing it, and causing so much damage that to this day, it is weakened in the wintertime.

**Lucas Stewart** – a young student at the Hero Academy. He's often used by the masters as a messenger because of his strong work ethic and reliability.

**Lucio Sanctus** (*LOO·chee·oh   SAHNK·toos*) – the Patr Pruma of the Vandan Church.

**Lusnauqua** (*loos·NOW·kwah*) – the rugged land surrounding Broken Reach, in the center of the eastern section of the continent of Promistala.

**Malatirsay** (*Mahl·ah·TEER·say*) – the hero who will defeat the animaru and save Dizhelim from the darkness, according to prophecy. The name means "chosen warrior" or "special warrior" in Alaqotim.

**Manandantan** (*mahn·ahn·DAHN·tahn*) – the festival to celebrate the goddess Danta, goddess of song.

**Marla Shrike** – a graduate of the famed Hero Academy, an experienced combatant in both martial and magical disciplines.

**Marn Tiscomb** – the new Master of Prophecy at the Hero Academy. He replaced Master Aeid, who was murdered.

**Maurius Gainet** (*MAW·ree·us   GAY·net*) – the Chief Steward of the king's castle in Metrovial.

**Mellafond** (*MEH·la·fond*) – a large swamp on the mainland to the east of Munsahtiz Island. The name *means pit of Mellaine*.

**Mellaine** (*meh·LAYN*) – goddess of nature and growing things.

**Miera Tannoch** (*MEERA   TAN·ahkh*) – Aeden's mother, wife of Sartan.

**Migae** (*MEE·jay*) – the God of magic. The word "magic" comes from his name.

**Mionn Bhais** (*MYOON BAJH*) – the Death Oath, a tradition set forth at the beginning of the Croagh clans. It consists of a magical ritual that binds the clan chiefs to either submit to one leader or to challenge that leader in combat to the death.

**Mora Davenson** (*MORE·ah   DAA·ven·sun*) – the queen of the Great Enclave, wife of Joceus Davenson

**Morningsilver** – the horse the Academy let Jia use, a pale grey horse whose coat shone in the right light.

**Moroshi Katai** (*mor·ROE·shee   kah·TAI*) – a mythological hero who battled the Dragon of Eternity to found the nation of Teroshi.

**Moschephis** (*mose·CHE·feess*) – the trickster god, from whose name comes the word mischief.

**Mudertis** (*moo·DARE·teez*) – the god of thievery and assassination.

**Munsahtiz** (*moon·SAW·teez*) – the island in the Kanton sea on which the Hero Academy Sitor-Kanda resides.

**Muscade** (*moos·CAWD*) – the horse the Academy let Aila use, a light reddish brown mare.

**Nanris** – the unofficial capital of Kruzekstan, more

important than the actual capital of Kruzeks because most of the wealth of the nation is centered in Nanris.

**Nasir Kelqen** (*nah·SEER  KEL·ken*) – the Master of the School of Research and Investigation at the Hero Academy.

**Nessa Shua** (*NESS·ah. SHOE·ah*) – one of Cara Moore's underlings, an unattractive woman who wears very tight clothing on her superbly fit body and fights with great flexibility.

**Nightheart** – the horse the Academy let Raki use in his travels, a black stallion.

**Nobleflame** – the horse the Academy let Lily use, a dark red gelding.

**Nyang Fu Mei** (*NYAHNG  FOO  MAY*) – daughter of the warlord of the Nyang tribe in ancient Shinyan.

**Olar Zeen** (*OH·lahr*) – the combat master who trained Aila in combat and how to use the vinci

**Omnisagnitio** (*OME·nees·ahg·NEE·shee·oh*) – the name of the Well of Power found in the cave system where Tsosin Ruus's cache of information was found, within the Aerie Mountains.

**Omri** – a fair sized city in northern Kruzekstan, one of the first of the cities to fall to the animaru.

**Osulin** (*AWE·soo·lin*) – goddess of nature. She is the daughter of Mellaine and the human hero Trikus Phen.

**Ossar Sattis** (*OSS·ahr  SAT·iss*) – the Blue-Cloaked Bastard, a slaver that Erent Caahs captured for a bounty when he was still a boy

**Pach** (*PAHKH*) – in Dantogyptain, it means five. As a proper noun, it refers to the festival of Manandantan that occurs every fifth year, a special celebration in which the Song of Prophecy is sung in full.

**Padraig Seachaid** (*PAD·reg SHAW·chid*) – the clan chief of the Seachaid Croagh clan.

**Patr Pruma** (*POT·er PROO·mah*) – the leader of the Church of Vanda.

**Pedras Shrike** – Marla Shrike's adoptive father, the groundskeeper for the administrative area of the Hero Academy.

**Percipius** (*pare·CHIP·ee·us*) – god of the dead and of the underworld.

**Phoenixarrow** – one of the Falxen sent to kill Khrazhti and her companions. A statuesque red-haired archer who had a penchant for using fire arrows.

**Pilae** (*PEEL·lay*) – a type of animaru that looks like a ball of shadow.

**Pofel Dessin** (*POE·fell DESS·in*) – a traveling scholar who meets Marla and Evon on their journeys.

**Pouran** (*PORE·an*) – roundish, heavy humanoids with piggish faces and tusks like a boar

**Praesturi** (*prayz·TURE·ee*) – the town and former military outpost on the southeastern tip of the island of Munsahtiz. The south bridge from the mainland to the island ends within Praesturi.

**Preshim** (*PRAY·sheem*) – title of the leader of a family of Gypta

**Promistala** (*prome·ees·TAHL·ah*) – the main continent in Dizhelim. In Alaqotim, the name means "first (or most important) land."

**Qozhel** (*KOE·shell*) – the energy that pervades the universe and that is usable as magic.

**Qydus Okvius** (*KIE·duss OCK·vee·us*) – the headmaster of the Hero Academy, Sitor-Kanda.

**Raibrech** (*RAI·brekh*) – the clan magic of the highland clans. In Chorain, it means "bloodfire."

**Raimund Bainer** (*RAY·mund BANE·er*) – one of the three High Itera of the Church of Vanda.

**Rainstorm** – the horse the Acaedmy let Urun use, a grey mare with black speckles.

**Raisor Tannoch** (*RAI·sore   TAN·ahkh*) – a famous warrior of Clan Tannoch, companion of the hero Erent Caahs.

**Raki Sinde** (*ROCK·ee   SINDH*) – grandson of Jehira Sinde, friend and training partner of Aeden.

**Ren Kenata** (*REN ke·NAH·tah*) – a Hero Academy adept who was is not only one of Quentin Duzen's associates, but also a member of the Dark Council.

**Rhaltzheim** (*RALTZ·haim*) – the nation to the northeast of the Grundenwald Forest. The people of the land are called Rhaltzen or sometimes Rhaltza. The term Rhaltzheim is often used to refer to the rugged land within the national borders (e.g., "traverse the Rhaltzheim")

**Ritma Achaya** (*REET·mah   ah·CHAI·ah*) – Fahtin's mother, wife of the Gypta family leader Darun.

**Roneus Lomos** (*ROE·nee·us   LOE·mose*) – the Master of the School of Stealth at the Hero Academy.

**Rougang** (*roo·GAHNG*) – one of the major cities in modern Shinyan, in former Xin tribe territory. In ancient Shinyan, it was a town, the headquarters for the rebel forces of Xin Tai Rong.

**Rumbler** – Joceus Davenson's old hound dog, brown with black splotches and big, floppy ears.

**Ruthrin** (*ROOTH·rin*) – the common tongue of Dizhelim, the language virtually everyone in the world speaks in addition to their own national languages.

**S'ru** (*SROO*) – the dark god of the animaru, supreme power in Aruzhelim.

**Saelihn Valdove** (*SAY·lin   VAHL·doe·vay*) – the Master of the School of Life Magic at the Hero Academy.

**Saevel** (*SAY·vell*) – the arba huntress who guided Urun's group through the Mellafond swamp.

**Salamus** (*sah·lah·MOOS*) – an ancient nation in which the legendary hero Trikus Phen resided. It no longer exists. Things of Salamus were called Salaman.

**Sartan Tannoch** (*SAR·tan TAN·ahkh*) – Aeden's father, clan chief of the Tannoch clan of Craogh.

**Sastiroz** (*SASS·teer·oz*) – an animaru lord, one of Kirraloth's two main commanders.

**Satta Sarak** (*SAH·tah SARE·ack*) – a city in the southeastern part of the continent of Promistala, part of the Saraki Principality.

**Scrapper** – the name Aila gave the small trebaxel they found in Sintrovis

**Seachaid** (*SHAW·chid*) – one of the five highland clans of the Cridheargla.

**Semhominus** (*sem·HOM·in·us*) – one of the highest level of animaru. They are humanoid, larger than a typical human, and use weapons. Many of them can also use magic. Most animaru lords are of this type.

**Senna Shrike** – Marla Shrike's adoptive mother.

**Senod** (*SEN·od*) – the owner of one of the finest mercenary organizations in the Great Enclave. He tried to steal Erent Caahs's knife when he was a boy and Erent scared him straight.

**Seoras Corcan** (*SORE·us*) – the clan chief of the Corcan clan of Croagh.

**Seren** (*SARE·en*) – the most common type of animaru, with sharp teeth and claws. They are similar in shape and size to humans.

**Shadeglide** – one of the Falxen sent to kill Khrazhti and her companions. She is small of stature but extremely skilled as a thief and assassin.

**Shadowed Pinnacles** – the long mountain range essentially splitting the western part of Promistala into two parts. It was formerly known as the Wall of Salamus because it separated that kingdom from Gentason.

**Shaku** (*SHOCK·oo*) – a class of Teroshimi assassins.

**Shalana Vabiros** (*shah·LAHN·ah  va·BEER·ose*) – one of Joceus Davenson's advisors, the only woman on the King's Council

**Shanaera Eilren** (*shah·NARE·ah  ALE·ren*) – the Master of Unarmed Combat at the Hero Academy.

**Shinyan** (*SHEEN·yahn*) – a nation on the northern tip of the western part of Promistala, bordering the Kanton Sea and the Cattilan Sea. Things of Shinyan (such as people) are referred to as Shinyin.

**Shu root/Shu's Bite** (*SHOO*) – a root that only grows in Shinyan, the key ingredient to the poison Shu's Bite.

**Sike** (*SEEK·ay*) – a class of Shinyin assassins

**Sintrovis** (*seen·TROE·vees*) – an area of high magical power on which the Great Enclave was built. In Alaqotim, it means *center of strength*.

**Sirak Isayu** (*SEER·ack  ee·SAI·yoo*) – a member of the Dark Council. He comes from the southern part of the continent of Promistala, near the Sittingham Desert.

**Sitor-Kanda** (*SEE·tor  KAN·dah*) – the Hero Academy, the institution created by the great prophet Tsosin Ruus to train the Malatirsay. The name means roughly "home of magic" in Alaqotim.

**Sittingham Desert** – a large desert in the southwestern part of Promistala.

**Skril Tossin** – best friend of Marla Shrike and Evon Desconce, a Hero Academy adept.

**Snowmane** – the horse the Academy lent to Aeden, a chestnut stallion with a white mane

**Solon** (*SEW·lahn*) – one of the masters in Clan Tannoch, responsible for training young warriors how to use the clan magic, the Raibrech.

**Souvenia** (*soo·VEN·ee·ah*) – an empire that was one of the world powers before the War of Magic, and one of the major players in that war. It no longer exists.

**Srantorna** (*sran·TORN·ah*) – the abode of the gods, a place where humans cannot go.

**Sudepta Sinde** (*soo·DEP·tah  SINDH*) – one of Raki's older brothers, the one whose birthday it was when Raki's family went out to get him a present and were attacked and killed.

**Sudin Torfan** (*SOO·din  TORE·fan*) – one of Joceus Davenson's advisors, the king's oldest friend

**Surefoot** – Marla Shrike's horse.

**Surus** (*SOO·roos*) – king of the gods.

**Sutania** (*soo·TAN·ee·ah*) – the nation south of the Kanton Sea, the capital of which is the city of Arcusheim.

**Suuksis** (*SOOK·sis*) – an animaru lord; Khrazhti's father.

**Tamo** (*tah·MOE*) – the name given the carved wooden masks the Shinyin Imperial Guard wear. They were named after the rebel Jee Ta Mo, who wore a similar mask in his service to Xin Tai Rong.

**Tannoch** (*TAN·ahkh*) – one of the five highland clans of the Cridheargla, the one to which Aeden was born into.

**Tarshuk** (*TAR·shuk*) – a semi-desert-like area to the southwest of the Heaven's Teeth range that has stunted trees and scrub.

**Tazi Ermengo** (*TAH·zee  air·MANE·go*) – the king of the doomed kingdom of Awresea. He taunted the god Fyorio and was destroyed along with his entire kingdom, which was renamed Fyrefall.

**Tere Chizzit** (*TEER  CHIZ·it*) – a blind archer and tracker with the ability to see despite having no working eyes. He is Aeden's companion in the story.

**Tero** (*TAY·roe*) – the Dragon of Eternity, one of the mightiest of all dragons who had ever lived and whose plummet to his death created the Astugi Sea.

**Teroshi** (*tare·OH·shee*) – an island nation in the northern part of Dizhelim. Things of Teroshi, including people, are referred to as Teroshimi.

**Thalia Fendove** (*THA·lee·uh  FEN·doe·vay*) – a member of the Dark Council.

**Thomasinus, son of Daven** (*toe·mah·SINE·us*) – the hero who banded the remnants of the troops of Gentason together to create the Great Enclave. Once they elected him king, he changed his last name to Davenson.

**Thomlin Byrch** (*TOM·lin  BIRCH*) – a member of the Dark Council.

**Thritur Nyhus** (*THRY·tur  NY·hus*) – a member of the Dark Council.

**Thunderlight** – the horse the Academy let Tere use, a black stallion with white markings that look like slashes.

**Toan Broos** (*TOE·aan*) – traveling companion of Erent Caahs and Raisor Tannoch.

**Tongqi** (*TOHNG·chee*) – the capital city of Shinyan, nestled in the bowl created by the mountains near Honor's Peak.

**Toras Geint** (*TOR·ahs  GAYNT*) – an old tracker and scout who befriended Erent Caahs when he was a boy and who mentored the young hero, training him to track and hunt, among other things.

**Touhas Ailgid** (*TOO·ahs  ILE·jid*) – the elder of the Ailgid clan of Croagh who was named their clan chief after much of their clan was destroyed by the animaru.

**Trebaxel** (*tre·BAX·el*) – ape like creatures that are rumored to exist in Sintrovis, in the Great Enclave.

**Trebhin** (*TREH·vin*) – one of the five highland clans of the Cridheargla.

**Trikus Phen** (*TRY·kus  FEN*) – a legendary hero who battled Codaghan, the god of war, himself, and sired Osulin by the goddess Mellaine.

**Tsosin Ruus** (*TSO·sin ROOS*) – the Prophet, the seer and archmage who penned the Song of Prophecy and founded Sitor-Kanda, the Hero Academy.

**Tuach** (*TOO·akh*) – one of the masters in Clan Tannoch, responsible for teaching the young warriors the art of physical combat.

**Tufa Shao** (*TOO·fah SHA·oh*) – the Master of the School of Body Mechanics and Movement at the Hero Academy.

**Tunin Ferrol** (*TOO·nen. FARE·all*) – one of Cara Moore's underlings. He is obsessed with food.

**Twilight** – the horse the Academy let Khrazhti use, a grey mare.

**Urtumbrus** (*oor·TOOM·brus*) – a type of animaru that are essentially living shadows.

**Urun Chinowa** (*OO·run CHIN·oh·wah*) – the High Priest of the goddess Osulin, a nature priest.

**Utrix** (*OO·trix*) – a colechna (snake-type) animaru who looks for the hidden cache Tsosin Ruus left for Aeden and Marla. He is a mage and obsessed with study to gain knowledge of the new world he has come to.

**Vadim Plesca** (*VAH·deem PLES·kah*) – a mage during the Age of Magic, a close associate to Aquilius Gavros.

**Vaeril Faequin** (*VARE·ill FAY·kwin*) – the Master of the School of Mechanista Artifice at the Hero Academy.

**Valcordinae** (*val·COR·di·nay*) – a series of extremely ancient tunnels with a well of magical power at its core. The word is ancient Alaqotim for *strong minds*.

**Vanda** (*VAHN·dah*) – a modern god, claimed by his followers to be the only true god. It is said he is many gods in one, having different manifestations. The Church of Vanda is very large and very powerful in Dizhelim.

**Vandictae** (*vahn·DIC·tay*) – the book of holy writings of the Church of Vanda.

**Vandictatorum** (*vahn·DIC·tah·TOR·um*) – the massive domed structure in Vandomus, the center of learning about the Vandictae. Essentially a university of the church's holy writings.

**Vatheca** (*VATH·ay·kuh*) – the headquarters and training center of the Falxen. It is a mixture of two Alaqotim words, both meaning "sheath."

**Veraugun** (*vare·ow·GOON*) – the name of the Well of Power found in Shinyan. It means true honor in ancient Alaqotim.

**Verona Gilcaryn** (*vare·OH·nah    gill·CARE·in*) – the Academy graduate who is the King of the Great Enclave's healer and mage

**Vesta** – a huge mythological beast that was too large to come down from the heavens to Dizhelim. Surus did battle with the monster to prevent it from destroying the world.

**Videric Dewitte** (*VEE·dare·ic   deh·VIT*) – the Master of the School of Magical Healing at the Hero Academy.

**Vincus** (pl. vinci) (*VEEN·cuss; VEEN·chee*) – Aila's chain blade weapons.

**Viro/Vira** (pl viri) (*VEER·oh / VEER·ah /  VEER·ee*) – a former Hero Academy student who has graduated with a mastery in at least three schools and no longer lives at the Academy or participates in its function.

**Vituma** (*vi·TOO·mah*) – the leader of the Dark Council. The name derives from the ancient Alaqotim term for *prophet's shadow*.

**Voordim** (*VOOR·deem*) – the pantheon of gods in Dizhelim. It does not include the modern god Vanda.

**Vora** (*VORE·ah*) – the Leaf Talker of the tribe of arba in the Mellafond swamp.

**Vulmer Liadin** (*VUL·mer  LEE·uh·din*) – the first headmaster of the Hero Academy, appointed by Tsosin Ruus himself to run the school for the Prophet.

**Wolfen** – large intelligent wolves that roam desolate areas in the Rhaltzheim.

**Wolfen's Rest** – the inn in Dartford, on the mainland not too far east from the bridge to the island of Munsahtiz.

**Xaviera Contanko** (*zaw·vee·AIR·ah cone TAHNK·oe*) – the Master of Artifice: Items of Power at the Hero Academy. She journeyed to the Dark Pinnacles with Raki, Jia, and Urun.

**Xin Su Jun** (*SHEEN SOO JOON*) – the current Shinyin emperor, son of the former emperor.

**Xin Tai Rong** (*SHEEN TIE ROHNG*) – the rebel leader who eventually defeated Chao He Ling's forces and became the first emperor of Shinyan.

**Yezras Farlingian** (*YEZ·rass far LIN·gee·an*) – the Master of the School of Conjuration and Invocation at the Hero Academy.

**Yoniko Takesi** (*YOE·nee·koe tah·KAY·see*) – a member of the Dark Council.

**Yralissa Zinphinal** (*eer·ah·LISS ah ZIN·fin·all*) – the Master of the School of Illusion at the Hero Academy.

**Yxna Hagenai** (*IX·nah HAG·en·eye*) – the Master of Edged Weapons at the Hero Academy.

**Zejo Troufal** (*ZAY·joe TROO·fahl*) – a hero who lived at the end of the Age of Magic. He was Erent Cahhs's idol when he was a boy, before he himself became a hero.

**Zhadril** (*ZHAD·reel*) – an animaru mage—former high priest of S'ru—who was defeated in battle by Khrazhti to lose his position. In Dizhelim, he was given permission to study corrupted magic in a swamp area.

# AUTHOR NOTES

Thank you for reading Hero's Strength! I hope you enjoyed it and liked the revelation in the book. For that matter, I hope it *was* a revelation. My editor and proofreader didn't comment on the surprise, which concerns me a little bit that maybe they'd figured out Aila's secret beforehand. In any case, it's no secret that authors like me need reviews from readers like you to increase the number of people who hear about my books. **Could you please leave a review?** Reviews and ratings are so important in creating word of mouth so other readers will try my stories. I would appreciate it immensely if you could help.

This year has been...interesting. As you may be aware, I signed with Oliver Heber Books (OHB) early in 2023 and they took over the rights to publish most of my existing books and those going forward. This is something new for me and the transition has been full of surprises and has inevitably resulted in me rearranging my normal schedule. Unfortunately, that included delaying the launch of this book and those following it (my fault, not OHB's).

One of the challenges of my new situation was this particular series. Originally, I wrote the first three books (Wanderer's Song, Warrior's Song, and Heroes' Song) as a separate trilogy and called it the Song of Prophecy series. Then, I shifted the way the books were written (mostly in the manner in which I wrote the different points of view and focused on a different main character for each book) and put those stories into a different, but connected, series called the Hero Academy series.

Upon the change, OHB and I decided to try to make the designation of the books in those two series a bit more streamlined. Though we still refer to the first three books as "prequels" (which is what they're named in the first omnibus edition) all of the books from the former Song of Prophecy series and the Hero Academy series are now one series: the Song of Prophecy series. Thus, those prequels are books 1-3 of the series and this current book is Book 10. It's a bit confusing, but from here on out, the numbering of the books will be clear and easy.

Things going forward should be smoother (and faster). As I get back to more of a regular launch cycle, I hope you'll stick around. I'll soon reach the point in the series I've alluded to before where the stories as originally planned will be doubled up, resulting in longer books as we close in on the finish to the series. I have the arc planned out, though there's still a lot of work to do on specifics like characters, locations, and exactly how I'm going to bring all the differing factions in to clash in a final maelstrom that will, hopefully, leave us with a world that is not a burned out husk of unlife. But who knows what that will look like?

Stay tuned and the answer will be: you.

I appreciate you sharing my stories with me and hope to see you in Dizhelim again.

P.E. Padilla

## The Great Prophet predicted you would want to read his story

Tsosin Ruus, the most renowned mage during the Age of Magic, wrote the Song of Prophecy to aid the world of Dizhelim as it would exist thousands of years after his life ended. But who was the Great Prophet, and how did he come to be the most important person in history...up until the present time?

And what of Erent Caahs, the most famous of contemporary heroes?

Get these two full-length companion novels to the Song of Prophecy and Hero Academy series for free and find out the fascinating stories that transformed ordinary boys into figures idolized by millions.

To get your free books and find out about upcoming books, please visit my website at https://pepadilla.com (top right hand corner of the page). Thank you!

# ABOUT THE AUTHOR

A chemical engineer by degree and at various times an air quality engineer, a process control engineer, and a regulatory specialist by vocation, USA Today bestselling author P.E. Padilla learned long ago that crunching numbers and designing solutions was not enough to satisfy his creative urges. Weaned on classic science fiction and fantasy stories from authors as diverse as Heinlein, Tolkien, and Jordan, and affected by his love of role playing games such as Dungeons and Dragons (analog) and Final Fantasy (digital), he sometimes has trouble distinguishing reality from fantasy. While not ideal for a person who needs to function in modern society, it's the perfect state of mind for a writer. He is a recent transplant from Southern California to Northern Washington, where he lives surrounded by trees.

pepadilla.com/
pep@pepadilla.com

SoP4 - Hero Dawning

SoP5 - Hero's Mind

SoP6 - Hero's Nature

SoP7 - Hero's Honor

SoP8 - Hero's Knowledge

SoP9 - Hero's Darkness

SoP10 - Hero's Strength (this book)

SoP11 - Hero's Anger (coming soon)

**Song of Prophecy Omnibus/Box Sets:**

Song of Prophecy Series Omnibus 1: The Prequels

Hero Academy Series Omnibus 2

**Tales of Dizhelim (companion stories to the SoP Series):**

Arrow's Flight

Song's Prophet

**Order of the Fire Series:**

Call of Fire

Hero of Fire

Legacy of Fire

Order of the Fire Boxed Set